Rave Reviews For Ana Leigh's Historical Romances:

"Angel Hunter is a lively, engrossing, action-packed romance filled with delightful characters that leap from the pages straight into your heart."

—*Romantic Times*

"Proud Pillars Rising is an absolute delight from first page to last! You'll laugh out loud and smile with surprise at this humorous, heartwarming love story."

—*Romantic Times*

"Sweet Enemy Mine will warm your heart with its touching story and leave you with the knowledge that love can truly conquer all."

—*Romantic Times*

"Paradise Redeemed has so many conflicts, memorable characters, intriguing plot twists, and adventures that readers will be captivated."

—*Romantic Times*

RUNAWAY LOVE

"I think I'm falling in love with you, Rory. When we're apart, I can't seem to get my mind off you."

"I have the same problem. This is a new experience for me. I never felt this way before." She gazed intently into his eyes. "You have to help me, Thomas. I'm a spoiled brat. I've been pampered and doted upon my whole life."

He drew her into his arms. "Don't sell yourself so short. I'm no saint, Rory. Far from it." He kissed her and she closed her eyes to savor the sensation of the excitement that surged through her.

"And since I always get what I want, I should tell you now that I want to marry you."

THE GOLDEN SPIKE

ANA LEIGH

LEISURE BOOKS ▌ NEW YORK CITY

This book is dedicated to my grandsons—
Justin and Brandon,
our future visionaries. So build your railroads, boys.

A LEISURE BOOK®

June 1994

Published by

Dorchester Publishing Co., Inc.
276 Fifth Avenue
New York, NY 10001

Copyright © 1994 by Ana Leigh

Printed in the United States of America.

"What was it the Engines said,
Pilots touching – head to head,
Facing on the single track,
Half a world behind each back?"
               —*Bret Harte*

Chapter One

Scraped and bleeding from numerous falls, she clambered laboriously to the top of the rocky rise, then halted for a few precious seconds to gulp mouthfuls of air into lungs that felt as if they were on fire.

Desperation gleamed in the green eyes that scanned the valley below. Cradled in a narrow passage blasted through the mountains, a single track of iron rail hugged the rocky terrain.

The pounding of her heart sounded like the thump of drums in her ears as Rory Callahan cast a fretful glance behind her. But she saw no sign of them. *Where were they?*

Dragging in several more much-needed breaths, Rory scrambled down the mountainside. Midway, her boots slipped on loose rocks. Unable to check her fall, she tumbled, down to the base of the steep declivity as jagged rocks and stones bruised and lacerated her arms.

Holding back her sobs, she painfully rose to her feet. Her hat had been lost in the fall, and she brushed aside a thick curtain of red hair to glance upward just as two horsemen in fast pursuit crested the rise. Instantly, Rory started to run along the track. Her urgency to escape the riders banished any awareness of pain.

Coming out of the gorge where the canyon flattened out for several miles, Rory raced along the track until her lungs felt near to bursting. Each ragged breath she drew seared them. Finally forced to halt, she dropped to her knees, gasping. A quick backward glance revealed that her pursuers had descended the rise, reached the track, and were coming at full speed toward her. She could not outrun horses. Rory knew it was just a matter of time.

Suddenly, as galvanizing as the trumpet of a cavalry charge, the blast of a train whistle pierced the silent valley. Green eyes glimmering with tears, she was buoyed with renewed hope. She rose to her feet and raced toward the distant puff of black smoke.

Terror kept her moving until she could no longer run. Still she stumbled forward, sights and sounds contorted by the blood pounding in her head. The hoofbeats behind her sounded louder than the train whistle ahead. At any moment, she expected to feel the agonizing pain of the death blow. Her vision blurred. Her steps became tottering. Rory lurched forward. *Please, God, just a few more minutes.*

After several more torturous steps, her mind and body gave up to darkness and she collapsed on the track. At the final instant, one hand reached out in desperation toward the hope for salvation steaming toward her.

Grimacing, Doctor Thomas Graham tossed several more hunks of wood into the engine's furnace as the voice of Caleb Murphy rose above the clatter of the train.

"Oh, my darlin', Oh, my darlin', Oh, my darlin' Clementine. You are lost and gone forever, dreadful sorry, Clementine."

For the last hour Graham had suffered Murphy's raucous singing and now had good cause to question the wisdom of hitching a ride to town in the cab of this discordant baritone.

Thomas Jefferson Graham, affectionately known as "T.J." to his friends in the East, shook a head of dark hair and tried to keep his amusement from showing in his warm, coffee-colored eyes.

He stretched to ease the muscles of his broad shoulders; stoking the boiler of a locomotive was a new experience for him. However, Thomas was not adverse to hard work. In fact, people meeting him for the first time tended to mistake this rugged Union Pacific doctor for one of the brawny linemen who were laying track.

Born and raised in Virginia, Thomas had lost his parents in an epidemic during his first year of medical school. After serving in the Confederate

Army during the war, he had become fascinated by the concept of a transcontinental railroad. The thirty-year-old doctor had accepted a position with the Union Pacific and had come West to be part of the momentous endeavor.

"Murph!" Thomas groaned when the locomotive engineer slipped into the next verse of the song.

Ignoring the complaint, Caleb Murphy suddenly cut off the tune and uttered sharply, "What in hell!" A stream of tobacco juice accompanied the expletive as he gave several quick jerks to the whistle cord. "Hey, Doc, take a look."

Thomas leaned out the opposite side of the cab. His steady gaze studied the track ahead. Once again Murphy yanked on the whistle cord with a long, steady warning blast. "What do you make of it?"

"Appears to be someone running on the track," Thomas replied. "From the looks of all that long red hair, I'd say it's a woman." His dark gaze suddenly sobered when two horsemen came into view. "My God, Murph, she's being chased by Indians! Can you get up any more speed?"

Spurred to action, Thomas grabbed the Winchester that Murphy kept mounted on the wall of the cab. "This rifle loaded?"

"Ain't there for decoration, Doc," Murphy mumbled, pushing the throttle to full.

"Dammit!" Thomas cursed after several attempts to draw a bead on the riders. Frustrated, he lowered the rifle. "She's dead center between me and them. I can't get a good angle from

14

here without the risk of hitting her." He put a warning shot above their heads. When it failed to stop them, Thomas slung the rifle strap over his shoulder and eased himself out of the open door of the cab.

"You're gonna kill yourself," Murphy hollered as Thomas climbed up the outside of the speeding locomotive.

Reaching the top successfully, Thomas lowered one knee to the roof of the cab and took aim just as the woman fell to the ground. His shot found its mark, and the Indian nearest the girl tumbled from his horse. The riderless animal continued to race alongside the track toward the speeding locomotive.

The other rider saw the wisdom of retreating and reined up. He now sped forward, allowed his wounded confederate to mount behind him, and they rode hard toward the distant hills. Murphy pulled on the brake. Thomas lost his balance, pitched forward, and rolled off the roof into the crib containing the supply of wood.

Amid the screech of metal on metal and belching clouds of hot steam, the single engine ground to a stop less than fifty feet from the crumpled heap on the track.

"You hurt, Doc?" Murphy asked with a side glance at Thomas. The train engineer grabbed a canteen and climbed down from the cab.

"Only my dignity," Thomas mumbled to himself, retrieving the Winchester. He managed to scramble out of the woodpile, picked up his medical bag, and followed Murphy.

15

* * *

As Rory slowly drifted back to consciousness, she felt the arms that slipped beneath her and effortlessly lifted her as if she were a feather pillow. With consciousness came remembrance, and her instinct for survival prevailed. In panic, she started to struggle in the arms of her captor.

The hold around her tightened at once, and she felt herself drawn against a warm wall of muscle. "Please, miss, don't struggle. You're safe now."

The soothing voice took her by surprise. It did not belong to any Westerner, but had the pleasant, rounded tone of a cultured Southerner. The warm timbre was as comforting as the strength in the arms that held her.

Lulled by a sense of security, her panic ebbed, and she relaxed. Daring to venture a peek, she lifted her lashes and met the gaze of the warmest pair of brown eyes she had ever seen. Dumbfounded, she stared, wondering if she could be dreaming.

Thomas offered a friendly smile of reassurance. "Don't be frightened. I'm Dr. Graham, miss. I'm only trying to get you out of the sun."

"Doctor? You're a doctor?" This surprising information added to her bewilderment. Not only was her rescuer handsome, he had the warmest eyes and the strongest arms she had ever known. And in addition, he was a doctor!

Convinced that she must be hallucinating, Rory surrendered to the fantasy as her weakness pulled her back into unconsciousness.

She awakened to discover herself lying in the shade of an aspen tree. Rory had no idea how much time had passed since she lost consciousness. She felt the loss of the strong arms that once held her; however, the warm brown eyes were still studying her.

"I want you to take a few sips of water." To Rory's immediate pleasure, she discovered that the husky timbre had not disappeared either.

Rory felt the return of his hands and arms, gentle despite their strength, as he slipped them beneath her back to raise her shoulders. He brought the canteen to her mouth, and she greedily gulped the welcome liquid.

"Easy there. Not so fast," Thomas cautioned. "Just sip slowly."

The cool slide of water down her throat shocked her out of her inertia. She jerked up to a sitting position. "Pete! Oh, God! Pete! I've got to get to him."

The sudden movement shot a bolt of pain to her head. Groaning, Rory clutched her head and fought the blackness that threatened to engulf her again.

"Just relax, miss, and tell us who you are." Thomas gently tried to force her back down, but Rory would have none of it. Her panic had returned and she began to fight him.

"Let me go. Pete's down with an arrow. We've got to help him."

"We will, miss, as soon as I finish with you." He handed her a pill. "Here, swallow this."

"What is it?" she asked. He raised the canteen

to her lips, and without further balking Rory popped the pill into her mouth.

"A salt tablet. You're dehydrated—which is probably causing your blackouts. You also have some deep lacerations that need attention."

"There's not time for that now," she cried, desperation creeping into her voice. "Didn't you hear what I said? Pete could be dying while you sit here shoving pills down me."

"'Pears there's no use in arguing with the lady, Doc," Murphy remarked. He had stood silently holding the Winchester across his chest.

Against his better judgment, Thomas reached out a hand to Rory and pulled the distraught woman to her feet. "All right, Miss . . ."

At this sign of capitulation, Rory smiled in relief. "Callahan, Rory Callahan."

"You any kin to T.J. Callahan of the Circle C?" Murphy asked.

"I'm his daughter." She turned slowly, her gaze sweeping the terrain. "Matter of fact, we're standing on Circle C land right now." She walked away.

At the sound of Murphy's long, low whistle, curiosity gleamed in Thomas's eyes. "What's this all about, Murph?"

"Looks like we've stumbled into a beehive, Doc, and caught ourselves the Queen Bee." The engineer's look of amusement before he turned and followed Rory added to Thomas's curiosity. He hurriedly gathered up his medical supplies.

"What happened to the two Utes chasing me?" Rory asked, when Murphy reached the engine, where she waited impatiently.

"Doc put a bullet in one of them, but they were able to ride off before he could get the other one."

Her eyes spat fire at Thomas as he walked up and joined them. "You let them get away? What about Belle?"

Thomas couldn't understand why such a beautiful woman chose to be so damned ornery. Being partial toward attractive redheads, he hoped her foul disposition was temporary, perhaps brought on by injuries and fatigue.

"Belle?" Thomas asked with sufferance.

"My horse. One of them was riding my horse," she replied irritably.

"What kind of horse?" Thomas asked hopefully, remembering a quick glimpse of a riderless piebald racing past the train.

"Belle's a sorrel mare," Rory snapped.

"Oh," Thomas said, abashed.

"Oh! And just what does 'oh' mean?" she asked querulously.

Redhead or not, Thomas was losing his patience with this spoiled brat. Didn't the woman have any gratitude—or reverence? Good God, he reflected, she had just been plucked from the hands of death! Couldn't she show some kind of thankfulness, if not to them, at least to her Maker? Thomas reasoned that she had to be suffering a reaction to her injuries. "I had hoped Belle was a piebald."

Murphy grasped his meaning at once and couldn't resist a pun. Chortling, he spewed a stream of tobacco juice. "Looks like you backed the wrong horse, Doc."

Nodding, Thomas added to the humor. "Guess so. Matter of fact, Murph, you could even say it was a horse of a different color."

When the two men erupted into laughter, impatient green eyes glared at them. Agitated by the cavalier manner with which they treated the loss of her beloved horse, Rory exploded in anger. "I can't see anything amusing about losing a mare I've raised from a filly."

Realizing that they were taking the matter too lightly, Thomas regained his composure. "I had hoped Belle was black and white."

"Pete's horse was. Why?"

"Because Pete's piebald is probably halfway back to the ranch by now," Thomas informed her.

"And Belle?" Rory asked suspiciously.

"Is probably halfway back to the Ute camp."

Before Rory could voice any further displeasure, Thomas took her arm. "May I help you board, Miss Callahan?"

Rory was dwarfed between the two men as the three of them stood crowded together in the small cab. As soon as Murphy got the engine rolling again, Rory pointed to a mountainous rise a short distance ahead. "That's where I came down into this flat. I'll get off there and climb back up to get to Pete."

"Murph, can you operate this engine without someone to stoke her for you?" Thomas asked as he opened the furnace door and added several more pieces of wood to the fire.

Murphy patted the wall of the cab. "This ole gal and me have been sweethearts for a long time, Doc. I stroke her real gentle-like, and she heats up like a two-bit whore on a Saturday night."

The remark brought a glare of displeasure from Rory. "He said 'stoke,' Mr. Murphy, not 'stroke,'" she corrected, disgusted by the crudity.

Murphy had heard enough of her sharp tongue. He expressed his displeasure by firing a stream of tobacco juice into the open furnace. The moisture sent up a sizzling hiss and dissolved into steam.

Thomas slammed the furnace door shut before Murphy could offer another demonstration of his annoyance. "I'm going with Miss Callahan. When you get back to town, get a message to Callahan's ranch to come looking for us."

"You two would be a heck of a lot smarter to go back with me. This here problem is Callahan's, Doc, not the railroad's," Murphy declared.

"That would take hours. By the time we got back to Pete, he could bleed to death," Rory argued. "Or what if those Indians went back to finish what they started?"

Murphy made no attempt to hide his irritation. "Or what if your friend Pete is dead already? Ever think of that, Miz Callahan? And you don't have to worry about those two Utes. One of those bucks is wounded. They headed home."

"And on my horse," Rory grumbled. She wouldn't listen to the man. Pete wasn't dead. He couldn't be dead. What would she do without Pete? He was like a father to her. If *she* were lying out there, there would be no question what Pete would do. If this obstinate man wouldn't stop the train, she would have to jump off it.

"We're almost there," Rory warned a short time later when they entered the narrow passage. To her relief, Murphy slowed down and the engine ground to a halt.

Turning to Thomas, she offered him the option to remain. "Mr. Murphy is right, Doctor Graham. This is not the railroad's problem. I don't expect you to come with me."

Even if he hadn't taken the Hippocratic oath, Thomas would never have considered allowing her to go off alone on this mission. "Miss Callahan, I'm a doctor," he said calmly. "If there's a wounded man out there, I've taken an oath to help him."

A spark of admiration gleamed in her eyes. Hiding the ache of her injuries, she hopped down from the cab and started to scramble up the steep hillside.

"What in hell did I get myself into?" Thomas grumbled, hooking the canteen around his neck. He picked up his medical bag and started to follow Rory.

"Better take this, Doc." Murphy handed him the Winchester. "You never know what you might run into."

"Thanks, Murph." Thomas slung the rifle strap over his shoulder.

"Looks like that Queen Bee is part mountain goat," Murph snorted with a glance toward Rory as he watched her struggle to scale the rocky terrain. "Gotta hand it to her, the gal's got grit," Murphy said with admiration. He reached out a huge paw to shake hands. "Good luck, Doc. I'll get you some help as quick as I can."

Murphy watched as they climbed the steep hill.

Midway up, Rory retrieved the hat she had lost earlier. The sign was clear enough for even Thomas's untrained eye to read; looking back down, he marveled how she had not sustained more serious injuries when she rolled down the hill.

As he envisioned a clearer picture of her flight from her pursuers, a deeper regard for the courageous young woman began to formulate in his mind. "You're lucky to be alive, Miss Callahan," he murmured, only to discover that she had already resumed the climb.

Blasting had sheared off the slope of the mountain, and the higher they climbed, the steeper the incline became. Much of the surface was granite shale, which made the footing perilous, and the high altitude added to the difficulty of breathing. With Rory encumbered by her injuries, and Thomas by his medical bag and the heavy rifle slung over his shoulder, their progress slowed to a snail's pace.

They offered one another a helping hand whenever needed, and when they finally crested the top, breathless and exhausted, Thomas took off his hat and waved to Murphy in the ravine below.

Caleb Murphy acknowledged the signal with

several blasts from the whistle, then pushed the throttle and the engine chugged away.

High above, the two figures sat down to regain their breath and silently watched the train disappear from view.

Chapter Two

Grateful for the few moments of rest, Rory relaxed and stared off into the distance. She was startled when Thomas took hold of her wrist. "What are you doing?" she exclaimed, trying to pull free. But he held her arm in a firm grasp as he examined the palm of her hand.

Grimacing, he shook his head. "Look at this. Climbing up here has irritated your injuries all the more. I'm going to treat these cuts whether you like it or not."

Rory didn't want to admit how much her hands burned. Despite her urgency to find Pete, she allowed Thomas to cleanse the injuries. He smeared an unguent on the scrapes and wrapped the hand in gauze.

"Now the other one," he ordered.

On the verge of balking, Rory met his dark gaze and realized that he would not tolerate any protest on her part. She relented without argument and noticed that his ministrations helped immediately. The stinging sensation had been greatly relieved.

She sucked in a gasp of pain as he dabbed a medicated piece of cotton to a cut on her forehead. "Ouch!"

"I'm sorry, but that cut needed cleansing. Probably could use a couple stitches to close it up."

"Not now, Doctor Graham." Rory jumped to her feet. "We're wasting valuable time."

She started off at a brisk walk. After closing his medical bag, Thomas had to run to catch up with her. He saw no sense in inquiring if she knew where she might be headed—Rory Callahan was decidedly a woman who knew where she was going.

After half an hour of scrambling over the rocky terrain, Thomas became convinced that Murphy had been right; the woman must be part mountain goat. Huffing, he called a halt. "Miss Callahan."

Rory cast an impatient backward glance to discover that he had sat down on a boulder. "Doctor, it's only a short distance farther." The sound of desperation and fatigue in her voice conveyed the same urgency as he saw in her drawn features. Thomas reckoned the girl would keep driving herself, with or without his help, until she found the wounded man.

Wearily, he rose and followed.

After another quarter of an hour, they finally reached the timberline along the edge of the rocky rise. Pausing momentarily, Rory took a quick drink from the canteen and continued at a vigorous pace on the more level ground.

"Would you mind telling me where we're going?" he asked when she finally halted again.

"We're here. This is where I hid him."

"Hid him!" Thomas exclaimed.

Without responding, she hurried over to a nearby rock formation. Dropping to her hands and knees, she crawled between the boulders. "Pete, can you hear me?" she called out. After a few seconds, her head reappeared. "Dr. Graham, I need your help. Pete's unconscious, but he's alive."

She tried unsuccessfully to budge the wounded man. "When Pete lost consciousness, I shoved him under here."

"Come out from under there, and I'll try to get him out," Thomas suggested.

"You're too big, Doctor." Grunting, she continued her efforts to free the unconscious man.

Thomas stretched out on his stomach and peered under the rock. "Can you get his arm free? Then I can help pull him out."

Rory's struggles finally succeeded in freeing Pete from the narrow crevice under one of the huge boulders. Grasping the man's hand, Thomas dragged him as she shoved him free.

Expecting a younger man, Thomas was surprised to find this Pete fellow considerably older than the girl.

"Why don't you tell me just what happened?" Thomas asked as he worked to remove the arrow from the unconscious man. The shaft had been broken off, but enough remained for Thomas to get a firm hold and yank out the arrow.

Watching the doctor work swiftly over the wounded man, Rory tried to concentrate on words. "Pete spotted some stray cattle, so we rode up here. We had just gotten off our mounts when we were ambushed by four Indians."

"Ambushed?"

"Well, I don't know what you'd call it," she said defensively. "But arrows started coming from a clump of trees behind us. They shot this arrow into Pete before he even got off a shot, but he held them off until all his shells were gone."

She halted as her mind recalled the scene of that desperate moment. "Pete told me to get mounted and head back to the ranch, but I wouldn't go without him. By that time he was so weak he could barely climb on his horse, then could hardly stay in the saddle. I had to lead him, so the going was slow. The Indians were between us and the ranch, so we had to go in the opposite direction, toward the rise. We only managed to escape because the Utes were on foot."

When she stopped as if the story had ended, Thomas glanced up briefly from his ministrations. "Go on."

"We got this far then Pete lost consciousness and fell off his horse. I dragged him between the rocks to hide him and then wiped away the tracks and rode off with both horses. I figured if the Indians followed the horse tracks, they'd never find him."

Admiration gleamed in Thomas's eyes as he again glanced in her direction. "You mean you deliberately made yourself a decoy."

"It wasn't quite as heroic as it sounds, Doctor. I knew I could make better time without Pete slowing me up. And it would have worked, too, if I hadn't fallen." She shook her head in disgust.

"Do you believe it? I fell out of the saddle. Remember those trees we entered a short while back? That's where Belle and I parted company. I came out of those trees hell-bent for leather and hit that drop too fast. Belle shied and I fell. Seems like I rolled darned near halfway down the mountain before I could stop myself. The two horses were still above, but I knew it would take too long to climb back up to them."

"So that's how the Indians got your horses."

Rory nodded. "They got the horses, but they had to skirt the rise to find a spot to come down. That took time and gave me a chance to get away."

"I only saw two Indians chasing you. You said there were four."

"Yeah, I guess Pete got two of them before he ran out of ammunition." Her worried glance shifted back to the wounded man. "Will he be all right, Doctor?"

"Well, I've done all I can for your friend. That's a mean tear in his flesh and muscle, but the shoulder bone seems intact. He's lost a lot of blood and his pulse is weak, but steady. I've dressed the wound, and barring infection, there's no reason why he shouldn't recover."

His dark gaze swept the lengthening blue shadows that had begun to surround them. "I better get a fire going. It'll soon be dark and will cool down quickly."

"I can do that for you," Rory offered.

"No, you'll dirty those dressings on your hands. Can you handle a Winchester?"

"Of course," Rory remarked.

Thomas handed her the rifle. "Then you stay here and keep an eye on Pete while I gather firewood. I'll be back soon." He started to walk away, but turned back, adding, "Don't take a shot at me when I come out of those trees."

Rory gave him an exasperated look. But upon seeing his smile, she realized that his fear that she would be too fast on the trigger might not be ungrounded.

Minutes seemed to pass like hours as she waited uneasily for his return. The night moved in, blanketing the Utah mountainside in darkness. Tall boulders loomed behind her like hulking behemoths. Her head jerked toward the screech of a grouse in the nearby trees. At the answering coo, her eyes rounded with alarm, wondering if it could be Indians calling to one another. She cocked the rifle.

And with the setting of the sun, the coolness came. Gooseflesh spotted her bare arms, but she kept a firm grasp on the rifle lying across her lap.

She jumped with a nervous start when a voice spoke at her side. "Sure glad to see that red hair of yours still in place, gal."

"Pete!" Rory's instant smile glowed with love as she swung her attention to the figure lying at her side.

"Where'd you get that Winchester, gal?"

"It's Doctor Graham's. He removed the arrow from your shoulder. How are you feeling, Pete?" she asked tenderly.

"Sure could use a drink." He tried to sit up, but fell back, too weak to rise.

"Stay still. The doctor said you've lost a lot of blood." She retrieved the canteen and raised Pete's head and shoulders so he could swallow.

"This place kinda looks familiar," Pete remarked, looking around as he lay back down. When his brain started to connect, he suddenly asked, "Doctor? Where'd a doctor come from up here? And what happened to those Ute bucks chasing us?"

"Oh, it's a long story, Pete. You'll never believe what happened."

"Gotta tell you, gal, I'm sure glad I'm still around to hear it and you're around to tell it to me." He picked up her hand to squeeze it and saw the bandages. "Yep, reckon you've got a story to tell all right."

At that moment, Thomas returned with his arms laden with firewood. He dropped the heap to the ground and hurried over to check his patient.

"I'm glad to see you've regained consciousness, Mr.—"

Suddenly, piercing shrieks rent the night air, and two figures dashed from the trees with raised tomahawks. Rory spun with the rifle, and her shot brought down the Indian nearest her. The other made a flying leap at Thomas.

The two men rolled on the ground as Thomas

struggled to release the Indian's grasp on the tomahawk. He felt a searing pain as the edge of the weapon grazed his arm.

The constant thrashing around prevented Rory from coming to Thomas's assistance. Helplessly, she watched the life-and-death struggle. She gasped with alarm when she saw the red stain darkening the sleeve of Thomas's shirt.

His clenched fist circled the savage's wrist and he began to slowly squeeze, finally forcing the Indian to loosen the grasp on the tomahawk. The weapon slipped through the savage's fingers.

The two rolled together, grappling for one another's throats. The Indian let out a grunt of pain as Thomas drove a smashing blow to the nose of his attacker. He felt the bone crunch beneath his fist, and two streams of blood gushed from the Indian's nostrils.

The two men scrambled to their feet. Thomas delivered another punch that sent the Indian reeling backward. Before Thomas could reach him, the savage dashed into the trees.

Thomas had no intention of chasing after him. He picked up the tomahawk and half-stumbled over to the other Indian Rory had shot. After a quick examination, he looked at Rory. "You're right, Miss Callahan. You can handle that Winchester. The man's dead."

Returning to the others, he slumped down on the ground next to Pete. The wounded man offered a grin and reached out a hand. "You must be the doc. Name's Faber. Pete Faber."

Still breathless, Thomas shook the man's hand. "T.J. Graham, Pete."

"T.J.?" Grinning, Pete cast a side glance at Rory. "Bet that ain't gonna set too good with your pa."

"I don't understand," Thomas remarked. His breath restored, he took the wounded man's pulse.

"My father's initials are the same as yours, Doctor," Rory offered in explanation.

"What she ain't telling you, Doc, is once you meet T.J. Callahan, you're gonna find there's only room for one 'T.J.' in this here territory." His mumbling ended as he dropped off to sleep.

"Doctor Graham, what about your arm?" Rory asked.

Thomas examined the wound. "It's just a surface laceration." He swabbed the cut with disinfectant and then wrapped it. "Miss Callahan, would you mind tying this off for me?"

Rory came over and knelt beside him. As she bent to the task, the faint fragrance of lavender drifted up to tease his nostrils. Rory raised her head, and for a long moment their gazes remained locked. Then she shifted her eyes back to his arm to finish tying off the ends of the bandage.

Her task completed, she quickly moved away, and Thomas set to building a fire. As soon as he succeeded in getting a blaze started, he glanced over at the young woman. An awkward silence had developed between them. "It's quite a coincidence that your father and I have the same initials, Miss Callahan."

Yawning, Rory stretched out as the fire began

to warm her. "I'd say so. But Pete's right, there's only room for one T.J. in this territory."

"I can assure you that I have no designs on your father's—ah, realm, Miss Callahan. I am merely a doctor, not an empire builder."

"That's well and good, Doctor Graham. That way you should get along just fine." Seconds later, she drifted into slumber.

Thomas shoved the Indian's body under the same rocks where Pete had been hiding. He then stayed awake to feed the fire and keep a watchful eye on his patients. Toward midnight, Rory began to whimper in her sleep. He hurried over and discovered that she was trembling.

Thomas lay down beside Rory and gathered her in his arms in an attempt to warm and calm her. Her trembling ceased immediately, and her rounded curves settled into his. She felt good in his arms, and he did not release her. Besides, a good rest was the best medicine for her at the moment, he told himself.

Once again he became aware of the faint scent of lavender that pervaded her hair and body. He drew her closer, allowing the pleasant fragrance to play with his senses and fantasies.

Keene MacKenzie smelled the fire long before he broke through the trees. He dismounted, tethered his horse, and proceeded to make his way through the spruce and cottonwoods. MacKenzie figured riding unannounced into a camp at night was a sure way of inviting a bullet.

His steady, gray-eyed gaze swung to the right

at the sound of creaking leather and the soft thud of hooves. Others were stalking the camp too.

MacKenzie faded back into the shadows as silently as he had appeared.

Awaking, Pete Faber slowly struggled to his feet. His legs wobbled and seemed barely strong enough to support him. But he couldn't ignore the call of nature any longer. Weak-kneed, he staggered into the cover of the nearest trees.

Minutes later, the galvanizing, telltale click of a hammer being cocked instantly woke Thomas. His eyes popped open, and he stared up into the barrel of a rifle.

"Take your hands off my daughter and sit up real slow-like." The command was as chilling as the steel-blue eyes that glared down at him from above the rifle stock.

In the dim light, Thomas could see that the speaker was big and broad. The man appeared to be in his sixties. "Yes, sir." Thomas attempted to raise his hands in the air. However, one arm remained encumbered by a very soft, very warm, and very feminine body. His mind fleetingly registered those facts as he discovered the reason for the warning. Rory Callahan lay on her side snuggled against him, one leg hooked over his and his hand riding possessively on the rounded curve of her derriere. He quickly slipped his arm out from under her, dumping her to the ground.

Rory awoke with a start. "What's wrong?"

Wordlessly, Thomas nodded toward the pointed rifle.

Rory screamed, then, recognizing the wielder of the weapon, her face split into a relieved smile. "Daddy!" Jumping to her feet, Rory rushed into her father's arms.

For several seconds the old man hugged her tightly, then he stepped back, frowning grimly. "You gave us one hell of a scare, daughter." The gruff reprimand did not mask the relief he tried to disguise.

As Thomas stood up, several men on horseback sat silently watching his every move.

"You've got some fast explaining to do, Bucko," Callahan snarled. "I don't cotton to finding you sprawled all over my daughter. What the hell are the two of you doing up here alone?" The lethal glint had returned to his eyes.

Thomas, ever a true gentlemen, did not want to point out to the outraged father that just the opposite had occurred; his daughter had been the one doing the sprawling.

"And where's Pete? His piebald came trotting back to the ranch."

"Tarnation, I'm right here," Pete grumbled, stepping into the clearing. "Damned shame a man can't take a walk in the bushes without you raising a fuss, T.J."

Thomas turned to respond, but he soon realized that Pete had been addressing Callahan. Nevertheless, his patient's welfare remained his primary concern. "Why didn't you call me if you needed help?" he asked the wounded man.

"Just who in hell are you, anyway?" Callahan asked gruffly.

"The name's Graham." Thomas stepped forward, but found his outstretched hand ignored by the rancher.

"Daddy, don't you know what happened? Mr. Murphy said he would get word to you."

"Who's Murphy?" Callahan asked.

"Caleb Murphy. He's a locomotive engineer with the Union Pacific," Thomas volunteered.

"The railroad!" Callahan exploded in anger. "Might have guessed the railroad's behind this mess."

Rory had suffered through too many of her father's tirades against the railroad to be intimidated by yet another. "Will you listen for just once in your life, Daddy," she declared. "Doctor Graham saved Pete's life. And if it weren't for him, I'd be dead too. We owe him a debt of gratitude."

T.J. Callahan was not a man easily swayed, especially in the presence of his riders. "From what I saw when we rode up, it appears you already did enough thanking for both of us."

The accusation made no sense to Rory. Confused, she glanced helplessly at Thomas. But he grasped Callahan's meaning at once—the old man had found them in a compromising position.

"You're mistaken, sir. It's not how it appeared."

"Daddy, Pete had an arrow in him, and if that train hadn't come along when it did, I'd be dead by now." Angrily, she brushed aside the curtain of hair that had shrouded most of her face. Callahan gasped in shock when he saw

37

the ugly gash across her forehead.

"If you don't want to listen to the girl, T.J., why don't you take a good look at her?" Pete advised.

Callahan's outraged parenthood dissipated at the sight of her injuries. In the flickering light from the campfire, he saw the dark bruises on his daughter's face and arms. Now, openly shaken, he reached for one of her gauze-swathed hands and held it in the cradle of his own callused hands. "My God, honey, what happened to you?"

Callahan had lost his ire and listened intently as Rory pieced together her fragmented account. "We were attacked by Utes." The arms that had protected Rory throughout her life closed around her. Now that she was safe again in the arms of her father, the strength that had driven the girl drained away. She buried her head against his chest. "I was so scared, Daddy."

With all eyes trained on the couple, no one noticed a tall man step out of the shadows. "Saw the fire and hoped it was your camp, Doc," he said with a brief nod at Thomas.

At the sight of the speaker, several of the riders started to reach for their Colts. The slight shift of the Winchester the man held was minor, but nevertheless threatening. "Don't try it, boys. Unless you figure it's worth dying over."

Callahan shook his head, and the men dropped their hands to their sides. None of them was eager to draw on Keene MacKenzie.

"What are you doing here, MacKenzie?" Callahan snarled.

"Came looking for Rory and the Doc." He nodded politely. "Evenin', Rory." Thomas noticed a softening in the scout's tone of voice.

"Hello, Keene," she said shakily.

"Pete, you well enough to sit a saddle?" Callahan asked. "We brought your piebald."

"I don't advise you to do that, Pete," Thomas interjected when the wounded man climbed on the horse.

"Well, I'll give *you* some advice, Doctor," Callahan barked. "Keep your advice out of Circle C business. I'm grateful for what you've done for Rory and Pete, but you're railroad. Which means you're not welcome here."

He lifted Rory onto his saddle and crawled up behind her.

Malevolence gleamed in his eyes as he turned back to the gunman. "As for you, MacKenzie, I'm giving you 'til dawn to get off the Circle C. If you're still around by then, my men have orders to shoot you on sight."

In a flurry of pounding hooves, Callahan and the Circle C riders rode away.

As the dust settled, Thomas emitted a long, low whistle. "So that's T.J. Callahan," he said reflectively, recalling the earlier warnings about the man.

MacKenzie did not respond to the remark. "I gotta get my horse." He disappeared into the trees only to reappear minutes later leading the dun gelding he always rode.

"Hungry, Doc?" He tossed Thomas a piece of jerky.

Thomas snatched it in mid-air and began to

chew voraciously on the strip of dried beef. "Don't suppose you've got a cup of coffee in your saddlebags?"

"Got the makings for one." MacKenzie dredged through his saddlebags and handed Thomas coffee and a battered pot. "Get it going while I unsaddle Duke here."

"Callahan told us to get off his land. I had the impression he meant it," Thomas remarked when MacKenzie appeared to be settling in for the night.

"Yep, reckon he did," Keene answered indifferently. "Still got time to grab a couple hours of shut-eye. We'll pull out at first light."

Thomas wasted no time pouring water from the canteen into the pot. "How'd you happen to find us, Keene?"

"I was in town when Murph arrived. He told me what happened and whereabouts he dropped off you and Rory. Hell, I know this area like the back of my hand, so I headed out."

As Thomas set the coffee to brew on the fire, several questions piqued his curiosity. "Keene, why is Callahan so bitter against the railroad? I'd think he'd be glad to see it come through."

"Reckon T.J. figures he's got his reasons, Doc," Keene said noncommittally, dumping his gear near the fire.

"He didn't seem too pleased to see you tonight." The statement was bold, but Thomas was still curious about MacKenzie's exchange with Rory Callahan; he had sensed an undertone of intimacy.

"There's some bad blood between us." Keene

stretched out his long, lanky body and covered his face with his hat to signal an end to the conversation. Thomas had known MacKenzie long enough to recognize that this man who had been hired by the railroad to scout, as well as hunt for the game to feed the work crews, had said all he intended to say on the subject.

Further sleep was an impossibility for Thomas. He didn't even attempt it. Instead, he sat before the fire sipping draughts of coffee from a chipped mug MacKenzie had produced. His glance shifted to the stretched-out figure by the fire. MacKenzie appeared to be sleeping; at least, he hadn't said a word to Thomas since he lay down.

Everything about the Union Pacific scout seemed bathed in mystery to Thomas. Although the two men were near in age, they were complete opposites in temperament. Gregarious by nature, with an infectious charm, the Union Pacific doctor thoroughly enjoyed people, whereas Keene MacKenzie was a reticent and private individual.

During the War Between the States, Thomas had encountered several soldiers similar to Keene. Close-mouthed and self-sufficient, they kept their own counsel, their private lives to themselves, their thoughts and emotions behind an impassive mask, and they competently performed what was expected of them in the line of duty.

Despite their differences in personality, the two men had liked one another from the time of their first meeting three months earlier. It hadn't been long before Thomas recognized and learned to respect the unique aspects of Keene MacKenzie's character, and he was not offended by the scout's aloofness.

As he milled over these thoughts, Callahan's departing threat intruded on Thomas's reflections. The "bad blood" between Callahan and the scout went far deeper than the rancher's quarrel with the railroad. Intuition told Thomas that the beautiful Rory Callahan somehow was mixed up in it too.

Chapter Three

All the while that she sat beside Pete on the seat of the buckboard, Rory Callahan was doing some heavy thinking. In fact, in the two weeks since her harrowing experience with the Utes, Rory had frequently drifted into deep thoughts of the good-looking Union Pacific doctor.

Closing her eyes, she conjured up the image of his dark-eyed handsomeness and the sound of the pleasant drawl that just seemed to roll off his tongue.

"I'd bet his voice could charm the skin off a snake."

"What did you say?" Pete asked.

Rory's eyes popped open in surprise; she hadn't realized she had spoken aloud. "Oh . . . ah, I'd bet . . . it's so warm I could swim in the lake."

"Pretty far piece to go just for a swim, gal,"

Pete remarked, visualizing the Great Salt Lake.

Amused, he shook his head. *Women; sometimes their moods took them almost over the edge.* "Last couple weeks seems like you've been acting a little tetched, Rory. Don't suppose you fell on your head when you slid down that mountain, do you?" he asked tongue-in-cheek.

Rather than pursue the conversation and thereby reveal too much to the shrewd old man, Rory dropped the subject and remained quiet during the rest of the trip to town.

Set amidst a forest of poplar, elm, and box elder, the once sleepy little town of Ogden had swelled into a boomtown since the arrival of the railroad. The latest terminus for the Union Pacific, the town bulged with newly erected storeyards to handle the tremendous influx of equipment and supplies.

A sawmill, telegraph office, saloon, company store, smithy, lawyer's office, surveyor's office, and a medical station quickly followed. A new three-story hotel had sprung up to accommodate the endless stream of "coming and going" railroad personnel.

And with the railroad came the camp followers, the scavengers who fed on the carrion of an advancing society—gamblers, prostitutes, swindlers, and hawkers.

As soon as the Circle C riders reached town, the two ranch hands who had come along for protection made a beeline for the saloon. "I'll help you get the supplies," Pete offered as his wistful glance followed the two lucky cowpokes.

"Oh, go along, Pete," she said with an impish smile. "I can take care of the supplies."

A sanguine grin splintered the weathered face. "Ya sure you don't mind, Rory?" When Rory shook her head, Pete didn't wait for further encouragement. He headed toward the saloon.

Rory entered the general store. Whenever she crossed the portal, Rory always felt like a child entering a land of enchantment.

The store was redolent of the mixed aromas of drying vegetables and peppermint candy, apples and candle wax, incense and freshly baked bread. Onions and garlic dangled on skeins from the rafters, and baskets heaped with apples and potatoes sat on the floor wherever there was space. Large glass jars filled with beans, licorice sticks, sugar, and coffee rested on a counter. Burlap sacks of grain and seed were stacked in corners next to small kegs of molasses.

Shelves holding everything from ammunition to unguents lined a wall behind a glass-enclosed counter that contained Colt pistols and wire-rimmed eyeglasses.

At the far end of the store were several racks of factory-made clothes in various sizes. Chalky-white, faceless, papier-mâché heads displayed the latest Parisian bonnets on a shelf above a row of brightly colored poke bonnets.

After presenting her list of supplies to the proprietor, Rory's attention was drawn to bolts of bright material and ribbon on a nearby table. For five minutes, she juggled a roll of green satin ribbon and another of white, trying to choose between the two. Finally making her choice, she laid aside the white ribbon.

"Either one would look lovely in your hair."

Startled, she turned to discover the very person who had been tormenting her recent thoughts. "Doctor Graham!" Rory exclaimed. Although she felt quite flustered, her genuine smile held a radiant welcome.

"Miss Callahan." He nodded, quickly tipped his hat, then replaced the Stetson on his dark head. "It's a pleasure meeting you again. And I'm glad to see all those bruises and cuts you sustained are fading."

By this time, Rory had regained her composure and bravely met the warmth of his dark eyes. "I never had the chance to properly thank you, Doctor Graham. I don't know what I would have done without you."

"How's Pete?"

"Oh, completely recovered from his wound. He came to town with me." Her eyes sparkled with devilment. "I think it was an excuse just to visit the saloon."

"Well, I imagine it's a welcome diversion from ranching."

"Do you have ranches in the East, Doctor Graham?"

"No, I can't say we do. We do have horse farms or cattle farms. But certainly none that run for thousands of acres."

"Do you ride, Doctor?"

"I'm a Virginian, ma'am." His eyes sparked with devilment. "In Virginia we learn to sit a saddle before we learn to walk. Finest thoroughbreds in the country. Matter of fact, I have a close friend who raises and races thoroughbreds."

"In Virginia," she said.

Thomas grinned sheepishly. "Well, no, ma'am. Actually his farm is in Missouri."

"Oh, then obviously he doesn't raise the finest thoroughbreds in the country," she teased. Her responsive laughter joined with his warm chuckle.

"Perhaps you would like to join us some day at the Circle C? I'd like to show you the ranch."

"I'd love to, ma'am, but I believe your father made his wishes on that subject quite explicit."

Her eyes brightened flirtatiously. "Oh, don't give that a thought, Doctor. I can be very persuasive when I want to be."

"I'm sure you can, Miss Callahan." His dark eyes stared deeply into the depths of her green-eyed gaze.

When she finally broke the fixed stare, she walked over to the counter and handed the roll of ribbon to the elderly shopkeeper. "Please add a yard of this to the rest of the supplies, Mr. Wyler."

"Sure will, Rory." Wyler put the ribbon on a heap of barrels and sacks piled near the door. "You've got enough here to fill a buck-board."

"Miss Callahan, I'd be glad to help load your supplies," Thomas offered.

"No thank you, Doctor. The boys will load them when we're ready to leave town."

"You be sure and save me a dance Saturday night, Rory," Wyler called out to her as she moved to the door.

Rory responded with a cheery wave. "I promise, Mr. Wyler. See you Saturday."

"Did I hear mention of a dance?" Thomas asked, clearly captivated.

Rory's eyes flashed in invitation. "Yes, Saturday night. Do you plan to attend, Doctor?"

He grinned roguishly. "I do now, Miss Callahan."

His unabashed candidness produced a coquettish blush of pleasure from Rory as he opened the door for her.

Outside, Keene MacKenzie leaned nonchalantly against a post. He straightened up when Rory stepped out of the store followed by Thomas Graham.

"Howdy, Rory." He nodded toward a nearby buckboard. "Hoped it'd be you when I saw the Circle C brand on that team."

"How have you been, Keene?" she asked. Their gazes lingered on one another.

"Can't complain. You're looking a lot better than the last time I saw you," he drawled.

"I have to say I feel a lot better too. I just thanked Doctor Graham for his help that day. I want to thank you too, Keene. I knew you'd come looking for Pete and me as soon as you heard we were missing."

An awkward silence developed between the two, and she flashed a nervous smile at Thomas. "Ah, thank you again, Doctor Graham." Then Rory turned back to MacKenzie. "Take care of yourself, Keene." She reached up, kissed his cheek, and hurried away.

"So that's the way it is," Thomas commented. "I'm glad I found out before I made a damn fool of myself over her."

"We're not sweet on each other, if that's what you're thinking," Keene replied.

In truth, another man's interest in a woman would not have discouraged Thomas Jefferson Graham. In matters of the heart, he followed the credo, "All's fair in love and war." Only a wedding band on her finger could deter him from pursuing a woman he admired. In fact, he and his best friend, Ruark Stewart, had carried on a long-time, friendly rivalry of wooing away one another's girlfriends.

That is, until Ruark met Angel, Thomas thought, grinning. The game had ended when his best friend had fallen hopelessly in love with the beautiful Angel Hunter.

Thomas shoved the Stetson off his forehead. "The two of you could sure have fooled me. It's none of my business—"

"You're right about that, Doc," Keene said succinctly.

He stepped off the stoop and hurried over to a young woman who struggled to hoist a sack of flour into a buckboard. "Let me give you a hand with that, Mrs. Rafferty."

Breathless, the tiny, fragile-looking woman stepped aside and allowed Keene to toss the heavy sack into the back of the wagon. "Thank you, Mr. MacKenzie."

In her mid-twenties, Kathleen Rafferty wore

a plain homespun gown. Her long black hair hung from beneath a poke bonnet that shaded a calm, blue-eyed gaze as she watched Keene load her supplies. Although the evidence of a life of hard labor and little luxury had begun to show on her face and thin body, the young Irishwoman's beauty was still undeniable.

Having followed Keene, Thomas began to help with the loading. "How are you feeling, Mrs. Rafferty?"

" 'Tis fine I am, Doctor Graham." Her voice carried a soft Irish lilt.

Frowning, he regarded her with a clinical stare. Having recently treated the woman after she suffered a miscarriage, her long medical history of hemorrhaging and miscarriages were of deep concern to him. "I asked you to come back for a checkup, Mrs. Rafferty," he said kindly.

Blushing, Kathleen Rafferty lowered her eyes. "I've been doin' fine, Doctor. There'd be no call for it, you see."

"What I see, Mrs. Rafferty, is a very ugly bruise on your arm."

Her eyes flashed with guilt as she covered the inflamed area with her hand. " 'Tis me own clumsiness, sir. I tripped and fell."

Thomas saw Keene stiffen momentarily, then continue to load the wagon. It was apparent that the scout didn't believe the explanation any more than he did. Her husband, Mike Rafferty, was foreman of one of the Irish crews, and the drunken brute's abuse of his wife was common knowledge.

"What's goin' on here?" a voice bellowed gruffly.

Speak of the devil. Grimacing, Thomas turned to greet the speaker. The unpleasant odor of whiskey wafted from the man.

"We were helping your wife load these heavy sacks, Rafferty," Thomas replied.

"I let ya alone for five minutes, an' as soon as me back's turned, you're throwin' yerself at whoever's in sight."

Rafferty raised his arm to strike his wife, but Keene MacKenzie reached out with lightning speed and caught the man's arm in motion. The two men silently glared at one another until Keene felt Rafferty relax. He released his grip, and the bully lowered his arm.

"Considering your wife's recent illness, Rafferty, I must insist as her doctor that you do not allow her to do this kind of heavy labor." Thomas knew his words were wasted. The stubborn, hard-headed Rafferty took no one's advice.

Thomas's gaze remained unwavering under Rafferty's black glare. "And I'm tellin' ya to mind your own business," Rafferty shot back. Then he added for his own defense, "I keep a roof over her head and food in her belly. Ain't too much to expect her to tote a few sacks now and then."

Rafferty picked up the final sack, tossed it into the back of the wagon and unhitched the horses. "Get in the wagon," he barked.

"Let me help you, Mrs. Rafferty," Thomas offered when Kathleen started to step up on the high buckboard.

"She don't need no help," Rafferty growled.

He climbed up, grabbed the reins, and goaded the team to motion before Kathleen was seated. The poor woman fell down heavily against the seat. Regaining her balance, she sat upright.

Thomas and Keene watched silently as the wagon rambled away. Stealing a side glance at MacKenzie, Thomas saw the scout's usually impassive expression now etched with anger.

Above the clamor of the music, for the past thirty minutes the small circle of men had been discussing the recent presidential inauguration of U.S. Grant. Although listening to the conversation, Thomas frequently lifted his glance to follow Rory Callahan as she whirled around the floor in the arms of one partner after another.

She looked breathtaking, dressed in a pale green gown which hung in swags over a white pleated tulle flounce. His appreciative gaze roved to her rounded bosom. A white tulle flounce with narrow puff sleeves added a modest touch to the bare shoulders and daring décolletage of the French gown. He felt a knot of rising passion in his loins and reluctantly shifted his attention back to the conversation.

But the attraction became too enticing to ignore. A short while later, he broke away from the group and wandered over to Keene MacKenzie, who stood leaning against a wall.

"You holding up this wall, Keene?" he gibed lightly. "Haven't seen you out on that dance floor yet."

"Reckon you won't either," the scout responded in a laconic drawl.

"You got something against dancing, Keene?"

"Have you, Doc? Ain't seen you out there hopping around like a drunken buck," Keene challenged.

Any further word that Thomas might have offered in his own defense was cut off when several screeching chords on the fiddle quieted the room. All eyes turned toward the town's mayor as he called for attention.

"Ladies and gents, it's time for what you've all been waiting for—a real, gen-u-whine, heel-stomping hoedown!"

Immediately the rush was on. To the twang of a banjo and the saw of a fiddle, people scurried to claim partners. A heavy-set woman with a wide smile and a purposeful gleam in her eye promptly approached Thomas. "Doctor Graham?" Clarissa Humphrey asked hopefully.

Thomas grinned at the wife of the mayor and accepted the invitation. "My pleasure, ma'am." He took her arm and led her onto the dance floor.

The spectators who were unfortunate enough not to have partners moved back and lined the walls as the dancers formed squares.

The mayor began to clap his hands to the beat of the music. "Bow to your partners," he called out in the vibrant resonance that had helped to get him elected.

"Gents, hold her tight, then circle to the right." The laughter of the crowd rose above the music as the couples circled the floor.

"Now turn her around and circle back. Make your feet go wickety-whack." The room resounded with the responsive stomp of the men's boots on the wooden floor.

As the music livened, so did the dancers' enthusiasm and enjoyment. The men lifted and swung their partners; the women reacted with shrieks of pleasure.

"Now all join hands and circle left, mind the music and keep the step," the mayor called out.

The hall rang with the clamor of music and gaiety as the spectators clapped their hands and stamped their feet in accompaniment. With lively laughter, Rory weaved from partner to partner, her red hair bouncing bewitchingly on her shoulders.

"Ladies to the center, men to the rear," Humphrey chanted. "Time to wave bye-bye 'cause you're gonna part here."

"Bye, Rory," the young telegrapher, who had luckily found himself briefly partnered with her, called out good-naturedly.

"Bye, bye, Randy." She waved gaily to him, her green eyes flashing with merriment.

"All you ladies join hands and circle the floor," the mayor shouted. "That sure looked purty, gals, so do it once more."

The ladies continued to move in a wide ring until told to stop and greet a new partner.

"Ladies, circle your partner. Now the gent to his right."

To Rory's surprise, she found herself facing Doctor Graham.

"Well, Miss Callahan," he said with a pleased

smile. They laughed warmly into each other's eyes.

As the dance drew to a close, Mayor Humphrey called out, "Gents, it's time to grab that lady and without a miss, give that little gal a thank-you kiss."

As shrieks and giggles from the women sounded around them, Thomas spanned Rory's waist with his hands. "Well, I'm glad I held out for the finish, Miss Callahan."

He slowly lowered his head. She closed her eyes and lifted her pursed lips to him. Startled, she reopened her eyes abruptly when she felt the kiss he pressed on her cheek.

"Thank you, ma'am," he said properly.

The faintest trace of a smile curved the corners of his lips, as if he had guessed her anticipation. Swept by a hot blush of embarrassment, she nodded. "Thank you, Doctor Graham." Then Rory turned and walked away from him.

Thomas followed and took her hand. "I think we both could use some fresh air, Miss Callahan."

Rory allowed him to lead her out a nearby door, but once outside, she withdrew her hand from his and walked ahead of him.

Thomas was content to trail behind, admiring the provocative swing of her hips. She stopped and leaned back against the trunk of a cottonwood.

As the soft glow of moonlight changed her red hair to auburn, he devoured the image of her and said softly, "Don't be angry with me, Rory."

The deep, smooth, honied sound of his voice

had a narcotic effect on her. Whatever annoyance she had entertained dissipated with his first word.

Rory turned to him. The beauty of her serene gaze momentarily robbed him of his breath. "Why would I be angry, Doctor?"

"You're a paradox, Miss Callahan," he murmured when he found his voice.

Her brow arched in amusement. "A paradox? In what way, Doctor?"

"I'm trying to decide which is the real Rory Callahan. I remember a desperate young girl dressed in jeans and boots scrambling up a mountainside. Now I'm gazing upon a serene beauty gowned in the latest Paris fashion, wielding a fan instead of a Winchester."

"What is so unusual about a woman dressing up for a dance, Doctor Graham?"

He moved closer to her. The faint fragrance of lavender toyed with his senses. "I'm just curious to know which is the real Rory Callahan."

She smiled as seductively as a Circe. "Surely you already know that a woman plays many roles, Doctor."

Chuckling warmly to withstand the assault, he changed the subject. "Doctor. Doctor Graham. Such formality. Won't you call me T.J.?"

Rory smiled at the absurdity of the thought. "I can't call you that. It would be like addressing my father." She cocked her head to a fetching angle and tapped her fan against her cheek. "You must have a name."

"Thomas Jefferson Graham, at your service, ma'am."

"Oh, no!" Her eyes sparkled with merriment.

Thomas grimaced. "Don't tell me. Let me guess," Thomas groaned. "Your father's name is Thomas Jefferson."

At Rory's nod, they both broke into laughter.

"It does appear we have a definite problem here. But surely, you haven't always been called by your initials?" she asked hopefully.

"Well, when I was younger, whenever I really misbehaved, my mother would frown and call me Thomas."

"Thomas." For a brief moment her green eyes deepened with reflection as she rolled the name on her tongue. "I like it. The name suits you much better than T.J. May I call you Thomas?"

"It would be my pleasure, ma'am."

"I imagine your mother misses you, Thomas."

"My mother's dead, ma'am. She and my father died twelve years ago."

Her eyes clouded in sympathy. "Oh, I'm sorry. I understand your sorrow. My mother died a year ago."

"Sorry to hear that, ma'am." His brown eyes had deepened to velvet. She felt enveloped by their warmth. "And your home is where, Thomas?"

"Virginia. When I got out of the Army, I returned there and set up a practice near Williamsburg."

"And what would lure a doctor from Virginia to come West with the railroad?" She began to stroll again.

"Well, the completion of the transcontinental railroad was something I just didn't want to miss. This is a great milestone in history. Just a few years ago, this nation was torn apart by a civil war, and now here we are linking one coast to the other—uniting the country as we've never been united before."

Rory stopped once again and leaned back against the tree. "You really feel strongly about it, don't you, Thomas?"

"It was easier for me to visit Europe than the west coast of America. But the railroad will change all that." He grinned. "I suppose this all sounds very boring to you."

"Not at all. I've never looked at the railroad in that light before. It's always been such an unpleasant issue with my father."

"Yes, I've noticed." His dark eyes danced with devilment. "When this offer from the railroad came along, I welcomed the opportunity to be a part of it." He took her hand. "Well, I've done enough talking about myself." They began to stroll. "Tell me about Rory Callahan. What does she want out of life?"

Rory smiled. "Well, I haven't really thought too much about it. I've always been very happy right here. I love the ranch. Can't imagine living anywhere else." She laughed lightly. "I've never been to Europe like you, Thomas. I've lived my whole life right here in Utah except for the two years my mother insisted I go to Missouri to a finishing school. And then I couldn't wait to get back to the Circle C."

They stopped in the shadow of an oak tree, and she leaned back against it. "My mother had been a schoolmarm when she married my father and she educated me—and Keene."

"Keene?" he said, surprised.

Rory nodded. "Keene's mother was our cook. We both grew up on the Circle C." She glanced sheepishly. "I'm spoiled rotten, you know."

"Really? I hadn't noticed," he said, amused.

"Well, it's not my fault," she added grinning adorably. "Men have always given me whatever I've asked for."

She felt her heartbeat quicken when his dark eyes gazed into hers. "That wouldn't be hard for a man to do, ma'am." He inched closer. "And what, for instance, have you asked for?"

Amusement brightened her eyes. "Ma'am. Miss Callahan. Such formality," she said, mocking his earlier remarks. "Why not Rory?"

"Rory." Her name on his lips had the potency of a caress.

The air felt charged with a hushed expectancy. "How old are you, Rory?" he asked.

Her heartbeat quickened as she felt his heated stare. She looked up into the dark-eyed gaze leveled on her mouth. "I'm twenty-one."

"And it hasn't occurred to you to get married?"

"Oh, it has occurred to me, Thomas, but I always heard you were supposed to be in love to marry." For a long moment they stared deeply in each other's eyes. "I've never been in love."

In the moonlight, her eyes glistened like green jewels. With a low throatiness, she asked, "What about you, Thomas? I can't believe you haven't married." She held her breath, fearful of his answer.

"No, never. I also believe love is essential to marriage," he said slowly. He moved nearer. The male essence of him encompassed her, sheathed her like a bond. He raised his hand and traced a finger down the delicate line of her cheek and across the sensitive curve of her lips. "So beautiful, Rory," he whispered softly. The husky cadence stroked her spine. Mesmerized her.

Unintentionally, she swayed toward him and he cupped her face in his hands. "Rory. Rory." He groaned the ragged entreaty. "You fire a man's blood, Rory Callahan."

Reluctantly, he released her and stepped back. "Good night, you redheaded temptress."

This time he was the one to walk away.

Chapter Four

Depending on how fast the rails were laid, Tent Town moved at least once a month.

Three mammoth cars, each eighty-five feet long, ten feet wide, and eight feet high formed the center of the town. One car contained multiple, three-tiered bunks which ran along the entire length of each side. The other two cars consisted of an office, a kitchen, and a dining room.

Several sidings branched off from the main track to maneuver the trains which daily brought the supplies that enabled the iron track to stretch ever westward like a silver snake slithering slowly across the continent.

Clustered a short distance away, but close enough for protection from Indians and wild animals, were the pitched tents of the families of the married men and any others who preferred

61

the risk of living outside to the smells and sights of the overcrowded sleeping car.

A large corral erected at one end of town enclosed the several dozen horses and mules, so vital in the railroad's construction. A dozen or more box cars containing food and supplies clustered together at the other end.

The favorite spot in town was the saloon tent. The makeshift bar consisted of nothing more than a long wooden plank supported by several barrels—but a place, nonetheless, where the men went in the evenings to drink and talk.

Each weekend from Saturday night until Monday morning, Jake O'Brien, who operated the saloon, brought in a dozen or more of his girls. For a small percentage of the action, the foremen would provide Jake with several partitioned boxcars equipped with cots so that the whores could "accommodate" the men.

But come sunrise on Monday morning, it was work as usual, and the grueling, back-breaking task would resume again until the following Saturday night.

Now on a Monday morning as the camp began to stir after a rowdy weekend, Michaleen Dennehy had already been working for hours.

Small in size and stature, Michaleen stood not much more than a foot taller than the elves and pixies who were said to inhabit the rolling emerald hills of his native County Down.

Born the seventh son of a seventh son, the probability of his inheriting even one rock of Irish soil was so remote that when the potato famine hit Ireland in the '50s, Michaleen abandoned digging potatoes for cooking them instead. He came to America and had worked as a railroad cook for the past fifteen years. Now at age fifty-five, there wasn't a single way of preparing a potato that Michaleen Dennehy had not attempted.

The top half of him appeared to be entirely covered with pure-white hair. For other than a pair of very round and very bright blue eyes, most of Michaleen's features were obscured under a wooly beard, shaggy mustache, and a set of bushy eyebrows woven together above the bridge of a red, bulbous nose furrowed with blue veins.

A bright red tam o'shanter, which Michaleen claimed had been worn by his great-great grandfather at the Battle of the Boyne, was always perched at a jaunty angle atop a head of unruly hair that grew as wide as it was long.

Now, as the brightening rays of dawn lightened the sky, Michaleen gave three quick yanks on the train whistle especially installed as a dinner bell. Then cupping his hands to his mouth, he shouted at the top of his lungs, "Come and get it!" The latter was hollered for his own satisfaction, since old habits died hard in Michaleen.

As if awaiting the cue, men began to fill the benches next to the many rows of long tables. Abundant trays of freshly baked bread and pots of hot coffee were there for the taking after Michaleen and his assistants quickly filled the workers' plates with beef, beans and potatoes. The menu rarely varied.

"Potatoes again!" one of the ex-Rebel crewmen complained. "Ain't ya'll ever heard of grits, Dennehy?"

When several other Southern soldiers added their hoots of disapproval, Michaleen said good-naturedly, "Now, now, laddies, listen to yer papa and eat yer potatoes. I'm guessin' about now ya all can use some starch in yer peckers."

Mike Rafferty sat nearby listening to the exchange. He hated the former Reb soldiers, but Rafferty hated Michaleen Dennehy more because the little man made no secret of his loathing for the crew boss.

Seeing an opportunity to harass the cook, Rafferty quickly added his gibe. "I think Dennehy's mother gave her little runt a potato to suck on instead of a tit," he snorted.

"Weel now, will ya listen to the likes of him," Michaleen remarked, arching a furry brow. "Jus' when did a black-hearted Irishman such as yaself get so wise, Rafferty? Considerin' the Dennehys were playin' harps in the Halls of Tara while Raffertys were still swingin' through trees."

"Don't be pushin' ya luck, runt," Rafferty threatened.

Unintimidated by the bully's threat, Michaleen's eyes brightened further with puckish rascality. "And by their tails, I've heard tell," he continued, adding fuel to the fire.

The men in earshot broke into laughter at the little man's scrappiness, but Rafferty did not take kindly to being made the brunt of the joke. He shoved his plate aside and jumped to his feet, hands balled at his sides. He wanted to slam his fist into the mouth of the smirking little man, but knew he would lose face in the eyes of the other men.

Michael Rafferty governed himself by a warped code of fair play—he balked at striking a man as small as Dennehy, but thought nothing of beating up his own defenseless wife.

"It ain't gettin' any earlier. Let's get movin'," he ordered with a thunderous growl to the men around him. Then he thumped out of the room.

With the efficiency gleaned from years of experience, Dennehy and his assistants swiftly disposed of the remaining crews. By the time the final spikers and bolters finished eating, preparation had begun for the next meal.

Standing at the entrance of her tent, Kathleen Rafferty watched the train puff away, carrying Mike and the last of the crew to "end of track" about ten miles away.

She was unmindful of the faint smile that softened her face as the morning breeze gently stirred the long strands of dark hair on her shoulders.

For this was the time of day Kathleen loved the most. The camp quieted, rid of the hundreds of men who crowded back at sunset with their shouting and fighting.

Her gaze wandered to the corral where Keene MacKenzie was preparing to ride out. She watched him mount with the effortless, lithe movement of a man born to the saddle.

As he ambled past on his gelding, Keene tipped a finger to the brim of his hat and nodded politely. "Morning, Mrs. Rafferty."

"And to you, Mr. MacKenzie," she replied. Her longing gaze lingered on the scout's back as he gently nudged his knees, goading the horse to a faster gait.

Kathleen felt the heat from the hot blush of guilt that swept through her. She knew the thoughts she harbored about Keene MacKenzie were sinful—adulterous in the eyes of her church. But despite her feeling of guilt, the reticent scout remained the center of her fantasies.

Kathleen had loathed Michael Rafferty from the time they were children on neighboring farms in County Kerry. Her thoughts often drifted to the rolling green countryside of her homeland. The smoky village of Kelso overlooked the sea and, on a clear day, she would sit on the edge of the steep cliff and watch the sea swallows dip and swirl above the rocks below.

Though poor, her parents were kind and loving, so Kathleen grew up wanting for nothing, content to tend the tiny flock of sheep on her parents' farm.

Then, eight years ago, a drunken Michael Rafferty had come upon her while she crossed the moor in search of a stray lamb. He raped her and when she found herself with child, her parents and the local priest had insisted he wed her. And from that time on, every day of her life with the drunken bully had been a living hell.

"Top of the marning, darlin'." The pleasant

cadence broke into her reverie.

Smiling warmly, she turned to the speaker. "Good morning, Michaleen."

Michaleen Dennehy stood beside her holding a plate. A smile gleamed lovingly from under his shaggy mustache. "I've brought ya some hot food, Kathleen."

"'Tis kind of you, Michaleen, but truly, I'm not hungry."

"But ya mus' eat, darlin', to gain back your strength," he insisted.

Michaleen worried about Kathleen's health as much as the doctor did. His loathing of Michael Rafferty stemmed primarily from the bully's brutal treatment of his gentle wife.

Taking her arm, Michaleen led Kathleen over to the stumps of two sawed-off trees. "Now sit yarself down and eat this food while it's still hot, darlin'."

To avoid further argument, Kathleen took a few bites of the bread and began to nibble at the potatoes. She left the beef and beans untouched.

As she ate, Michaleen studied her face for any evidence of fresh bruises. "I see the Black Dev'l didn't abuse you this weekend."

She was not shocked by his bluntness. Michaleen was the only person to whom Kathleen confided, admitting things to him that she no longer even confessed to the priest.

The elderly clergyman, who came weekly to say the Mass, professed to be sympathetic, but when she had complained about her husband's beatings, he mentioned her vows, advising she had best try to obey Rafferty. And at a later date, when Kathleen almost died from hemorrhaging after a miscarriage, the goodly priest reminded her that her wifely responsibility was to continue in the attempt to bear a child.

Under this burden of despair and loneliness, Kathleen had discovered the unlikeliest of friends—Michaleen Dennehy. His sympathy and understanding helped to assuage the misery of her marriage.

"Michaleen, you know I see little of Mike at week's end," she admitted with a sigh of relief. Both knew her husband's preoccupation with the visiting whores.

Unable to swallow another bite, Kathleen handed him the plate. "Thank you, Michaleen."

He sighed, eyeing the half-eaten plate of food. "Ah, Kathleen," he said sadly, "what's a man to do with ya?" Patting her hand, Michaleen rose to his feet. "I'll come back later, darlin'."

Smiling fondly, Kathleen watched him cross the camp to return to his cooking duties. Then, wearily, she rose and returned to her tent.

Upon entering, her attention was caught by the shirt Mike had flung on her cot before he left. He had ordered her to replace the buttons ripped off the front in the heat of passion by one of the whores.

Kathleen went to a small trunk which held all her worldly possessions and dug out a small woven basket. The kit contained needle and thread, but where would she ever find the buttons to repair the shirt?

*   *   *

Not more than five miles due north from the makeshift town, T.J. Callahan glared at his daughter across the breakfast table.

"And I don't ever again want to hear of a daughter of mine sneaking out with any of that trash from the railroad."

"Daddy, I did not *sneak* out. Dr. Graham and I stepped outside for some fresh air," Rory argued back. "We weren't gone more than five minutes. If that nosey banker's wife was so damned worried about it, why didn't she come out and join us?"

"You watch your tongue, gal. A lady don't use dirty words. And I never said Agatha Pebbles was the one who told me."

Rory flung down her napkin, her green eyes flashing with anger. "You didn't have to. I'm sure Mrs. Busybody Pebbles couldn't wait to ride out here to tell you. And furthermore, Dr. Graham is a perfect gentleman."

"You don't know anything about him," her father accused.

"And neither do you," she shot back defiantly.

"He works for the railroad. I don't have to know any more than that."

Father and daughter glared at one another. Two strong-willed people, they were both used to having their own way.

"Since Mother died, you make snap judgments about everyone. Your hatred and suspicions are destroying you. First Keene—"

Callahan's fist slammed down on the table, cutting off her words. The impact splashed a dark coffee stain on the tablecloth. From a face red with fury, his eyes seemed to bulge out of his head. "I have forbidden that name to be mentioned in this house. I will not have you disobey me."

His shouts did not intimidate his determined daughter. "And I will not be ordered around like one of the hired hands. I'm not a child."

"You're lucky you aren't, gal, or I'd be warming your britches right now."

The ludicrous threat diminished her anger. For even as a child, no matter how mischievous her deed, nor his degree of anger at the time, her father had never raised a hand to her.

She began to feel pangs of regret over their cross words. However, the issue was not closed; she intended to see as much of Thomas Graham as she could.

"Daddy, you know you've never spanked me in my life," she said gently.

Callahan, too, recognized that the spat had ended, but he had to have the last word. "And I can see now, a swat or two might have hewed you down a might. You sure don't have your mother's gentle ways."

He shook his head wistfully at the thought of his wife. Her tragic death had left Callahan with an unhealed wound in his heart.

In 1842, Thomas Callahan had left Missouri with not much more than the shirt on his back. He settled in Utah and started the Circle C. With hard work and determination, he had fought every obstacle in the demanding country to keep the Circle C running. By the time the Mormons arrived in the territory five years later, the ranch had already begun to show signs of becoming one of the largest spreads in Utah. The first time Callahan saw Sarah Coventry, he fell in love with the gentle, young Mormon girl. Feeling the same way about him, she had forsaken her religion to marry the rancher, and Callahan had remained devoted to Sarah until her death. Her memory haunted every moment of his life.

"Hope you two are through yellin'," Pete Faber announced, interrupting Callahan's thoughts as he walked into the room. "Heard you clean down to the bunkhouse." He sat at the table and poured himself a cup of coffee.

Callahan leaned back in his chair and lit a cigar. Each day over morning coffee, the rancher and his foreman discussed the plans for running the huge ranch.

"I want those mavericks branded and driven to the east pasture," Callahan declared as Pete rolled a cigarette.

Pete nodded. "Good idea. There's plenty of grass for grazing."

As they talked, one of the hands knocked on the door and with hat in hand stepped hesitantly into the room. "Got bad news, T.J. I was riding the south boundary near that Tent Town. The fence we strung's been torn down."

"Dammit," Callahan cursed. "Bet that railroad trash is responsible again. They get liquored up on Saturday nights and all hell breaks loose."

"Curly, would you like a cup of coffee?" Rory offered graciously, interrupting her father's tirade.

71

"No thank you, ma'am." Despite the girl's sincerity, acceptance was taboo. The hands on the Circle C knew their place, and no one accepted any hospitality from the ranch house unless T.J. Callahan extended the courtesy. The only exception was Pete Faber, but he was the foreman and had been with the Circle C from the time Callahan started the ranch.

Pete gulped down the remains of his coffee and got to his feet. "I'll take a couple of the boys and we'll see to mending the fence. Let's go, Curly."

With a bashful smile, the young cowpoke nodded to Rory and backed out awkwardly. "Thanks for the offer, Miss Rory." He slapped on his Stetson and hurried after the foreman.

An hour later, accompanied by Rory, Callahan rode up to the group of Circle C riders. The four men were at the task of mending the wire fence which ran for three miles parallel to the railroad tracks.

Every time Tent Town moved, Callahan moved the wire fence, making sure it extended a mile beyond each end of the town limits.

Still frustrated, blaming the railroad for the damage but having no way to prove it, Callahan barked at the crew who were hard at work. "You men gonna take all day mending a few feet of wire?"

Unruffled, Pete Faber glanced up at the ranch owner. "Now just shed those spurs, T.J. We're working as fast as we can," he said in his easygoing drawl. "We gotta replace some of the poles."

"Well I want those cows branded and moved today," Callahan declared. He glanced up in disgust when a train came around the bend and chugged into view.

From the cab of the train, Caleb Murphy squinted ahead as he sighted the ranchers. "Hey, Doc, ain't that the Callahan gal up yonder?"

Thomas Graham had his nose buried in a medical journal. His head shot up. "Rory." He leaped over to the other side of the cab and peered out.

"Murph, stop the train!" he shouted excitedly when he recognized Rory Callahan.

"Stop the train?" Murphy hollered back gruffly, but he slowed the locomotive and ground to a stop across from the Circle C riders.

"Good morning, Rory," Thomas called to her from the door of the cab.

Pleased to see him again, Rory returned the greeting. "Good morning, Thomas."

"Mr. Callahan," Thomas said, acknowledging the rancher. Callahan mumbled an expletive under his breath.

Spying Pete Faber among the group, Thomas called to him. "How's your shoulder feeling, Pete?"

The foreman grinned and waved. "Just fine, Doc. You patched me up real good."

"What's the wire for?" Thomas asked out of curiosity.

Rory was horrified when her father, who had ignored Thomas until then, quickly jumped on the reply. "Want to make sure all you railroad trash stay on the other side of the track where you belong. Don't want to see any of you on the Circle C."

"Yes, sir, I remember you made those particular wishes quite clear at our last meeting," Thomas said good-naturedly. He had no intention of engaging in a verbal sparring match with the rancher.

"See that you don't forget," Callahan warned.

However, Caleb Murphy did not share Thomas's caution, and he promptly spewed a stream of tobacco juice out the window of the cab. "'Pears to be a peck of work for nothin'—you'll just have to move the fence again in a couple of weeks."

"'Pears to be my business, railroad man, not yours." The retort was made with a black glare from Callahan. "Get moving; you're holding up my crew."

Thomas had already climbed down from the cab of the train, and Rory rode over to the fence and dismounted. "You're looking very lovely this morning," he said.

She blushed with pleasure. "Thank you."

Somehow his dark-eyed gaze always seemed to convey more than the casual words that crossed his lips. She felt like a schoolgirl in his presence. She had been around men all her life and never felt uncomfortable with any of them. Yet his masculinity challenged her own femininity, making her more aware of the physical differences between man and woman—and more intrigued by these attracting differences.

Remembering those few intimate moments they had shared in the garden the night of the dance, Rory couldn't help but imagine what it would be like to have Thomas tell her he desired her . . . or even more thrilling, that he loved her.

"Of course, you always look lovely." The pleasant cadence drew her out of her musing. "This morning is no exception, Miss Callahan."

"You flatter me, Doctor Graham. I imagine you could charm the skin off a snake," she remarked. She dredged up the earlier criticism of him as a defensive measure to remind herself to be wary of his magnetic appeal.

"What an unflattering analogy, Miss Callahan. Surely you aren't comparing yourself to a cold-blooded serpent?"

"On the contrary, Doctor. I feel more like the lamb being led to the slaughter."

When Thomas threw back his head in laughter, she took the opportunity to study his face. The rugged lines had been changed to boyishness by his engaging smile. Her gaze shifted to the firm outline of his mouth with its full, sensual lips. The thought of those lips covering her own brought another blush to her already glowing complexion.

"I see you only as a very lovely woman. And a very desirable one," he added truthfully.

"Do you always flirt so outrageously, Doctor?"

"Just telling it as I see it, ma'am." The words were accompanied by another devastating grin.

Callahan chose that moment to ride over to them, and Thomas offered a friendly nod, only to be ignored again.

"You coming, Rory?"

Incensed and embarrassed by his rudeness, she shook her head. "I'll ride back with the crew."

Father and daughter exchanged an angry glare. He wheeled his horse around, spurred his mount, and rode away.

Murphy gave several blasts from the train whistle. The clamor ended any further conversation between Rory and Thomas, who hurried back and leaped onto the step of the cab as the train began to inch forward.

Rory mounted and nudged her horse to keep pace with the locomotive. "Something looks different about you, Thomas. What is it?"

"Must be this gun belt." Thomas laughed and motioned to the Colt now slung at his hip. "I learned a man can't roam around this country without one."

"We'll make a real Westerner of you yet, Thomas," Rory shouted. She reined up and waved good-bye.

Thomas cupped his hands to his mouth. "When can I see you again, Rory?"

"I don't know." Rory knew she still had some convincing to do with her father.

"How about next Sunday?"

Shaking her head, she called back, "I can't hear you."

Thomas leaned out the cab to repeat the question but she was already out of earshot. "Oh, hell!"

He raised his hand and waved.

Chapter Five

The unusually warm spring day had prompted
Michaleen to move part of his kitchen outside.
As Thomas stepped off the train, the smell of
frying potatoes permeated the air. Despite the
early hour, the cooks were already hard at
work preparing the noon meal. Once completed,
the fare would then be packed up and taken
by Murphy to end of track, where a hungry
crew would consume it on their hour-long
lunch break.

Amazed, Thomas paused to observe the operation. The smokestack of an abandoned steam
shovel had been sawed in half, lengthwise. The
two sections had been placed on metal tripods.
Grates had then been set over low-banked fires
in the bottom of each section. Michaleen and
his assistants now shuffled from one frying pan
to the other, flipping over the potatoes heaped

in the heavy, cast-iron skillets that lined the makeshift grill.

Not a day passed that trains or wagons did not haul in tons of food. And wherever or whenever possible, representatives from the railroad negotiated with local farmers to procure fresh fruit and vegetables to fill the stomachs of this massive army inching its way ever westward.

"A good day to ya, Doctar," Michaleen called upon spying Thomas.

"The same to you, Michaleen." Thomas liked the scrappy little cook, as he did most of the diverse and unconventional people involved in the monumental task of building the transcontinental railroad.

Abandoning the cooking duties to his assistants, Michaleen beckoned Thomas to his side. "Doctar, will ya be takin' a look at Mrs. Rafferty?" he whispered to avoid being heard by other ears. "The dear child is not well, I'm thinkin'."

The weight of the world appeared to be resting on Michaleen's shoulders as the barely visible slit of his mouth puckered into a grim line. "I can't get the woman to eat."

Michaleen had raised this issue often with Thomas. Just as concerned as Michaleen over the health of Kathleen Rafferty, Thomas nodded in understanding. He squeezed the little man's shoulder to offer him some assurance. "I'll see what I can do, Michaleen."

At the sudden sound of shrill cackling, both men turned to see Caleb Murphy approach with a wire cage of squawking hens in each hand. Michaleen's gloom dissipated at first glance, and a wide Irish grin split his furry countenance.

"Murphy! Ya've brought me chicks!"

"That I did, and I hadda been out of me mind to agree to the doin' of it," Caleb grumbled. "I'll be glad to be rid of these stinking chickens."

"Ah, ya're a good man, Caleb Murphy," Michaleen avowed. He winked at the engineer. "And I've a bottle of Irish in me tote. I'm thinkin' ya'd not be adverse to a good nip, 'bout now."

"Well, you're right about that, you old piece of buzzard bait. I've had me fill of listening to these cackling hens."

Having just suffered through Murphy's singing, Thomas was hard pressed not to consider the cackling hens a fair trade-off.

Michaleen patted one of the cages. "Now dan't be speakin' so disrespectful of me darlin's here," he cautioned. "Soon we'll be enjoyin' the taste of fresh eggs in the marnin'."

His bright eyes glowed warmly. "Will ya be carin' to join us, Doctar?"

Thomas waved off the invitation. "Next time, Michaleen. I've got a lot to do right now." Grinning, he walked away.

"Ah, what a fine man he is," Michaleen said as the two men watched Thomas hurry toward the line beginning to form outside the door of his makeshift clinic.

"On that we agree," Murphy concurred.

Poking Murphy in the side with his elbow, Michaleen offered a sly wink. "And 'tis time we get on with our business, too."

Grinning, each of the men picked up a cage of chickens.

*   *   *

Patching up the injuries and wounds of the men were not Thomas's only responsibilities. The families of the crew often required medical attention as well. It was not unusual for him to deliver a baby in the middle of the night or set an arm or leg of a youngster who had fallen out of a tree.

Delivering a newborn life into the world was a satisfying and welcome diversion from the more serious and grim accidents of the railroaders, which often ended in death or dismemberment.

Several hours later, Thomas finished treating his last patient, a five-year-old girl who had punctured her foot while running barefoot. After treating and bandaging the infected area, he tousled her head of blond curls. "Now you keep your shoes on, young lady," he advised, pulling out a piece of peppermint candy from a drawer.

The youngster's eyes glowed with pleasure at the sight of the sweet. Shyly, she reached out and accepted the offering. Then, giggling, she popped the mint into her mouth.

"God bless you, Doctor," her mother said as the girl scampered off to join her playmates.

Thomas closed his medical bag, then walked to the door. Crossing his arms across his chest, he leaned on the casement. Murphy had pulled out, taking several cooks to serve lunch at the end of track. Now, with the hustle of preparing lunch completed, and only a skeleton crew remaining, the camp had again quieted down—

until the evening when once again the returning railroaders would swarm over the camp.

Michaleen's words of concern for Kathleen Rafferty still troubled Thomas, but she had not appeared for an examination. He decided to seek her out.

Thomas found Kathleen with her arms elbow-deep in a tub of water, scrubbing on a washboard. "Good afternoon, Mrs. Rafferty."

Kathleen blushed, knowing he would lecture her for not following his instructions. "And to you, Doctor Graham."

He fulfilled her foreboding with his next statement. "I had hoped to examine you today, Mrs. Rafferty."

She lowered her eyes. "I mean no disrespect, Doctor, but I've not the need for it."

"Kathleen, you are not looking well. I would like to reexamine you."

Her eyes shifted in guilt. "Michael says I'm not to be runnin' to you with me ailments, Doctor. He says I'm usin' ill health as an excuse not to be doin' me proper work."

After witnessing the incident in town, Thomas showed no surprise at the order from the insensitive bully. "Kathleen," he said gently, "we both know better. I wouldn't concern myself if I believed you were in good health."

Closing her eyes, Kathleen forced aside her thoughts. How she wanted to tell him the truth— that her conscience ailed her more than her body. But she was not going to unload any of her problems on this kindly man.

"But 'tis true, Doctor. I'm feelin' fine. 'Tis only

me appetite's been ailin', not me body. That's why I'm lookin' so peaked lately."

Obviously, her husband's displeasure was a greater threat to the woman than the danger of her own failing health. Thomas saw the uselessness of further argument.

"Well, will you at least promise me you will try to eat three meals a day, Kathleen?"

She raised her eyes and met his probing gaze. "Aye, Doctor, I promise."

"And one more promise, Kathleen." Thomas slipped a bottle of tonic into her hand. "I want you to take one teaspoonful of this daily."

Her eyes widened with uneasiness. "A tonic! What is this for, Doctor Graham?"

"A vitamin supplement. It will help to increase your appetite as well, Kathleen."

"But if Michael knew I was takin'—" She cut off her words, realizing she had said too much already.

"Your husband need not know, Kathleen. But I'd be glad to explain to him your need to take it."

"Oh, no, don't do that," she cried out. He heard desperation in her tone and saw the fear in her eyes. She shoved the bottle into the pocket of her gown. "I'll take the tonic, Doctor, I promise. But please don't tell Michael."

Thomas thought of plenty he would like to tell Michael Rafferty, but before he could say anything further, the sound of a gunshot broke the quiet of the afternoon.

He spun around to the diversion. Bowed low over his dun, Keene MacKenzie rode at a full gallop toward Tent Town. The scout thundered into the camp, leaping from the horse before the gelding had come to a full stop.

At once, women, children, and the five other men who had remained in town anxiously surrounded him.

"There's a big war party headed this way," Keene shouted. "All you woman and children, get into the sleeping car, now!"

Several in the crowd started screaming in panic, but they were quickly quieted by the more stalwart members. The women began to herd together their children.

"Glad to see you here, Doc," Keene said when he spied Thomas.

"What do you want me to do?" Thomas asked, relinquishing authority to the experienced scout.

"Town's spread out too much to defend all of it. We'll build a barricade in front of the sleeping car." The men immediately ran to stack railroad ties.

Keene shouted to the women entering the car. "How many of you ladies have fired a rifle before?" Several women raised their hands.

"I'm sorry, but we'll need your help. Round up all the rifles." Kathleen rushed inside to get at the rifles and ammunition the railroad kept strapped to the ceiling of the sleeping car.

Grimacing, Keene added, "I need a good rider to get to the end of track for help. Gotta warn whoever goes, those Utes aren't so dumb they won't try to stop you."

"I'll go, Keene," Thomas volunteered.

"Figure before this is over, we're gonna need you right here, Doc."

"Pa says I'm part horse, sir," a thirteen-year-old boy spoke up.

"Oh, no, Jimmy," his mother sobbed, tugging at her son's shirt sleeve.

The drumming of hooves and wild yelping cut off her protest as a band of more then fifty savages rode toward camp. Without a further word, the young boy shrugged off his mother's hand and leaped on the back of Keene's gelding. Goading the horse to a gallop, he sped away as several women forced the grief-stricken mother into the railroad car.

The six men had barely finished the barricade of railroad ties when a flood of arrows and even a few bullets began to whiz past them. Michaleen dashed to safety toting the cages of chickens as the whooping and hollering Indians charged the small, outnumbered defenders.

The blasting gunshots, thundering hooves, yelping war cries, and screaming children intensified the horror and confusion of the attack.

Keene's timely arrival had thwarted the Indians' plan to hit the small garrison and overrun the camp on the first charge. Now, under a relentless hail of bullets, the attackers were driven back and forced to take cover among the trees.

Yelling oaths, a few braves began to run from tree to tree. "They're just trying to draw your fire," Keene warned. "Hold your shot 'til you have a sure target."

Within minutes, streams of flaming arrows

began to streak the sky like lightning bolts. The tents and structures became engulfed in flames.

"There goes O'Brien's whorehouse," Keene reflected with irony when several of the abandoned boxcars began to burn.

"My God!" Thomas suddenly shouted. "My medical bag. Cover me."

"Doc, get back here," Keene yelled, but Thomas had already dashed toward his burning clinic.

He dodged behind a block of kegs and eyed the distance to the clinic. With still about fifty feet to go, he saw that there was no other cover between him and the burning building. The Indians spotted him, and arrows smacked into the barrels, the long feathered shafts embedding themselves in the wooden casks.

It was now or never. Thomas drew a deep breath, crouched low to make himself a smaller target, and dashed from the protective cover. Arrows flew around him, narrowly failing to strike their mark as he zig-zagged toward the burning hut.

Brandishing war clubs, several of the more aggressive Indians dashed from the trees and headed toward the burning hut. A rapid fire from Keene felled the lot.

Flames licked at the floor and walls of the blazing clinic as Thomas flung himself through the door. His eyes and nose burned from the astringent black smoke. He fumbled for his medical bag and uttered a prayerful thanks when his groping produced not only the bag, but the gun belt he had removed while examining his patients. Snatching the Colt out of the holster, he slung the belt over his shoulder and grabbed the medical bag.

Turning quickly to leave, Thomas froze at the sight of a painted savage blocking the doorway. With a blood-curdling war cry, the Indian raised a tomahawk and lunged at him. Thomas fired reflexively and got off two shots. The brave fell at Thomas's feet and the savage locked his arms around Thomas's legs, pulling him down. For a long moment, the two rolled together until Thomas succeeded in delivering a punch to the chin of his attacker. The blow freed him, and he crawled on his knees until he located his dropped medical bag, pistol, and gunbelt.

With the building on the verge of collapse, Thomas ran out the door. Coughing from the smoke in his lungs, he raced toward the stack of barrels. A well-aimed shot from Keene sent another brave at Thomas's heels sprawling to the ground.

Arrows and bullets kicked up the dirt around him as Thomas sprinted toward the barricade. He felt as if his lungs were ready to burst as he dove over the top and hit the ground. Dragging in deep breaths, he listened to the sound of his pounding heart in his throat.

"You're a damned fool, Doc. A damned lucky fool," Keene drawled.

"Will ya be lookin' at that," Michaleen sighed when he saw that the food supply boxcar had caught fire. Angrily, the little man stood up and shook his fist at the attackers. "I'm warnin' ya blasted heathens, ya'll be facin' the wrath of Michaleen Dennehy if ya meddle with me kitchen."

"Get down, Dennehy, before you get killed," Keene snapped, then turned suddenly at the sound of a thud.

One of the men had dropped his rifle and keeled over, an arrow protruding from his chest. Thomas quickly moved to the man. After a brief examination, he shook his head.

Kathleen Rafferty darted from the car and picked up the dead man's rifle. Crouching, she hurried over to Keene. He gave her a side glance of concern. "Mrs. Rafferty, what are you doing out here?" he questioned with a worried frown.

"I can load the rifles for you."

"It's too dangerous. Get back inside where you'll be safe."

"I'm not afraid, Keene," she said with firm conviction.

For a moment their gazes met and lingered. "Well, keep your head down," he warned and returned his attention to the battle.

Once again the Indians pulled back, giving the defenders a temporary respite. Keene used the time to assess the ammunition supply.

"Can you fire a rifle at all?" he asked.

"I can fire one, but I'm thinkin' I'd not be hittin' what I'd be aimin' for."

"At close range, it's pretty hard to miss," he said solemnly.

The portent in his words was not hard to grasp. "Do you think Jimmy Kelly got through?" she asked softly.

Keene shrugged. "Hard to say. My gelding's fast. Don't think anyone could catch him, once he got past them."

"If he did, will we be able to hold out until help arrives?"

Keene looked at her squarely. His gut reaction was to lie to her, to give her false hope. But the serenity in her eyes convinced him she wanted to hear the truth.

"We're getting low on ammunition, Kathleen."

She smiled, savoring the sound of her name from his lips. Would God forgive her for preferring to die with Keene MacKenzie at her side rather than her rightful husband? Would she ever—

A blood-chilling cry from the distance dismissed her thought. Whipping their horses and rending the air with war whoops, the Indians charged again from the cover of the trees. Despite being outnumbered, the small group of defenders fought on with determined courage.

The Circle C riders had just loaded up to return to the ranch when they heard the sound of gunfire echo down the canyon. Pete Faber lifted his head. "Sounds like gunshots coming from Tent Town."

His weathered face hardened. "Take a look at that." He pointed to the pillars of black smoke drifting across the sky. "Dammit!" he cursed. "Gotta be redskins. They must be burning the camp."

"There's women and children in that camp," Rory said, appalled.

"You ain't telling me nothin' I don't know," Pete grumbled, resigned to what had to be done.

"And I seen the train carrying the men leave there this morning, Pete," Curly added.

"Reckon if the town's burning, ain't too many of them women and kids still alive," one of the cowpokes added solemnly.

"From the sound of that gunfire, somebody's still alive," Pete replied.

"Thomas!" Rory suddenly cried out. "Thomas is there. Remember, he was headed that way this morning." She turned frantically to Faber. "Pete, we've got to help them."

"Reckon we don't have much choice considering there's women and children. Let's get moving, boys."

When he saw Rory had already mounted, he shook his head. "You ain't coming, Rory. We're riding in against hostiles. You'd best get back to the ranch and bring help."

"Like it or not, I'm coming with you, Pete," Rory shouted. She goaded her horse to a full gallop.

"Damn-fool girl," Pete mumbled, swinging into the saddle. "She's gonna get herself killed."

Rory had never ridden so fast. Her heart seemed to thunder as loudly as the horses' hoofbeats. She hated to think what destruction they would find. And Thomas. Was he still alive?

Concentrating on the small circle of defenders,

the Indians didn't see the Circle C riders until they were already in the town.

"Riders coming in," Keene shouted.

"Riders?" Thomas asked in surprise. "Who are they?"

"Looks like Circle C. Dammit," Keene suddenly cursed, "that fool Rory's among them." Thomas gaped in disbelief.

With drawn pistols, the men had formed a phalange with Rory in the center. Riding through the fracas, they fought off the Indians who swung battle axes or tried to pull them out of the saddle. The riders leaped their horses over the barricade of the makeshift fortification.

"Howdy, Pete," Keene said simply as the riders dismounted. Then the scout returned to pick off the nearest target.

Rory's anxious gaze sought out Thomas. "You're bound and determined to get yourself killed, aren't you?" he declared when she hurried over to him. "Riding right through the middle of a band of hostiles is one of the most foolhardy things I've ever seen."

"I'm glad to see you too, Thomas." She grinned, despite the havoc. "Besides, didn't you tell me you wanted to see me?"

Thomas was not amused. "You're damn right I do, but not under these circumstances." His concern for her exploded in anger. "If you wanted to help so badly, why didn't you ride back to the ranch and get help? Riding in here the way you did, you might have been killed."

"But I wasn't, was I?" she fired back.

"It ain't over yet," Keene added tersely.

"So you're mad at me, too," she remarked to him.

"Nope. I've known you too long," Keene responded. "Wouldn't be like you to think before you acted."

Under the additional hail of bullets from the new arrivals, the Indians quickly pulled back to regroup for another charge.

"Why'd you come here, Rory?" Thomas asked during the lull.

"I would think that was obvious. We heard the shots and saw the smoke. We figured you were under attack."

As he loaded cartridges into his rifle, his dark eyes rested on her face. "I don't mean to sound ungrateful, but why didn't you just high-tail it back to the ranch? This is no place for you, Rory." He glanced up and met her gaze. "I don't want to see you hurt."

For a lingering moment, they stared deeply into one another's eyes. "We'll get out of this. I know we will," she said softly.

He put aside the rifle and began to reload his pistol. "We better. You and I have some unfinished business to attend to."

"Unfinished business?"

He reached for her pistol and checked the chamber. "That kiss I passed up the other night," he said with a grin.

Rory blushed, remembering how much she had hoped he would kiss her the night of the dance. "Was I that obvious?"

"I'd hate to think I'd never have the opportunity again." His gaze shifted to her mouth.

"I'd hate to think you wouldn't too," she said in a throaty whisper.

Taking a lesson from the cowboys, the Indians rushed the fortification on horseback. Many were cut down, but this time a few succeeded in leaping the barricade. The hand-to-hand fighting became too close for shotguns or pistols.

Springing from his saddle, a brave leaped on Keene. The two men rolled together, locked in a death struggle. Unable to fire for fear of hitting Keene, Michaleen picked up a cast-iron frying pan and swung the heavy skillet at the head of the savage.

"I warned ya, ya'd be answerin' to Michaleen Dennehy," the little man declared.

As the Ute slumped over, Keene rolled free and finished off the attacker with a knife.

Running over to the sleeping car that sheltered the women and children, Rory and Kathleen began to extinguish several burning arrows embedded in the side of the car. Kathleen screamed as one of the braves snatched her by the hair and raised his tomahawk to cleave her skull. Keene spun around at the sound of her cry. Fanning his Colt, he put two shots into the head of the savage.

Meanwhile, another Ute had thrown Rory to the ground. As he raised a knife to plunge it into her heart, Thomas sprang at him, knocking the Indian aside. The two men fell, grappled, and rolled about. Thomas managed to keep a firm hold on the savage's wrist gripping the battle axe. Seeing Thomas's plight, Pete Faber rushed to his aid.

The attackers who had daringly penetrated the defenses were disposed of in quick order. The remaining force of hostiles recognized the uselessness of continuing the siege. They scrambled to retrieve their dead and wounded. Then, frustrated, they released several more shots and arrows at the defenders and rode off in a cloud of dust.

The small force stood up and looked around at their own battered ranks. One of the railroaders lay with a tomahawk in his skull, another dead from an arrow. Keene's arm was bleeding from a knife wound suffered during his struggle.

"Doctor Graham," Kathleen called softly. Thomas turned to her, and his heart leaped to his throat at the sight of Rory lying motionless with her head cradled in Kathleen's lap.

An ever-widening circle of blood stained her blouse.

Chapter Six

"Don't look so grim, Thomas," Rory weakly remarked as he inspected the shaft protruding from her shoulder. She smiled, despite the pain. Concerned by the pallor that had replaced the natural golden glow of her face, he did not return the smile.

"Dammit it, Rory, this is nothing to take lightly," he asserted. "It may have missed your heart, but that arrowhead could be poisonous."

"Is there anything I can do, Doc?" Keene asked, standing helplessly aside. His own shirt sleeve was stained with blood.

"I should take her back to town, but if that head is poisonous, I don't dare delay. Let's make her as comfortable as we can," Thomas said to the scout.

"Still getting yourself into fixes, aren't you?"

Keene remarked as he tenderly lifted Rory in his arms.

"And you're still getting me out of them," she teased lightly. But she appeared to be getting paler and weaker by the moment.

Keene's worried glance conveyed his concern when he looked at Thomas. "Where do you want her, Doc?"

Glancing around the area, Thomas saw that all the buildings, railroad cars, and tents had either burned or were burning, with the exception of the sleeping car. But he ruled out using that car since it was the only safe place for the children to remain until all the fires in camp could be extinguished.

"Mrs. Rafferty, will you get a mattress from the sleeping car? We'll lay her under the big cottonwood over there. At least she'll be out of the sun."

"Of course, Doctor." Kathleen hurried off and returned immediately with one of the light pallets used on the bunks.

After making Rory as comfortable as possible, Thomas sterilized his instruments. Kneeling beside her, he said gently, "I'm going to have to dig out the arrowhead, Rory."

"I know, Thomas." Trying to ease his burden, she forced a game smile, but her green eyes were round with apprehension.

"I'm sorry, but I haven't any anesthetic in my bag. It was in my clinic."

"I kind of suspected as much," she replied.

Outwardly, Thomas remained clinical, but his thoughts wrestled with the return of a hellish nightmare—those closing months of the war, the Confederacy's exhausted medical supplies, bullets, limbs removed from the wounded without the merciful aid of anesthesia.

He shifted his glance to Keene. They exchanged a wordless message and the scout put his hands on Rory's shoulders to hold her down. When Kathleen Rafferty reached out and took her hand, Rory smiled, trying to hide her fear behind a facade of bravado.

"We've never met, I'm Rory Callahan."

"I'm Kathleen Rafferty," the Irishwoman said kindly.

Rory clenched her lips to keep from crying out when Thomas cut off the extended shaft of the arrow. But the worst was still ahead—removing the arrowhead embedded in her shoulder.

"Mrs. Rafferty is the wife of one of the foremen," Keene said to distract Rory.

"I appreciate your help, Mrs.—" Her words were cut off as Thomas made his first probe. Gasping with pain, she clenched Kathleen's hand and tried to keep from screaming. The next shock of pain hit her like a black wave sweeping from her brain and she passed out.

"Thank God," Thomas murmured as he continued with the task and finally dislodged the embedded tip.

While Thomas bandaged the wound, Keene MacKenzie examined the arrowhead just removed from the shoulder of the unconscious girl.

"It's been painted, Doc. Hard to tell if it's poison or not. Indians like to paint everything."

He handed the tip to Pete Faber. "What do you think, Pete?"

The foreman studied the sharp point carefully, then shook his head. "Don't know. My gut feeling says it's poison."

Keene nodded in agreement.

"What kind, do you think?"

"Probably rattler," Keene said.

"Or deer liver?" Pete ventured.

Thomas looked up in surprise. "Deer liver?"

"Yeah. They let the liver rot 'til its tainted," Pete informed him.

"Lot easier killing a deer, Doc, then milking a rattlesnake," Keene drawled.

"Can she be moved, Doc?" Pete asked. "I sent the boys to fetch the wagon we left a mile or so down the track. We'd best get her back to the ranch if we can."

"I guess that would be the wisest thing to do," Thomas agreed. "And while they're gone, let me treat that arm of yours, Keene."

"It's just a scratch, Doc."

At the sound of a train whistle, Kathleen Rafferty raised her head, her face wreathed in a hopeful smile. "Jimmy Kelly must have made it through safely."

Caleb Murphy had the locomotive at full throttle as the train came barreling up to what remained of Tent Town. Carrying loaded rifles, pick axes, and shovels, the railroaders leaped off the sides and the tops of the railroad cars.

The women and children came rushing out of the sleeping car and dashed into the arms of their men. For several minutes, chaos reigned until all the families were reunited.

In the meantime, the rest of the astonished men walked around shaking their heads in disbelief at the burned-out town. Seeing his wife, Mike Rafferty went over to the small group under the tree. "You okay?" he asked Kathleen. She nodded and followed him when he walked away.

A short while later, the Circle C riders returned with the wagon. Thomas and Keene helped them carefully load Rory. "There's nothing more I can do here," Thomas said. "I'm coming with you."

"I'm not leaving her either, 'til I know she's gonna pull through," Keene announced.

Pete Faber looked dismayed. "Things are gonna be rough enough when we bring Rory back all busted up like this. You two showing up with her is sure gonna put the boss in an uproar."

"I don't give a damn what he says," Keene commented laconically.

"And I can't leave my patient," Thomas said firmly. "If that arrowhead was poisonous, the next twenty-four to forty-eight hours will be critical. So, like it or not, we're coming with you."

"I've got no quarrel with that, Doc. Just remember I warned you about T.J."

Keene took the reins of his gelding from Jimmy Kelly, who had just unloaded the horse from the train. He patted the young man on the shoulder. "You done good, son. And you've got a good eye for horseflesh, too."

Thrilled with the compliment, the young lad

glanced at Keene reverently. "Gee, thanks, Mr. MacKenzie."

"Didn't expect you to be riding in the wagon," Thomas remarked after Keene tied his horse to the back of the wagon, climbed into the bed, and plopped down beside him.

"I figure I better rest my gelding. When we get our butts kicked off the ranch, old Duke there will have to carry both of us."

Keene's quip and Pete Faber's concern had been well founded. As soon as the wagon pulled up in front of the ranch house, T.J. Callahan came bursting out of the door. "What in hell are you two doing..." The words died in his throat at the sight of Rory lying unconscious.

"What happened to her?" His accusing glare fell on Keene.

"She took a Ute arrow in the shoulder," Keene said, hopping off the back of the wagon.

The older man's glare swung to Thomas. "How bad is she?"

"No way of telling at this time, sir. I removed the arrow, but if the tip was poisoned, there could be some far worse effects. The next two days will tell."

Before he could explain any further, Pete and Curly dismounted and joined them. "Utes jump you while you were working the fence?" Callahan asked the ranch foreman.

"Naw. They hit that Tent Town, and we went to help out."

Callahan's face reddened with anger. "You tellin' me you *took* her there?"

"Told her to head home, but you know Rory," Faber replied.

"Never mind your damn-fool excuses. Long as you're riding for the Circle C, your job is to keep Rory safe, not help out the railroad. They're not paying your wages."

Pete Faber eyed him sadly. "I've been ramroding the Circle C for twenty years, T.J., but that don't mean I'm gonna stand by and let women and children get massacred just 'cause you've got a grudge against the railroad. If you can't live with that, then I reckon it's time I pack up and ride on."

"Same goes for me, T.J.," Curly said, moving to Pete's side.

For a moment, the embittered rancher glared at the mutinous hired hands, then backed down. "Nobody's telling anyone to ride on. Man's got a right to think of his own daughter first, ain't he? Any of the other hands get hurt?"

When Pete shook his head, Callahan snapped an order to the men lifting Rory out of the wagon. "Be careful what yur doin' there." He moved to take a closer look. "Take her to her room."

Callahan's hand shot out and stopped Thomas when he went to follow the men into the house. Here was someone upon whom he *could* vent his frustration. "You ain't going any farther. I told you once, greenhorn, I don't want to see you or that *railroad scout* on the Circle C."

"Mr. Callahan, I have a responsibility to my patient, and I take that responsibility seriously," Thomas advised. "I intend to remain with Rory until I'm sure she's out of danger."

Annoyed, for a moment Callahan eyed the doctor as he would a persistent fly buzzing around him. Despite his bias toward the railroad, the rancher recognized character in a man. Instinctively, he decided that, Westerner or dude, this railroad doctor meant every word he said. He dropped his hand.

"Okay, go on in." He angrily jabbed his finger at Keene. "But that bastard ain't putting one foot across my threshold."

Unwavering, Keene's gray-eyed gaze met that of the vitriolic rancher. "Then you best get your boys to stop me, T.J., 'cause I ain't leaving 'til I know Rory's okay. Follow me, Doc," he said without a backward glance.

Having carried Rory to her room, Pete and Curly had returned to the porch in time to hear this latest heated exchange between Keene and Callahan. The two cowboys stepped aside for the determined man to pass.

Without hesitation, Keene mounted the stairway, turned to his right at the top of the stairs, then strode past several rooms and entered a bedroom at the end of the hallway.

As Doctor Thomas Graham followed Keene, his curiosity was piqued. He wondered why the scout was so familiar with the precise location of Rory's room.

By evening, Rory was thrashing in the clutches of a high fever. Several times, in the throes of delirium, she called out to Thomas. He worked relentlessly through the night, trying to reduce her temperature with quinine and alcohol rubdowns.

Callahan made repeated visits to his daughter's bedside, but would not consider remaining in the same room with Thomas and Keene.

"Is there something I can do, Doc?" Keene asked, after sitting by helplessly for hours.

"I'm going to try a cold bath to cool her down. I'll need a tub about half-filled with water."

"Gotcha, Doc." Keene hurried out of the room. Thomas had Rory wrapped in a sheet by the time Keene returned.

"All set, Doc. Bathroom's down the hall on the right."

Callahan stopped Thomas in the hallway as he carried Rory to the room. "Just a minute there, greenhorn. What are ya gonna do with her?"

"I'm going to give her a cold bath to cool down her body temperature," Thomas explained impatiently.

The rancher's glance took in Rory's apparent nakedness under the sheet. "You mean naked?" When Thomas nodded, Callahan declared, "It'd be a sight more proper for a couple of the women to do."

"Mr. Callahan, I am a doctor. I am accustomed to nudity—male or female."

"Yeah. Well that don't make you a damn eunuch. I seen you all wrapped around my daughter when she wasn't ailing."

"Sir, please step aside so I can take care of my patient. You are wasting valuable time. Why don't you return to your room? I'll call you if there's a change in her condition."

Grudgingly, Callahan stepped away. Thomas kicked the door shut in the rancher's face before the man could voice any more of his suspicions.

"I ain't budging 'til you come out of there," Callahan shouted from the other side of the door.

Rory opened her eyes at midday and glanced around at the familiar room. Bright sunlight streamed through the window where Keene sat asleep in a chair. Thomas dozed in a chair next to the bed.

For several moments, she studied his sleeping face. As if sensing her stare, Thomas opened his eyes. For a silent moment, his dark gaze remained locked with her steady stare. Then she smiled. He rose to his feet.

"You gave us quite a scare, Rory Callahan," he said tenderly. Before she could say more, he stuck a thermometer into her mouth. Her green eyes danced above the instrument as he picked up her wrist and counted her pulse.

"Temperature's almost back to normal," he said after reading the thermometer. "Let's listen to that heart."

Thomas sat down on the bed and pressed the stethoscope to her chest. Her eyes rounded with shock when she realized that she was naked under the sheet.

"Hmmm. . . . Heartbeat's faster than it was just seconds ago when I took your pulse."

"No wonder, Thomas. I've just discovered I'm naked beneath these covers," she declared with a hot blush.

"Really, Miss Callahan? I never noticed." He grinned.

Awakened by their voices, Keene ambled over to the bed. "She giving you a hard time already, Doc?"

"Well, it's very embarrassing to wake up and find yourself naked in bed," she declared, struggling with feminine modesty. "You could at least have put a nightgown on me, Thomas." She turned her face aside on the pillow.

"Rory, I've already gone through this argument with your father. I had to give you cold baths and alcohol rubs all night to keep your temperature under control."

"You did what?" she exclaimed. "How could you? I was unconscious. Why, that's taking advantage of me!"

"That's it, Doc," Keene declared. "She's well enough to be spittin' out that snake venom in her, so I reckon I can leave now. Her name wouldn't be Callahan less'n she told you what you did wrong." He glanced purposely at Rory. "Before offering a thank-you for saving her life."

Keene stopped at the doorway and shoved his hat off his forehead. He flashed one of his rare smiles. "Glad to see—and hear—you're back to normal, Rory." Then he shifted his glance to Thomas "You gonna ride back with me, Doc?"

Thomas nodded. "Let me check her wound. I'll be right along."

"Okay. I'll saddle up Duke."

After Keene left, Rory pulled up the sheet and tucked it under her chin. Her face set in a contrite smile. "Thank you, Thomas. And I'm sorry if I sounded ungrateful."

Grinning, Thomas sat down on the bed. "I didn't go into the medical profession because I wanted thanks, Rory. There's a great deal of satisfaction derived from helping people when they can't help themselves." His dark eyes flashed with devilment. "Now tell me, Miss Callahan, do I have to wrestle you to get another look at that wound?"

Rory hadn't realized how tightly she had been clutching the sheet. Flustered, she released her grip. Thomas pulled it down and removed the dressing.

Despite her embarrassment, she lay docilely, admiring the competent way he went about the task. His fingers were firm, yet his touch was gentle—and exciting. "Looks okay, but keep this covered," he advised, putting a fresh dressing on the wound. "We don't want any infection."

Closing his medical bag, he picked up her hand and squeezed it lightly. "You're dehydrated from the fever. I want you to drink plenty of fluids. I'll be back in a couple of days to check the wound." Grinning, he added, "That is, if your father lets me on the ranch."

Thomas walked to the door, then stopped and looked back. "Ah . . . do you want any help putting on a nightgown?"

"No thank you, Doctor Graham, I can do it myself," she said with an emphatic toss of her red head.

He snapped his fingers and grimaced. "Doggone it!"

"Besides," she added with a flash of her green eyes, "I'm sure you're faster at getting it off then you are at putting it back on."

His dark eyes lit with devilment. "We'll have to put that to a test sometime, won't we, Rory Callahan?"

True to his word, Thomas showed up on the Circle C two days later. "Well, I can see you didn't suffer any relapse," he said when a vibrant and smiling Rory greeted him at the door. "How's that shoulder doing? Any sign of infection?"

"Not that I can see, Doctor," she said.

"I'd like to look at it, Rory,"

"Well, since there's no privacy here, perhaps we'd be better off going to my room."

"To prevent your father from kicking down your bedroom door, why don't you ask your cook to accompany us?" Thomas suggested.

Rory's eyes lit with mischief. "If you prefer, Thomas. Although I don't see what purpose would be served by having Charlie Toy there."

"Charlie Toy?" Thomas asked.

"Our cook . . . Chinese . . . about sixty years old," she added, suppressing a smile.

With a long-suffering glance, he followed her up the stairway, the doctor in him clutching tightly to his medical bag—the male in him sorely tempted to swat the trim little derriere preceding him.

After examining the wound, Thomas put on a fresh dressing. "Looks good, Rory. You should have full use of the shoulder in a week." He closed up his medical bag and they returned to the parlor.

"Can I offer you a drink or a cup of coffee or tea, Thomas?" she asked. She didn't want to say good-bye.

"No, but are you up to a short walk, Rory?"

"Am I! I've been cooped up in this house too long already."

"Well then, your doctor definitely advises fresh air to facilitate your recovery."

They walked at a leisurely pace toward a nearby copse of blue spruce and box elder. The ridge sloped into a deep declivity, tinged with colorful blossoms of white, yellow, and purple.

Despite the spring sunshine, a chill lingered in the air. Rory's brief shiver brought a quick response from Thomas. "If you're uncomfortable, we can go back to the house," he said, slipping his jacket around her shoulders.

"Oh, not yet, Thomas. Usually this time of year we're still up to our knees in snow. But this spring, the mountains are so beautiful with all these wildflowers in bloom."

His glance swung to the snow-capped peaks of the towering range surrounding them. "This certainly is beautiful country, I can't deny that."

"But . . . ?" she added with a questioning smile.

"It's not Virginia."

Rory smiled. "So, you're homesick, Thomas." She sank down in a patch of warm sunlight.

Thomas took a deep breath of the crisp mountain air, then lowered himself next to her. "I guess I would have to admit, I am. Those rolling, green hills of Virginia will always have a hold on me."

Rory's green eyes flashed coquettishly. "Doctor Graham, how unflattering of you. I would have thought a Southern gentleman like yourself would have told me that I'm enough of a diversion to take your mind off your home."

"Doctor Graham?" His dark-eyed gaze remained steadfast. "You have a tendency to be so formal, Miss Callahan. The time has come to lay down some ground rules."

"Ground rules?" she asked guardedly.

"No more games, Rory. We both know I'm here as Thomas Graham. I left the medical bag back at the house. So if you're going to play the coquette and bat those long lashes at me, be aware of the risk involved."

For the brief moment of her indrawn breath, Rory wondered if she were playing with fire. Rory was headstrong and spoiled. Men had always jumped to her bidding as long as she could remember. Even Keene MacKenzie had endured her domination with a restrained tolerance. Her instincts told her that Thomas Graham would not readily fall into that assembly.

But he had thrown down the gauntlet, and she was not one to ignore the challenge. A faint smile tugged a curve to her lips. "I'm well on the way to recovery. I have no further use for a doctor, Thomas Graham."

Their gazes remained locked as he slipped his hand beneath the mantle of her thick hair. The slight pressure on her neck pulled her forward. She drew a deep, shuddering breath and a musky whiff of bay and shaving soap teased her nostrils. Closing her eyes, she parted her lips.

His firm lips covered hers, and a pleasant warmth fluttered through her body as his mouth moved to take command. He slipped his tongue into the moist chamber of her mouth, eliciting her small groan of response. The flutter of warmth surged to a throbbing heat, and instinctively her tongue joined the play.

When he released her, Rory felt a mixture of fright and passion. This man had aroused emotions within her that she found as alarming as they were exciting. She tried to conceal this disturbing fact behind a glare of anger.

Thomas saw the rise of outrage in her emerald eyes. "Anger, Rory? You knew I intended to kiss you."

"You forced more than a kiss, Thomas," she accused him, rising to her feet.

"Forced? Excuse me, Rory. Your response was anything but forced." He stood up. "I think it's time we return to the house." He started to walk away.

A blush colored her cheeks as she followed him. "Well . . . I'm not myself."

He stopped and turned back to her. "Oh, I see. Your response is strictly the result of the altitude and a weakened condition," he mocked. Then he shook his head. "You disappoint me, Rory. I've been led to believe that honesty is your strong suit."

"Then I apologize, Thomas, if I've led you to believe you could force—"

His next move caught her by surprise. His

hand reached out and snagged her hair, pulling her toward him. His descending mouth trapped any further protest and he ground his mouth on hers, his probing tongue filling the chamber of her mouth.

She tried to twist her head away, but his grip only tightened. She was aghast at his brutal treatment and, despite the underlying excitement from the contact of his lips and tongue, she fought to resist him.

Thomas raised his head. The anger in his eyes matched the fury in hers. "Did you like that, Rory?"

"Of course not," she retorted angrily. She turned her head aside to avoid looking into his eyes.

He cupped her cheek to shift her gaze back to his. "I didn't either. But *that* was *forcing* a kiss on you. I hope you see the difference?"

For several seconds, she wrestled with her emotions as she looked into the unrelenting pair of deep-brown eyes. She couldn't fool herself any more than she could him. Her earlier response to his kiss had been an instinctive and reciprocal reaction to an exciting and tantalizing sensation—and they both knew it. Traces of a smile danced at the corners of her mouth and in her eyes as she nodded.

Thomas grinned and his eyes deepened with warmth. "Rory," he whispered. His thumb toyed with the curve of her lips, then he dipped his head and his tongue teasingly traced the sensual curve.

A swirling warmth within her began to coil

and spread toward her loins. "Oh, Thomas," she sighed. Slipping her arms around his neck, she closed her eyes as he nibbled and stroked her lips.

The heady rush of his warm breath was an aphrodisiac. "Kiss me, Thomas," she pleaded, unable to bear another moment of the tantalizing torment.

Their lips molded together. An exquisite sensation swept through her, arousing a sensual appetite she had never experienced before. She responded ravenously, sliding the tip of her tongue past her parted lips to seek the contact of his.

When he finally lifted his head, she felt unsated, still hungry for more. For a few interminable seconds, Thomas gazed down into twin green pools of desire. Then her eyes clouded when she was struck by the shock and reality of her unrestrained response to him.

He leaned into her. Despite his clothing, his body heat seemed to sear the spot where his shoulder pressed against her flesh.

She felt she no longer could trust herself. Frightened, she met his steady stare as his dark head hovered above hers, his mouth so close that their breath mingled.

Seeing the fright in her eyes, he asked in a husky murmur, "What are you afraid of, Rory?"

"Myself, Thomas. My feelings . . . my response. That kiss was a mistake."

"You know it was no mistake. I've waited and thought about this moment since the first time

I looked into those green eyes of yours."

Slowly, sensuously, he circled her lips again with his tongue. She gasped as a shudder swept her spine. He slipped his tongue between her parted lips and ravaged the vulnerable chamber with hot, demanding thrusts and sweeps.

She ignited, and her tongue duelled aggressively.

Her nipples hardened, aching for his touch. When the hand at her waist slid higher and cupped the mound of her breast, an erotic tremor swept through her and she shifted, pressing harder against his heated palm.

His firm and insistent mouth closed over hers in a long, drugging kiss which left her gasping, but still wanting more. He traced a trail of kisses to her ear, then back again to claim her lips.

Her fingers splayed the flexing muscles of his back and shoulders, and her shuddering sigh of pleasure made him bolder. His mouth followed the slim column of her neck, and as he grasped her shoulders, he unexpectedly encountered an obstacle. Through eyes clouded with arousal, he raised his head and stared dully at the bandage on her shoulder. The sight had the effect of plunging him into ice water. Thomas released her and stepped away. Befuddled, she opened her eyes.

"I'm sorry, Rory. I momentarily forgot about your wound."

"My wound?" she asked, perplexed.

He reached out and grasped her by the elbows, pressing a light kiss to her lips. His dark eyes crinkled at the corners as he grinned, unable to let the opportunity pass. "But it would appear you have regained most of your strength."

Rory felt no embarrassment, no tinge of girlish modesty. For the few brief moments in his arms, she had experienced the undeniably strong stirring of womanhood. She felt sheer relief at not having to hide the attraction she felt for him.

"When can I remove that bandage, anyway? My shoulder feels fine."

"The stitches can come out in about five days," he commented, picking a dried twig out of her hair. He took her arm, and they began to walk back to the ranch house.

"Will I have a scar, Thomas?"

"At first, but it will gradually fade."

"That's good news. I hate to sound shallow and vain, but a big red scar would sure ruin the looks of my shoulder."

He shook his head. "Honey, it would take a lot more than a scar to ruin that décolletage of yours."

Blushing with pleasure under the intimate compliment, she exclaimed, "Why, Doctor Graham, is that a professional opinion?"

"No. That is a Thomas Graham opinion. But please don't quote me to your father."

After retrieving his medical bag from the house, he lingered over a good-bye kiss. "You're a fever in a man's blood. You know that, don't you, Rory?" he groaned. Her tongue circled his lips in a reply.

He stepped away quickly and with a lithe move swung into the saddle. "Keep doing that and I'm going to forget my good intentions. So consider yourself warned, Rory Callahan."

"That's what I'm hoping. So consider yourself warned, Thomas Graham," she responded with a seductive smile.

His bold glance swept her flushed face and curved bosom. "And from where I'm sitting, that décolletage of yours looks mighty tempting, honey." He kneed his horse and rode off with a smile.

Rory stood with her arms crossed over her chest and watched him ride away. Her green eyes lit with devilment. "Yep. And I sure wouldn't want anything to happen to that décolletage, Doctor. I've got a lot of convincing to do and I'll need all the help I can get. But by the time I'm through, Thomas Jefferson Graham, those rolling, green hills of Virginia will be the farthest thing from your mind."

Chapter Seven

The railroad brought in boxcars and tents for the unfortunate residents of Tent Town. With all their personal belongings destroyed, the families were desperate for household items and clothing. When word of their crisis reached the ears of the citizenry, the people in Ogden and the surrounding community rallied to the call.

A town social was planned for the distribution of the many generous donations. By coincidence, the affair fell on the very day set aside by the Irish to commemorate the patron saint of Ireland.

And to the sons of Hibernia, how better to celebrate St. Patrick's Day than with a parade?

The streets of Ogden had never before been lined with so many spectators. The area's leading ranchers, accompanied by their families, had come to town for a meeting concerning the government's recent treaty with the Utes. The Mormons had rallied their faithful to see none other than Brigham Young himself, who would be a participant in the parade.

Spying Kathleen Rafferty in the crowd, Rory climbed down from the wagon, waved good-bye to her father, and hurried over to thank the thoughtful woman for her kindness on the day of the Indian attack. Since the parade was about to begin, Rory remained with Kathleen to watch the event.

With the shrill pipe of her whistle and the resounding peal of her bell, Caleb Murphy's "Betsy" led the parade. Bedecked in brightly painted paper shamrocks and green ribbons streaming from her smokestack and smokebox, the engine slowly puffed down the track. Sunlight blazed off the polished, golden brass of her dome covers, handrails, whistle and bell. Caleb Murphy waved to the crowd from one window while Jack Casement, the main construction boss for the Union Pacific, waved from the other.

With a sprightly step, Grand Marshal Michaleen Dennehy proudly walked behind the engine swinging a shillelagh in his right hand and clamping a long cigar between his fingers in the other. The little man waved and offered a "Top of the marnin'" to familiar faces among the spectators.

Boasting the current record for the most laid rails, Mike Rafferty's crew had the distinction of being the first crew in the procession. Several other work crews were strung out behind them.

The Ogden School Band, tooting their trumpets, flutes, and trombones, marched next in bright red uniforms trimmed with white fringe.

In gratitude to the railroad for the progress it would bring to the community, Brigham Young, the spiritual leader of the Mormons and former governor of Utah, rode in an open carriage waving to his clapping and cheering disciples.

Several more railroad crews marched behind him, followed by Father Quinlivin from Our Mother of Good Hope along with the children of the parish all waving small flags.

The band from a traveling medicine show, which by good chance happened to be in the nearby town of Brigham, had come to join the parade. And finally, the rear was brought up by the last of the Irish work crews.

"We haven't had this much excitement in Ogden since the first engine arrived," Rory exclaimed when the crowd began to disperse. "Kathleen, do you have any immediate plans?"

Kathleen knew her husband would head for the tavern if he wasn't already there. And once he began drinking, he wouldn't give a second thought to leaving her on her own for the rest of the day. She smiled at Rory. "No. I thought I'd just be takin' in the sights."

"Well, how about joining me for a lemonade or iced tea?" Rory asked. "Then we can take in the sights together."

"That'd be pleasin' me," Kathleen said quietly, but inwardly she was happy for the attention.

Kathleen's shy reserve, coupled with the unpleasant situation in her marriage, had

117

discouraged any close friendships with the other women of Tent Town. But she had liked Rory Callahan from the first moment she met her and envied the self-confidence and strength of character that Rory possessed.

Kathleen Rafferty was too self-deprecating to recognize the character and fortitude she displayed herself by enduring Michael Rafferty's constant physical and mental abuse. Her husband's constant castigation in the six years of their marriage had destroyed any self-esteem the poor woman had ever possessed.

Rory linked her arm through Kathleen's, and the two women walked arm and arm down the street.

While the festivities continued, many of the ranchers and local businessmen gathered at the Town Hall. Foremost on the tongues of all was the recent treaty negotiated between the Utes and the United States government.

"We teach our kids the three R's," Callahan grumbled. "Reading, 'riting, and 'rithmetic. While all them lazy Utes wanna teach their dumb *papooses* is the three B's—bulls, blankets, and blacksmiths. What kind of crazy treaty is that? And what the hell do they need blacksmiths for anyway? They're conivin' to be stealin' our horses, that's what."

"There's plenty of wild horses in the mountains, T.J.," one of the men ventured.

"Sure. And have you ever seen any of them Utes try to catch and break one? No. And you never will. 'Cause they're too damn lazy. It's easier to steal ours that are already broke."

"Lazy? Maybe them Indians are more smart than lazy," one of the men said. "My son busted his arm just yesterday trying to break a bagtail." A low rumble of laughter followed the comment.

"Well, we oughta start hanging 'em. Most states, they hang white men for horse thieving or cattle rustling. 'Bout time we start doing it to these thieving Utes."

"Ah, come on, T.J. They only steal enough steers to feed themselves. It's never been a serious problem before. Railroad's got 'em a little stirred up, that's all. But they don't cause no real trouble."

Callahan's black glare turned on the man. "You wanna go to the cemetery and tell my Sarah that?"

The rancher lowered his head. "Sorry, T.J. Forgot about your missus."

"Well, I ain't. And a couple weeks ago we hadda dig an arrow out of my daughter's shoulder. Our women ain't safe no more. What do you think woulda happened to them women and kids at Tent Town if my Circle C riders hadn't showed up? It woulda been a massacre. Although I don't know which is worse—the Indians or that railroad trash." Callahan cast a pointed glare in the direction of Thomas Graham and Keene MacKenzie, who were leaning against the wall, listening.

The room suddenly quieted when Brigham Young and his clerk entered the room. Despite the cane he used for a painful arthritic condition,

Young exuded the same authority that he had demonstrated ever since becoming the spiritual leader of the Mormons twenty-five years before. Sitting down, he removed his tall black hat and carefully placed it beside him on the table.

Thomas stared openly. This was the first opportunity he had had to closely observe the renowned preacher.

The stocky, broad-shouldered preacher could not be called refined. Dressed in a plain, homespun suit of black wool, his only adornment was the watch chain on his vest. A full but neatly cropped beard with stiff chin whiskers extended to his long gray sideburns, but he wore no mustache. He had a craggy face with knitted brows over closely set eyes, a long nose, and a small mouth.

No longer governor of Utah, the Mormon leader was still the most influential force in the territory. And not a man in the room, including T.J. Callahan, presumed to challenge that authority.

Although acknowledged to be one of America's greatest colonizers, due to the polygamy doctrine of his religion, the Mormon leader was severely impugned by critics who considered him to be nothing more than an uneducated, debauched preacher. The man had already fathered fifty-six children on his sixteen wives.

True, the preacher had a limited education, but those who knew Brigham Young, politically or religiously, were aware that this maligned preacher was neither a religious fake nor a libertine.

Brigham Young practiced what he preached, setting an exemplary and inspirational example for others to follow. He devoted his every waking hour toward achieving the "Kingdom of the Almighty God."

And not unlike Moses, who centuries before had led his followers out of Egypt to the Promised Land, in 1846 the Mormon leader's strength and religious conviction had helped him to guide his persecuted faithful from Illinois across the prairie to the rugged splendor of Utah, where he founded Salt Lake City a year later. Under his guidance, the city had blossomed with roads, canals, and countless social, economic, and educational institutions. In the twenty years that followed, he founded another three hundred and fifty communities in the Far West.

As always, in accordance with his religious doctrines, Brigham Young declined any offer of tobacco, liquor, coffee, or tea, accepting instead a glass of plain drinking water.

"Please continue your conversation, gentlemen," he insisted with a friendly nod.

Continuing to stare transfixed at the Mormon leader, Thomas realized that he was in the presence of greatness and recalled the time Robert E. Lee had visited the field hospital during the Civil War. Although Brigham Young's physical appearance was just the opposite of the distinguished, aristocratic mein of the Confederacy's great general, the young man sensed the same stateliness in both leaders.

"Those goddamned Utes have no claim to this land," Callahan declared, resuming his tirade.

"They're nothing but a wandering band of murdering and thieving gypsies."

Religiously opposed to any form of cursing, Young raised his hand. "We cannot presume the Almighty has condemned these wandering souls, Mr. Callahan. Therefore, we must not use His name in vain."

Callahan ignored the subtle chastisement. "The government makes treaties with the Sioux Nation, with the Cheyenne Nation, with the Ute Nation," he continued to rage. "Hell, these ain't no *nations*. England's a nation. Prussia's a nation. These Indians are just tribes of lazy savages who don't want to work. They're good for nothing except murdering innocent women and stealing livestock."

He shoved aside his chair and thumped across the room. "Why should we always be negotiating separate treaties with them? If they wanna live in this country, they oughta have to live by the same rules as the rest of us."

"And be subject to the same privileges," Keene interjected.

"Don't give me any of your smart talk, boy," Callahan glared, pointing an accusing finger at the scout. "That damned railroad you're hired out to is what stirred up these Utes to begin with."

"Well, I can see how laying a railroad track across their land could easily be interpreted as an act of war, Mr. Callahan," Young commented.

Callahan's bitterness was beyond reasoning. He lunged over and slammed his fist down on the table next to the Mormon leader. "It ain't their land. It's our land. We came out here and turned this wilderness into a civilization. What did they ever do with it, huh? Did they try to farm it, like your people, Young? Or ranch it, like us cattlemen? Naw. They were even too lazy to build themselves decent huts to live in."

Pounding himself on the chest, he bellowed, "Hell, for over twenty-five years I've worked my ass off building up the Circle C to one of the biggest ranches in the territory. And each year I'd cut a half-dozen cows out of my herd just so their kids wouldn't go hungry all winter. 'Cause I knew for damn sure they were even too lazy to hunt in order to put food in their kids' bellies. And what thanks did I get for it? The rotten savages killed my wife—and now they almost killed my daughter."

He stomped to the door. "Well, I don't give a good goddamn what treaty the government *negotiates* with them. I'm ordering my ranch hands to shoot any of the murdering bastards on sight." He slammed out of the room.

After Callahan's bombastic departure, Brigham Young sat for a lengthy moment shaking his head. "Mr. Callahan has suffered an irrefutable loss, but such bitterness will ultimately destroy him. I can only hope the treaty will bring an end to this temporary conflict. The Indian and the white man have co-existed peaceably in Utah in the past, and I am sure they will be able to do so in the future."

"Mr. Young," Thomas said, stepping forward. "We've never met, sir. My name is Thomas

Graham. I'm a doctor with the Union Pacific. I realize I have no personal stake here, and I certainly can sympathize with Mr. Callahan's grief. Matter of fact, I was at Tent Town at the time of the attack when his daughter was wounded. I don't wish to minimize what disaster might have occurred. But it takes a great lack of vision to protest the linking of the Atlantic and Pacific Oceans by a transcontinental railroad. It will probably be the greatest achievement this country will ever know and will have far-reaching effects on the world as well."

Brigham Young nodded. "I agree with you, Doctor Graham. But we must try to understand that at the moment Mr. Callahan is reeling under the despair of personal grief. He is reacting to this situation emotionally, not rationally. He and the Indian have much in common. They both feel threatened by this iron monster creeping across their land—and by the armies of invaders which follow it. But the flow of progress and civilization cannot be stemmed. Not by us. Not by the Indian."

Brigham Young rose to his feet. "However, the death of a loved one causes a catastrophic despair. At such time of sorrow, every man needs a time for mourning. We must all pray that with the help of the Almighty our brother will pass through this dark valley before any further misery ensues."

He shook Thomas's hand. "A pleasure to meet you, Dr. Graham. And your home is where?"

"Virginia, sir."

"The Cradle of Liberty," Young said. He

slapped him on the shoulder in dismissal.

Rejoining Keene, Thomas said excitedly, "Well, I'll sure have some interesting stories to relate when I get back home."

"Maybe by the time this railroad's finished, Doc, something might have caught your fancy and you won't want to return to that Cradle of Liberty," Keene murmured.

The scout's words made Thomas Graham return his thoughts to a certain headstrong redhead with incredible green eyes. "Something . . . or *someone?*" he remarked. "Let's go and see how the festivities are progressing."

Rory and Kathleen were listening to a medicine drummer expound the virtues of his elixir, which he claimed could cure everything from hives to frigidity in women.

"Which do you suffer from?" Thomas asked, moving to Rory's side.

"Thomas," she exclaimed with pleasure. "I don't think I suffer from either."

"I'd have to agree," he said.

"Really?" Her eyes sparkled with deviltry despite a faint blush. "Are you speaking as Doctor Graham or Thomas Graham?"

Grinning, he spread his arms to show her his empty hands. "No medical bag. This is a holiday for me, the same as it is for you."

He turned his attention to Kathleen. "And how are you, Mrs. Rafferty? Enjoying the fair?" Flushed with excitement, there was a healthier glow to Kathleen's cheeks then he had ever seen.

Ana Leigh

"Oh, yes, Doctor Graham," Kathleen replied. Her glance shifted to Keene MacKenzie. "A good afternoon to you, Mr. MacKenzie."

Keene nodded. "Mrs. Rafferty."

"And what are you two lovely ladies about?" Thomas asked.

"Oh, we're just enjoying the sights," Rory offered casually.

"Do you object to more company?" Thomas asked.

Rory's eyes flashed coquettishly. "Are you referring to yourself?"

"Well . . . Keene too," Thomas said, grinning.

Rory slipped her arm through his. "We'd love it. Right, Kathleen?"

"Ah . . . well yes, of course," Kathleen stuttered, flustered by this unexpected turn of events.

The sudden saw of a fiddle attracted their attention, and the four people moved to where a dozen couples were dancing an Irish jig.

None was more vigorous and enthusiastic than Michaleen Dennehy. With one of the local whores as a partner, the little cook soon became the center of attention as the other dancers faded to the sidelines to watch him. The crowd clapped and cheered him on, and the louder they clapped, the more spirited became Michaleen's step.

Keene MacKenzie looked down at Kathleen Rafferty as she laughed and clapped in rhythm to the music. The dark-haired woman had never looked lovelier to him. Her blue eyes sparkled, and her flushed face radiated an excited glow.

The dance finished and Michaleen grabbed his partner and lifted her off her feet.

"Well, I'd say, little man, you and I oughta go back to my place and see what you can cook up there," the whore said with a suggestive arch of her brow.

"And she ain't talking about potatoes, Dennehy," one of the railroaders hooted.

Michaleen slipped an arm around the whore's waist. "Well, me blue-eyed calico cat, if cookin's yer fancy, darlin', Michaleen Dennehy is the man with salt and pepper in his shaker." Giggling, they walked away.

Kathleen Rafferty blushed, astounded by a side of her cherished friend she had never seen. She hurriedly walked over to a ringed area where children were competing in a three-legged sack race. When the relay was over, the director of the activities called for adult couples for the next three-legged relay.

"You game?" Thomas asked Rory.

Rory hung back. "Oh, I don't know."

"Back home, I excelled at three-legged races. Come on, Rory Callahan, where's your adventuresome spirit?" He grabbed her hand and towed the reluctant girl behind him.

A cheer and applause sounded from many of the spectators when Thomas stepped up to participate. The likable doctor was popular not only among the railroaders, but he had made many friends among the townsfolk as well.

"Trust me, Rory, this will be as easy as a snap of the fingers," he assured her and snapped his fingers to prove his point.

"Well, just so as to make it more interesting, folks," the relay organizer said, "each one of you is to put on one of these." He reached into a box and pulled out sets of snowshoes.

Thomas's confidence waned quickly. "Snowshoes? I've never worn snowshoes in my life. And besides, there isn't even any snow."

"Well, Thomas, you've got us into a fine fix now," Rory declared with hands on hips.

"Well, which one do you prefer?" Thomas asked her, good-naturedly. "Right foot or left?"

"Right foot, if you don't mind."

He knelt down and attached the snowshoe to her right foot before putting the other on his left foot. "Well, it won't be that much different. Since there's no snow, we just have to hop with it the same as we would in a regular three-legged race," he assured her. "The important thing is for us to stay in step together."

"Your confidence is inspiring, Thomas," Rory drawled, slipping her left leg into the burlap bag. Thomas put his right leg in next to hers, then holding the bag up between them, they began to hop at the sound of the starting signal.

Cheered on by their friends in the crowd, the couple were making a successful effort, leading the other contestants, when midway through the course Rory lost her grip on the bag. The sagging burlap tripped Thomas, preventing him from raising the awkward snowshoe high enough to clear the ground. He fell against Rory, instinctively grabbing at her to keep from falling. Clutching her in his arms, they both tumbled to the ground.

Laughing, they sat up. Discarding the snow-shoes and burlap bag, Thomas helped Rory to her feet. "You aren't hurt, are you?"

"No, of course not," Rory replied, brushing off her clothes. "But I do hope this is the end of any relays you have in mind for us."

"Well, confidentially, I do have one other in mind, but we need privacy," he whispered in her ear. She flashed him a saucy grin and walked over to where Kathleen and Keene were waiting.

However, one of the people watching the event had not been quite as amused. Unexpectedly, T.J. Callahan strode up to the four people.

"What the hell do you think you're doing, Rory? You've made a public spectacle of yourself rolling around on the ground with this railroad trash you've been running with. Get to the wagon, girl, we're going back to the ranch."

"Sir, it wasn't her fault. I apologize for—"

"I've said all I intend to," Callahan declared, cutting off Thomas's attempt at an apology. "Now!" he barked in a sharp command to Rory and strode away.

Rory smiled to hide her embarrassment. "I guess it would be wiser if I left," she said. She squeezed Kathleen's hand. "I'll come to visit you," she said.

"Rory, I'm so sorry. I didn't mean to spoil your day," Thomas said.

"You didn't, Thomas. Really," she assured him.

"Why do you keep taking his guff, Rory?" Keene grumbled.

"You should understand why, more than any other. He's lonely and he's bitter, Keene. But he is my father. And I know he loves me." Rory left without any further good-bye.

Kathleen Rafferty watched Rory move hastily through the crowd to catch up with her father. "I'm thinkin' a woman's station in life doesn't much matter. The Lord puts all of us at the mercy of one man or another." She smiled sadly. "Good day to you, gentlemen."

Much later that evening, exhausted from a long, lonely day of wandering on her own, Kathleen Rafferty entered Jake's to approach her husband.

Mike Rafferty was occupied in a beer-drinking contest with some of the other men. He had already drunk more than his limit. To the hoots of the crowd, he downed another full mug of beer non-stop and followed it with a shot of whiskey. His opponent conceded defeat.

"Okay, who's next? Mike Rafferty is man enough to out-drink any man in the place," Rafferty boasted. Annoyed, he glared at Kathleen when she tugged at his sleeve. "What is it, woman?"

"Mike, may I be talkin' to you private?" she said softly.

"Whata ya want?" he snarled. "Can't you see I'm busy?"

"Better see what your wife wants, Mickey," a nearby whore taunted.

"Well, speak up, woman," he demanded, irritated.

Kathleen was too embarrassed to look at the amused circle of faces. She kept her eyes downcast. "Mike, 'tis tired I am. Will you be thinkin' of leavin' soon?"

He slammed the beer mug down on the bar. "I'll be back." Grabbing her arm in a painful grasp, he hurried her outside.

"I oughta beat the hell out of ya," he snarled. "Whata ya tryin' to do, shame me in front of my friends?"

"Please, Mike, let go of my arm. You're hurtin' me," she pleaded.

"I'll hurt more than yar arm, woman, if ya ever do this again." His fingers dug deeper into her flesh. Kathleen felt as if the bone would snap if he didn't release her. "And I'll be the one sayin' when it's time to leave. And I'm not ready, yet," he announced.

He raised an arm and backhanded her across the face. Backing away, Kathleen covered her smarting cheek with her hand. With clenched fists he lumbered toward her.

"Rafferty." Keene MacKenzie stepped out of the shadows.

"Whata ya want?" he asked, turning around and snarling like a madman.

"Couple of the guys are waiting for you inside. They want a rematch," Keene good-naturedly. Mike Rafferty's cruel mouth curled in a smirk. Hiking up his pants, he shoved past the scout and went inside.

Kathleen couldn't look Keene in the eye when he helped her to her feet. "Well, I stopped his abuse this time. What about the next time?"

Forcing back her tears, she mustered her pride and glanced up at him. "'Tis grateful I am to you, Mr. MacKenzie. But 'tis not your problem."

Keene stared into her eyes, luminous in the moonlight. "Why don't you leave him, Kathleen?" he asked gently.

"Because we are joined in the eyes of the Church," she half-whispered.

For a long moment, they stared deeply into one another's eyes. As she struggled with her emotions, a single tear slid down her cheek. Keene slowly reached out a finger and wiped it away.

After a long, lingering look into his steady, gray-eyed stare, she hurried away.

Chapter Eight

Rory was just preparing to leave the house when the sound of approaching hoofbeats caused her to glance out the window. She broke into a smile of pleasure at the sight of the rider. After a quick peek in the mirror, she hurried outside to greet him.

"Well, hello, Doctor. Is this a business or social call?"

Grinning, Thomas motioned to his saddle. Only a rifle scabbard was attached. "No medical bag, Rory."

She smiled up at him. "You must feel naked." She felt elated. Just his presence excited her, and she could feel her heart thumping in her breast. "So this is purely a social call."

"Admittedly, a much-needed social call." His grin narrowed and his brown eyes deepened. "I've missed you, Rory."

For a long moment, their gazes locked. "I've missed you too, Thomas." She was unaware of the throaty catch in her voice.

"I thought I would dare the wrath of T.J. Callahan and take you up on that offer of a ride."

"Well, you've picked a good time. My father rode out to the west range today."

"Then for the sake of peace and tranquility, I recommend that you give me a tour of the *east* range," he teased.

She giggled delightfully. "My very thought. I'll saddle my mare."

Once mounted, they followed the bank of a river through a forest of juniper and piñon pine to where it narrowed to snake through a canyon of granite walls. In the valley below, Circle C cattle grazed contentedly. Thomas and Rory dismounted, and for a long moment they stood in silence, admiring the tranquility of the pastoral scene.

"It's very pleasant here," he said. "Hard to believe all the activity going on just a few miles away."

Rory glanced askance at him. "As pleasant as your Virginia, Thomas?"

He took her hand and they walked to the shade of a tree and sat down. "Miss Callahan, nothing is as beautiful as *my* Virginia."

"Someday I'll have to go to your Virginia and see it for myself."

He toyed with her fingers. "I hope you will." He glanced down at her hand in his. "I would like that very much, Rory." He lifted her hand

and pressed a kiss to her palm. Warmth washed through her from the pleasant sensation of the touch of his lips. For a long moment she stared down at her hand in his.

Then she looked up and met his gaze. "What's happening between us, Thomas?"

"I think I'm falling in love with you, Rory. When we're apart, I can't seem to get my mind off you."

"I have the same problem. This is a new experience for me. I never felt this way before." She gazed intently into his eyes. "You have to help me, Thomas. I'm a spoiled brat. I've been pampered and doted on my whole life."

He drew her into his arms. "Don't sell yourself so short. I'm no saint, Rory. Far from it." He kissed her, and she closed her eyes to savor the excitement that surged through her.

"And since I always get what I want, I should tell you now that I want to marry you."

He grinned in amusement. "You're sure about that, are you?" He lowered her to the ground and kissed her.

When they parted, she said breathlessly, "I can see you're not taking me seriously." She laced her fingers through his hair and lay looking up at him. "I'm only trying to warn you, Thomas."

He raised his head and his dark eyes sobered. "Rory, my feelings for you are just as confusing to me. There's a deep attraction between us that I know goes far beyond just wanting you physically. But right now, honey, all I can think about is how much I need to kiss you."

"Then why don't you?" she whispered seductively. She slid her arms around his neck, drawing him closer. "No one has ever kissed me like you do."

He cupped her cheek in his hand and smiled down at her. "I hope not. I'd like to believe I was the first to arouse this kind of response in you. You fire my blood, Rory," he rasped hoarsely. Lowering his head, he leaned over her, closing the gap that separated them. She shut her eyes and parted her lips to accept the ardent and voracious mouth that took possession of her own.

They had repressed their passion since the promise of their first kiss. Now their pent-up desire erupted with mutual intensity.

Every nerve in her body was attuned to the male essence of him now. The devouring hunger of his kiss consumed her. Devastated by the assault of his mouth and hands, her passion spiraled. Breathlessly, she clung to him.

His lips left hers, only to blaze a heated path to the hollow of her throat as his hands joined the ravishment of her senses. They seemed to be everywhere: sweeping down her spine, cupping her breasts, pressing her tighter against him. Her clothing was a poor shield against the hot touch of his inflamed body.

With a sensuous purr of rapture, she lay back in his arms as he trailed moist kisses down the column of her neck. She tightened her arms around his neck and his hard, muscular body pressed her soft curves into the ground in a further bombardment of her already devastated senses.

Raising his head, he stared down at her, his long spiky lashes screening his passion-filled eyes. He began to lightly nibble and tug at her lips. At her groan of pleasure, the corners of his dark eyes crinkled with the warmth of a smile, and he tenderly cupped her cheek.

Her hand on his neck, she pulled his head back down to hers. Their mouths opened to one another and her lips yielded to the galvanizing intrusion of his hot tongue. He slid his lips down the column of her neck as his hand swept her body.

Her arms dropped to her sides and she offered no resistance when he began to release the buttons of her bodice. He slipped it off her shoulders and she lifted her head as he pulled off her chemise. The nubs of her breasts hardened to peaks, a temptation he did not ignore.

Lowering his head, he rasped them with his tongue, then bit one lightly and sucked it into his mouth.

"Oh, God!" she moaned. Her back arched responsively as a tremor swept her spine.

Under the mindless ecstasy of his toying, she felt the slide of her skirt past her hips. His mouth and tongue tugged and suckled at her breasts as he slid his hand to the core of her sex and began to stroke her between her legs. Gasping, she bit down on her lower lip to keep from groaning aloud when his fingers probed the opening. The exciting sensation continued to curl and, unconsciously, she parted her legs, her hands clutching the brawn of his shoulders. As her taut body trembled, he reclaimed her lips, draining her of her remaining breath.

She pressed her nakedness against him. Stretching out her full length, she gloried in the sensuous delight of her nakedness beneath him. With her body enveloped in a hot flush, her passion continued to coil like a spring.

"Take me, Thomas. Now. Take me now," she pleaded, gasping for breath as she sought release.

He rose to his knees and pulled off his shirt. As he started to unbuckle his pants, he suddenly lifted his head.

"What? What is it?" she asked.

"Horses. Get up, quick, Rory."

She jumped up, yanking her skirt over her hips as Thomas pulled her chemise over her head, then her bodice. As she buttoned the bodice, he quickly donned his shirt.

"Let's get out of here." He led the horses into the concealment of a copse of trees just as a band of Utes broke into the clearing. There were several women and children with the group.

"Wow!" he murmured when the Indians had disappeared from view. "A couple of minutes more, and I'm afraid we would have been easy game for them."

"I don't think they were dangerous. They didn't have any paint on. And they had their wives and children with them. They were probably just crossing the ranch to head north." She finished putting her clothing in order. "I can't help but feel sorry for most of them. They're so lost. They don't understand what's happening. They're being driven out of these mountains that have been their home for generations."

"Well, just the same, I'd better get you back to the house."

They swung up into their saddles, and he glanced over with a grin. "This wouldn't have happened in Virginia, Miss Callahan. The only wild man you'd have to worry about is the one you're with."

She offered him a saucy smile. "You make Virginia sound more interesting by the minute, Doctor Graham." Goading her horse, she moved away. Thomas shoved his Stetson to the back of his head and followed.

Rory Callahan rode away from Tent Town, once again disappointed at not seeing Thomas Graham. She had had no contact with him since the day of their ride the week earlier and she missed him desperately.

She found some consolation in knowing that Thomas had tried to see her several times, even though he had been turned away by her father. Rory knew that, sooner or later, drastic action would have to be taken. Her mind was made up—Doctor Thomas Jefferson Graham was the man she intended to marry, whether her father liked it or not.

The task ahead would be to convince Thomas of the same idea, for despite what he had said, he still appeared to be a man who had something other than marriage on the mind. But how could she fault him, when she wanted the same thing?

The moment they were together, she felt this mating urge—more reason why they would have to get married as soon as possible. But it seemed next to impossible to carry on a romance, much less extract a marriage proposal, from a man whom she rarely saw.

Back in her bedroom, she sat down and wrote Thomas a letter, informing him that she would be gone the next two weeks but hoped they could meet upon her return. Then, desolately, Rory finished her packing. Arriving in Ogden early the next day, she slipped the envelope under the door of the tiny office Thomas maintained in the town. Her eye caught his name painted on the office door, and she sighed, not entirely enthusiastic at the thought of the long trip ahead—away from him.

Thomas had thought about Rory Callahan throughout most of the long trip back to St. Louis. He had tried to see her before leaving Ogden, but her father's interference had made the attempt unsuccessful. In the short time he had known her, she had come to mean much more to him than just the prospect of a casual affair. He grinned fondly. There was nothing casual about Rory Callahan. *No, this is the one*, he told himself. *The woman you don't walk away from*. The woman he had been hoping for his whole life. He had sensed it the moment he picked her up in his arms and carried her to the shade of the tree that first day they met.

Funny, how you know it as soon as you meet her, he thought.

He shoved his musing to the back of his mind as the train chugged into Union Station. Peering out of the window, he immediately spied the tall figure of his best friend. Ruark Stewart's dark handsomeness and urbane bearing made him an easy stand-out in any crowd.

As Thomas stepped off the train, Rory Callahan, the distant territory of Utah, and the building of the transcontinental railroad were temporarily forgotten, replaced by a flood of memories from the past—memories of a friendship formed during prep school and then college. Of a comradeship that the Civil War could not sever, even though the two men had fought on opposite sides; memories of a shared camaraderie and rivalry. And of wooing away one another's sweethearts. Of Angel Hunter, who had brought an end to that particularly competitive sport. Of the joy and pride he'd felt delivering the first-born child of these cherished friends.

For a lengthy moment the two comrades shook hands, grinning at each other like school-boys. Ruark was the first to speak. "Glad to see you're still wearing your scalp."

"And my pants, ole friend," Thomas added.

Ruark made a casual swipe at the gun belt strapped on Thomas's hip. "And I see you're packing iron, Buffalo Bill."

"A necessary evil, I assure you," Thomas replied. He wanted to kick himself for forgetting to remove the gun belt. Aware of Ruark's propensity toward teasing, Thomas knew that now he would never hear the end of the matter.

After getting his baggage, they ambled over to a waiting carriage. "Hello, Daniel, how are you doing?" Thomas said, shaking the driver's hand.

"Pleasure to see you again, Dr. Graham."

"Is your rheumatism still bothering you?"

"Not as bad, sir. That tonic you recommended helps to ease the pain." Daniel disposed of the baggage while Thomas and Ruark climbed into the carriage.

"So, fill me in, old friend. What's the empire builder been up to lately?" Thomas asked, once the carriage was underway. "Still have that Midas touch?"

Ruark chuckled. "Added to the fact that I own a successful racing stable, my business investments are multiplying, I'm married to the most beautiful woman in the world, and I have the brightest soon to be three-year-old son imaginable."

"Whom I happened to have delivered," Thomas interjected.

"Ah, yes. I do admit your contribution in that one accomplishment, old chum. Nevertheless, how is it, despite all my personal accomplishments—and all are extraordinary I might add—you still will not admit I have any brains?"

"I have never said that, friend. I've only implied they're between your legs," Thomas quickly refuted.

"Ah, jealousy. Still eating away in the poor man's breast."

"I have to say though," Thomas conceded, ignoring the challenge, "you did have enough sense to marry Angel. Of course, I had to beat that sense into you."

"Like hell you did. I sure didn't need *you* to convince me to marry the woman I love."

"Well, if it weren't for me, you'd still be trying to figure out how to convince her to marry you." The bantering gleam left Thomas's eyes, and his face softened. "How is she, Ruark?"

Ruark's dark eyes glowed with the depth of his emotion. "Lovelier than ever, T.J. She's looking forward to your visit. So is Nana."

"And Nana Sarah." Thomas grinned at the thought of Sarah Stewart. "How is my sweetheart doing? Her health's still holding up, isn't it?"

"Just as healthy and feisty as ever. She's been planning a party for her eighty-fourth birthday coming up this summer," Ruark said.

As they turned into a driveway, Angeleen Stewart stepped out onto the porch. The wind caught her long black hair, whipping it to the side in black, satiny streamers. Laughing, she brushed some of the strands off her cheek and raised her hand to wave at the approaching carriage.

Lord, it feels good to see Angel and Ruark again, Thomas thought.

He practically leaped out of the carriage door as soon as they stopped. "Hello, Angel Face," he said tenderly, taking her into his arms. After a kiss and a hug, he stepped back, holding her hands in his, and studied her face.

Ruark hadn't exaggerated. If possible, Angeleen had grown lovelier in the past year.

143

Even yet, his first glimpse of her flawless face, sapphire eyes ringed with thick, dark lashes, alabaster skin, and black hair as dark as ebony took his breath away.

With tears of joy glistening in her eyes, Angeleen studied Thomas intensely. His face was deeply tanned, and his dark eyes, the color of brown velvet, still danced with deviltry.

"You look wonderful, T.J.," she exclaimed. "I hope you're back to stay?"

Suddenly a dark-haired youngster came running out the door. Thomas squatted down and shook the boy's hand. "Well, Tommy! How's my godson doing? You're sure growing fast. Pretty soon, you'll be as tall as your daddy."

Grinning with pleasure, the three-year-old looked proudly up at his father. Thomas hugged the youngster, then Ruark scooped up his son in his arms and kissed the lad's cheek.

"You remember Doctor Graham, don't you, honey?" Angeleen asked.

With childhood honesty, Tommy Stewart shook his head. "Don't feel bad, Sport. Doctor Graham has that effect on many people," Ruark said. He put down his son and the lad scampered away.

"My God, they grow up fast," Thomas exclaimed. "And he's the spitting image of his father."

"I know," Angeleen remarked. "But I love him just the same."

Laughing, Ruark slipped an arm around her waist. "Have you told him our good news, sweetheart?"

"Tommy is going to have a baby sister or brother," Thomas answered before she had a chance.

"How can you tell?" Angeleen glanced down at her slim stomach and hips. "Please don't tell me I'm showing already?" she groaned.

"No, I just figured that blinding glow you are radiating couldn't be from loving this character." He pointed a finger at Ruark. "Tell me, Angel, has this Yankee been treating you properly, or does he need another punch in the jaw?"

"Sounds to me like *this Yankee* might have to put the long-lost Reb in line again. That gun belt doesn't scare me, Buffalo Bill," Ruark declared.

"You put me in line? Hey, ole buddy, everyone knows that I was the one who put you in line."

"Boys," Angeleen said, flashing a tolerant but loving smile. Stepping between them, she hooked arms with each of them and marched the two men into the house.

Much later that evening, after the others had retired, Thomas and Ruark lingered over a late brandy and cigar. "I'd say it's time to hang up that gun belt, friend, and come back home, settle down and get married."

"Boy, misery sure loves company," Thomas grimaced. "Why is it that once a confirmed bachelor gets married, he tries like hell to sell the same catastrophe to his friends? Tell me this, oh Mighty Empire Builder, am I expected to proceed in the exact order you laid out for me?"

They had been friends too long for Ruark not to be able to separate the chaff from the wheat.

Grinning, he said, "You've found her! You're in love!"

Throwing up his hands, Thomas immediately protested the accusation. "No. No. No. I did not say anything about love. But I have met a girl who's—ah, quite interesting." He grinned. "I'm working on it, that's all, buddy. But don't say anything to Angel and Nana Sarah, or the two of them will start planning the wedding."

Ruark Stewart regarded his friend with a renewed gleam in his eyes. This was more of a confession of love than he had ever heard before from Thomas Jefferson Graham.

Thomas spent the next day ordering medical supplies to be shipped to Ogden. That evening he accompanied the Stewarts to the wedding ball for the son of one of Ruark's business associates.

Upon hearing of his connection with the railroad, Thomas was immediately converged upon by a circle of men who were eager to hear a firsthand report of the progress being made.

"Well, right now, the two railroads are only a couple hundred miles apart."

"I heard tell there's been a few fingers in a few pots," one of the men slyly remarked.

"I'm no businessman, sir," Thomas said. "But I can't imagine an undertaking of this scope without some kind of graft."

"A flagrant waste of the government's money, I'd say," Mason Denning, a local banker, commented. "And I bet Thomas Durant and Grenville Dodge aren't exactly clean."

"And don't rule out the Central Pacific either. I'm sure the Big Four aren't lily-white," another man added cynically.

"Well, in a month or so the tracks will link up, and it will all be over," Thomas said.

"What a celebration that will launch," Ruark remarked.

"A well-earned celebration, gentlemen," Thomas declared. He spread out his arms to convey the scope of his words. "The magnitude of the endeavor is incomprehensible. You'd have to see it to believe it. Six years of laying eighteen hundred miles of track. Tunneling through mountains, blasting passages where there were no passages. Ploughing through twenty-foot snow drifts in the winter and choking on alkali dust in the summer. They built snowsheds through gorges, spanned rivers with bridges through the Laramie Hills, the Cheyenne Pass, the Rockies, the Wasatch Mountains, the High Sierras. . . ."

The circle of men stood silently, fascinated by Thomas's impassioned discourse. "And thousands upon thousands of laborers, gentlemen," he continued to expound. "Surveyors, graders, railers, spikers, bolters, cooks, soldiers—armies of Irish Tarriers, Chinese coolies, Johnny Rebs, Yankee Bluecoats, and devout Mormons, just to name a few.

"And always the endless caravans of mule-driven wagons bringing in food, supplies, dismantled engines, iron rails, wooden railroad ties. Hauling in wagonloads of dirt for ballast, then hauling away the wagonloads of rock and stone.

147

"And throughout the whole time, they fought rain, snow, sleet, wind. The heat. The cold. Landslides, flash floods, Indians, insects, herds of thundering buffalo . . . and each other."

Thomas halted, suddenly realizing that he had been monopolizing the conversation. With a smile of chagrin, he added a final word. "It will be interesting to see how history records this amazing feat."

"Doctor Graham, I think you've got quite a story to tell," the publisher of the local newspaper, *The Missouri Democrat*, declared. "I'd like to carry this message to my readers. Would you object if I sent one of my reporters over to interview you tomorrow morning?"

Thomas raised his hand to ward off the suggestion. "Sir, I'm flattered. But I'm just a doctor. My contribution has been minor. You should be looking for interviews a month from now when some of those men start returning. They'll have the real stories to tell." He made a hasty departure and hurried over to Angeleen and Sarah Stewart.

The orchestra had just struck up the first waltz of the evening. "Since that husband of yours is not available, may I claim the first dance, Mrs. Stewart?"

Looking breathtaking in a gown the exact color of her sapphire eyes, Angeleen rose to accept the offer. However, Thomas was quickly nudged aside. "Over my dead body. The first waltz is mine." Ruark Stewart took his wife's hand and led her to the dance floor.

"I meant you anyway, Nana Sarah," Thomas

said to the regal-looking, gray-haired dowager who remained.

The grande dame eyed him skeptically. "Don't try that Southern charm on me, you rapscallion," Sarah Stewart declared. "Besides, at my age, each breath is too precious to waste waltzing around on a dance floor."

Thomas sat down in the chair vacated by Angeleen and clasped her hand. "That doesn't mean we can't share the first dance. Who says we have to spend it waltzing?"

"Ah, Thomas, you are a charmer," Sarah said. Her clear blue eyes lit with unconcealed pleasure. "Isn't it about time you found yourself a good woman and got married? You're not getting any younger, you know."

He pressed a kiss to her blue-veined hand. "I've already found myself a good woman. I figure if I wait long enough, I'll soon be old enough to avoid any scandal when I marry you, sweetheart."

"Mercy me, Thomas. How you do carry on!" Nevertheless, with a twinkle in her eye, she patted his hand and was obviously pleased by the flattery.

As her grandson and his wife waltzed by, Sarah's face softened into a smile. "Aren't they a handsome pair, Thomas? I remember the night I saw them waltzing together for the first time. I knew then what the outcome would be."

Thomas grinned, recalling his own initial meeting with Angel Hunter. "The first time I saw them together was at Delmonico's in New York. After five minutes, I knew they were in love with one another, although both of them tried hard to disguise their true feelings."

Sarah leaned over and patted his hand again, her face wreathed with a smile. "But what a time we had getting them wed," she exclaimed.

"We sure did," he agreed. He flexed his jaw. "Your grandson sure packs a wallop."

Sarah clasped her hands together. "Oh, what a glorious fight that was," she enthused.

The waltz ended, and he saw Ruark and Angeleen step outside onto the veranda. "Excuse me, my love, I'm going to try and claim the next waltz with Angel."

Stepping outside, Thomas spied Ruark and Angeleen in the shadows of a nearby tree. The married couple were engaged in a fervent kiss.

Thomas crossed his arms and leaned back against the door, intentionally discouraging anyone else from stepping out to interrupt the intimate scene. When Ruark and Angeleen finally drew apart, Thomas cleared his throat. "Don't you two get enough of that at home?"

Ruark lifted his head, but didn't look around. Instead, he nibbled at his wife's ear. "I think if we ignore him, Angel, he'll go away."

Straightening up, Thomas walked over to them. "Not until *he* gets to dance with your wife."

"Look, T.J., there must be plenty of single women at this wedding. Can't you attach yourself to one?" Ruark grumbled.

Thomas shook his head sympathetically and grabbed her hand. "Come with me, darlin'. How can you suffer such demonstrative possessiveness? No wonder the guy had to coerce you into marrying him."

Angeleen cast a backward glance at her disgruntled husband. With a helpless shrug, she allowed Thomas to tow her behind him. Grinning and shaking his head with tolerant sufferance, Ruark followed them back to the ballroom.

As he whirled Angeleen around the floor, Thomas glanced across the room and glimpsed two men standing with a redheaded bridal attendant. The woman's back was turned to him, but her auburn-colored hair and the set of her shoulders reminded him of Rory. Each time they passed the group, he glanced longingly toward the three people, the men's heads bent attentively above the woman.

"What's wrong, T.J.?" Angeleen asked.

"Wrong? Nothing. What made you ask?"

"Because sometime during this waltz, I suddenly found myself dancing alone," she said. A serene smile graced her face. "Where did you disappear to, T.J.?"

"Someone looked familiar, that's all."

"Could that someone be female?" she asked.

He winked. "Could be. And I intend to check out the situation when this dance is over."

Angeleen laughed lightly. "That sounds like the man we've all learned to love," she replied.

"Ah, Angel . . . do you know the bridal attendants?" he asked casually.

"All but one. There's the bride's sister, the Sheldon twins, Carissa Dandridge, and a school

151

friend of Laura's, a Rory Callahan. Come to think of it, I understand she's from Utah." Her eyes suddenly lit with awareness. "Small world, isn't it?"

Thomas felt his pulsebeat quicken. "Smaller than you think, Angel."

As soon as the dance finished, he returned Angeleen to the waiting arms of her husband. "Excuse me," he said and hurried away.

"Where's he running off to in such a hurry?" Ruark asked.

"I believe he said he saw someone he knew."

"Oh, yeah?" Ruark asked, suddenly interested. He stretched his neck to follow Thomas's progress through the crowd. "Male or female?"

"My very same question," Angeleen said with light laughter.

Across the room, Thomas approached the three people. He stepped up behind the woman. "I believe this is our dance, Miss Callahan."

Rory recognized the slight Southern accent at once. "Thomas!" Smiling, she turned around. "Thomas, what are you doing here?"

"Taking in this extraordinary event, which is becoming more beautiful by the moment."

Dressed in a pale green gown of silk organdy with a filmy flounce draping her shoulders, she looked like a breath of spring. Her green eyes were alight with merriment, and her glorious mane of red hair was pinned to the top of her head, adorned at the back by a band of woven lilies of the valley.

"And I have to say this is a most unexpected, but pleasant surprise." He reached for her hand.

"Excuse us, gentlemen." The two young men appeared annoyed as he led her away.

When Thomas and Rory entered the flow of the dancers, he dropped all semblance of formality and expressed a warm, heartfelt sentiment. "You look lovely, Rory." Rory *felt* lovely under his dark-eyed gaze. He always had the ability to make her feel that way. "I missed you."

She was too happy to see him to be coy. "I missed you too, Thomas."

"I tried to see you, but your father wouldn't let me near you."

"I know. I went to Tent Town several times, hoping to see you, too. Did you get my note?"

"Note? No, I didn't," he said.

"It doesn't matter. It was just to tell you I'd be in St. Louis for a couple of weeks."

He continued gracefully gliding her around the floor. "Where are you staying?"

"At the home of Laura's parents. And you?"

"With the Stewarts. They're close friends." He suddenly blurted, "Rory, let's get out of here."

She looked at him astounded. "I can't leave, Thomas. I'm one of the bridal attendants."

"Tell them you're ill or tired. Tell them anything, but let's get out of here."

For a long moment, she stared into his eyes. She saw the urgency in his eyes and heard it in his voice. "Oh, this is unforgivable of me. But give me a few minutes to make my excuses."

"Good girl," he said, relieved.

She frowned solemnly. "No, I'm not. But that's not the issue here, is it?"

He squeezed her shoulders. "I'll meet you outside."

The dance ended, and she hurried over to talk to the host and hostess. Thomas sought out the Stewarts and told them he was leaving.

"Rather sudden, isn't it?" Ruark asked.

"I'll explain later," Thomas said.

At the serious look on the face of his friend, Ruark did not stop to banter. "Take our carriage. Just tell Daniel to come back about ten o'clock."

Thomas slapped him on the shoulder. "Thanks, old friend."

Outside, he paced anxiously. Seeing Thomas, Daniel approached him. "Did you want the carriage, Doctor Graham?"

"Yes, Daniel." When the driver turned away to go for the carriage, Thomas stopped him. "Ah . . . Daniel, if a person wanted to be alone for a short while, where's the best place to go?"

"Mr. Ruark always had me circle the park a few times," Daniel said succinctly. The carriage was waiting by the time Rory appeared.

"Around the park, Daniel," Thomas ordered as he and Rory climbed into the carriage.

"Yes, sir," the driver replied. His expression remained inscrutable as he closed the carriage door.

Chapter Nine

The darkened carriage secured them within its confines like a snug cocoon. Thomas pulled Rory into his arms and his mouth closed over hers at once. From the first touch of his lips, nothing else mattered to her. Sighing with pleasure, Rory gave herself up to the kiss.

"I've missed you, Rory. For weeks I've done nothing but think about the feel of you, the taste of you," he murmured. He followed the declaration with a stream of kisses to her ear.

He reclaimed her parted lips and his probing tongue filled her mouth, intimately exploring the sensitive chamber as the intensity of the kiss increased. Quivering with rapture, she molded her curves to his muscled body.

"Thomas, I don't know what comes over me when I'm with you," she breathed with a sigh as he traced a trail to the throbbing pulse of her slender neck. "I've never felt like this before with anyone."

He pulled her onto his lap and she lay in his arms. For a long moment, he stared into her passion-filled eyes. "I can't believe no man has ever lit the fire within you, Rory. You're so much woman," he said, smiling tenderly.

His nearness intensified her longing for him, and she nestled deeper against him. Reaching up, she ran a finger along the chiseled line of his jaw. "I guess I just never met the right man until now. But I like what I feel when I'm in your arms." Her gaze returned to the warmth of his smile. "Kiss me again, Thomas," she murmured, parting her lips in invitation.

With a smothered groan he complied, claiming her lips in a deep, drugging kiss. Relaxing in his arms, she surrendered to the excitement of the kiss. When they were forced to separate, her eyes were hazy, like emerald pools of desire.

"Lord, Rory. I can't get enough of you!" he groaned. His mouth slid down the column of her neck as he slipped his hand under the filmy flounce of her gown and cupped the fullness of a breast.

Closing her eyes, she lolled back, her body throbbing with blissful sensation. "What are you thinking about, Rory? I wish I could guess what thoughts are running through that beautiful head of yours."

"I'm afraid they aren't very ladylike, Thomas," she said hesitantly, but her impish smile and candor were signs of encouragement. "I'm thinking of how much I enjoy being in your arms."

His hands dropped away when she sat up but did not move from his lap. "And I'm thinking of what a brazen hussy I've become." She released the flounce and shoved it off her shoulders. "Open my gown, Thomas." She turned her back to him.

His firm hands cupped the curves of her shoulders as he drew her back against the wall of his chest, and his husky voice at her ear became yet one more sensuous assault. "Are you sure this is what you want, Rory?" His warm breath ruffled her hair as he nibbled at the delicate shell, sending a shiver down her spine.

She turned her head to glance back at him. Eye to eye, they stared deeply at one another and she felt a rising blush of uncertainty. "Isn't it what you want too?"

He chuckled lightly and she basked in the exciting intensity of his dark-eyed gaze. "I've wanted to make love to you from the first moment I saw you."

Her emerald eyes offered an unmistakable invitation. "Then what are you waiting for, Thomas?"

He released the buttons and the gown dropped to her waist. Lying back in his arms, she slipped her arms around his neck, her breath quickening when his hand swept the curve of her breast.

Lowering his head, he began to tantalize the sensitive peak with his tongue. A groan slipped past her trembling lips when his mouth closed around the other peak. Soon overcome with a feeling of ecstasy, she began to writhe beneath him.

Their gazes met and locked for a few seconds. She glowed under the blazing passion she read in his dark eyes, unaware of how her own eyes glittered with expectation. He did not ignore the invitation.

Once again his mouth covered hers as he slipped his hand beneath her gown.

Her passion surged, meeting the power of his, and their tongues coupled in a heated duel, her urgency intensifying at the feel of his heated palm caressing her thigh.

"Thomas. Oh, God, Thomas," she groaned aloud as he palmed the throbbing chamber of her loins. His mouth stifled her moans, his tongue filling her mouth as his fingers began to stroke and probe. When he found the sensitive nub, his name became an incessant moan on her lips that increased his passion all the more.

Sliding his mouth to her breast, he laved and nibbled at the exquisite mounds, now full and heavy with her own passion. A wave of hot, blinding sensation enveloped her and then exploded in spine-shuddering tremors.

When his arms slipped around her, she slumped breathlessly against him, gasping for much-needed breath. He nibbled a trail of kisses along the column of her neck, and she shifted her head to allow him freer access.

She felt the renewed stirring of arousal. "Oh, God, Thomas, I'm depraved. I love this too much," she whispered.

Her throaty admission sent a surge of hot blood to his loins. He lightly tugged at one of the taut nipples with his teeth and then closed his mouth around it.

She slid her hand down the wall of his chest and his rapid heartbeat under her palm incited a need to feel his naked flesh. With trembling fingers, she released the studs of his shirt and slipped her hand into the opening.

Her fingers tingled as the hair on his chest brushed at her fingertips. His movements ceased. Waiting. His body taut with tension.

With renewed wonder, she followed the trail of hair down his lean stomach until it disappeared into the top of his pants. Hesitating, she sought his glance for reassurance.

His eyes were hooded with passion. "Yes, sweetheart, yes," he rasped, encouraging her to continue.

The husky plea further elevated her confidence. He sucked in a breath when she slid her hand lower and palmed the heated mound she encountered. She marveled at the feel of it—the swollen bulge, restrained by his pants, seemed to throb with its own pulse and heat. Her own loins tightened in instant response.

In the sensual but hypnotic throes of sexual exploration, she sought to remove any barriers. Her fingers began to fumble with the buttons of his pants.

But suddenly, a jolt of the carriage threw her off his lap. The carriage had abruptly halted.

"Oh, no!" he groaned in utter dismay.

Reaching for her, Thomas lifted her to the seat and yanked up her gown to cover her exposed breasts.

"What happened?" she asked, confused and still breathless as he hurriedly buttoned her gown. Then quickly restoring his own clothing, Thomas opened the carriage door.

"What is it, Daniel?" he asked.

"I don't know, sir. But there appears to be someone lying in the road ahead," Daniel replied. He blew several times on a shrill-sounding whistle, then climbed down from his seat.

Both men hastened from the carriage and ran toward the form. Just as the two men reached the fallen figure, the toot of a police whistle sounded in response to Daniel's summons.

Before Thomas could examine him, the man rose to his feet. "What happened, sir?" Thomas asked.

"Just a dizzy spell," the man murmured.

"Perhaps I can help. I'm a doctor," Thomas offered. But the man hurried away before Thomas could stop him.

After a quick explanation to the two policemen who arrived on the scene, Thomas climbed back into the carriage. Rory had restored her appearance, and the disruptive incident had restored their composure as well.

Thomas delivered her to the home of her host with the promise of calling on her the following afternoon.

Astride Bold King, the black stallion that had played such an important role in bringing Ruark and her together, Angeleen joined Thomas and Ruark the next morning for an early morning ride.

Despite his curiosity, Ruark Stewart did not bring up the subject of Thomas's hasty departure the previous evening, having been well-coached and chided earlier by his wife. But when Thomas tried to appear casual as he mentioned Rory Callahan, he didn't fool his two friends for a moment.

Eager to meet the young girl, Ruark suggested they dine together and then go to the Olympic Theater to attend the St. Louis debut of a new musical.

As Thomas knew they would, Ruark and Angel liked Rory's down-to-earth naturalness at once. The four people got along famously throughout the meal.

Later, during the intermission of the musical which starred the three Worrell sisters and their entire New York company, Thomas and Ruark savored a glass of wine while the two women went to freshen up.

"So, Rory's father is a rancher in Utah," Ruark remarked. "You planning on going into the cattle business, old friend?"

"Is that your heavy-handed way of asking me what my intentions are toward Rory?" Thomas asked. "Thank God you're married, or you'd be planning right now how to move in on her."

Ruark raised his hand in protest. "Nothing to worry about, buddy. Those days are behind me. I haven't looked or thought about another woman from the day I met Angel. Can you blame me?"

"No. You'd be a damn fool if you did." Thomas's dark glance swept the lobby. "Say, is your fly open, buddy, or is mine? We seem to be under close inspection of some sort."

"Feel naked without your gun belt, Buffalo Bill?" Following the direction of Thomas's glance, Ruark discovered that they had attracted more than casual interest from several circles of women. He flashed a grin at Thomas. "Reminds me of our college days. Looks like we've still got it, old friend."

Glancing again around the room, his dark eyes suddenly lit with a gleam of interest. "And so have they."

His slight nod was directed toward Angeleen and Rory. As they crossed the lobby, the two attractive women drew lingering glances from the many men observing them. With an enamored smile, Ruark walked forward to meet his wife.

Shaking his head, Thomas followed. Ten years earlier, he would have bet his soul that no woman could ever have that effect on the debonair and womanizing Ruark Stewart. But that was before Ruark met Angel Hunter.

Later, when the performance had ended, the two couples strolled to their carriage. Ruark had given Daniel the evening off and forsaken the heavy carriage for the lighter, open rig which he was driving himself.

"So what did you think of those Worrell sisters, T.J.?" Ruark asked. "That Jennie isn't too hard to look at, is she?"

"She was okay, but I thought her sister, Irene, had it all over her."

"Oh, I think you're both wrong," Angeleen remarked. She winked an eye at Rory. "Sophie was much more impressive."

Realizing that the conversation had become nothing more than a word game between them, Rory added, "Yes, indeed. Especially the time when she crossed her eyes and sang through her nose."

Ruark groaned. "I think you've met your match, old buddy," he said with a warm chuckle. He slipped his arm around Angeleen's shoulders. "You know, if we didn't have to chaperon these other two, we could stop in the park and do some sparkin'."

"Far be it from us to thwart the course of true love," Thomas replied. "Rory and I are more than willing to flag down a carriage of our own."

"Just because my husband is talking crazy is no reason why you should too, T.J.," Angeleen declared. However, her saucy grin at her husband belied the feigned indignation.

Ruark grabbed Angeleen and kissed her; then, swooping his wife off her feet, he swung her into the seat. "Ruark Stewart, you're incorrigible," she lamented with a heated blush. "People are watching."

"Only with envy, Angeleen," Rory quickly interjected.

Ruark's head jerked up. "Envy! Aha!" he cried out with a shout of victory. "Just as I've always contended. And remember, that testimony was unsolicited."

"Lady, you're going to pay the price for feeding the vanity of that egomaniac," Thomas warned, making a grab for Rory.

"I don't know what you're talking about,"

Rory squealed. "Besides, I wasn't referring to myself." She ducked away as Thomas began to stalk her.

"Rory, I think you and I should be the ones to take a different carriage and leave these two characters to their vices," Angeleen suggested.

Rory couldn't reply because Thomas had her backed up against the carriage, kissing her soundly.

To any passerby, the foursome sounded like drunken sailors as they rode through the streets harmonizing one of the songs from the burlesque they had just seen.

"What the hell!" Ruark suddenly blurted out, cutting off his contributing baritone. "Looks like a body lying in the road." Their gaiety ceased at once as he reined up quickly.

"The same thing happened to us last night," Thomas remarked suspiciously. "You two ladies stay in the carriage."

The two men climbed out of the wagon, and Thomas bent down to examine the body. "Why, this is the same man we saw last night," Thomas said. At the sound of scurrying feet, he glanced up to see several men rushing at them from the shadows.

"Ruark, look out," Thomas shouted.

The man on the ground suddenly opened his eyes and grabbed at Thomas's arm to pull him down. Ruark shoved the fellow away with his foot, enabling Thomas to jump up.

They were outnumbered five to two, and fists flew furiously as Thomas and Ruark attempted to dodge blows while making every punch they threw count.

The pair of bays pulling the rig whinnied and stamped as the fighting men crashed into them. Angeleen Stewart grabbed the reins and struggled to hold the team in check.

"Angel, get out of here," Ruark shouted.

"I'm not leaving you," she shouted. One of the thieves jumped up and tried to drag her out of the wagon.

Not one to sit idly by at any time of emergency, Rory sprang to action. With her opera pump in her hand as a weapon, she climbed over the back of the front seat and began to smack the scoundrel in the head and face. Forced to release his hold on Angeleen, he fell back, clutching at his eyes.

Meanwhile, Thomas shoved off two of the thieves who had wrestled him to the ground. Rising to his feet, he threw a solid uppercut to the chin of one of the thugs and knocked him out cold.

Ruark and Thomas finally succeeded in reaching each other so they could fight back-to-back. "Where the hell are your damn smoking pistols when we need them, Buffalo Bill?" Ruark grumbled, delivering a solid punch to the nose of one of the attackers. A bone crunched under his fist, and blood began to stream from the nostrils of the scoundrel. Holding his bleeding nose and mouthing vile curses, the man disappeared into the shadows.

Thomas and Ruark made quick work of dispatching the two remaining assailants, then with clenched fists and heaving chests, the victorious gladiators glanced around at the strewn figures on the street. Ruark stuck out a hand to Thomas. "Yep. Gotta admit, we've still got it, old friend."

Grinning, the two men shook hands.

A short time later at their home, Angeleen entered carrying a tea tray as Thomas treated Ruark's injuries.

"Let them have their brandy, Rory. I made us a pot of tea."

Ruark winced as Thomas applied some antiseptic to a cut on his brow. She quickly put down the tray and rushed to his side. "How is he?" she asked with a worried frown. Picking up Ruark's hand, she pressed a kiss to the palm.

"He'll live," Thomas snorted.

"And what about you, T.J.?" Angeleen asked.

"How do I know? I don't have the luxury of a doctor's examination." He grabbed his drink, stretched out on the floor before the fireplace, and closed his eyes.

"Oh, the poor baby," Rory teased. Holding her tea cup, she sat down on the floor beside him. "I'll listen to your tale of woe. Why don't you tell me where you hurt, Thomas?"

He raised a lid and eyed her mischievously. "Promise to kiss it where it hurts?"

Rory blushed and glanced up, embarrassed at the amused couple observing them. "Are you sure I'm not inconveniencing you by staying the night?" she said, quickly changing the subject.

"Of course not," Angeleen replied. "We have

plenty of room. I've laid out a gown and robe for you in the room directly at the right of the stairway, Rory. And the police inspector promised to inform the Bacons that you are spending the night with us."

She slipped her arm through Ruark's. "Well, it's late. And I've had enough excitement for tonight, so we'll say good night." She yanked Ruark to his feet. "Won't we, darling?"

"Oh . . . yeah, of course," Ruark said. "Good night, you two." He slipped his arm around her shoulders, and as they climbed the stairs, he whispered in her ear. "You sure you've had enough excitement for the night?"

"I'm open for negotiation, counselor, if you can show me enough evidence to strengthen your case."

Ruark's dark brow arched suggestively, accepting the challenge. "Every man's entitled to his day in court, you know."

"Or night." Angeleen Stewart's sapphire eyes flashed with the provocative gleam that always managed to play havoc with her husband's libido.

Rory smiled as the couple disappeared upstairs. "I like your friends, Thomas. I bet they had an interesting courtship. Will you tell me about it?"

Thomas sat up and downed the remains of the brandy. His dark eyes mellowed with the warmth of rich memories.

"Well . . . once upon a time there was a rich Yankee . . . an impoverished Southern belle . . . and a black stallion named Bold King." Rory

167

sat with her knees tucked under her chin and listened enthralled.

" . . . and they lived happily ever after," Thomas said, fifteen minutes later as he finished the story.

Rory sighed and smiled. "And Angeleen is so beautiful."

He raised his arm and cupped her nape, drawing her head down to his. "And so are you, Rory." His kiss was lazy, but sensual.

"I don't think we should do this, Thomas," she warned. "This isn't the time or place."

"Nothing will happen that you don't want to happen," he whispered, trailing a string of kisses to her ear. A shiver went down her spine when he began to nibble at the sensitive shell. "I have great control. You should know that by now."

"But I don't," she whispered in a throaty sigh as his lips slid down the slender column of her neck. She shoved him away in panic and rose to her feet. "So, I'm getting out of here, too. And quickly," she added.

With a resigned groan, Thomas sat up. "Just like I said, who ever tries to heal the doctor?"

Over breakfast, Thomas and Rory discovered they both·had return tickets to Utah for the following day.

In order to observe a daring surgical procedure scheduled for that morning, Thomas left for the Good Samaritan Hospital. Rory wanted to do some final shopping for the early spring styles not yet available in Ogden. Angeleen agreed to accompany her, and Ruark went into his business office. They all agreed to meet for lunch.

Later that morning, as soon as Rory and Angeleen entered the dress salon, a small man with a pencil-thin moustache, receding hairline, and round black eyes rushed up to greet them.

"Ah, Madame Stewart," the man exclaimed eagerly.

"Monsieur Dubonnet," Angeleen acknowledged warmly. The Frenchman bowed and kissed her hand.

After Angeleen introduced her to the salon's owner, Rory wandered away, her attention drawn to a day dress of green-and-white muslin with an underdress of green grenadine.

"The dress would look lovely on you, mademoiselle." Rory had been so engrossed in studying the gown, she had not been aware that Angeleen and the couturier had moved to her side.

"This is a lovely gown, sir. I am sure it would flatter anyone," Rory agreed.

Not just anyone, Dubonnet would have liked to say. He frequently had to suffer the vanity of his female clientele. A large waistline, small breasts, or a pair of wide hips could often present a design challenge. However, he doubted this lovely young girl had any one of these problems; her figure appeared perfect to his practiced eye. *Actually, delightful,* he thought with admiration. *Her youthful glow is pure enchantment.* His eyes shifted to the woman next to her. *As is Madame Stewart's,* he marveled.

"Would you like to try on the gown, mademoiselle?" Dubonnet flitted around Rory, pointing out the quality of the material and richness of the color.

"I don't think so," she declined. "Besides, I am sure you wouldn't want to sell your sample gown."

"And why not? Madame Stewart has mentioned that your stay in St. Louis is limited."

"Limited indeed, Monsieur Dubonnet. I am leaving in the morning," Rory said good-naturedly.

"Then I insist you try on the gown." When Rory nodded her acceptance, he clapped his hands. Instantly, a seamstress appeared and led her to a dressing room. The gown required only a slight adjustment at the hips, and the couturier assured Rory it could be done within the hour.

"Oh, Rory, the gown does look lovely on you. We could finish our shopping and come back," Angeleen suggested. Rory willingly agreed. She dressed and rejoined Angeleen in the salon.

Upon passing a table filled with colorful bolts of material, Rory stopped to admire a roll of garnet-colored satin embroidered with pink, white, and green flowers. "How lovely. And what an unusual shade." She picked up a corner of the material and examined the intricate stitchery.

Dubonnet rolled his eyes heavenward. *"Oui, mademoiselle.* Is it not exquisite! And the shade is the newest fashion."

Rory sighed and let the fabric drop through her fingers. "How I wish I had discovered you sooner, Monsieur Dubonnet," she said forlornly.

"Now I'm practically on the train back to Ogden."

Before departing, Rory decided to purchase a gift for Kathleen Rafferty. She bought her friend a pair of white silk stockings embroidered with red vertical stripes. Her final purchase was a Tyrolese brown felt hat. The fashionable chapeau, trimmed with brown velvet, sported a velvet cockade and green feathered plume.

"I'll be the most fashionably dressed woman in Utah," Rory exclaimed as they left the store.

Ah, young women! Dubonnet lamented as the two lovely ladies laughed gaily and continued on their jaunt. *When will women learn their beauty makes its own fashion—not the dictates of a French dress designer.*

Later, after an exhausting, but enjoyable, morning of shopping, the two women waited in the dining room of the hotel for Thomas and Ruark to join them.

"I've had such a delightful time, Angel," Rory remarked. "I can't thank Ruark and you enough for your hospitality. It's no wonder Thomas loves the two of you so much."

"I suppose we appear to be self-satisfied elitists to you."

Rory was shocked at how close Angeleen had come to touching on a part of the truth. "No, of course not. But I do admit, there were times I felt like an intruder. The three of you are so close."

"I know exactly what you mean, Rory, and I can't blame you for feeling that way. I remember that I felt like an outsider too when I first met

171

T.J. That bond between him and Ruark appeared to be impregnable."

"But Thomas told me the two of you became friends immediately."

Angeleen's lovely face sobered. "Did he tell you what happened to me in New York?" Rory nodded. "And when Tommy was born?" At Rory's look of affirmation, Angeleen reached for her hand. "Then you've probably guessed that underneath that wide grin and Southern charm is a rock of strength. Looking back at that time, the uncertainties, I don't know what I would have done without T.J."

While listening to Angeleen, Rory watched the expressive emotions flit across the woman's lovely face. Rory could see how Angel Hunter had brought the wealthy and womanizing entrepreneur, Ruark Stewart, to his knees. She would have liked to witness the development of that volatile relationship. For a second, Rory's thoughts drifted to Thomas Graham. Would their romance take a similar rocky course?

"I think I understand what you mean. Thomas has seen me through several crises in the short time I've known him," Rory remarked.

"There are all kinds of heroes, Rory," Angeleen said. "I'm hopelessly in love with Ruark. I worship and adore him. He's a brilliant business-man. His vision and foresight never cease to amaze me. I think he could move mountains, if he had to." Her eyes sparkled with impishness above the graceful hand she brought to her mouth. "And I'm thrilled with the lovable rogue's continual posturing to try and impress me. But

confidentially, Rory, T.J. will always be a hero
to me, too." She laughed gaily. "But I'll deny I
ever said so if you breathe a word of it to either
of them."

Angeleen's sapphire eyes brightened like jewels. "Oh, I know Ruark and T.J. have been
acting like schoolboys, but don't be misled by
their antics. They both are men of strength and
courage."

"They haven't fooled me for a moment, Angel.
I know Thomas and Ruark are just happy to see
each other," Rory said.

Angeleen squeezed her hand. "Thank you for
understanding, Rory."

"It's like coming home for him. Thomas told
me you Stewarts are the only family he has."

Smiling, Angeleen said, "By the way, I like
Thomas much better than *T.J.* Sounds more dig-
nified." She glanced across the room. Momentarily, the conversation was forgotten and her
eyes deepened with warmth as she watched
the tall figure of her husband cross the room
toward them.

That evening, after Tommy had been put to
bed and Sarah Stewart had retired, the foursome
sat long into the night sharing the warmth of
camaraderie.

The next morning, Ruark and Angeleen
accompanied Thomas and Rory to Union Station. The two men lingered over their handshake.

"You'll be seeing us sooner than you think.
We're coming out for the big rail-linking ceremony," Ruark said. "I've invested in a mining

173

operation near Ogden, and we're moving some heavy equipment out there. I thought I'd combine business with pleasure by bringing Angel and Tommy with me. Wouldn't want my son to miss history in the making."

"Then I'll see you next month, old friend," Thomas replied.

And as the train pulled out of the depot, Ruark shouted in a final warning, "And try to stay out of trouble until then."

Chapter Ten

Rain began to fall as the train pulled out of St. Louis. The train was crowded. Thomas buried his head behind the covers of a medical journal. Rory tried to concentrate on the new novel, *Little Women*, which she had intentionally purchased in St. Louis to read on the return trip. She was unsuccessful.

She peered through the rain-streaked window but found the drab landscape not varied enough to hold her interest. In fact, she thought, the countryside appeared downright dull compared to the splendor of Utah. Dull, black, and dreary.

Around noon, the baby in the seat opposite them began to cry and continued nonstop for the next hour. In sympathy, Rory offered to hold the infant for the poor harried mother— only to be rewarded for her charity when the child proceeded to regurgitate on her. By the time she returned from sponging off her gown, Thomas had lulled the child to sleep by stroking its stomach.

"Understand it works with alligators, too," he informed her with a pleased grin.

A short time later, he fell asleep beside her, and Rory finally succeeded in reaching that mellow state of dozing when sound fades into a distant background.

"Pow! Pow! You're dead!"

Her eyes popped open. A young boy, not much older than eight or nine, stood over her pointing a carved toy gun in her face. After firing the coup de grace into her temple, he raced off to join his brother, who was "shooting up" the opposite aisle.

After another hour of the "James Boys," the besieged passengers were at their wit's end—Everyone except Thomas Jefferson Graham, who had managed to sleep through it all.

One of the boys knocked her hat off the seat and then trampled it. Rory gave them both a sound tongue-lashing and ordered them to sit down and behave themselves.

The two boys ran sobbing to their mother, who stomped back clutching a hand of each of them. "She's the one, Mama," the oldest boy declared, pointing a shaking finger in Rory's direction as his sniffling brother clung to his mother's skirt.

The indignant woman threatened to pull out every hair on Rory's head for frightening her little boys. And Rory Elizabeth Callahan was just in the mood to tell her to try and do it.

Their shouting woke Thomas. Only the calm intervention of Doctor *Pied-Piper-of-Hamelin* Graham, who patiently showed the two boys how to fold torn-out pages from his medical journal into boats and hats, prevented the hair-pulling bout which might have ensued.

Things only got worse as the day progressed. Several times, breakdowns or rescheduling required them to change trains or routes, resulting in lengthy delays and adding to Rory's growing disgruntlement. Even the few facilities that offered food were always out of everything except coffee and bread.

But for Rory, the final indignity occurred when, after changing trains for the third time, a ventilator that had negligently been left partially open sprayed cinders over her new hat and gown. She was able to wipe the grime off her face, but her gown and already crushed hat were stained with black soot. Glancing at Thomas, she discovered that there wasn't a speck on him.

Finally, tired and hungry, they arrived at Council Bluffs. All that remained was to take the ferry over to Omaha, where they would spend the night and then board the Union Pacific early the next morning.

Standing on the deck of the ferry, Rory covered her mouth to stifle a yawn as she anxiously waited to reach the other side. She cast a grateful glance at Thomas, who was making arrangements for their trunks to be taken directly to the depot. Thankful for his presence, she wondered how he could still be in such good spirits so late at night.

Sighing, she turned back to stare listlessly at the river. Bright moonlight cast silver rays on the mighty Missouri River and, even in her tired state, she could not help but admire the stunning sight.

The ferry passed midstream, approaching the opposite shore. She glanced in disgust at "Jesse James" and his brother "Frank," the names she had secretly dubbed the two rambunctious boys, who even at this late hour were running around still creating a disturbance.

Suddenly the youngest boy tripped and fell. Rory made a grab for him but was too late to keep the unfortunate child from tumbling overboard.

The boy's mother turned her head in time to see her son tumble over the side. "Joey!" she screamed. "Help! Somebody help him. He can't swim," she cried out piteously.

Thomas swung around at the sound of the woman's cries. Shucking his gun belt, he pulled off his boots and dived into the swirling water. The current had already caught the boy and had begun to carry him downriver.

As soon as the ferry touched shore, several of the crew raced along the river bank in pursuit. Aided by the swift current, Thomas's strong strokes rapidly closed the gap between him and the boy, and he finally succeeded in overtaking the flailing youngster.

Grasping Joey firmly by the shoulders, Thomas fought his way to the shore. The current and the panicking boy began to take a toll on Thomas's waning strength. The men on shore threw out several lines and he managed to grab one. Moments later, the rescuers succeeded in towing the pair out of the water.

As Thomas lay gasping for breath, the group huddled around him and the youngster. One of the crewmen turned the young lad over and began pumping the water out of him. A murmur of relief swept the circle when the boy began gagging. Within minutes, a couple of the crew had Joey on the river bank regurgitating all the water he had swallowed.

Shivering, Thomas gratefully accepted the blanket tossed to him. "Be sure that youngster is wrapped firmly," he warned the sailor who picked up the boy to carry him back.

Rory rushed up to the men returning to the ferry. Hearing Joey bawling for his mother, she knew the young boy was not harmed and rushed over to hug Thomas "Are you all right, Thomas?"

He managed a grin. "I'm fine," he murmured through chattering teeth.

Once back on the ferry, Joey was snatched up by the arms of his crying mother as Thomas ordered her to get the wet clothes off the boy at once.

He got himself some items of dry clothing out of his trunk, and ten minutes later he rejoined Rory on shore. "Well, what an appropriate end to a totally miserable day," she remarked, putting her arms around him. "That was a heroic thing you did, Thomas."

"Anyone would have done the same thing, honey," he said, brushing aside his role in the incident. "I'm just glad the youngster is okay. But perhaps the deed does warrant a kiss," he remarked with a mischievous grin.

"I would certainly think so," Rory said. Her green eyes danced with amusement. She slipped her arms around his waist. "I'll call back the boy's mother to bestow one on you. It will also give her the chance to thank you for saving her son's life."

"Well, I'm sure the poor woman was just so relieved to get her son back alive that it never crossed her mind. But you make a most attractive emissary," he said. "so why don't you take her place?" he suggested, drawing her into the shadows of the wharf.

The tenderness in his eyes was more of a devastating assault on her than his lips and hands could ever be, and her body began trembling with passion.

He slowly leaned toward her, closing the gap that separated them, and his head lowered. Her lips parted to accept the tender and warm mouth that closed over her own, drawing an instant response from her.

His lips mercifully left hers, only to trail a heated path to the hollow of her throat. "Oh, Thomas," she breathed rapturously as he cupped the round mound of her breast. His hand felt like a flame through the fabric of her gown.

Every nerve in her body was attuned to the male essence of him now. She felt consumed by the ravishing hunger of his kiss, resistance incinerated by the heat of their mutual passion.

His hand played havoc with the tingling nerves

of her spine as he repeatedly swept her back, pressing her tighter against his own heated body. She felt his arousal pressing against her, and her own passion responded to the exciting pressure of it. She slid her arms around his neck, pulling him even tighter to her, his long, hard body molding to her soft curves.

"Thomas. Oh, Thomas," she moaned, his name a sensuous purr on her lips.

"I want you, Rory. I want to make love to you."

"Oh yes, yes," she whispered.

"Tonight, Rory. I can't wait any longer." He raised his head and stared down at her, his long spiky lashes hooding his passion-filled eyes.

"Neither can I." At the sight of her tremendous smile, the corners of his dark eyes crinkled with the warmth of his own smile.

He cupped her face in his hands and their mouths opened to one another, his tongue electrifying her with fiery probes. He slipped a hand to her bodice and began to release the buttons.

"Oh, lord!" he murmured when her firm breast filled his hand. He withdrew it swiftly. "Let's get a room quick."

"Sorry, folks. Ain't no rooms available," the night clerk informed them a short time later when they tried to check into the hotel. "Rented the last one not more than ten minutes ago."

Appalled, Rory stared at the young man, then at Thomas. After sixteen hours of hard train seats and even harder depot benches, then driven to distraction by her need for him, she had anticipated relaxing in a warm bath to wash off the soot, then stretching out in a comfortable bed and having Thomas make mindless love to her.

Seeing her distress, Thomas inquired, "Is there a possibility of another hotel, or even a boarding house?"

The man shook his head. "You folks should have stayed in Council Bluffs."

"That's an understatement," she groaned.

"Come over on the ferry?" he asked. At Thomas's nod, the clerk remarked, "Heard tell a boy almost drowned."

"That's right," Thomas said and quickly changed the subject back to the current problem. "Are you certain there's not a room available somewhere?" he asked, casting a sympathetic glance at Rory.

"No, sir. This town's picked clean."

Desolately, Rory turned away. Her passion quelled, she now faced the prospect of another hard bench in still another train station. And eight hours remained before they could board the Union Pacific heading west.

She went over to a worn mohair settee. Sagging and lumpy from frequent usage and broken springs, she saw the coiled tip of a spring poking through the fabric near the base of the couch.

But at least it was a momentary respite from the hard train benches she had endured throughout the day, Rory thought, sinking down into one of the concave contours which had been restructured by the sizes and weights of various posteriors. She was beginning to agree with her father's contempt for the railroad.

Thomas remained at the desk talking in low tones with the night clerk. Wiping a cinder out of the corner of her eye, Rory threw a glare at the two men, who continued chatting amiably together. She knew she was acting like a spoiled brat, but in her present mood, Thomas's inexhaustible good humor and imperturbability exasperated her as much as the numerous setbacks of the day. Five minutes ago he was so fired with passion, he had practically made love to her on the wharf.

Grinning broadly, the very object of her rancor ambled over to her. "I have some good news, honey."

"You got a room," she said. Her hope buoyed.

"Well, no, but Fred has—"

"Fred?"

"Fred Granger, the night clerk. Seems like a real nice guy," Thomas informed her.

"Oh, of course, your ole buddy Fred," she intoned with acerbity. "What about him?"

"Fred's swapping his bed tonight for my treating a festering boil on his a—ah, rear end."

Her eyes lit with restored faith. "A bed!" She clasped her hands together and threw her glance heavenward. "Oh, thank You, Lord. Thank You. Thank You."

Jumping to her feet, she fixed an adoring look on Thomas. How could she have ever doubted him? "Where is it?"

"You've been sitting on it," he said.

Rory's smile vanished as quickly as it had

appeared. "This is his bed?"

"Well . . . yeah. When he's on duty. There's not too much for a night clerk to do during the night." When she continued to stare aghast, he said defensively, "Hey, I think it was kind of nice of him to make the generous offer."

"Generous offer?"

Maidenly modesty kept her from pointing out to him that while ole Fred was getting his butt lanced, she would probably get a broken spring in hers. Why were women naive enough to put their trust in men? Crossing her arms over her chest, she plopped back down on the couch.

She heard a spring pop.

The next morning as they ate breakfast, Rory leaned over the table and whispered, "Thomas, don't you think she's acting strange?"

"Who?" Thomas asked with an amused, whispered reply.

"That woman over there in the corner," Rory said.

Thomas threw a casual glance toward a woman sitting alone at a table drinking a cup of coffee. "I never noticed. Why do you ask?"

"Well, she keeps looking out the window as if she's looking for someone."

"Maybe she is," he said.

"Or maybe she is avoiding someone," she added with a meaningful toss of her red head.

Rory dawdled with the large cut of beef on her plate, her attention continually straying back to the woman in the corner. After a few more minutes, she again leaned over and whispered.

"And furthermore, all the women I know drink tea." Her eyes gleamed with a smugness born of the assurance of her own conviction. "She's . . . *drinking . . . coffee.*"

Thomas forced back his laughter by swallowing a bite of steak. Patting her hand, he whispered in concern, "Yes, I see, my dear. Let me guess . . . that would make her either a Russian princess or possibly an escapee from a Turkish harem. You could be on to something, Miss Pinkerton."

"But what would a Russian princess be doing in—" She stopped. "Oh, Thomas, be serious."

He grinned broadly. "Oh, but I am, my dear. If you want to play sleuth, I'll play along. I'll play any time you like," he added with a glint in his eye.

He answered her look of dismay by changing the subject. "Speaking of sleuthing," he said, motioning toward the practically untouched piece of beef on her plate, "are you going to finish that steak?" When Rory shook her head, Thomas forked the piece of meat and transferred it to his plate. While he finished his meal, she sat drumming her fingers on the table, trying to think of a worthy retort to his disparaging remark about her detective skills.

They had time for a short walk around the town before having to board the train. When they returned to the station, they found the depot had turned into a beehive of activity.

Some of the passengers were crowded around a peddler hawking merchandise from the back of his wagon, while others had been attracted to a man in a spotless white uniform selling boxed lunches.

"All aboard!" the conductor yelled.

As Thomas stopped to buy two of the lunches, Rory observed several unsavory-looking men leaning against a building and scrutinizing the passengers. They looked suspicious to her. Since the notoriety of Jesse James and his gang, the incidence of train robberies had been on the rise. All she needed was another attempted robbery, she reflected, recalling the harrowing experience in St. Louis.

Three buckskin-clad men with shaggy beards and drooping mustaches were supervising the loading of their horses into the baggage car.

"That's a friendly-looking trio," Rory whispered aside to Thomas when he joined her. "They smell worse than their horses. Hope they aren't riding in our car."

"Look like buffalo hunters," he said. "I've seen a lot of hunters on this line. The railroad hires them."

"Oh, you mean like Keene?"

Thomas shook his head. "Not really. Keene's function is to scout and hunt game for fresh meat. These men are hired just to shoot and kill the buffalo. They're slaughtering them by the thousands. The railroad wants the animals destroyed or completely driven away."

"But the buffalo are the Indians' major source of food," she argued.

"Yep. That's the idea. Get rid of the buffalo and you get rid of the Indians."

Much to Rory's relief, the buffalo hunters

moved to a different coach. But as they boarded, one of the hunters turned his head and imperviously spewed tobacco juice, narrowly missing Rory's shoe. He continued on without so much as a side glance, much less an apology.

The luxurious Pullman's Palace Sleeping Cars offered cushioned seats, ornate ceiling lights, pillows, bunks, tables, draped windows, and even men's and women's dressing rooms.

The sleeping car was divided into two sections, each containing three sets of double seats on both sides of the aisle. The sets of double seats faced each other, so that a party or family of four could remain together.

Since the train wasn't full, Rory and Thomas had the complete double seat to themselves. "Which seat do you want, east or west?" Thomas asked when they entered the car.

She smiled bewitchingly, her own good humor restored by the prospect of a comfortable ride. "I can't decide whether I want to see where I'm going, or where I've been. You sit where you prefer."

"I prefer to sit with you," he said with a rakish grin. "And since I like to see where I'm going, because I know where I've been, I'll take the seat facing west." He patted the seat beside him. "But I'll let you have the window."

"Why do I feel that remark has a slight innuendo," she laughed, and shifted over to sit down beside him.

Rory noticed that the woman she had observed in the diner was one of the occupants of their sleeper car. A short time later, when the woman got up and went into the dressing room, Rory nudged Thomas, who once again had buried his head behind a medical journal.

"There's something definitely strange about her," she whispered.

"Who?" Thomas asked, lowering the magazine.

"That woman," she whispered. "Just watch her when she comes back."

"Rory," Thomas said patiently, "the woman is not disturbing anyone. Why are you concerned about her?"

"Maybe she has something to do with those train robbers I saw at the station."

"Train robbers!" he said, surprised and somewhat amused.

"Well, they looked like train robbers anyway," she relented. "But maybe she's working in cahoots with them, and we're all about to be held up."

"Did they board the train?"

"I don't know, I was too busy watching the buffalo hunters."

"Well, if your train robbers are going to try to take on those buffalo hunters, they've got to be the biggest fools in the world," he commented lightly, dismissing the whole issue.

A short time later she poked his arm. "I figured out what's different about her. It's her *walk*," she said emphatically.

Thomas lowered his magazine. "You'd walk differently too if you'd lived in a Turkish harem." She looked at him, annoyed by his nonchalance. "Honey, all women do not walk alike. Trust me."

188

"Well, you're supposed to be a doctor. Can't you tell the difference?" she demanded.

"The difference in how women walk?" he asked, amused. "Certainly. Some take small steps, some large strides, some wiggle their hips, some swing their arms—"

"I'm talking about the difference between a man and a woman," she hissed impatiently.

"I've never had a problem telling one from the other," he contended. "*You*, my dear, are definitely a woman."

"Well, I'm telling you, that woman walks like a man, and she's probably just as strong too. I wouldn't be surprised if we all get our throats cut tonight while we're sleeping."

Thomas drew a deep, suffering breath. "Rory, if this is the—uncomfortable time of the month for you, I can give you a pill that will ease your tension and irritability."

"You are mistaken, Doctor Graham. And furthermore, that is a very indelicate subject to broach with a maiden," she replied.

"A maiden, through no fault of mine," he added.

Seeing that he continued to take her suspicions lightly, she crossed her arms and leaned back. "Well, just don't say I didn't warn you, Thomas Graham."

"I won't be able to if my throat is cut, now will I?" He picked up his journal and returned to reading.

A young lawyer, Dave Seller, and his wife, Barbara, who were sitting in the section across the aisle from them, suggested a game of whist.

As soon as the porter put up the table, Rory and Thomas shifted over, pairing off against the couple. The next two hours passed swiftly as the foursome laughed together, enjoying one another's company.

Suddenly, a rumble of excitement passed through the car. The passengers had clustered at the windows, apparently fascinated by activity outside. The nearby hillside had indeed become a spectacle to witness, as before their eyes stretched a solid sea of buffalo. Realizing that the roaming herd would be a new experience for most of the passengers, the train conductor brought the train to a slow stop, enabling everyone to take a longer look.

"My God, there must be thousands of them," the young lawyer remarked. "What a sight."

Then the unexpected blast of rifle fire startled everyone, and Barbara screamed as the buffalo began dropping to the ground.

Thomas guessed the reason at once. He rushed to the door and found the three buffalo hunters blasting away at the herd from the observation platform of the attached coach.

"You're going to spook that herd," Thomas shouted to the three men. But engrossed in their "sport," the hunters ignored him. In spite of repeated attempts, Thomas's warnings fell on deaf ears, and with the next series of shots, his fears turned into reality; the buffalo started down the hill and within seconds were stampeding toward the train with earth-shaking ferocity.

Seeing the danger too late, the train engineer

frantically pushed the throttle of the engine, but the train gathered speed more slowly than the horrendous black wave swept toward it.

The ground shook with the ponderous vibration of an earthquake; only then did the passengers recognize the impending catastrophe. People began to scramble and scream, but could find no way to escape the tidal wave of shaggy beasts sweeping down on them. One hope remained—if only the train could gather enough speed to outdistance the buffalo before they reached the track.

Thomas raced back to Rory, shoved her face down in the seat, and threw his body over her. "Keep your head buried in those pillows," he ordered.

The train crawled along as the buffalo rumbled toward it in a cloud of swirling dust. The deafening sound exploded amidst the screams and chaos.

While the engine, tender, and most of the coaches slipped by the thundering rampage, the horde slammed into the caboose at the rear. The violent collision upended the car, which then derailed the baggage car and one of the coaches. The coach tipped and slammed to the ground. A score of buffalo fell and were immediately trampled under other pounding hooves before the massive herd swung around the obstruction and thundered past.

The train was enveloped in a swirling dust cloud. "Are you okay, Rory?" Thomas asked, lifting her to a sitting position. She nodded, too scared to speak.

"I've got to leave you, honey. I'm sure I'm needed outside," he said. Grabbing his medical bag from below the seat, Thomas climbed off the train and joined the engineer, brakemen, and porters racing down the track toward the wreckage. And Rory was right behind him.

Screams and crying could be heard from within the overturned coach. Unmindful of the broken glass, people scrambled to climb through the windows to get out of the car.

Miraculously, the baggage car was still upright, the back end of the car resting in the base of the incline that ran parallel to the track.

Dazed and shaken, the passengers plopped down on the hillside. Many were bloodied and disoriented. Reunited families hugged and grabbed one another, crying in relief at the sight of their unharmed loved ones.

The whinny of frightened horses joined the shouts and cries as the horses of the buffalo hunters were led off the baggage car.

In an extraordinary bit of good fortune, only two of the passengers in the damaged coach sustained serious injuries, one a broken arm and the other a mild concussion. Many others suffered cuts and abrasions from the broken glass they encountered climbing out of the windows. Through all Thomas's ministrations, Rory stayed at his side, moving among the wounded and lending an assisting hand wherever possible.

It took another hour to retrieve the mail bags and load all the passengers and their luggage into the remaining coaches. To the dismay of no one, the buffalo hunters got their gear and mounted their horses to follow the herd. "Good riddance," Rory remarked as the three instigators of the stampede rode off.

Thomas had the two injured men brought into their car, where he could keep an eye on his patients. The passengers had to double up in the other cars but did not mind the inconvenience, since all were relieved that no one had been killed in the disaster.

Later, however, Rory wasn't too joyous when she was told she would have to double up in the berth to sleep with the mysterious woman passenger so that the injured men could have her bunk.

She let Thomas know what she thought of the arrangement as the two stood alone on the observation platform before retiring.

"Rory, it's only for tonight. I'd gladly give the man my bunk, but it wouldn't solve the problem," he said. "You two are the only women.

"Of course, you and I could always double up," he teased.

"Well, I would prefer that arrangement to the one I'm stuck with."

He drew her into his arms, and she found his long, drugging kiss the perfect remedy to calm her fears after the near tragedy. And as the kiss deepened, the combination of his body and lips overpowered her, sensation spilling from the core of her womanhood—sweet sensation, too exquisite to deny.

Sighing his name, she molded herself to him and nuzzled her cheek against the wall of his chest.

"I don't think I could resist the temptation of your lying next to me, Rory," he whispered.

He gazed into her trusting green eyes and knew he was right. If Rory climbed in with him—bed or berth—given the chance, he would try to make love to her. The situation had gotten out of hand between them. Their relationship had gone beyond the point where either of them was content with just kisses.

Moonlight cast an auburn glow onto her red hair. As he looked into her eyes, he struggled with a much greater, deeper realization. There was no use trying to kid himself—he was in love with Rory Callahan. The magnetic redhead had him totally captivated. And when he made love to her, and Thomas knew it would only be a matter of time before he did just that, it would not be in the berth of a railroad car filled with passengers.

He reached for her slowly and with leisurely deliberation drew her into his arms, pulling her with him as he leaned back against the wall of the train. Once again his mouth closed over hers, his tongue invading the honeyed chamber in sensuous sweeps. When his hand swept the curve of her spine, she trembled at his electrifying touch.

Thomas Graham was the only man who had ever aroused this passion in her. Groaning, Rory gripped his shoulders, her fingertips tingling at the feel of the corded strength concealed beneath the fabric of the coat.

"Oh, Lord, Rory," he groaned, his breath fluffing the hair at her ear, "I want you so much, I ache," he murmured. His hands slid up and cupped the fullness of her breasts.

He placed a quick kiss of desperation on her forehead, then firmly moved her away. "Get thee to bed, Satan."

Chapter Eleven

One dim light glowed above the door when they entered the car. All of the other passengers had already retired. With sagging spirits, Rory changed into her night clothes in the women's dressing room and then approached the berth. She was not looking forward to this night, for she still had her doubts about the strange woman.

During the events that followed the wreck, she had seen no sign among the passengers of either of the dubious-looking men she had noticed in Omaha. But as far as she was concerned, that did not take any suspicion off her sleeping companion. Not once throughout the emergency had she seen the woman giving assistance to the injured. That alone gave rise to uneasiness.

The porter brought her the stairs, and Rory climbed up into the upper berth. The woman lay on her side with her face to the wall. If she was awake, she made no effort to acknowledge Rory's presence. Rory removed her robe and lay back.

So maybe the woman wasn't a train robber, she conceded as she lay trying not to move a muscle. Maybe the woman had been ill. Maybe she was ill with some contagious disease—like the Black Plague! *And here I am, lying right next to her in this small berth, probably catching whatever she's suffering from*, Rory thought, horrified.

She shifted even closer to the edge of the berth. Instead of counting sheep, she began counting what possible maladies the woman might have. Somewhere between numbers twenty-one and twenty-five, Rory fell asleep.

She had no idea how long she had slept when her sleeping companion woke her by turning over in the berth. The woman now lay on her back, and her steady breathing indicated that she was sound asleep.

Rory's curiosity about the woman ran rampant. It was too dark in the berth to make out her features, but by opening the drapes slightly, Rory figured she could get a good look at the woman. She parted the drapes.

The interior of the chamber lay in shadows. In the eerie glow cast by the dim light above the door, currents of air swayed the dark drapes lining the aisle. The muffled snores emanating from behind the draped berths sounded like deep moans. The mysterious darkness unnerved Rory, who had never feared darkness before.

She turned and looked at her companion. Her eyes widened in horror, and she clamped her hand over her mouth to keep from screaming.

Without making any attempt to climb down, Rory leaped from the high berth. She raced through the aisle to Thomas's berth and scaled it easily without benefit of stairs.

"Thomas. Thomas," she whispered, shaking him lightly.

Startled, Thomas opened his eyes and bolted up, slamming his head on the ceiling of the berth. "What is it, Rory? What's wrong?" Despite his surprise, he remembered to whisper.

"Thomas, that—that person in my berth is a—is a *man!*" she stammered. "I told you, I told you there was something suspicious about that woman. She's a man—I mean, he's not a woman."

Relaxing, Thomas lay back. He remained relaxed for all of ten seconds before becoming aware that Rory had stretched out on top of him with her body pressed against him and her arms firmly locked around his neck.

His hands swept her spine and came to rest on her derrière. He liked the feel of it, and his palms cupped the warm cheeks.

"What makes you think the woman is a man?" he asked.

"He's got whiskers." She ran her hands over his bristled cheeks. "Just like you have now. He needs a shave."

"Did you feel them to make sure they're whiskers?"

"No, of course not. I got out of there as soon

as I discovered she was a man."

"Well, maybe she's the bearded lady in a circus," he said, trying to humor her. His hands began moving again, unintentionally inching up her gown.

"Thomas, I am trying to tell you that *she* is a *he*," Rory hissed.

He gave no credibility to her story. One of the qualities he found most refreshing about Rory was her lack of coyness. "Look, honey, I'm flattered, but this is not the time or the place."

Rory might have become angry at his skepticism, or even insulted by his vanity, if he hadn't already raised her gown practically up to her waist and curved his warm palms around the bare cheeks of her rear end.

"I'm not lying to you, Thomas." She tried to assure him, but her throaty denial became even deeper when he turned her over on her back and raised himself onto one arm. He shoved the bunched-up gown higher, and his hand closed around her breast.

"Thomas, what are you doing?" she sighed as his thumb rasped her nipples to hardened peaks.

"What does it feel like?" he whispered, lowering his head. His tongue took up the play before he closed his moist mouth around one of the hardened nubs.

"Feels wonderful," she sighed.

"Does to me too," he agreed.

He pulled the gown over her head and she closed her eyes, reveling in the feel of lying naked in his arms. Thomas sat up and shoved aside the blanket and sheet, then shifted her weight beneath him.

He began to struggle in the cramped berth to get his long legs out of his underwear. "Damn it, I told you this wasn't a good idea," he hissed sharply. "I can't get the damn things off."

She started to giggle and he clamped his mouth over hers, stifling the sound. Within seconds, her arms slid around his neck. "What can I do to help?" she asked softly.

"Stay the hell out of my bed," he grumbled into her mouth. He sat up, retrieved her gown, and pulled it back on over her head.

"Rory," he said softly. Her green eyes were barely discernable in the darkness. "This just isn't working out. We have to stop this."

"I don't understand. What do you mean?"

"I mean we're going to have to do this right. Get off this damn train, get married, and get a room."

The unexpected proposal took her by surprise. "What did you say?"

His teeth flashed in a grin. "Translated that means, I love you, Rory. Will you marry me?"

He had said the words she had hoped for, prayed for; but now she suffered with doubt. She didn't doubt her feeling; she doubted his. "Did this proposal come about because you were unable to get your underwear off?" she asked lightly.

"Rory, there's been a physical attraction between us from the time we first met." He gathered her into his arms and kissed her lightly. "But we've played this game to its limit. I want more than some stolen moments in the back of a carriage or the berth of a train. More than just going to bed with you. I want to wake up in the morning and find you next to me every day."

His hand cupped her cheek. "I wish I could see you now . . . those green eyes of yours looking at me trusting and straightforward."

He lowered his head and her eyelids drooped as he placed a kiss on each of them. "And I want you to have my baby, Rory. I want to walk through a door and see you holding our baby, nursing it at your breasts. I want us to grow old together, watching our children grow."

Even in the darkness she could feel the intensity of his brown-eyed gaze, "Will you, Rory? Will you marry me?"

"I think you ought to marry him, Rory," Dave Seller's voice declared from the bunk across the aisle.

"Yeah, Rory. Tell him you'll marry him so we all can get some sleep," Barbara Seller added. The muffled laughter of the couple carried across the aisle.

"Oh no," Rory groaned. "Do you suppose they've been listening all the time?"

Thomas chuckled warmly. "Them and probably the rest of the car. Now I'll have to make an honest woman out of you. What about it, sweetheart? Will you marry me?"

She slipped her arms around his neck. "What do you think? I've thought of nothing else but marrying you from the moment I first laid eyes on you, Thomas Jefferson Graham."

After a long, and near-disastrous kiss, they

agreed to wed the next morning when they reached Cheyenne. Then, clasped together in each other's arms, the two lovers dropped into slumber.

The next morning, Rory towed Thomas by the hand down the aisle to the last berth. She would prove to him once and for all the truth of her story.

"See for yourself," she declared dramatically, parting the drapes.

The berth was empty.

She put her hands on her hips in contemplation. "I bet he's getting dressed. Look in the men's dressing room," she said.

"Who am I suppose to look for, honey?" Thomas said patiently. "I wouldn't know him if I saw her," he said, purposely confusing his gender.

"Don't try to be funny, Thomas. He wouldn't dare go to the women's dressing room again. I'll go look just to be sure. But you come with me."

Rory was dumbfounded when neither dressing room produced any sign of the mysterious passenger. "He's hiding somewhere on this train. We might still get our throats cut," she declared.

"Sam, did any passengers get off the train during the night?" Rory asked the passing porter.

"No, Miz Callahan," he said with a wide grin. "Cheyenne in ten minutes. Best be hurryin', ma'am." Rory had to put aside her investigation and scramble to get dressed.

The Rollins House appeared to be the only

hotel in town. One look at the ramshackle building was enough to convince Thomas and Rory they would wait to be married in Laramie later that day.

They ate a hasty breakfast and then the shout of "All aboard!" sounded again from the conductor.

Rory climbed back on the train while Thomas said good-bye to his two patients and the other displaced passengers from the wrecked coach.

Rory's glance immediately sought out the mysterious passenger, but the corner seat was now occupied by a woman and two young children.

Once the train resumed its passage, Rory tried to turn her attention toward the unusual rock formations as they continued their climb through the Rockies. However, the euphoric awareness that this would be her wedding day and that tonight she would be in Thomas's arms were foremost in her thoughts.

Some reservations danced through her mind: not having her father there to give her away, her friends and the ranch hands present to witness the event . . . and Keene. But postponing the wedding to satisfy her longing for the presence of family and friends was never a serious consideration; she wanted to get married as quickly as Thomas did.

Shortly after midday, the train reached Stevens, Wyoming, cresting the highest point they would have to surmount before beginning the descent into the desert. The town teemed with Army personnel, and the train slowed to toss out a mail pouch.

As Rory glanced out the window, she couldn't help but feel sorry for the lonely men stationed in the middle of nowhere. Yet the presence of the military was absolutely necessary because of the unrest the railroad had stirred up among the Indians. She smiled and waved to the many soldiers as they passed.

When they resumed speed, her heartbeat quickened in her breast. The next stop would be Laramie. Experiencing the same surge of excitement, Thomas picked up Rory's hand and squeezed it.

Kathleen Rafferty raised a hand to her brow to ward off the sun's glare, and her blue-eyed gaze watched Keene MacKenzie ride into town. Unintentionally, she had been watching for him for the past week since he rode away. Relieved to see him return, she felt the tension ease from her body. It was unusual for him to be gone for so long, and she had begun to fear the worst.

Her gaze remained fixed on the tall figure as she watched him slowly dismount and climb the tall stairway to the room he rented in town. Something seemed different about his step, and she began to fret again.

Since Tent Town had been destroyed, the men had moved into the sleeping car at the end of track. Their families remained in Ogden, where it was safer. Kathleen liked the arrangement since her husband was only in town from sundown on Saturday evening to sunrise on Monday morning. After claiming his conjugal rights upon arriving, he always headed for Jake O'Brien's, returning only to attend Sunday morning Mass with her. Then he would disappear again. Late Sunday night, he would stagger back to the tent in a drunken stupor, sleep it off, and be gone early the next morning.

Of course the new arrangement had its disadvantages too. Kathleen missed Michaleen Dennehy's daily visits. She had not realized how much she had looked forward to those moments with the little man.

Ya nay miss the sunshine 'til the rain starts fallin', Kathleen thought, recalling the wisdom of her mother's favorite axiom. Sighing, she turned away. "That rain has its advantages too, Momma. At least I won't have to see Michael Rafferty for six more days."

By sunset, Kathleen had not seen any further sign of Keene coming or going. His gelding stood patiently, still tied to the hitching post. She had observed Keene's habits often enough to know that he always unsaddled his horse if he didn't intend to ride it.

To avoid being seen, she waited until dark. Then, venturing forth, Kathleen climbed the stairway leading to Keene's room and tapped on the door. When there was no reply, she decided she must have missed him. Kathleen started to turn away, but then her instinct caused her to turn back. She tried the handle and found the door unlocked.

Enough light filtered through the open door for her to see Keene lying on the bed. Instantly, she knew something must be wrong. Keene MacKenzie's senses were always so well-tuned that surely, awake or sleeping, no one could enter his room without his knowing it.

Quickly stepping inside, she closed the door, and for several seconds Kathleen did not move as she waited until her eyes adjusted to the darkness. Then she crossed to a bedside table. After much groping, she succeeded in finding matches to light the lamp.

Keene lay on his stomach.

His shirt appeared to be soaked. At first Kathleen thought the moisture water, but, struggling to turn him over, she realized that it was perspiration. He was burning with fever. Then a gasp slipped past her lips when she saw that the whole left front of his shirt was stained with blood.

"Mr. MacKenzie, can you hear me? 'Tis Kathleen Rafferty."

Keene opened his eyes and, reaching out, he grabbed her arm. His eyes were glazed with fever, and the heat from his hand burned through the fabric of her sleeve.

"I'll be gettin' you a doctor, Mr. MacKenzie," she said worriedly.

Despite his weakened condition, his hold grasped her like a vise. "Is Doc Graham back yet?" he murmured faintly.

"No. But there's a Doctor Jensen at the other end of town."

"No. No doctor," he said.

"But 'tis feverish, you are, Mr. MacKenzie. And you've lost a lot of blood."

"No doctor," he repeated. "I'll be okay." He tried to sit up, but fell back.

Kathleen quickly moved over to the ewer. The pitcher of water had to be a week old, but she partially filled a glass just to get some liquid down him. Hurrying back, she held up his head and Keene greedily gulped down the water. "Not too much right now," she cautioned. "I'll be gettin' some fresh water for you."

Setting aside the glass, Kathleen put her hand on his brow. He felt so hot, she hated to think of how high his temperature must be.

Keene closed his eyes. "Your hand sure feels good, ma'am."

"If you be so against me gettin' a doctor, will you at least be lettin' me look at your wound, sir?" He gave her a slight nod. "Then I'll be needin' a scissors to cut away that shirt."

"Scissors? Never had no call for 'em. My . . . knife," he began, but slipped into unconsciousness before he could finish.

Her hands trembled as she unsheathed the knife at his waist and sliced open the seams of the shirt. The bloodstains and the jagged rip at the shoulder made it useless to attempt salvaging the garment.

To stem the flow of blood, Keene had packed the wound with a red bandanna. Kathleen gingerly peeled away the padded, sodden cloth.

The flesh was red and inflamed around what appeared to be a knife wound. Some of his flesh was caked with blackened splotches of dried blood; apparently the jagged cut had bled, stopped, and then bled again.

Kathleen rooted through his chest of drawers for anything she could possibly put to use. Her effort produced a half-empty bottle of whiskey, but more beneficial, a bottle of carbolic acid and bandages that Thomas had given Keene for an earlier wound.

After cleansing and bandaging the wound, she covered him with a sheet, grabbed the ewer, and left to get fresh water.

Once outside, the sight of Keene's gelding reminded Kathleen that the horse had not been fed or given water all day. She led the animal away and turned it over to the stable boy. Familiar with the gelding, he promised to see to the horse's needs.

Kathleen then returned to her tent, filled the ewer with fresh water, and hurried back to Keene's room. He appeared not to have moved since she left.

She poured a portion of the cool water into a basin and tenderly began to bathe the usually bronze face, now ashen and wan. Gaunt from fever and pain, his beloved features were further shadowed by unshaven whiskers.

When she finished sponging his face and neck, she put a damp cloth across his fevered brow.

Kathleen then removed his boots and socks, but the most difficult task still lay ahead. She knew she must get him out of his trousers, but the act seemed improper to the moral young woman whose only sin was harboring a secret and forbidden love for him. Praying for the Lord's forgiveness, she released his belt and pulled the Levis off each long leg.

Next she sponged his chest and discovered Keene's ranginess was deceiving; he had a lithe and muscular body without an ounce of useless fat. Dark hair trailed into his underwear.

His chest bore the scars of many past wounds. The vivid scar on his arm from the Indian attack on Tent Town still looked puckered.

When she finished bathing him, his long, muscular body remained motionless. Kathleen covered him with a quilt, for the room had cooled down considerably.

Keene became restless during the night and tossed in delirium. Fearing his thrashing would dislodge the bandage or start the wound bleeding again, Kathleen dared not leave him. With no chair in the room, she sat stiffly at the foot of the bed. Maintaining her vigil throughout the night, she changed the cloth on his brow many times and constantly moistened his fevered lips.

At dawn, when it appeared that he had relaxed into a placid slumber, Kathleen felt it was safe to leave. Pausing at the bedside, she gazed tenderly for a few minutes at his sleeping face. Her hand caressed his cheek, and she brushed back the tousled hair from his forehead.

Bowing to a forbidden temptation, she leaned down and pressed a tender kiss to his lips. Then she slipped out the door and returned to her tent.

Having been heaved and tossed by torturing billows, Keene now floated on a sea of tranquility. He felt a soothing touch on his brow and then the soft pressure of lips. Kathleen?

Listlessly, he opened his eyes but saw no sign of her. He was alone. Through the sluggish haze of fever, he reasoned that his wretched nightmares had been transformed into sweet dreams. He closed his eyes and drifted back into the torpid obscurity of slumber.

As she waited for a kettle of water to boil, Kathleen stirred the bubbling pot of stew. Keene had slipped in and out of sleep throughout the day, and although still feverish, he was fully coherent when he awoke. However, his wound had begun to show signs of festering, so she decided to put a hot poultice on it. When the water came to a rolling boil, she grasped the handle of the kettle with a towel and carried the pot up the stairway to his room.

Keene became upset the moment she entered carrying the heavy kettle. "Mrs. Rafferty, you're not strong enough to be toting that kettle upstairs. And you could burn yourself besides."

Puffing from the climb, she put down the heavy vessel. With arms akimbo, she declared firmly, "I have much need for hot water, Mr. MacKenzie, and the totin' of it is the only means for the gettin' of it."

He grinned at the feisty response, so out of character for the docile woman. Kathleen was just as surprised at herself. She knew that such a rebuttal to her husband would have drawn a backhanded blow.

An embarrassed blush brought color to her cheeks. She hastily poured some hot water into a basin and sat down on the bed.

"How did you get this gash?" she asked as she applied hot cloths to the festering wound.

"Got careless and let a Ute buck get his knife into me."

She knew Keene had said all he intended to about the incident that had almost cost him his life. When the water began to cool, Kathleen cleansed the wound again with carbolic acid and covered it with a fresh bandage.

Keene lay and watched the movements of her slight body as she bustled about his room. The sight brought him pleasure. Soon he closed his eyes and drifted back into sleep.

Kathleen sensed the moment he dozed off. She turned her head and smiled at the sleeping figure.

Later that day, she brought him a plate of stew and slices of freshly baked bread. He declined to eat the food, asking only for a cup of coffee.

"If you're to be regainin' yar strength, Mr. MacKenzie, I'd be sayin' 'tis important to be eatin'," she chided, one hand on her hip, the other shaking a spoon at him.

The sight was too appealing for even the reticent scout to ignore. "Well then, Mrs. Rafferty, I'd be sayin', you should be practicin' what you're preachin'," he replied, mocking her Irish lilt. Then his steady gaze locked with hers. "So I'll make a bargain with you. I'll eat, if you eat."

Her blue eyes lit with Irish laughter. "I'm thinkin' thar be a bit of the devil in ya, Keene MacKenzie."

"And I'm thinkin' you may be right, Kathleen Rafferty."

She sat down on the bed and fed him a spoonful of the stew. His gray eyes never wavered as he waited. Hesitantly, she scooped up a spoonful and put it in her mouth. Then she offered him a bite of bread, and he waited for her to take one as well. Grinning at each other, the two continued the exercise until the stew and bread were gone. Then he lay back and closed his eyes.

In the days that followed, Keene and Kathleen took their meals together. And in the shared moments of this intimate compromise, Keene MacKenzie succeeded in doing what Thomas Graham and Michaleen Dennehy had tried so hard to accomplish—Kathleen Rafferty began to eat three solid meals a day.

The following Saturday, Kathleen was just in the process of removing Keene's laundry from the clothesline when Mike Rafferty arrived back.

"You're home early, Mike," she exclaimed, dismayed by his unexpected appearance.

"We ran out of rails," he grumbled. Mike frowned and grabbed her arm as she started to shove Keene's trousers into the clothes basket. "Hold up, woman." He snatched the Levis out of her hands. "These ain't my pants."

Flustered, she started to stammer. "I . . . ah, took in some laundry."

Rafferty's black glare fell on her. "Took in laundry. Whose laundry? Whata ya talkin' about, woman?"

"Mr. MacKenzie's," she said softly. "He's wounded and is payin' me to tend to him." The last was a blatant lie, but Kathleen knew

Mike Rafferty could not be considered a charitable man.

His grasp tightened on her arm, and he twisted it behind her. "Payin' ya. What else is he payin' ya for, whore?"

"Mike, please, you're hurtin' me. And you've no cause to call me that."

His backhand caught her across the cheek, knocking her off her feet. "Don't be lying to me, whore. I've seen the cow eyes ya give him." She tried to rise, but he drew back and smacked her in the face again.

"I'll take care of this myself," he snarled.

"Please, Mike, I'm beggin' you not to be makin' a scene," she pleaded, rising to her knees and clutching at his arm.

"Ya should have thought of that sooner, ya whorin' bitch." Kathleen raised her hands to try to ward off his next blow.

Rafferty grabbed a fistful of her hair and half dragged her into the tent. "There's just one way to treat a whorin' bitch like you," he cursed violently, jerking her against the hard wall of his chest. His mouth ground on hers in a punishing kiss.

She struggled to free herself, and he slapped her again. Rafferty felt himself grow hard. With a grunt of satisfaction, he picked her up as if she were weightless and threw her on the cot. Kathleen began to sob, and he backhanded her across her face.

"Shut up that whimperin', you whorin' bitch," he growled, ripping at her clothing. "Ya gettin' what ya deserve."

When he finished with her, he pulled up his trousers and, without a backward glance, left the tent to pursue further pleasures.

Sobbing, Kathleen curled up in a despondent heap and lay drowning in a sea of pain and mortification.

Chapter Twelve

Thomas and Rory were married in a small church in Laramie with David and Barbara Seller as witnesses. Rory's eyes misted when Thomas slipped his mother's gold wedding band, which he had worn as a watch fob, on her finger. The four people then hurried back to the depot in time for the Sellers to board the train.

As the newlyweds waved good-bye to the friendly couple, Rory felt a sadness in knowing she would probably never again see these two people who had shared the most important day of her life.

"Do you want to send your father a wire?" Thomas asked as they entered the telegraph office.

"No, we'll be back in Ogden tomorrow. I'd rather tell him the news to his face."

"I'm sure he'll be delighted when he learns

you've married me," Thomas said with a skeptical glance at his appealing wife. "He'll probably come after me with a shotgun."

After writing out a wire to send to the Stewarts, the closest people he had to a family, Thomas glanced askance at Rory. "You understand, Mrs. Graham, Ruark and Angel will never forgive us for not getting married in St. Louis while we were there. Expect to hear about it the next time we see them."

Rory giggled. "Do you think they'll be surprised when they get the wire?"

"I doubt it. Ruark already figured out I intended to marry you. I don't know how he did it."

She slipped her hand into his. "I think it's wonderful that you have friends like Ruark and Angel." She sighed with pleasure.

"They're your friends now too, honey. Don't ever forget it. And if ever you have a problem and I'm not there for you, go to them."

Her eyes glistened. "This is our honeymoon, Thomas. Please don't sound so gloomy. You're frightening me."

He squeezed her hand and tucked her arm under his. "You're right, sweetheart. Nothing is going to happen to either of us. This is just the beginning for you and me. We've got our whole lives ahead of us." He glanced down at her. "But right now, we've only got about twelve hours before the train arrives. Let's get to that hotel."

They ate their wedding breakfast in the hotel's dining room, ordering the salty, tough steak and fried potatoes that had become the main staple along the train route. Seeing Rory struggle with the unappetizing food on her plate, Thomas reached over and clasped her hand.

"As soon as I complete my contract with the railroad, we'll go on a honeymoon to England and France, sweetheart. We'll dine in the best restaurants, and you'll be able to savor some of the finest cuisine in the world."

Her eyes gleamed with pleasure. "A honeymoon in London and Paris. Oh, that sounds wonderful, Thomas. Have you been to Europe before?"

Thomas nodded. "Ruark and I made the Grand Tour when we finished college. Of course, that was in our carefree bachelor days," he added playfully.

She shook her head. "I can just see the trail of broken hearts strewn across Europe."

"And most of the British Empire. But those days are gone forever," he added with a teasing grin. "Ruark and I are old married men now."

She stared at him for a long moment. "Are you . . . sorry, Thomas?"

"Sorry? About what, honey?" he asked, mouthing a bite of steak.

"Our getting married."

Surprised, he glanced up. "What makes you think that?"

Her eyes remained fixed on her plate. "I think I pursued you shamelessly and . . . maybe I rushed you into getting married."

"Rory, look at me." She raised her eyes to meet the warmth of his dark brown eyes. "Honey, I know that I appear to you to be easygoing to a fault. But I assure you, I have a mind of my own. You'll notice I never *rushed* into marriage before. I had to make certain I was in love." He eyed her intently and gave her hand a squeeze. "You having second thoughts or just bridal jitters, honey?"

Her face shifted into a loving smile, and she curled her fingers around his. "No second thoughts, Thomas. I love you."

"Well, you know it's still not too late. If you'd rather have the fancy gown, veil, and all the trimmings, I'll understand, honey. We can hold out a while longer."

She rolled her expressive eyes. "Maybe *you* can."

"Well then, it's a done deed. So what are we doing down here, Mrs. Graham, when there's a bed waiting upstairs? No mountain passage overrun with Indians, no small train berth with prying ears. A big, soft, *private* bed of our own is just waiting for us." Casting aside their napkins, they raced up the stairs laughing.

Thomas grabbed her at the top of the stairway, swooped her up in his arms, and carried her up the next flight to their room. When the bridal couple burst through the door, a shocked chambermaid turned around at the sound of Rory's squeals.

Thomas lowered Rory's feet to the floor. "Oh, excuse us. We thought the room was empty."

"I'll soon be done here, sir," the woman said with an understanding smile. She had worked in hotels too long not to recognize newlyweds when she saw them.

Thomas winked at Rory. "Want to go back and finish that steak you were enjoying so much?"

"No, I think I'll go to the dressing room." She snatched up her valise and scurried down the hall with a quick, but saucy, backward glance at her husband. Feeling awkward, Thomas hastened from the room to the bathroom on the floor below.

Once behind the privacy of the locked door, Rory's hand trembled as she pinned up her hair and shed her clothes. Thomas was right; she did have bridal jitters. In an effort to calm herself, she took advantage of the indoor plumbing and drew a hot bath, adding a generous measure of lavender bath salts.

The water did have a soothing effect, and she lolled back in comfort. Another quarter of an hour passed before Rory realized that she probably appeared to be dawdling. Hastily finishing her bath, she pulled on her robe.

When she returned to the room, Thomas stood at the window staring at the street below. He had partially closed the draperies to ward off the bright morning sunlight and turned when she entered. "This is a busy town," he commented. "Couple of medicine show wagons just arrived."

Drops of moisture glistened on his hair from his recent bath, and she thought he looked exceedingly handsome in a navy blue robe that enhanced his dark good looks.

Her heart began to pound when he walked to

219

the door and slid the bolt, locking the two of them together in the semi-dark room. Then he took her in his arms.

"This is it, Rory. Nothing's going to stop us this time. I don't care if the damn hotel burns down around us."

She had waited for this moment as long as he. Every nerve end throbbed with a mounting need for this man who was holding her, yet she found herself trembling now that the moment had finally arrived.

He sensed her tension and understood the reason for it. Despite Rory's outrageous boldness, which he found to be as refreshing as it was arousing, she still was a maiden experiencing the pangs of trepidation on her wedding night.

He began to remove pins from her hair. The thick mass dropped to her shoulders like an auburn curtain. He lightly combed his fingers through the thick strands.

"You smell so good, sweetheart," he murmured, his breath warm and tantalizing at her ear. "Don't be nervous, love. Just think of how much we both want this moment."

Rory slid her arms around his neck as he pressed her closer. Delicious sensations flooded through her when his mouth closed over hers. The nervousness that had gripped her only seconds before was replaced with the different tension that his kisses and touch always evoked. When breathlessness forced them to part, she sighed and buried her head against the solid wall of his chest.

His warm palms caressed the nape of her

neck as he reclaimed her lips with a light kiss. Then, cupping her cheeks in his hand, he tilted her head to meet his tender gaze. The heated intensity of his look inflamed her.

"I've thought of nothing but this moment for so long," he murmured, lazily sliding his lips to her ear. He trailed them to the hollow of her throat.

His husky whisper sounded like an erotic caress, and she shifted her head to give him freer access to her neck. "I have too, Thomas," she sighed. She trembled when he slipped the robe off her shoulders.

The absence of his touch caused her to open her eyes. She blushed when she discovered that he had removed his own robe. With outstretched arms, he grasped her hands and stepped back.

"Look at me, Rory. Know my body. Because I already know yours. And from this moment, my nakedness must never make you uncomfortable."

She had never seen a man fully naked before. He appeared to be all muscle and hair, molded and sculpted in a powerful, magnificently proportioned symmetry. She marveled at the splendor of him. And the sight of the engorged muscle extending from the core of that sinewy might appeared equally wondrous to her.

"You're beautiful, Thomas," she said, simply.

"Men aren't beautiful, honey," he chuckled. "But a woman's body like yours . . . is very beautiful." His soft Southern drawl stroked her like a caress.

"Why, Thomas? If a woman's body is beautiful . . . or a picture or a song . . . or even a poem, then why can't a man's body be just as beautiful?" she said solemnly.

Uninhibitedly, she stepped nearer to him. "I think your body is beautiful." Her hands caressed the wide shoulders down to his chest, her fingertips tingling as they lightly grazed the sinewy firmness.

With a growing sense of urgency, he reached out and cupped her face, covering her lips with his. She could feel the power in his arms when he lifted her and carried her to the bed. Their kiss remained unbroken as he laid her gently on its downy softness.

She slowly raised her eyelids and found a pair of brown velvet eyes gazing down adoringly. Savoring the sight of them and the love she saw in their depths, she reached out and stroked his cheek. He slipped his arms under her and pulled her tighter against him.

His lips lowered to hers and seemed to devour her, their pressure increasing as his passion mounted. The same excitement spread through her, and she felt a knot in her fluttering stomach.

"Oh, God, Rory, I love you," he whispered between kisses.

His mouth moved to claim a breast and close around the quivering globe. The fluttering in her stomach spread to her loins. The pressure of his mouth increased as he felt her rising eagerness. Responding to her smothered groan, he returned to reclaim her quivering lips.

She reveled in the feel of his sensuous exploration of her nakedness. "Thomas," she sighed. "Don't stop. Don't ever stop," she pleaded.

His mouth and hands continued to explore and probe her quivering flesh, and the blood pulsing through her veins felt like liquid fire that would surely consume her. But the thought of his ceasing this ravishment became an even greater threat to heightened senses driven beyond the point of no return.

Shivering with ecstasy, she felt his firm hand close around her hips and draw her tighter between his thighs. Her need had become as great as his, and her legs shifted restlessly. Slipping her arms around his neck, she clung to him and parted her thighs to accommodate him.

His own fevered desire now raged through his body, but he forced himself not to rush this moment. He knew there would be pain for her. Tormented by the thought of hurting her, he tried to make this first time as painless as he could. He stroked her moist sex until her body writhed beneath him, contracted, and then erupted in spasmodic shudders. Only then did he slip into the heated sheath.

His first attempt to enter her brought a muffled cry of pain, and she started to panic. "Don't struggle, honey. This will only hurt for a moment."

She tried to relax, but her body remained taut with tension. "Honey, you're moist and ready for me. Just trust me," he assured her. Kissing her, he slid his hands down to her hips and cupped her buttocks. Then he penetrated her, piercing

223

her maiden shield. She gasped with pain, but did not cry out.

For several seconds he did not move, but felt the heated blood pulsating in his throbbing organ. He lifted his head.

The green eyes that once gazed so trustingly into his were now shrouded with suspicion. "The worst is over, sweetheart," he assured her.

Under the passionate remorse she read in his dark eyes, her expression softened with renewed trust. For a few seconds, their gazes locked, and her emerald eyes glittered with sensuous allure.

Once again his mouth covered hers. "Now the pleasure begins," he said in a husky whisper and began to move inside of her.

He kissed her hard and passionately as his own excitement neared a fever pitch. Their tongues coupled in a heated duet, her passion quickly building to match the intensity of his. Their bodies melded together—bodies and needs becoming one driving urgency for both of them. The perfect rhythm of their dance built to a mind-shattering crescendo when the hot evidence of his love flowed into her.

Many minutes passed before he raised his head to gaze down at her. He brushed back the hair clinging to her cheeks, then, unable to resist the temptation, he dipped his head and pressed a light kiss on the end of her nose. Her emerald eyes met his loving glance with open frankness, tugging a smile from the corners of his mouth. Raising a hand, he gently caressed her cheek and his smile broadened.

Her gaze shifted to his mouth and she traced

Thrill to the most sensual, adventure-filled Historical Romances on the market today...

FROM  LEISURE BOOKS

As a home subscriber to the Leisure Romance Book Club, you'll enjoy the best in today's BRAND-NEW Historical Romance fiction. For over twenty years, Leisure Books has brought you the award-winning, high-quality authors you know and love to read. Each Leisure Historical Romance will sweep you away to a world of high adventure...and intimate romance. Discover for yourself all the passion and excitement millions of readers thrill to each and every month.

Save $5.⁰⁰ Each Time You Buy!

Six times a year, the Leisure Romance Book Club brings you four brand-new titles from Leisure Books, America's foremost publisher of Historical Romances. EACH PACKAGE WILL SAVE YOU $5.00 FROM THE BOOKSTORE PRICE! And you'll never miss a new title with our convenient home delivery service.

Here's how we do it. Each package will carry a FREE 10-DAY EXAMINATION privilege. At the end of that time, if you decide to keep your books, simply pay the low invoice price of $14.96, no shipping or handling charges added. HOME DELIVERY IS ALWAYS FREE. With today's top Historical Romance novels selling for $4.99 and higher, our price SAVES YOU $5.00 with each shipment.

AND YOUR FIRST FOUR-BOOK SHIPMENT IS TOTALLY FREE!
IT'S A BARGAIN YOU CAN'T BEAT! A Super $19.96 Value!
LEISURE BOOKS *A Division of Dorchester Publishing Co., Inc.*

GET YOUR 4 FREE BOOKS NOW—A $19.96 Value!

*Mail the Free Book
Certificate
Today!*

Get Four Books Totally FREE— A $19.96 Value!

▼ Tear Here and Mail Your FREE Book Card Today! ▼

PLEASE RUSH
MY FOUR FREE
BOOKS TO ME
RIGHT AWAY!

Leisure Romance Book Club
65 Commerce Road
Stamford CT 06902-4563

AFFIX
STAMP
HERE

a finger along his sensuous lower lip. "I love you, Thomas."

His handsome face slashed into an appealing grin. "You took the words right out of my mouth."

"You mean we're both in love with you, Thomas?" she said, her eyes dancing with devilment.

He groaned, then levered himself above her to do battle. He changed his mind as soon as he stared down at her. For several seconds he marveled at her exquisite loveliness; her face was tinged with a blush of passion, her eyes slumberous.

She ran her hands down the sides of his sloping shoulders to the powerful chest. "You know, Thomas Graham, without your medical bag and with your clothes off, you don't look too much like a doctor."

He lay back, pulling her into his arms. "And how many naked doctors have you known, Mrs. Graham?"

"Hmmm . . . Mrs. Graham. I kind of like the sound of that."

"You took the words right out of my mouth," he repeated in teasing warmth. "I like the sound of it too," he said, before she could offer another gibe.

She returned to stroking the firm wall of his chest. "Thomas, now that I'm your wife, will you please tell me how you developed your fabulous chest. I'm jealous. I'm sure it's larger than mine." Her finger began to trace the trail of hair down his chest, across his flat stomach.

"I did a lot of boxing in college," he rasped as her movements began to arouse him. "And my chest may be larger than yours, but it sure as hell isn't as appealing. But for the sake of science, I'll be glad to measure," he said, cupping her breast in his hand.

He let her continue her examination. After all, he had told her to become comfortable with his nakedness and Rory was doing just that. So comfortable, in fact, that after several moments of a most intense exploration, he growled huskily and rolled over, trapping her beneath him.

His mouth claimed hers, and within seconds the tempo of their movements increased.

Entwined, they fell asleep, waking a few hours later to make love again. It was sunset when they finally rose and dressed. In a couple of hours, their train was due and, as much as he would have liked to spend another day in Laramie, Thomas had an obligation to return to work.

"If there hadn't been that train wreck, we could have spent the night here," Rory moaned as she closed her valise.

"Honey, if it wasn't for the train wreck, we wouldn't be married. Remember?" he reminded her.

"Oh, yes. My sleeping companion." Her face twisted in reflection. "I wonder where that scoundrel disappeared to?" she said.

"So do I. Whoever he or she may be certainly deserved an invitation to the wedding."

They deposited their luggage, then ate an early supper before the dining room filled up with train passengers. With still more than an hour remaining, they wandered over to the medicine show.

Laramie boasted a fair-size population as well as a temporary army garrison. Hand in hand, Thomas and Rory strolled among the other participants taking in the sights.

A barker tried to lure them into a tent that promised the sights of a sword swallower, a bearded woman, and a snake woman, part-human, part-serpent.

"I'll pass, if you don't mind," Thomas remarked to her.

They moved on to another tent where several soldiers were testing their marksmanship at a shooting gallery. Thomas watched the good-humored joking and jostling among the men as they missed the target.

Luring the largest crowd was a trained bear that performed the amazing feat of taking food in its paws from anyone brave enough to venture forth to feed it—the food, of course, purchased from the animal's trainer. Despite prodding from Thomas, Rory refused to be enticed to the attraction.

Instead, she found herself drawn to the wagon of Professor Omnipotent, "The Renowned and Unrivaled Astrological Physician," she read aloud from the bold letters painted on the side of the wagon.

"I'm impressed," Thomas drawled.

"And," Rory declared, after reading more of

the message exhibited on the wagon, "Professor Omnipotent not only is thoroughly acquainted with the Egyptian, Arabian, and Persian astrological readings, but he even understands the astrological science of the Persian Magi." Her brows rose suggestively. "And the sublime mysteries and secrets of the Hindu philosophers," she added.

Clucking sympathetically, Thomas shook his head. "Terrible burden for one man to have to carry around."

"Why, you sound skeptical, Doctor Graham." She stuck out her hand. "Give me fifty cents. I intend to have the good professor prepare me a horoscope."

Thomas shoved a coin at her. "Well, I hope the professor is *omnipotent* enough to do so before the train arrives." He wandered back to watch the antics of the chained bear, while Rory disappeared into the astrologer's wagon.

The Union Pacific was just puffing into town when she rushed up to him a short while later and clutched his arm, her eyes wide with excitement. "Thomas, I saw him again."

"Saw who, honey?" he asked.

"That man who was impersonating a woman. I saw him in Professor Omnipotent's wagon."

"Having his fortune told?" he asked, amused. "Sure it wasn't the bearded woman instead?"

"No. It was him. Dressed up as Professor Omnipotent."

"You mean your would-be assailant has swapped robbing trains for hustling fifty-cent horoscopes?"

"Don't make jokes, Thomas. Maybe he murdered Professor Omnipotent or something gruesome like that. Just come with me, and I'll show you."

"Rory, we don't have time for that now. We have a train to catch. And right away, too." Taking her arm, he steered her to the depot.

"But it's him. I'd know him anywhere," she protested, glancing behind helplessly as he maintained a firm grasp on her arm.

The now familiar "all aboard" sounded above the snort of steam and rumble of rails. And a short while later, as the train chugged out of Laramie, Rory was still declaring she was right.

By the time they climbed into their berth later that evening, the train had descended into the desert. What appeared to be an unending stretch of alkali desert and wild sagebrush now lay ahead.

Restrained by the size of the berth and the proximity of the others around them, the romantic endeavors the married couple would have liked to pursue were somewhat curtailed.

"You know, honey, ten years ago when Ruark and I were . . . ah, carefree bachelors with only one thing on our minds, this berth wouldn't have been any challenge to me. And without a doubt, despite his size, Ruark would have figured it out without blinking an eye. That guy would have found a way to be intimate standing on his head if he had to."

"Well, this berth certainly isn't any smaller

than a carriage seat," she whispered with a giggle, trying to free her legs which were already tangled in the sheets.

"Yeah, but less head room," he complained, clutching his head after bumping it against the top of the berth for the dozenth time.

With Thomas grumbling and Rory giggling against his chest, the couple finally abandoned any attempt at making love. Wrapped in each other's arms, the newlyweds got a good night's sleep instead.

Bright sunlight streamed through the train windows the next morning. Rory dressed hurriedly and with enthusiasm. Before the day's end, they would reach Ogden.

Soon the scenery took a dramatic change. In the distance, the snow-capped peaks of the Wasatch Mountains reached up to touch a brilliant blue sky. Walls of sandstone loomed on each side of the track as the train snaked through multicolored canyons on a winding corridor carved out by God—and the Union Pacific.

Silhouetted against the sun stood natural stone arches, domed cliffs, and eroded pillars of red rock commanding a view of narrow gorges forested with floors of towering box elders and pines.

And far in the distance, past the peaks and walls of sandstone canyons, they could catch an occasional glimpse of a shimmering sea of salt.

When the train chugged into Ogden, Rory

could hardly contain her joy. It felt good to be home again. She glowed with enthusiasm as she waited for Thomas to claim their luggage. Looking about her with a beaming smile, she took in the familiar sights of the town. She jerked to attention as she glimpsed the back of a figure moving through the crowd. The man's walk and the set of his shoulders looked familiar to her. She stretched her neck to try and get a better look.

Rushing over to the baggage counter, she glanced around frantically for Thomas. He had just worked himself up to the front of the long line. Without a word, she grabbed his arm and pulled him out of line.

"Where are we going, Rory?" he asked.

"You'll see."

Returning to the spot where she had seen the elusive scoundrel, Rory drew up abruptly. Her glance darted around the crowd in search of the man, but she saw no sign of him among the hustle and bustle of activity.

"Who or what are we looking for, Rory?" Thomas asked patiently.

Her shoulders drooped in despair. "It was him."

Crossing his arms, Thomas nodded tolerantly. "Professor Omnipotent?" Rory nodded.

"Uh-huh," Thomas said with the patient sufferance he had unintentionally adopted on the issue of Rory's ambiguous stranger.

"Well, now that you've dragged me away from my place in line, do you have any objection if I return and start all over again?"

Her jaw jutted out at a pugnacious angle. "He was here just a moment ago, Thomas. I know I saw him," she muttered as her husband took a new position at the end of the line.

Chapter Thirteen

After they claimed their luggage, it was too late for the ride out to the Circle C that day. "We'll go out first thing in the morning," Thomas told Rory as he unlocked his office door.

The living quarters behind the office he maintained in town had always been large enough to accommodate him, but now Thomas knew he would have to make different arrangements.

"I thought we would be staying at the ranch," she remarked upon viewing the small lodging, which consisted of an examination room, his bedroom, and a tiny room containing a slop pail and a tub for bathing.

"Rory, I work for the railroad, remember? I have to make myself accessible whenever I'm needed in the event of an emergency. This office is not only convenient to the railroad tracks, but to Tent Town. I couldn't live at the ranch. Not

233

only is it inconveniently located, but your father won't allow anyone from the railroad near the ranch."

"Of course, I never thought of that." She looked around the sparsely furnished bedroom containing a bed, a dresser, and a nightstand. "We'll just have to make this do until your contract with the railroad ends." Her smile did not erase her puckered brow. "What do you cook on?"

"I usually have been eating my meals at camp or the diner. But you can heat water for bathing on the potbelly stove in the examination room. Or use the public bath," he added with a chagrined glance in her direction. He knew Rory would probably never consider a public bath.

Her disappointment was evident. Thomas slipped an arm around her shoulders. "This has always been adequate for me, but our marriage came rather unexpectedly, honey. I'm sure we can find something larger in town."

Rory went over to the bed and sat down. Her green eyes lit with devilment. "At least the room has one necessary item."

Thomas pulled off his coat and tossed it aside. His tie quickly followed. Desire gleamed in his dark eyes as he walked toward her, unbuttoning his shirt. "And it's a damn sight larger than a train berth."

Later that night, they were sound asleep when suddenly the door burst open and several figures rushed into the darkened room. Rory screamed, and as Thomas tried to get out of bed, several men overpowered him, shoved a gag into his mouth, and yanked him to his feet.

In panic, Rory leaped up, intending to get Thomas's pistol, but her foot caught in the bedding and she fell forward, striking her temple on the bedpost. She was knocked unconscious, blood trickling from a wound on her temple.

Struggling to reach her, Thomas was able to shrug aside one of the attackers. He socked the other in the face, sending the man reeling backwards. Immediately, two more pounced on him, driving him to the floor. Another joined him, and they held Thomas down while still another bound his arms behind his back. After quickly pulling trousers on him, they bound his legs together while another intruder wrapped Rory in a blanket, picked her up, and carried her outside to a waiting wagon. Thomas was tossed in beside her.

The men climbed on their horses, and the wagon silently rolled out of town. The whole incident had taken only a few minutes and had gone unnoticed by anyone.

Thomas struggled with his bonds but could not loosen them. The cool night air attacked his bare chest and feet. He began to shiver. He had no idea who these men were, nor could he fathom their motive for abducting Rory and himself. Robbery certainly wasn't the reason since none of them had bothered to search the room.

Glancing at Rory, he saw that she was still unconsciousness. Worriedly, he rolled over to her. Bound and gagged, he couldn't do much more than put his head against her chest. He said a silent prayer of thanks when he was able to discern her heartbeat. Helplessly, he could only lie quietly and continue to try to free his hands.

The driver pulled to a halt after thirty minutes and Thomas was hauled out of the wagon. He stared in shock when the huge figure of T.J. Callahan stepped out of the shadows on the porch of the Circle C.

"What happened to her?" he growled when he saw the figure of his unconscious daughter.

"We didn't touch her, T.J. She tripped and fell getting out of bed," one of the men replied.

"How bad is she hurt?" Callahan asked, bending over Rory. His voice was fraught with concern. "Get her into the house and toss that bastard in the barn 'til we're ready for him." Callahan didn't even glance in Thomas's direction.

The next thing Thomas knew, he was hauled to the barn and tossed on the floor. The door slammed closed and he lay in the darkness.

He intensified his efforts to free himself, but the knots had been tied securely. His mind had been put to rest about the identity of their abductors, but he was deeply concerned about the seriousness of the blow to Rory's head.

Gray light had begun to filter through the cracks of the barn when the door opened. Several of the ranch hands entered, hauled him to his feet, then dragged him to a tree outside the barn.

My God, are they going to hang me? Thomas

wondered in a state of shock. Then one of the cowboys drew a knife and cut the ropes binding his arms and legs. The rough bark of the tree scraped his chest as his arms were roughly pulled around the tree trunk and his wrists tied together.

When he heard a door slam, he turned his head and saw Callahan striding from the house. Thomas's glance shifted to the coiled whip clutched in the rancher's hand. Shocked, he guessed the man's intentions.

The gag was removed from his mouth. Thomas drew several deep breaths, filling his lungs with much-needed oxygen. Finally, he was able to find his voice.

"Rory? Is she okay?"

"Through no fault of yours," Callahan snarled. He uncoiled the whip and drew back his arm. The snap of the whip sounded like the crack of a gunshot, kicking up the dust at Thomas's feet.

"Callahan, you're insane," Thomas shouted.

"You railroad trash come out here stirrin' up all kinds of trouble. Well, you ain't messin' around with my girl and gettin' away with it. I'm gonna teach you a lesson you won't forget," the rancher shouted.

A shock of hot, searing fire streaked to Thomas's brain as the whip slashed his back. He sucked in his breath to keep from crying out. For several seconds his vision blurred with pain. "You don't understand. Rory and I are—"

The words were cut from his mouth as sharply as the lash cut a bloody swath across his shoulders. He hugged the tree, his flesh burning under the punishment. The rough bark ripped at his cheek, scrapping and gouging like the bruising bite of the leather strap on his back.

Rory slowly opened her eyes. Groggily, she looked around and recognized her bedroom at the ranch. Her head was throbbing and when she slipped her hand to her head, her fingers encountered the gash on her forehead, the blood now dried. Stunned, she lay back, gathering her thoughts. Then she remembered everything.

Thomas! She sat upright, then clutched her head as pain shot to her temple. *What had happened to Thomas? And how had she gotten to the ranch?*

Rory slid her feet over the side of the bed and gingerly stood up. Her legs wobbled as she moved to the window. Seeing no one, she got a robe out of her armoire and hurried downstairs.

She saw no sign of her father, so she wandered out to the kitchen. Charlie Toy was gone as well. For several moments she stood perplexed, telling herself she must be dreaming the whole thing. Soon she would wake up next to Thomas in their bedroom behind his office.

In this soporific state, she walked to the window and gazed out. Finally, moving figures invaded her dream. She recognized her father . . . Charlie Toy . . . several of the Circle C riders. Her eyes languidly shifted to the focus of their attention.

Then she screamed.

Her throbbing head was forgotten. Tears

streaked her cheeks as she raced down the path to the barn. "Stop it! Stop it," she cried out.

T.J. Callahan turned around and glared angrily at the shouting figure dashing toward him. "Ain't you got no shame, girl? Get back in the house where you belong," he barked. "I'll take care of you later."

Breathlessly, she reached the small circle of men. "What have you done?" she cried out. She raced over to Thomas. His back was criss-crossed with several bleeding welts. Her frantic glance swung to one of the ranch hands. "Release him at once."

Unsure of whom to obey, the confused cowpoke glanced at the rancher. "I ain't through with the bastard yet," Callahan shouted. "When you inherit the Circle C, you can do what you want, but right now, I run this ranch, girl, and I give the orders here."

Stunned, Rory tugged at the rope binding Thomas, trying to release the knotted ends. "Why are you beating him?" she cried out.

"As long as I'm your pa, you'll do what I tell you to do," Callahan declared. "Thought you could sneak back into town without being seen, didn't ya? Well, no man's gonna mess around with the daughter of T.J. Callahan without payin' the price."

"My God, Callahan, Rory and I are married," Thomas ground out, his voice showing the strain of the beating.

Callahan's eyes appeared to bulge out of his head. His glance swung to his daughter. "Married? What in tarnation? I don't believe it.

No daughter of mine would—" With a look of disbelief, his glance swung to his daughter. "Is he tellin' the truth or just tryin' to weasel out of the rest of the beatin' he's got coming?"

"He's telling the truth." Brushing aside her tears, she turned a scathing glare on the nearest ranch hand. "Give me your knife."

The young man's head lolled in shame as he pulled a knife out of its sheath. "Sorry, Miz Callahan. I wuz only obeyin' orders."

The cowhand cut Thomas's bonds. Rory reached for his hand. For a long moment she stared into his eyes, her own eyes welling again with tears. "Oh, God, Thomas, I'm so sorry."

"I'll be okay." His gaze shifted to the ugly bruise on her forehead. "How's your head, honey?"

Smiling at him through her tears, she shook her head. "Don't worry about me, Thomas. We have to take care of your back."

Callahan still appeared stunned from the shocking news. "Well . . . you can't blame a man for protecting his daughter's honor," he said in a defensive growl.

Rife with contempt, Thomas's dark gaze came to rest on the rancher. "You can't uphold honor with an act of dishonor, Callahan."

T.J. Callahan saw a look in the eyes of the easygoing doctor that only a few men had ever witnessed. "I'll say this only once, Mr. Callahan. If any one of your men ever puts a hand on me or my wife again, I'll kill him."

Callahan was rendered speechless by the violent threat, and after an intense and silent pause,

Thomas turned to Rory. "Let's go, honey."

"But what about your back, Thomas?" she protested. "It needs to be treated."

"We can treat it at my office."

Just then Pete Faber and Curly Evans came galloping up to the circle of people. When the foreman saw Thomas's bleeding back, he swung his stunned gaze to Callahan. "What's goin' on?" he asked. No one answered the shocked foreman.

"I'm taking the wagon, Father," Rory declared. "You brought us here in it. We'll leave in it."

The rancher made an awkward move in her direction, then turned instead and stomped back to the house. The other Circle C riders slipped away, leaving only Pete and Curly. "Curly and me's been out all night chasin' strays. Somebody gonna tell me just what happened here?" Pete asked.

"Dad had Thomas whipped," Rory declared.

Curly pulled a garment out of his saddlebags. "Here, Doc, I've got this extra shirt. You're welcome to it," the young cowpoke said.

"Thanks," Thomas said gratefully. He draped the shirt across his back and shoulders. "I'll see that you get it back."

"Why did T.J. have the Doc beaten?" Pete pursued, trying to get to the root of the problem.

"He thought that Thomas . . . had taken advantage of me," Rory replied, climbing up next to her husband. She picked up the reins of the wagon.

The foreman's weathered face turned to Thomas. He didn't like what had occurred, but he wasn't going to jump to any conclusions either. "That true, Doc?"

Rory thrust out her left hand. The wedding ring glinted on her finger. "Does that look like he took advantage of me?"

"Rory and I were married in Laramie," Thomas said tersely. He had said all he intended to for the moment. "Let's go, Rory."

The two confused cowboys watched the wagon rumble away.

Suffused with a feeling of guilt and shame, Rory sat silently on the ride back to town. Immersed in his own feelings of outrage, Thomas rode beside her, unaware of the emotional struggle she was waging with herself.

"Rory, let's rest for a moment," he said when he glanced over and saw her look of remorse and humiliation,

She pulled up on the reins and Thomas climbed down. When she stepped down, Rory hung back at the wagon, feeling more shame than she had ever known.

"Honey, come over here," Thomas said.

Hesitantly, she walked over to him. He hooked a finger under her chin and raised her head to meet his loving gaze. Seeing the anguish in her eyes, he asked gently, "What's wrong, sweetheart?"

"How can you even ask?" she murmured. Her chin quivered as she fought to contain the tears she desperately tried not to shed. "I'm so ashamed, Thomas. I don't know what to say to you."

"You're not responsible for your father's actions, Rory."

He lowered his head and his mouth claimed her trembling lips. The kiss was exquisitely tender, yet it transmitted as much love as all the passion they had shared.

Inundated with love for him, she slipped her arms around his neck. Her chest throbbed with an ache too painful to bear. All the words of love she wanted to say to him were caught in a suffocating ball in her throat.

Once again he lowered his mouth to hers. This time his kiss was more insistent. He slid his hands to her hips and drew her tighter against him.

She felt her rising response to him, an urgency too powerful to be thwarted by her feeling of remorse over her father's actions. Enveloped by the passion in his kiss, she momentarily forgot her feeling of contrition and glided her hands over the bulging muscles of his arms to the back of his shoulders.

His tortured nerve ends twitched beneath her fingertips, reminding her of the bloody welts that criss-crossed his back. With a strangled sob, she wrenched her mouth from his and fled back to the wagon.

He hurried after her and caught her arm. Turning her to face him, he looked into her eyes. "Honey, the scars will heal."

Rory lifted her head. "Which ones, Thomas?"

"In a week we'll forget this ever happened."

"I'll never be able to forget it," she said solemnly. "The scars on your back will be a constant reminder." She withdrew from his arms and climbed back up on the seat. "We better get to town and take care of those welts before they become infected."

When the wagon rolled into Ogden, more than one head turned in surprise at the sight of the disheveled couple—Thomas half-dressed, Rory in a night robe.

Once in the office, Rory's tears returned, trickling down her cheeks as she sponged Thomas's back and applied ointment to the open welts. "Oh God, Thomas, I'm so sorry," she lamented, dabbing at a particular ugly welt. "I can't believe my father did this to you. I don't know what got into him."

He took her in his arms. Hooking a finger under her chin, he tipped her face to met his steady gaze. "Honey, I told you before—I don't blame you. This wasn't your fault. You're not responsible, so stop feeling guilty."

"How can I not feel guilty when my father took a whip to you." She gave him a beseeching look. "I don't understand why he wouldn't believe you."

"He never gave me a chance to explain," Thomas said. He kissed her lightly, then stepped away. "I have to get dressed now. Knowing how upset you are, I hate to leave you, but I have to get to my job."

Rory sat on the bed watching Thomas's stiff movements in his efforts to dress. And despite his denial, she knew that the first serious obstacle had materialized in their marriage. Whether either of them acknowledged the truth or not,

T.J. Callahan had driven a wedge between her and Thomas. Rory's feeling of guilt intensified.

Thomas suffered with the same pangs as Rory. He figured the only solution to the problem that had risen between them would be to get her away from her father. As long as the unreasonable bastard was in the picture, there would be a conflict in their marriage, with Rory always in the middle between him and Callahan.

Thank God the railroad is almost completed, he thought with relief as he left his office. Soon he could take her back to Virginia, where they could start building a life together.

As he neared the tracks, he saw Kathleen Rafferty hauling a pail of water from the well. Thomas walked over to her. "Good morning, Mrs. Rafferty." He took the heavy pail from her. Thomas felt the pull on his aching back as soon as the weight of the bucket settled in his hand.

"A good mornin' to you, Doctor Graham," Kathleen said, keeping her head lowered.

"How have you been feeling, Mrs. Rafferty?" he asked.

"Fine, Doctor."

"Where would you like this?" he asked when they reached her tent.

"Just put it there, Doctor," she said, pointing to a nearby stool. "And thank you for your kindness." She glanced up with a smile, and Thomas grimaced when he saw several ugly bruises on her cheeks. "Kathleen—"

"I'm grateful to you, Doctor," she said hurriedly, cutting off anything further he intended to say. "Good day to you." She turned and hastened into the tent.

For several seconds Thomas hesitated, tempted to call her out to talk to her. Realizing her embarrassment, he put down the bucket and left.

Thomas decided to find Keene MacKenzie. Maybe the scout would be able to update him on what happened while he was gone. And what Keene didn't know, Thomas figured, Michaleen Dennehy would be sure to know, as soon as he could make contact with the little man. He climbed the stairway to Keene's room.

"Come on in," Keene shouted in response to Thomas's knock.

Keene sat on the edge of the bed pulling on his boots. He threw Thomas a casual glance. "Hi, Doc. Welcome home."

"Can't say it's good to be back. What happened to you?" he asked, noticing the scout was favoring his shoulder.

Keene stood up and strapped on a gun belt. "A Ute buck stuck a knife into me," he said indifferently.

"Well, let me take a look at it," Thomas said, putting down his medical bag.

"It's okay now, Doc. This is my first day on my feet, so I'm a little wobbly, that's all."

Thomas shook his head. "How long do you expect to keep dodging the bullet, Keene?"

" 'Til my luck runs out, Doc." He picked up his hat and plopped it on his head. "Had breakfast yet?"

"Come to think of it, I haven't," Thomas said.

"Let's go find some. I'm hungry enough to eat a horse."

"Got some news to tell you," Thomas said as they walked to the diner. "Want to make sure you're sitting down before I tell you, though."

However, before they got any farther, a burly figure stepped into their path. Michael Rafferty glared at the two men. "Keep away from my wife or I'll kill ya," he growled, then staggered away before either man could say a word.

Not knowing what had transpired between Keene and Kathleen, Thomas assumed the threat was just another unreasonable action directed at him. Normally, he would have been able to laugh off the accusation, but the patience he had tried to hold on to throughout the night now dissipated and he released his frustration in an explosion of anger.

"Damn! All I did was carry a goddamn bucket of water for his wife. I've reached the limit of my patience with a couple of these bastards around here."

Keene had never witnessed any kind of outburst from the easygoing doctor. Surprise now registered on the usually enigmatic face of the railroad scout. "Maybe he meant me, Doc." But embroiled in anger, Thomas entered the diner and didn't hear him.

"This tastes like river-bottom sludge," Thomas grumbled after they were seated and cups of black coffee set before them. "Can't even get a decent cup of coffee around this place. I'll be glad to get back to Virginia."

" 'Pears like you're not too happy to be back,"

247

Keene said, more amused then disturbed by Thomas's personality shift. "You horny, Doc, or just feelin' downright ornery?"

Thomas shoved his hat to the back of his head and leaned back in his chair. "I used to pride myself on being a rational man, Keene, but I'm beginning to doubt that."

"Has all this got anything to do with that big news you talked about?" Keene asked.

Thomas took several more sips of the bitter coffee. "Well, I guess part of it does." He lifted his head and looked Keene in the eye. "I don't think you're going to like what you hear, but there's no easy way of saying it. Rory and I were married in Laramie a couple days ago."

Whatever effect this announcement had on Keene MacKenzie lay masked behind a pair of unwavering gray eyes. "Well, congratulations, Doc. You got yourself a great gal."

"I know that, Keene."

"How did T.J. take the news?"

"Not well," Thomas said. He did not tell the scout about the whipping. Rory was hurt and embarrassed enough about the incident without adding to her distress by relating it to others. It would be bad enough the next time the Circle C riders came to town and spread the word.

When the waitress brought each of them a plate of bacon and eggs, the two men ceased talking to concentrate on their food.

"You plannin' on heading back East?" Keene asked after several minutes, swabbing the egg yolk with a piece of freshly baked bread.

"As soon as this damn railroad is finished," Thomas replied.

Keene glanced up with a level stare. "Rory know that?"

Thomas frowned. "We've never discussed it, but I would assume she knows that would be my intention." He grew even more wary when Keene silently nodded, but said nothing further. "Pete Faber once commented that this territory wasn't big enough for me and Callahan. I'd have to agree with him."

Not wanting to pry, Keene tossed a coin on the table and rose to his feet. "Well, I gotta get movin'. Been laid up for a week."

"You heading out to end of track?" Thomas asked. At Keene's nod, Thomas stood up. "I'll rent a horse and ride along with you, since Murphy's pulled out already."

Chapter Fourteen

When Thomas and Keene reached end of track, Mike Rafferty was engaged in a shouting match with Sean Cassidy, the foreman of one of the crews responsible for laying the wooden sleepers that the rails rested upon. Both men appeared to be on the verge of exchanging blows.

"Your damn crew just ain't doing their job," Rafferty accused the other man.

"Are ya callin' me a liar, Rafferty?" Cassidy exclaimed.

"Well, if ya laid the sleepers the way you claim, then where are they?" Rafferty challenged. "I'm thinkin' maybe that crew of yours just quit early, Cassidy."

"An' I'm tellin' ya for the last time, Rafferty, we laid a mile of sleepers Saturday before we left for town."

"Then whadda ya be thinkin' happened to

them, Cassidy? Termites eat 'em?" Mike Rafferty smirked. "'Cause it's for shur there be no sign of 'em now."

The short, barrel-chested sleeper foreman shrugged his broad shoulders. "Maybe the Indians carried them off." That theory brought an outburst of laughter from Rafferty's crew, who were standing nearby listening to the argument.

"Well, my crew can't lay rail on rock, Cassidy, so I'm advisin' ya to haul your ass out of here and get them sleepers laid," Rafferty declared. "'Cause me and my crew'll be close enough to be smellin' your armpits in a couple of hours."

Hearing the exchange between the two foremen, Jack Casement walked over to them. "Rafferty, simmer down," he ordered. "Can't you see the man's telling the truth?"

"Oh, hell!" Rafferty said. He turned to leave and saw the two mounted men. Rafferty's eyes gleamed with malice as he glared at Keene and Thomas before stomping away.

Keene and Thomas dismounted and tied their horses to a nearby tree. "Top o' the marnin' to you," Michaleen Dennehy greeted them pleasantly when the two men approached him.

"Same to you, Michaleen," Thomas replied, shaking hands with the little man.

"What was all the shouting about?" Keene asked the cook.

"Cassidy laid a mile of sleepers last Saturday, and half o' 'em be missin' this marnin'. Rafferty's kickin' up a fuss fearin' the sleepers won't be down when he's ready for 'em. Now who would you be thinkin' would want them ties?" Michaleen asked.

"Don't sound like Indians," Keene remarked. "But anything's possible. Guess I better ride ahead and see what I can find." He climbed back on his horse. "See you later, Doc."

"Would you be wantin' a fresh egg, Doctar?" Michaleen asked with an affectionate smile toward his cages of chickens.

"No thanks, Michaleen. I ate breakfast in Ogden."

"And how is me darlin' Kathleen?" the little man asked. "I miss seein' the dear child."

"I saw her briefly this morning, Michaleen." The question made it apparent to Thomas that Michaleen was uninformed about anything regarding Kathleen. Rather than try to fend off any further questions about her health, he quickly changed the subject. "I guess I better get to work here."

Later, after treating the smashed finger of a bolter and then the scalded hand of a cook, Thomas strolled from the medical tent to watch the laying of the track. The five-hundred-pound iron rails had been unloaded from the train onto horse-drawn flat carts. The beds of the carts were equipped with rollers to help convey the heavy rails forward.

Then Rafferty and his crew went into action. Watching a crew as skillful as Rafferty's, Thomas experienced the same respect and awe he felt when observing an efficient medical team in operation—each individual was trained to do a specific job as quickly and efficiently as possible.

As soon as the horses hauled the cart to the end of the track, two men stepped up and each man seized the end of a rail. As they moved these ends forward, aided by the rollers in the cart, four more pairs of men stepped up and helped to carry the two rails until the thirty-foot-long sections cleared the cart. On command from Rafferty, the five-man teams lowered the rails in place on the previously laid sleepers. The procedure took only thirty seconds.

As the railers hurried back to repeat the operation, the gaugers hastened onto the track with their notched wooden gauges and aligned the pairs of rails a distance of four-feet, eight-and-one-half inches apart. Then, like grasshoppers, the gaugers leaped to the next set of rails as the spikers moved in behind them. With three precisioned blows of their heavy sledgehammers, they nailed the rail to the sleepers with long spikes.

When the spikers shifted to the next rail, the bolters dashed in to attach the fishplates, bolting the railends together. Finally, the ballasters followed with shovels and wheelbarrows, adding crushed rock and gravel to firm up the rail beds between the ties.

And the skillful band played on—three strokes to a spike, ten spikes to a rail, three-hundred-and-fifty-two rails to a mile. For eighteen-hundred miles, from the muddy banks of the Missouri to the surf-tossed shores of the Pacific, the clang and ring of sledges and shovels hammered out the notes of the Iron Horse Symphony.

"*A grand Anvil Chorus playing across the plains,*" Thomas quoted to himself, recalling the words written the previous year by an Eastern newspaper reporter.

He shook his head in tribute. "I wouldn't have missed this marvel for anything," he murmured aloud. His earlier disillusionment with the whole affair was momentarily forgotten.

With his good humor restored, Thomas returned to his medical tent.

Rory hitched up the team to return to the Circle C. She knew Thomas would be upset when he found out that she had gone to the ranch alone, but she wanted to get the matter resolved before his return that evening. Besides, she in no way expected him to ride out with her. After what her father had done to him, Rory felt she would be lucky if Thomas ever talked to her father again.

There was no sign of her father when she arrived at the ranch house. Charlie Toy nodded a greeting and hurried back to the kitchen, so Rory went up to her room.

She packed some additional clothing in a valise. Since Thomas's room provided so little space, she picked out only the clothing she would need until they could find bigger living quarters.

Resigned to leaving behind some of her favorite gowns, Rory quickly closed the valise and hurried downstairs. Her father waited at the dining table.

"Movin' out, daughter? Gonna live in a tent like the rest of that railroad trash?" he growled.

"It's customary for a wife to be with her husband, Daddy."

"Husband!" he snorted. The chair strummed a shrill chord against the wooden floor as he shoved away from the table and bolted to his feet. "Who married you, some kind of itinerant preacher?" Callahan snorted angrily.

"No, Daddy. Thomas and I were married in a church in Laramie. It was all legal and proper."

"May have been legal, but it sure weren't proper, gal. Ain't proper for a daughter not to have her daddy there when she weds." Rory saw moisture glistening in his eyes. "Thought you loved me, gal."

Her own eyes misted with tears as her heart reached out to him. "Oh, I do, Daddy."

"Is that why you snuck off and got yourself hitched to railroad trash?" he challenged.

"That's not how it happened. Thomas and I never planned to elope. We met by accident in St. Louis and things kind of . . . moved fast after that." She put her hand on his arm. "I'm sorry, Daddy. I never intended to hurt you. I love you, but I love Thomas too."

"Yeah. Well, wouldn't surprise me if that eastern dude married you just to get his hands on the Circle C someday."

"That's not true. Thomas loves me. And if you love me like you say you do, you'll try and make your peace with him. Although I don't know how he could ever forgive you for what you did to him."

"I ain't sorry for what I did to him. Any father would do the same to a man messing around with his daughter. Far as I'm concerned, you ain't married 'til I say you're married. I don't want the bastard in this house."

Her hand slipped off his arm. Rory walked to the door and picked up her valise. Turning, she looked back at him. "First Keene and now Thomas. How many more people must you hurt before you'll admit you're wrong?" Callahan's glare remained inflexible and unrepentant. "Good-bye, Daddy."

He did not reply.

Dispirited, Rory returned to town. As she unpacked her clothing and added it to her other garments in the armoire, she retrieved the gift she had purchased for Kathleen Rafferty in St. Louis. With the package in hand, she headed for the cluster of tents next to the railroad tracks. When she entered Kathleen's tent, she was shocked at her friend's appearance.

She reached out to embrace the other woman. "Kathleen! What happened to you?"

Kathleen raised her hand, attempting to cover the ugly bruises on her face. "'Tis nothing. I fell."

"Has Thomas examined you?"

"Thomas?" Kathleen asked, sitting down on the cot.

"Doctor Graham," Rory explained.

To ease the poor woman's obvious embarrassment, Rory briefly changed the subject. "I have some exciting news, Kathleen. Thomas and I were married on the trip back from St. Louis."

Kathleen's face broke into a warm smile. "'Tis happy I am for you, Rory. The doctor is a fine man."

"I think so too," Rory said, pleased. But not one to be diverted for long, she added, "But tell me, did you show that fine man the bruises on your face?"

"Yes. I saw him this morning," Kathleen replied, stretching the truth to avoid any further discussion.

"Well, then I'm sure you're in good hands." Grinning, she handed Kathleen the colorful package. "This is for you. I bought it in appreciation for your help when I was wounded."

A blush of surprise and pleasure enhanced Kathleen's face. "For me!" She was unaccustomed to receiving gifts. As pleased as she was, she felt self-conscious and awkward untying the gaily wrapped package with Rory watching her.

Her blue eyes widened with delight when she lifted a pair of fancy hose out of the box. "Oh, my! I've never had such finery before," she exclaimed. "'Tis most thoughtful of you."

She started to reach out to Rory, then shyly drew back. Seeing the gesture, Rory opened her arms and Kathleen hugged her. For a long moment, the two women silently embraced.

The young Irishwoman forced back her tears. She had not realized how much she longed for a friend until this moment. Knowing she now had one, Kathleen wanted to open her heart to Rory, but her shyness kept her from saying the words. Sensing Kathleen's sentiment, Rory felt a salty tear glisten in her own eye.

A short while later, after persuading Kathleen to accompany her, they headed for the newspaper office. "If there's anything available to rent, Mr. Rose would be the first one to hear about it," Rory said. But much to her distress, the editor informed her he knew of nothing in the vicinity.

Returning to her room, Rory sat down, leaned her elbows on the table, and rested her chin in cupped hands. Her troubled glance swept the spartan room. "I knew it would be a wild goose chase," she lamented.

Having lived in a thatched-roof hut with an earthen floor in Ireland and nothing but a canvas tent since coming to America, Kathleen Rafferty considered the four walls and firm bed of the lodging to be quite luxurious. But her heart sympathized with Rory, knowing the girl was accustomed to the comfort and spaciousness of the ranch house in which she had been raised.

"It appears to have a good, solid roof overhead," she said, hoping to cheer up her despondent friend.

"I know I must sound spoiled and unappreciative to you, Kathleen. But you see, I want to make everything as perfect as I can for Thomas. Our marriage has started out very badly. My father disapproves of my marrying Thomas."

"Disapprove! How could anyone disapprove of a man as fine as Doctor Graham?" Kathleen said, astounded.

"Well, mainly because Thomas works for the Union Pacific. Daddy blames the railroad for stirring up all this trouble with the Indians. He's been treating Thomas just horribly." Her worried glance swung to Kathleen. "I'm afraid Thomas won't tolerate his actions too much longer. What would you do, if you were me, Kathleen?"

Feeling intensely the disaster of her own marriage, Kathleen shook her head. "I'm afraid I'm not the one to be askin'. But I'm thinkin' you're frettin' for naught, Rory. The good doctor is happy just havin' you," she said kindly. "He'll not be carryin' grudges for what your father does."

Rory sighed. "I know. Thomas is too fair a person to allow Daddy to come between us," Rory said, trying to muster enough confidence to dissolve her doubts. It wasn't that she doubted Thomas's intentions. Her fear lay in the belief that her father's actions would get considerably worse before they got better. Would Thomas's tolerance be enough to endure then?

Her eyes suddenly lit with a renewed sparkle, and her face split with a delighted grin. "Of course, Daddy's disapproval of him never discouraged Thomas before we were married." Then her spirits drooped as her glance swept the room. "But that doesn't solve my problem about this room, does it?"

"Well, seein' as you can't make the room any bigger, I'm thinkin' there's nothin' stoppin' you from makin' it prettier," Kathleen said.

Rory jumped to her feet. "You know, you're absolutely right." She linked her arm through Kathleen's. "Let's go to the diner and have a cup of tea. Then we'll go shopping. By the time

Thomas returns tonight, he won't recognize this place."

After ordering tea and slices of freshly baked apple cobbler, the two women put their heads together and decided what would be needed to perk up the gloomy room. Rory's pert face curled in a thoughtful frown. "What I should begin with is a coat of white paint on the walls."

"Well, there's no call for the doin' of it today, is there?" Kathleen asked. "Why not be havin' it painted when the doctor leaves in the mornin'?"

"Kathleen, will you please refer to my husband as Thomas? The Doctor sounds so pretentious and . . . intimidating."

Frowning, Kathleen reflected for a moment, then her chin jutted to a determined angle. "Well, I'll give it a try, but I've got to be sayin', 'twill not be an easy thing to do."

The first stop they made on their shopping foray was at the Mormon church, where the sisters were conducting a fund raising. Rory was able to obtain crocheted doilies, a hooked rug, a patchwork quilt, and several embroidered hand towels—as well as an added treat of a chocolate cake as a surprise for Thomas that evening.

A trip to the general store produced paint, brushes, blue-and-white chintz for curtains, thread, and a pair of hurricane lamps. A stop at Ethan Billing's carpenter's shop resulted in a used rocking chair and a small hutch. In addition, Ethan promised that he and his son would paint the two rooms for her the next day.

The purchase of the hutch necessitated a return to the general store, where Rory bought a vase and some dried wildflowers. After congratulating Rory on her marriage, Abner Wyler assured her he would deliver the items in the morning as soon as Thomas left for end of track.

After succeeding in accomplishing results far beyond their expectations, Rory and Kathleen returned to the office, measured the bedroom and office windows, and proceeded to cut the chintz into the proper lengths. Then Kathleen gathered up the material and thread and hurried back to her tent to begin sewing the curtains.

Thomas arrived back in Ogden at twilight on Murphy's "Betsy." His body ached and his back felt on fire. "I'll ride out with you in the morning, Murph," he said to the engineer as he unloaded his horse from one of the freight cars. Wearily, he led the animal to the stable and then returned to his office.

Rory greeted him with a big smile and a deep kiss. The moment his arms closed around her and the kiss began, Thomas felt the surge of blood to his loins, banishing his tiredness. He released the buttons of her blouse and slipped his hand under her chemise. As he cupped one of the firm globes, his thumb grazed the taut peak and a heated sensation spread through her. Shoving up the chemise, he lowered his head and laved her breasts, then he took the nub into his mouth.

Weaving her fingers through his thick, dark hair, she pressed tighter against him. "I missed

261

you today, Thomas. I thought you were never coming home for dinner," she whispered.

"I'm glad you kept the kettle boiling," he teased. Returning to claim her lips, his tongue swept her mouth, inciting her to a greater urgency.

Her groping hands freed his shirt, and her fingers tingled from the feel of his nakedness as she reveled in the power contained within the sinewy tautness. She pressed her nakedness against him, the patch of dark hair on his chest brushing against the sensitive peaks of her breasts. As he slid his lips down the column of her neck, his hand swept the curves of her body. Wallowing in the sensuous delight of her nakedness against him, she felt passion spiral up inside her, winding ever tighter like a coil. The exciting sensation continued, and she stepped away from him.

"You hungry, Thomas?" She lightly stroked his chest.

"Can't you tell?" he asked, pulling her back into his arms. He kissed the tip of her nose and then released her. "So what did you do all day?" he asked, walking into the bedroom. Painfully, he shrugged off his shirt.

She gasped at the sight of his shoulders. One of the welts was bleeding. "Oh, Thomas, your back!"

"How about putting some more unguent on it, honey?" he asked.

"Lie down on the bed."

"You don't have to ask me twice." He stretched out on his stomach as she filled a basin with water. After sponging off his back, Rory applied salve to the welts, then put gauze over the one that had broken open. By the time she finished, Thomas had fallen sound asleep.

She removed his shoes and stockings, then his trousers. Finally, with much effort, she succeeded in working the sheet and blanket out from under him so she could cover him. She stood smiling tenderly at his sleeping form.

Then, with tears glistening in her eyes, she whispered lovingly, "Who ever takes care of the doctor?"

Thomas slept through the night and was all apologies the next morning. Rory, of course, was all smiles and understanding as she hurried him off. She couldn't wait to begin the remodeling.

Thomas continued to try to make amends as his dutiful wife walked him to the station. "Honey, I'm really sorry about last night. I'll make it up to you tonight," he promised with a grin.

"You bet you will," she informed him with a saucy smile. As the train, loaded with rails and supplies, pulled away, Rory offered a final wave to her husband, then rushed back to the office. Kathleen was already waiting for her.

Meanwhile, at end of track, Michael Rafferty was encountering his own problems. A crew of graders from the Central Pacific Railroad had appeared and begun grading tracks parallel to the Union Pacific. Because of the stiff competition that had developed between the two railroad lines, each crew kept on with what they were doing instead of stopping to resolve the obvious mistake. The tension grew worse when the Central Pacific began grading right above the heads of the Union Pacific crew working below them.

Rafferty stormed up the hill. "If I was you, O'Leary, I'd be pulling those slant-eyed Crocker Coolies back where they belong," he said, his voice rising to a roar. He spat on the ground, and his face contorted with contempt as he pointed a finger in the direction of the Chinese crew recruited by Charles Crocker of the Central Pacific.

"And I'm tellin' ya for the last time, Rafferty, I take me orders from Jim Strobridge of the Central Pacific. Try chewin' on your own advice and pull back where you belong, 'cause we're going to start blastin'," the man barked, unintimidated by the big Irishman.

"My orders are to lay track, and that's what I'm doin'," Rafferty shouted. Then he accused the Central Pacific crew of being the culprits responsible for the missing Union Pacific sleepers.

"I don't know what in hell you're talkin' about, Rafferty."

"You're a liar," Rafferty shouted and stomped away, turning back to let loose a final stream of tobacco.

He no sooner reached his crew when an explosion rocked the earth above their heads. When the dust settled, coughing and sputtering, the workers crawled out from under the rock and dirt. The dead body of one of the Union

Pacific workers was pulled out of the rubble, and several more men had been struck in the head by flying rock.

Only the timely arrival of the train bearing Jack Casement and Thomas prevented a further clash between the two factions. As Thomas tended to the wounded, Jack Casement convinced the Central Pacific foreman to return to his own camp.

"You know, Rafferty, you could try using reasoning sometime instead of threats," Casement chastised the Irishman when the other crew pulled out. "What did your belligerent mouth get you but a dead crewman and several more wounded?"

Bright and early, Abner Wyler delivered the paint and supplies as promised, and Ethan Billings and his son, Samuel, arrived with ladders. The two men set to work at once, and by midday the dingy office and bedroom sparkled with a coat of white paint.

Unaccustomed to household chores, but not to hard work, Rory followed Kathleen's guidance as they scrubbed and polished the floor. While the floor dried in the bedroom, they did the same to the office and bathroom.

The two women worked tirelessly for hours, striving to restore the rooms to order before Thomas returned home. By day's end, the sparkling bedroom was arrayed with a colorful hooked rug, a bright bedspread, and curtains on the window. A rocking chair now stood near the window. The recently purchased hutch added a cozy touch against the wall. The vase with the cluster of bright flowers offered an added cheeriness to the room.

Smiling with satisfaction, the two exhausted women stepped back to admire their handiwork just as the distant whistle announced the arrival of the train.

"I can hardly wait until Thomas sees the change in this place," Rory said proudly.

"I best be gettin' back to my tent," Kathleen said. "I'll not want to spoil the moment."

"I can't thank you enough, Kathleen." Rory gave her a final kiss and hug before Kathleen hurried away.

Tingling with expectation, Rory waited for Thomas to arrive. As a last-minute gesture, she put the uneaten chocolate cake on the table. When a knock sounded at the door, she rushed to open it, a wide smile on her face.

Caleb Murphy doffed his hat. "Evening, Miz Calla—ah, Miz Graham. Doc got held up back at camp." He handed her a folded piece of paper. "He asked me to give this to you."

Disappointed, Rory read the letter from Thomas.

Honey, I'm sorry, but a couple of the men were seriously injured and I have to remain here with them. I know you'll understand and I promise I'll make it up to you. Hopefully, I'll see you in a couple of days. I love you,

Thomas

* * *

Despondently, Rory walked back and slumped down in the rocking chair. She slowly rocked back and forth, staring forlornly at the chocolate cake. Long shadows darkened the room before she finally rose and lit the lamp.

Chapter Fifteen

Kathleen arrived back at her tent at the same time as Mike Rafferty. "Where've you been?" he grumbled.

Shocked, she asked, "Mike, what—what are you doin' here?"

"Some new men comin' in. Gotta take 'em back tomorrow and try to make railroaders of 'em." He smirked. "Casement sent the best man for the job." His face shifted into a grimace. "Asked you where you've been, woman."

"Just on an errand," she said, hesitant to tell him of her relationship with Rory.

"Sure you ain't been with that scout?" he growled accusingly. Rafferty knew better, having seen Keene MacKenzie still at camp when the train had left. But he enjoyed tormenting her.

"No, of course not, Mike," Kathleen protested.

"Will you be wantin' something to eat?" she asked, quickly changing the subject.

"I ate at camp," he said.

To Kathleen's dismay, she saw that she had neglected to put away the pair of hose Rory had given her. She walked over and threw her shawl over the stockings.

"Should I be heatin' you some water for bathin'?" she asked.

"What's the matter, woman, don't you like the smell of a real man? You've been sniffin' around that scout too much." He grabbed her and painfully pinched her cheek, then pulled her into his arms. His mouth closed over hers in a hard kiss, his tongue plundering her mouth as his huge paw groped under her gown. Pushing her down on the cot, he shoved her dress up past her waist.

"Christ, you're a skinny-ass bitch. Ain't you ever gonna have something to grab?" he grumbled, pawing at her breasts.

After having his way with her, Rafferty climbed off the bunk. Kathleen curled up with her knees to her stomach, waiting for him to leave.

He went over to the carton that served as a dresser for them. As he started to root for clean clothes, he shoved aside her shawl and saw the pair of hose.

Picking up the stockings, Rafferty examined them. "Where in hell did these come from?"

He spun around and turned his black glare on her. Walking over to the cot, he jerked her up by the hair. "Where'd you get these, woman?" he shouted, shaking them in her face. "They look like whore stockings to me."

Kathleen grasped her head, trying to ease the pain from his hold on her hair. "'Twas a gift from the doctor's wife. Please, Mike, let go of me hair, you're hurtin' me," she pleaded.

"You're lyin', bitch. Why would she be givin' you a gift? Your boyfriend give you these to parade around in, didn't he."

"No. 'Tis not true. Mrs. Graham gave me them in thanks for helpin' her when she was hurt. 'Tis the truth, Mike. I swear on the Blessed Virgin."

"You stay away from her. You hear? You got no call to be mixin' with her kind." Shoving her away, he walked over and picked up the scissors Kathleen had used making the curtains. He cut up the stockings into several pieces. "Here's your fancy stockings," he sneered, and threw them at her.

Then, grabbing his clean clothing, he headed for the public bath. It wasn't Saturday, but he could still make a good night of it.

Rory awoke before dawn. As she lay thinking about Thomas, a daring thought crossed her mind. She jumped out of bed and quickly dressed. At the stroke of six, she hurried to the diner. After a grumbled complaint, the proprietress agreed to her request.

Exhilarated, she hurried from the diner and rushed to the train station. After a short conference with Caleb Murphy, she rushed back to the diner.

A half-hour later, when "Betsy" steamed out of

Ogden, Rory was on board, carrying a big picnic basket.

Thomas had not fallen asleep until dawn. He was dreaming of Rory, of her soft hands stroking his brow, her exciting lips pressing light kisses on his face.

The dream was so real he could feel her, smell her, taste her. Groaning with arousal, he shifted restlessly and willed himself to wakefulness.

Opening his eyes, the very image of his fantasy was before him, her green eyes smiling down at him.

"Hi, honey. Am I dreaming, or what?" he asked.

"Tell me what the 'or what' means and then I'll be able to answer." She lowered her head and kissed him.

"We're still at camp, right?" She nodded. "Any minute some gauger or bolter's going to come through that door, right?"

"Not without knocking," she whispered, nibbling at his neck.

He groaned. "Oh, Lord! I'm in trouble. Deep trouble. I hope you're planning on climbing in this bedroll with me."

She stood up. "In any other circumstances, I'd accept the invitation. But that camp out there is already teeming with activity."

"God, woman, you're evil and devious. Thanks to you, I can't move right now—it would be too embarrassing. And I wouldn't want to spoil my image." Lying back, he closed his eyes. "How'd you get here? And please don't tell me you rode out here alone."

"I made the morning run with Mr. Murphy. I thought we could have breakfast together."

"Yeah, us and a couple hundred other people."

She picked up the picnic basket from the floor. "I brought breakfast with me." Her eyes sparkled impishly. "I thought we could find a nice quiet spot somewhere and be alone."

He immediately grasped the wealth of opportunity in the suggestion and bolted to a sitting position. "Let's go." He jumped to his feet.

"You're moving much more agilely than you were a moment ago, Doctor. A remarkable recovery. Worthy of being written up in one of those medical journals you've always got your head buried in."

Before more could be said, they were interrupted by a frantic knocking on the door. "Doctor Graham, come quick! Barnaby's taken a turn for the worse."

Thomas and Rory exchanged a knowing glance. "I'll wait," she said.

"Sorry, honey." He gave her a quick peck on the cheek and grabbed his medical bag.

Two hours later, Thomas had not returned. The crepes were soggy, the whipped cream was runny, the bacon was greasy, and the coffee was cold.

Caleb Murphy tapped on the door. "I'm heading back to town, Miz Graham. Are you still planning on going back with me?"

Rory picked up the picnic basket. "Yes, Mr.

Murphy, I'm going back with you."

"Sorry you never got a chance to have your picnic, ma'am."

"Oh well, it was a dumb idea anyway," Rory said despondently.

Dejectedly, she climbed up into the cab of the train.

Later that day, after preparing lunch, Michaleen Dennehy climbed into the cab of Caleb Murphy's engine to make the lunch run with him to end of track.

"Where will you be goin' when this job is finished, Michaleen?" Caleb asked as the train chugged along the newly laid track.

"This is just the beginnin'," Michaleen replied. "They'll be layin' track for the next ten years. Soon there'll be rails criss-crossin' this whole country." He cocked a bushy brow. "So I'm thinkin' the railroad will always be needin' a good cook such as meself."

"Ain't you ever plannin' on settlin' down?" Murphy asked.

"Same day as you do, Murph," the little man said with a toothy grin.

As soon as the train arrived at the site, the men broke from their labor and quickly laid a turnaround for Murphy's engine while Michaleen set up a makeshift kitchen. After they ate the usual fare of beef, beans, and potatoes, most of the men stretched out to relax and enjoy the rest of their hour lunch break.

Suddenly, a rifle blast from one of the men on

273

guard threw the camp into action. Men scrambled for cover as a band of Indians raced down on them from the concealment of the surrounding rocks. The combat became hand-to-hand as the men grappled with the attackers. Finally, a few of them reached the protective cover of the engine. Rifles and pistols soon began to pick off the attackers.

Having set up his makeshift kitchen in the shade of a cottonwood tree, Michaleen, now pursued by one of the braves, ran toward the train. But the Indian overtook him, and with a swing of his war club, he knocked Michaleen to the ground. The savage leaped upon him and delivered another blow to Michaleen's head. Stunned, the little Irishman felt a searing pain as the Indian cut a circular swatch and ripped off a patch of his scalp.

Whooping triumphantly, the savage jumped to his feet, waving the bloody trophy in the air. He slapped Michaleen's red tam on his own head and started to run back to the cover of the rocks.

Horrified, Caleb Murphy had seen his friend clubbed to the ground. By the time he could take aim and fire, the distraught man had been too late to prevent the savage from lifting Michaleen's scalp. But Murphy's shot found its mark, and the Indian pitched to the ground.

Still alive, Michaleen raised his head and saw the body of his attacker lying nearby. The red tam had fallen off the savage's head and lay on the ground. All the plucky little man could think of was retrieving the tam that his great-great-grandfather had worn at the Battle of the Boyne.

Dazed and bleeding, he crawled to where it lay and reached for it, drawing it to his chest. His head felt on fire, and he began to pray in preparation for meeting his Maker. Michaleen turned his head and the words of the prayer caught in his throat when he saw his own piece of bloody scalp still clutched in the hand of the dead Indian.

Michaleen Timothy Dennehy had never felt such outrage.

His precious Maker would just have to delay his calling until this indignity could be rectified. He staggered to his feet. As he bent over, a wave of dizziness almost caused him to black out, but Michaleen's fortitude prevailed. He snatched the scalp from the hand of the savage. Sinking to his knees, the indignant little man brushed the dirt off the piece of skin, then he stretched out on his stomach with his precious scalp and tam clutched beneath him.

The grim hand-to-hand combat continued as men fell around him, some from battle axes, others from rifle shots. The air hung heavy with smoke and the smell of sulfur from gunshots. Once most of the construction crew reached the train, they were able to set up a forceful barrage of fire that drove back the attackers. The Indians withdrew and the attack ended as swiftly as it had begun.

Caleb Murphy hurried to where Michaleen knelt in the dirt. The engineer's face was fraught with grief. "Saints preserve us," he exclaimed.

Blood streaked the white hair and beard of Michaleen as he held up the gruesome object. "Look, Murphy. Look what the heathen bastard did to me."

Murphy shook his head. "I thought sure you were a goner, Michaleen."

"Will ya be bringin' me the water pail, Murphy?"

The engineer moved quickly to comply. He hurried back, toting the pail. When he held up a ladle of water to Michaleen, the cook brushed it aside.

"I don't want it for drinkin', man." Michaleen thrust the scalp into the bucket of water. "I'll not be goin' to meet my Maker with part of me scalp missin'," the plucky little Irishman said. "Get me back to the doctar so he can be sewin' me back together."

Michaleen stood up on shaky legs and the flabbergasted engineer helped him back to the train. He wrapped his friend's head in a towel and laid him down on the flatcar. While the wounded and dead were loaded on the car with him, Michaleen lay quietly, clutching his precious tam in one hand and the handle of the pail in the other.

When everyone was loaded, Murphy steamed back to camp.

The arrival of the train carrying the wounded and the remaining crew caused a flurry of excitement. Thomas had his hands full giving medical attention to the wounded. He was momentarily shocked when Caleb Murphy carried the last patient into the makeshift office.

Thomas removed the bloody towel from Michaleen's head and examined the wound. After shaving away some of the surrounding hair, he thoroughly cleansed the injury. "Looks to me like you can pull through this as long as we can prevent infection. You're a lucky man, Michaleen. Not too many men can be scalped and live to tell about it."

Michaleen grinned broadly. "'Tis the luck of the Irish, Doctar."

When Thomas prepared to bandage the wound, Michaleen stopped him. "I want you to be sewin' my scalp back on, Doctar," the little man declared. "I've kept me headpiece in the bucket to keep it from drying out."

"But the hair will never grow back, Michaleen," Thomas said kindly.

"That's of no matter, Doctar. Me tam can always cover the spot. But I'll have me head which is all I'll be grateful for."

Thomas retrieved the piece of scalp from the bucket. Shaking it out, he closely examined the patch of skin and hair. The piece of flesh was intact, and the edges were well defined. "Well, I'm not making any promises, Michaleen."

Once again he wielded the razor and removed all the hair. Then threading the needle, he placed the skin over the wound and began to suture it down with tiny stitches.

For the next hour Thomas snipped and cut, meticulously applying over a hundred sutures. Throughout the ordeal, Michaleen uttered nary a sound of pain or complaint. Finally, with a sigh of relief, Thomas put aside the needle and thread, spread an ointment on the seams, and wrapped a bandage around the top of Michaleen's head.

"As I said earlier, Michaleen, I'm not making any promises. I advise you to stay off your feet for the rest of the day. You've lost a lot of blood. I'll look in on you later tonight."

Grateful, Michaleen clutched Thomas's hand and shook it. "I'm beholdin' to you, Doctar. As I've always said, you're a fine gentleman and the dear Lord has blessed us for just the knowin' of you."

Opening the door of the office, Thomas motioned to Murphy, who waited anxiously outside. "Take him back to his quarters, Murph, and see that he gets into bed."

"Will he . . . be okay?" the worried man asked.

"There should be no problem, if he stays in bed and rests," Thomas said.

"Murph, will ye be stoppin' your treatin' me like I've one foot in the grave," Michaleen grumbled, shrugging aside the concerned man's helping hand.

"And will you be minding the doctor's orders," Murphy shot back and followed him. "I've got more to do than fuss over a stubborn old fool who ain't got enough sense to die after being scalped by a redskin."

Shaking his head in amusement, Thomas crossed his arms and leaned against the doorjamb as he watched the two men move across the clearing. Then, stretching, he flexed the aching muscles of his shoulders and turned away to write Rory another letter of regret that he would not be home until the next day.

Later that night, he stretched out in his bed-roll and lay staring at the ceiling. His thoughts were on Rory. Somehow he would have to make it all up to her for these disappointments and separations. He smiled, recalling the good times they had shared in St. Louis. It would be like that again. Once they were away from here.

With any luck at all, the railroad would link up within a week or so. Then he would be free to leave, to take her back home to Virginia where they could begin to build a normal life together. Where T.J. Callahan would no longer be a threat to their peace of mind.

The moment Keene picked up the fresh tracks, he knew that Indians had not carried off the railroad sleepers. Earlier, the prints had been mixed and jumbled with those of the railroaders. But with these new tracks, he recognized a hoof print he had seen before. No worker on the Union Pacific would have reason to come this far away from the railroad bed—and no Indians wore boots or drove a wagon.

Keene continued to track the tell-tale sign for another hour, but he had long since guessed where it would lead. He finally dismounted and continued on foot.

He followed the tracks to the rim of a canyon. Keene tied Duke to a nearby conifer and walked over to the edge. Hunching down, his gray-eyed gaze swept the face of the steep declivity. Just as he suspected, Keene saw the missing railroad ties strewn haphazardly along the ragged slope below.

He stood up and walked back to his horse. Mounting Duke, he rode away from the Circle C.

Chapter Sixteen

Preparing to ride back to town the following morning, Thomas had just saddled his horse when Keene MacKenzie returned to camp. When the scout saw Thomas, he rode over to him.

"You comin' or goin', Doc?"

"Going," Thomas said. "I'm heading back to Ogden now. Haven't seen my wife in days. There's been a lot of excitement around here since you've been gone; some men were hurt in a blast, and there was some trouble with the Indians. I'm looking forward to getting back to a hot bath and a comfortable bed."

"Bet that ain't all you're looking forward to, Doc," Keene said, grinning.

Thomas arched a brow. "Yeah. Peace and quiet."

"Well, if you want company, I'll ride back with

you. I'll just be a couple minutes."

"You bet." Thomas swung down from the saddle and tied his mount to a tree to wait for Keene.

Michaleen came over to them, his head swathed in a bandage and his red tam sitting on top of the dressing. "A good day, gentlemen."

"What in hell happened to you?" Keene asked.

"One of them black-hearted heathens lifted me scalp," Michaleen declared. "And the doctar sewed it back on."

Keene's incredulous glance swung to Thomas. Laughing, he said, "You sewed it back on?"

Thomas shook his head. "I told you. I can't make any promises, Michaleen. The roots will die and you'll lose the hair."

"Hell, who'll be able to tell with that bush he's got on top of his head," Keene said.

"At least I'll have me scalp altogether," the little man said proudly. "Would you be likin' a fresh egg for breakfast, Mr. MacKenzie?"

"You got time for me to eat before we go?" Keene asked. Thomas nodded. "How about throwin' in a steak with those eggs, Michaleen?" Keene said.

The cook was elated. "And some fried potatoes?"

"Sure, why not," Keene agreed. "Haven't had anything 'cept a piece of jerky since yesterday morning."

"What about you, Doctar?" Michaleen asked.

"Well, maybe a couple of eggs and a few of those biscuits you just baked," Thomas replied.

"No potatoes?" the little man asked, somewhat aghast.

"Not this time, Michaleen."

"You find those missing risers?" Thomas asked after Michaleen departed.

Keene nodded. "Looks like it was somebody from the Circle C—or somebody who made it look that way. One thing's for sure, it wasn't Indians."

Thomas emitted a long, low whistle. "Hope Callahan knows what he's doing. Destroying railroad property can get him in trouble. He'll end up with the government on his back."

"Yeah," Keene said.

"You going to report it to Jack Casement?"

"I thought I'd try and talk to T.J. first. If he does it again, guess I'll have to report him," Keene said solemnly.

As they spoke, Murphy arrived with the morning supply train. Mike Rafferty climbed off with six men and immediately began barking commands at the new crewman to unload the supplies.

"Hey, Murph, you going back to town?" Thomas said to the engineer.

"Yeah, as soon as I get unloaded. Casement's in town waiting for the payroll to come in."

"We could ride back with him," Thomas suggested to Keene. "You got room for a couple passengers?"

"My pleasure, Doc," Murphy declared.

"Murphy, me friend," Michaleen called out. "Would you be likin' some fresh eggs this marning?" He set down a tin plate before Thomas and Keene.

"Ate in town," Murphy said.

Michaleen frowned. "Why wud ya be wastin' your hard-earned money when you could be enjoyin' the cookin' of Michaleen Dennehy? You'll be dyin' a poor man, Murphy."

"Yeah, but I'll be dying a lot later in life," Murphy joked.

The remark produced a round of laughter, but the smile left Michaleen's face when Rafferty came marching over to them. "Dennehy, as soon as these greenhorns finish unloadin' this train, I'll have a couple of those eggs of yours," the crew boss declared.

"Just used the last one, Rafferty," Michaleen said.

Mike Rafferty's mouth curled with a snarl. "You're lyin', you little runt. I oughta find them and shove them down your throat, shells and all." He hiked up his trousers and stomped away. "All right, you men. Get those cars unhitched," he shouted to the new arrivals.

The men scurried to unhitch the freight cars and shove them to a siding. "Come on, move your asses," Rafferty ordered. "We ain't got all day."

He pointed to one of the new arrivals. "Unhitch that car."

"I never did it before, sir," the young man said.

"Then it's about time you learn," Rafferty declared. He stepped between the two cars and pulled the heavy metal pin out of the coupling that linked the cars together. "All right, get this car off the track." The six men shoved the car to the siding.

"You come to work or to watch?" he snarled to the young man. "Unhitch the next car."

The man moved quickly to obey. He stepped between the two cars as he had seen Rafferty do and pulled the pin from the coupling. Before he could step away, the car rolled back into the other one, crushing him between the two cars. His pitiful cry of pain jolted the others to action.

They shoved the car forward, and the hapless man slumped to the ground.

Thomas bolted to his feet at the sound of the man's cry. Retrieving the medical bag tied to his saddle, he knelt over the unconscious man. After a quick examination, he glanced up at the circle of men around him. "This man has internal injuries. He needs extensive care. We've got to get him back to town."

Murphy didn't wait to hear any more. He jumped into the cab of the train while the others unhitched the cars. After he turned the train around on a siding, a flatbed was coupled to the tender. Using a cot as a makeshift litter, the men lifted the injured man onto the car.

Not wanting to waste any more time by loading the horses, Keene waved them on. "I'll bring your horse back to town, Doc."

Murphy raced "Old Betsy" back to Ogden.

Rory and Kathleen were in front of the office when the train screeched into town. Startled, the two women stepped aside as the men carrying the cot hurried past them.

"Thomas, what happened?" Rory asked.

"Later, Rory. I don't have time to talk now," he said, brushing past her.

Having not seen him for a day, Rory recognized his urgency but felt a sense of disappointment at his sharp tone. When the men traipsed out of the building, Kathleen asked her husband what had happened.

"The damn fool got himself crushed between two cars," Rafferty grumbled. "Come on and fix me somethin' to eat. Haven't had a bite yet this mornin'." With a sympathetic backward glance at Rory, Kathleen left with him.

For the next hour, Rory paced back and forth in front of the door. The only entrance to their quarters was through the office, and she didn't wish to disturb Thomas.

Meanwhile, Caleb Murphy wasted no time reporting the latest disaster to Jack Casement. Small in stature, the forty-year-old ex-general looked threatening as he headed toward the medical office. Seeing his approach, Rory tapped on the office door, then opened it.

Thomas was washing his hands. "Thomas, Mr. Casement is here." At the sight of his grim look, she glanced at the examination table. The still figure was covered with a sheet. Her compassionate glance swung back to her husband. "I'm sorry, Thomas. I'm sure you did all that was humanly possible."

Jack Casement appeared in the doorway. "Doctor Graham, I heard that one of my . . ."

His words died when he took in the scene.

"He was just a kid, Casement. Couldn't have been more than fifteen or sixteen. There was no reason for him to lose his life." The construction boss went over and lifted up the sheet to look at the face of the dead man.

"He should have been properly trained for the job he was given to do," Thomas said. Angrily, he tossed aside the towel he had been using to dry his hands. "Don't you men have any conscience? Doesn't a young boy's life mean anything? Why, when you're this close to being finished, do you continue to jeopardize lives?"

"I feel just as badly about it as you do," Casement said. "From the time we left Omaha, I've watched good men die. Young and old alike. The building of this railroad has been like waging a war. These men have died for a good cause, Doctor."

"You think so, Mr. Casement? Is there really a *good cause* worth the sacrifice of life, sir?"

"Didn't you serve in the recent war, Doctor? You must have felt your belief was worth dying for."

"I was a survivor, sir. The answer to your question is buried with the ones who didn't survive."

"I suppose you're right, Doctor." He stepped outside and issued orders to the men who waited. Four of them came in and removed the young man's body.

"Rafferty," Casement called out when the foreman returned and joined the others.

The group halted and the big Irishman

stepped forward. "Yeah, watta ya want?"

"Rafferty, pick up your wages and get out. I'm tired of the trouble you're always causing. It's getting so that I hear complaints about you every day. This latest accident is your fault."

"You sayin' it's my fault the damn fool got himself killed?"

"That's right. Only a veteran switchman can uncouple cars, and you damn well know it. You had no business ordering that greenhorn to do it."

"Sure, now that your damned railroad is almost finished, Mike Rafferty ain't good enough to work for ya. Didn't hear ya complainin' when my crew was layin' more track than the others."

"Rafferty, I'm not arguing with you. You're through as of now." Casement walked away, followed by the others, and Mike Rafferty was left standing alone casting black glares in the direction of the construction boss.

Rory and Thomas watched him from the door of the office. After a glowering look in their direction, he stormed off toward the tents.

"Poor Kathleen," Rory said sorrowfully. "That brute will probably take his frustration out on her."

"Not if I can help it," Thomas said. He followed the man. When Rafferty turned off toward the saloon, Thomas started to return to the office.

Suddenly a Circle C cowpoke stepped into his path. Thomas recognized the man as one of his abductors the night Callahan had whipped him.

Clearly inebriated, the cowboy swayed unsteadily on his feet. "Thought you'd be long gone by now, greenhorn."

"Well, as you can see, I'm not, cowboy."

" 'Pears T.J. didn't teach you a good enough lesson." His words were slurred. "Never did have much use for you Eastern dandies, much less a damn Reb."

"I have to say I feel the same way about loud-mouth drunks."

The confrontation had begun to attract attention. A small crowd had assembled and were listening to the exchange. From the doorway of the office, Rory saw the mob and hurried over to see what was happening.

The Circle C cowboy raised his clenched fists. " 'Pears I'm gonna have to teach you a lesson on my own."

The unsettled score with these men was still a sensitive issue with Thomas. And feeling the after-effects of the recent unfortunate death of the young man, he now had no patience for mincing words with this drunken cowpoke.

"Cowboy, you couldn't do anything on your own except piss in your pants." He took his open palm, shoved it into the face of the cowboy, and sent him reeling backwards. Water splashed in all directions as the cowboy plopped down into the horse trough.

Without a further word, Thomas turned and walked away. Rory chased after him.

"Thomas, that's Gus Jennings. He rides for the Circle C. You shouldn't have humiliated him that way."

Exasperated, he stopped, turning his angry glare on her. "Is that so? Well, your Mr. Jennings happens to be one of the men who abducted us."

"Gus was only following my father's orders, Thomas; he's the one to blame."

"Well, Gus appears to take pleasure in carrying out those kinds of orders."

"You don't understand us at all, Thomas," she explained. "When you ride for a ranch . . . well, you develop a special kind of loyalty to that brand."

For a long moment he stared at her, appalled. "No matter what you're told to do?"

"Well . . . yes."

"That's not the way I operate, Rory. That kind of loyalty could be misbegotten." He resumed walking.

"What happened with Rafferty?" she asked as soon as they entered the office.

"Rafferty?" He had already put that issue out of his mind. "Oh . . . he headed for the saloon."

Yawning, Thomas sank down on the bed. "God, I'm tired." Lying back, he closed his eyes and within seconds had fallen asleep.

Disappointed, Rory tiptoed over to the bed. He hadn't said more than a few sentences to her since his return—and those had been said in anger. No matter how much he denied it, he held her accountable for her father's actions, the same way he held Gus Jennings. The rift between them was widening.

Sighing, she pulled off his boots and covered

him with a light quilt. They would have to talk when he awoke.

With Thomas asleep in the bedroom, she decided to visit with Kathleen. Inasmuch as Michael Rafferty had been fired from the railroad, there was no telling how much longer her friend would remain in Ogden. Kathleen was surprised to see her.

"Have you heard the bad news, Kathleen?" Rory asked. Her green eyes were dark with despair.

"The young man died, I'm fearin'," Kathleen said.

Rory nodded. "And Mr. Casement has fired your husband."

Kathleen sank down on the cot. Her eyes welled with tears. "Then I'm thinkin' we'll be leavin' soon."

"Do you have any idea where you'll be going?" Rory asked.

Kathleen shrugged. "I've not a notion."

"Stay here in Ogden, Kathleen," Rory blurted out. "You can't possibly love Michael Rafferty. Don't go with that brute."

"I can't do that," Kathleen said sadly. "He's my husband. We are joined in the eyes of the church."

Kathleen was near to crying, something she had schooled herself against doing. The thought of never seeing Rory again—or Keene—was heartbreaking to her. In her heart she'd known that she would have to face this moment someday, but the time had come so unexpectedly, she was unprepared for it.

Forcing back her tears, she rose to her feet. "You best leave before Mike returns. I'm thinkin' his mood will be a nasty one."

"You'll come to stay good-bye before you leave, won't you?"

Kathleen nodded. "Aye, Rory."

Fearing she would break down and upset Kathleen more, Rory hurried back to the office.

With every drink Mike Rafferty swallowed, his mood grew blacker. He felt he had been treated unjustly by Casement. For the past two years, he had worked his ass off for the railroad and this was the thanks he got. He thought of the struggle fighting the Sioux, the arduous passes of the Rockies, the Wyoming hills. Now, when the job was almost done, they had no more use for him.

The more he thought about it, the angrier he became. He'd talk to Casement one more time. Maybe the construction boss had cooled down enough by now to regret the hasty action of firing him. The railroad still had need of a good worker like Mike Rafferty. Slamming down his glass, he stormed out of the saloon.

When Rafferty reached the special car used to transport the payroll, he pounded on the door.

A stoop-shouldered old man wearing a visored hat over a head of shaggy gray hair peered out through the bars of the metal window grill. "Whatta you want?"

Recognizing Mike, the man unlocked the door and returned to dividing the payroll into various piles on the table. "Close the door," the timekeeper ordered when Rafferty climbed into the car.

"Where's Casement?" Mike grumbled.

The man motioned his head in the direction of the town. "Went to get some sandwiches and coffee. He'll be right back."

"Wanna talk to him," Rafferty declared.

"Then go outside and do it. Casement don't like anyone inside when we're dividing payroll."

"Got some wages comin' myself."

"Talk to Casement," the timekeeper replied. "I just count the money. He's the one who doles it out. Now get out of here. Nobody's got any business in here except Casement."

Turning to leave, Rafferty clenched his hands into fists. His anger boiled over. Now even this little bastard thought he could tell him what to do. Suddenly, Rafferty was struck with how he would get even with Casement, the railroad, and this little bastard ordering him about.

Before the man could guess his intent, Rafferty turned and smashed his fist into the man's face, knocking him off his stool. Blood spurted from the teller's nose, and he opened his mouth to shout for help.

The cry came out in a gasp as Rafferty shoved a knife into the chest of the unfortunate man. Haphazardly, Rafferty shoved the money into the black payroll bag. Then he slunk out of the car and hurried back to his tent.

"Let's get goin'," he ordered Kathleen.

"Goin' where?" she asked. "I haven't packed yet."

"Just grab a change of clothes," he said,

shoving a few belongings into saddlebags. "We don't need any of the rest of this junk. Quit yer cacklin' and hurry up!" he bellowed angrily.

"I promised to say good-bye to Mrs. Graham."

"Ain't time for that. Let's go or I'm leavin' ya behind." He gripped her arm in a painful grasp and hustled her to the livery.

The livery boy saddled two horses for them. Then, to Kathleen's shocked gasp, Rafferty hit the boy over the head and the young man slumped to the ground.

"What are you doing?" she asked, horrified.

"Just get mounted and let's go," he shouted. The two riders attracted little attention when they rode out of town.

A grim-faced Jack Casement bent over the dead body of the timekeeper. "It had to be someone he knew. Why else would he let anyone in here?" Angrily, he kicked aside a chair. "And the bastard's got the whole payroll too."

At that moment, one of the railroad crew came running up the car. "Mr. Casement, you better come to the livery. The stable boy's got a lump on his head the size of an apple, and he's sayin' that Mike Rafferty stole a couple of his horses."

The men hurried back to the livery, and after listening to the boy's account of what had happened, he nodded. "Well, it ain't hard to guess who stole the payroll."

He turned to the man beside him. "O'Rourke, go find that scout, MacKenzie."

Chapter Seventeen

Upon rising in the morning, Thomas walked to the window. As he started to brush aside the curtain to glance out, he stopped and fingered the checkered piece of gingham in his hand. His gaze swept the rest of the room appreciatively, marveling at the change. "I can't get over what you've done to this place, honey. It actually looks livable now."

Lying in bed, Rory leaned on her elbow and propped up her head. Her long, disheveled hair dropped over her shoulders and breasts. "Kathleen and I tried to get it all done in a single day. Had I known my beloved husband would not be home for days, we could have taken more time and done a much better job."

"Well, you two ladies are to be complimented. I'll have to think of a way of rewarding you."

"I'm afraid there's not much time for that now

that Kathleen will be leaving. I'm going to miss her so much. And I feel so sorry for her, married to that brute."

Hopping out of bed, Rory moved behind Thomas and slipped her arms around his waist. She pressed a kiss to his shoulder. "How is your back feeling?"

"How does it look?" he asked.

Her fretful glance traced the outline of the reddened welts. "Terrible."

"Well then, it feels better than it looks." He turned. Pulling her into his arms, he kissed her lightly.

When she tried to prolong the kiss, he broke away and held her at arm's length. "No you don't, you temptress. I've got to go or I'll miss the train."

Rory sighed. "Since we've returned, I see you less than before we were married." She started to walk back to the bed.

Thomas grabbed her and pulled her back into his arms. "Honey, I feel bad about leaving you alone so much. I know you're lonely."

"It's not the loneliness, Thomas. It's the boredom. I'm not used to being so inactive. I always had a lot of work to do on the ranch. I guess I'm not cut out for city life."

Thomas kissed her, then released her and began to get dressed. "You'd better get used to city life, Rory. You married a doctor, remember? When we return to Virginia, I'll be setting up my practice again." Turning around, he grinned. "But not before we go on that honeymoon I promised you. As soon as my contract's up with the railroad, we'll go to England and France," he said, hurriedly pulling on his clothes.

Returning to the bed, she slumped down on the edge. "Can we at least have breakfast together?"

"I'm late already. I'll grab something at camp." He shaved using cold water, and in less than five minutes he was bending over to give her a quick kiss. "Be good, honey. See you later tonight." At the sound of several toots from the train's whistle, he rushed out, grabbing his medical kit on the way.

Lying back, Rory sighed at the prospect of another long, lonely day ahead of her. The inactivity of city life got on her nerves, making her feel edgy and irritable. Despondent, she rose and dressed. Then she went to the diner for breakfast.

"What does your husband think about the murder and robbery last night, Rory?" the gray-haired proprietress asked, placing a pot of tea on the table before Rory.

"What murder and robbery?" she asked, surprised.

Eagerly, the woman pulled out a chair and sat down at the table to relate the incident. "You mean you haven't heard? Why the railroad's payroll was stolen and the teller murdered."

The older woman picked up the menu and rapidly began to fan herself. "Mercy me, it'll soon not be safe for a woman to walk down the street alone. Ever since this railroad's come to town, we've had nothing but trouble."

"And a lot more business, Mrs. Jackson," Rory

297

reminded her sharply. "Ogden has become a boom town since the arrival of the Union Pacific, and all you local merchants are profiting from the growth."

Callie Jackson offered a belly laugh and patted Rory's hand good-naturedly. "You're right about that, honey."

"Did the sheriff catch the culprit?"

"No. Sheriff's out of town. The two made a clean getaway, but this Casement fellow from the Union Pacific sent Keene MacKenzie to track them down."

"There are two of them?" Rory asked, alarmed. Her concern was for Keene's welfare.

"The killers are one of those railroaders and his wife. Some Irish name. Ryan or Ra—"

"Rafferty? Michael Rafferty?" Rory asked, her eyes wide with dread.

"Yeah. Rafferty. That's it."

"Oh no! It can't be," Rory said in disbelief. "I know Kathleen Rafferty very well. We've been in your diner together often. Kathleen is no robber and certainly would never be a party to any killing. If she went with her husband, I'm sure he forced her to go. The man is a brute."

"Is she that skinny little dark-haired gal you came in here with a couple days ago?"

"Yes, that was Kathleen."

"Mercy alive, she looked afraid of her own shadow. I would have thought that timid little thing couldn't hurt a fly," Callie declared. "But young Joey Ross at the livery said this Rafferty and his wife stole two horses and rode off with them."

"Well, I know Kathleen Rafferty well enough to know she was no party to any killing or robbery."

"I wonder what will become of her now that they're on the run. Oh well, if Keene doesn't find them, it's most likely Indians will." Shaking her head in sympathy, Mrs. Jackson rose to her feet. "What are you having this morning, Rory?"

"Just a couple of biscuits and jam," Rory said. Her troubled thoughts were on Kathleen. Rory's only comfort was knowing that if Keene found them, he wouldn't shoot first and ask questions later the way a posse might do.

After leaving the diner, Rory wandered around the town peering into shop windows. She thought of a dozen things she had left behind on the Circle C that could occupy her time. Then she returned to her bedroom and played solitaire.

That evening a note arrived from Thomas saying he had to remain in camp with an injured workman. In desperation, she tried to read one of his medical journals but ended up returning to a game of solitaire.

The following morning, her day took an unexpected turn when she met Pete Faber and Curly Evans on her way to the diner. Rory decided to ride back with them to the Circle C and bring back some more of her belongings.

When she told Pete her intention, he shook his head gravely. "Ain't such a good idea, Rory. Your pa's been as mean as a grizzly since you left."

"Well, I'm not going there to make a social call, Pete. And I can't believe he'd order me off the ranch." Her eyes sparked with impishness. "Besides, I've been through enough of Daddy's black moods to know how to handle him. You don't have to worry about me."

"Well, I reckon you're just as stubborn as T.J., so it don't make no sense to try and talk you out of it. Soon as we eat some grub, we're headin' back. If you're coming with us, you best get movin', girl."

"I'll change and be ready to go in a few minutes," Rory called, already heading for the door.

When they rode into the Circle C, Pete and Curly went about their business and Rory entered the house hoping to find her father. She regretted the harsh words they had exchanged at their last meeting, although she felt his beating of Thomas was unforgivable.

Finding no sign of her father, she packed up a few more of her belongings and tied them to her saddle.

Thomas returned to Ogden early in the afternoon. Finding no trace of Rory, he set off looking for her. She wasn't in the diner, general store, or the apothecary. No one recalled seeing her. Thomas even went to Rafferty's tent and Keene's lodging, knowing he wouldn't find anyone at either site.

Then he realized that the one place he should have checked out was the livery. Joey Ross told him Rory had rented a horse to ride out to the Circle C. Thinking she had ridden out alone, Thomas was beside himself with frustration.

Within minutes, he was on his way to the ranch. Rory was on the verge of leaving when Thomas thundered up on his mount.

"Damn it, Rory, what in hell do you think you're doing? These hills aren't safe for you to ride around alone."

Taken aback by his aggressive greeting, she reacted defensively. "Thomas, I've ridden these hills since I was a child. The trail between here and town is safe. The Indians never come that close to town."

"It only takes once," he grumbled. "I want your promise that you won't do this again," he said worriedly.

She glared at him angrily. "Don't speak to me as if I'm a child, Thomas. I'm perfectly safe. I know this country."

"You've got a short memory, Rory. The day I met you, you were running for your life."

Rory put her foot in the stirrup and swung up on the back of her mount. "I'm a big girl, Thomas. I can take care of myself." She goaded her horse to a gallop. Thomas wheeled his horse and followed.

"What in hell are you so mad about?" he declared, riding up beside her.

"I already have one father. I don't need another. Of course, I shouldn't complain, should I? This is the first time you've put my interests ahead of your patients."

"Did you pull this damn fool stunt just to get my attention, Rory?"

"Now you're really being ridiculous, Thomas.

301

How would I know when you were coming back to town today?"

Thomas grabbed the rein of her horse and pulled up. "I was worried about you. Is that so ridiculous?"

"I guess not. But I don't understand why you would think I would risk my life on a whim."

"Well, you have been known to be rather impetuous at times."

"Like when I married you," she snapped.

"I don't think you mean that, Rory." Both of them were feeling injured, and one disagreeable word was leading to another.

Suddenly, a rifle blast ended any further argument. "Stay here, Rory, and I'll check it out," Thomas said. Drawing his Colt, he headed toward a nearby rise. He turned at the sound of hoofbeats behind him. "Damn it, Rory, I told you to wait behind."

"Next time, try asking," she snapped and goaded her horse forward.

They crested the rise and reined up. Nearby, T.J. Callahan and several of the Circle C riders were gathered under a tree holding two Indians captive. The small circle of men swung their attention to the approach of the riders.

One of the Indians used that brief moment to dash toward the cover of trees. Callahan raised his rifle and took aim.

"Callahan, stop!" Thomas cried out. But the rancher ignored him. Callahan pulled the trigger and the Indian fell to the ground.

Thomas dismounted and hurried over to the figure on the ground. After a quick examination, he shook his head and stood up. "He's dead." He glanced in contempt at the rancher. "He's just a boy, Callahan. Unarmed. It wasn't necessary to shoot him in the back."

"He tried to get away," the rancher growled.

"Anyone on horseback could have ridden him down," Thomas said. "What did he do?"

"I ask the questions around here, railroader," Callahan snarled. "I warned you to stay away from here. 'Pears I didn't teach you lesson enough."

"Daddy, he came with me," Rory interjected, stepping between the two men. She put her hand on his arm. "What happened here, Daddy?" she said gently, distracting her father's attention away from Thomas.

"Caught these two young bucks on the Circle C. They're up to no good, I'm sure."

"But they're unarmed, Daddy, and they're not wearing paint," she pointed out.

"That don't matter none. I don't want any of these thieves and killers snoopin' around my ranch." He threw a disgruntled glance at Thomas. "Same goes for you railroaders. Get movin'."

Thomas walked back and mounted his horse. Seeing Rory had remained at Callahan's side, he said, "Let's go, Rory." He motioned to the Indian, a young boy in his early teens. "Come on, son, you can ride behind me."

"That redskin ain't goin' nowhere 'til I'm through with him. String him up, boys."

As one of the riders tossed a rope over the branch of a tree, two of the other men grabbed the boy and tied his hands behind his back. "You're insane, Callahan," Thomas shouted. "You aren't the law here. Furthermore, this boy's committed no crime."

"And he ain't gonna have the chance to either," Callahan smirked. "That's Stalking Moon, Spotted Deer's son. Hanging the son of the chief will teach these rotten savages to ride clear of the Circle C. Get him on a horse, boys."

The cowhands lifted the boy to the back of a horse and led the animal over to the dangling noose.

Rory gasped aloud when Thomas drew his Colt and pointed it at the rancher. "I won't let you do this, Callahan. Release him now." The cowboys waited for the word of their leader.

Callahan smirked. "You're bluffin', railroader. You don't have a chance against my boys. You'll have a dozen bullets in you before you even hit the ground."

"Maybe so. But I will get off a shot, won't I, Callahan? If you think hanging that boy is worth dying over, then call my bluff," Thomas said calmly.

"Why should it stick in your craw anyway, railroader? You Johnny Rebs never have any fret about hanging darkies when it suits your fancy."

"Callahan, I don't think you should try to judge all Southerners by the actions of a few, anymore than I'd judge all Westerners by the actions of a bastard like you."

"Well, you shoot me and Rory will never forgive you," Callahan boasted confidently.

"Won't much matter if I'm dead, now will it, Mr. Callahan?"

Rory had listened to the exchange as long as she could. "Daddy, please. Do what Thomas says before someone gets hurt."

Everyone waited tensely as the two determined men tried to stare each other down. Finally Callahan nodded. "Okay, boys, cut the sonnabitch loose." A cowhand slashed the bonds of Stalking Moon.

"All right, son. Ride out of here," Thomas ordered.

The young boy spoke for the first time. "I take Eyes of Hawk." He led the horse over to the body on the ground.

"Couple of you men give him a hand there," Thomas ordered.

Two of the cowhands lifted the body and laid it across the boy's lap. With a final look at Thomas, Stalking Moon rode away.

Thomas holstered his pistol. "What did I tell you, girl? You gonna be happy married to a man who was willin' to gun down your pa?" Callahan asked triumphantly.

Rory's stomach was tied in knots. It now appeared to her that the rift between her father and Thomas was unbreachable. "Thomas would never have shot you, Daddy." The tone of her voice lacked conviction, and Callahan recognized that.

Smiling smugly, he looked at Thomas. "Reckon you just hung yourself, railroader. I know my daughter. She ain't ever gonna forget the sight of your gun pointed at her father's head. Hanging you was more pleasurable than hanging any redskin," he boasted.

Thomas looked at his wife. "You coming, Rory?" For a fraction of a moment she hesitated, as if to say something. "Or is this still another example of misbegotten loyalty?"

She climbed on her horse, and Callahan's booming laughter followed as they rode away.

Rory and Thomas spoke very little to each other on the trip back to town. The sun had set by the time they reached Ogden. Thomas returned the horses to the livery, and by the time he got back to the office, Rory had retired.

"Don't you want something to eat, honey?" he asked.

"No. I'm not hungry, Thomas. I would just like to go to bed."

"I think we should talk, Rory."

"Tomorrow, Thomas," she said. Rory closed her eyes. When he left and went into his office, she opened them, staring at the ceiling, deep in thought. She had a problem to resolve. But how?

Later when Thomas came to bed, Rory pretended to be asleep. He made no attempt to pull her into his arms. She lay on her side on the far side of the bed without moving a muscle until the steady pattern of his breathing indicated that he was asleep.

Tears streaked her cheeks as she continued to stare into the dark. The battle between Thomas and her father was building a wall between her and her husband. She didn't know what to do. She didn't know what to say. She wanted to sit down and have a good cry, hoping that the tears would flush away the problem.

Rory finally fell asleep sometime near dawn. She didn't hear Thomas get up in the morning and never felt the kiss he pressed on her lips when he departed.

She awoke to another day of loneliness. Another day of nothing to do, no one to talk to. Kathleen gone. Keene gone. Thomas always off with the railroad.

She paced the floor, wondering if she should ride out to the Circle C to try to talk some sense into her father. Remembering how upset Thomas was the previous day with her for riding out there discouraged any further consideration of . that idea. How she regretted that hasty act now. If she hadn't gone there yesterday, Thomas would never have followed. And if Thomas hadn't followed, they never would have encountered her father. Or Stalking Moon.

Some good comes out of every bad, she told herself. But what good could come out of the senseless slaying of a young boy and the near tragedy of Thomas and her father almost killing one another?

Frustrated, she threw herself on the bed. She began to sob and buried her head in the pillow. Sometime, as the sun began to sink below the granite peaks, she fell asleep.

Returning home that evening, Thomas was surprised not to see the reflection of a light from either the office window or the bedroom.

The door was unlocked. Cautiously, he turned

the handle and stepped into the darkened room, uncertain of what he would find. He felt a rising feeling of alarm.

He moved silently to the closed door of the bedroom. His chest felt constricted as he eased open the door. The shaft of moonlight revealed the figure on the bed. For a moment, he felt a sense of panic and rushed over to the bed. Then he saw the even rise and fall of her chest and realized that Rory was only sleeping.

Momentarily, he closed his eyes in a quick gesture of relief. As he stood in the darkened room, lit only by a shaft of moonlight gleaming through the lone window, Thomas studied the sleeping face of his wife.

Sometime in her sleep, Rory had turned over on her back. Her auburn hair was splayed in glorious disarray across the white pillow. Her features were cast in shadows, but the curve of the exquisite cheeks, the delicate sweep of her jaw, the slender nose, and the soft, sensual lips were all blazoned on his mind.

He shucked his gun belt and tossed aside his jacket and boots, then he lay down beside her.

Rory stirred in her sleep and felt her body responding to the sensuous slide of warm lips down her neck. She felt the pleasant tightening of arousal drawing at her loins, and the peaks of her breasts hardened. A moan of pleasure escaped her, and she parted her lips.

A firm, exciting mouth closed over hers and brought an instant response. Her lips yielded to the probing intrusion of his tongue. Reaching out instinctively, she embraced the hard body that moved to cover her.

She trembled, every nerve end in her body now attuned to the male essence of him as his mouth continued to consume her. Under the ravishing hunger of the kiss, her passion spiraled out of control.

Slowly, he raised his head, his dark eyes fixed on the sensual invitation in her eyes. Then he slowly closed the gap that separated them. Once again she parted her lips to accept the tender and warm mouth that closed over her own.

She felt crazed with lust. He had intended to make tender love to her, but all the pent-up frustration and energy she had been struggling with erupted into a fiery, tempestuous response that sent his own passion escalating.

Their tongues dueled as they pulled at one another's clothing until they were naked. There was no attempt to make love, only to mate.

His mouth ravished her breasts and she wrapped her legs around him, grinding herself against him. Her hands groped for his hard arousal, to drive it into herself. He rolled on his back and she now straddled him, pressing against him, the mat of dark hair on his chest brushing the sensitive peaks of her breast.

His mouth closed around her breast and he feasted on one and then the other. Stretching out her full length, she delighted in the feel of her nakedness against his.

He slipped his hand lower to the core of her desire, and she groaned aloud when he probed the opening. In mindless ecstasy she mounted him, and their taut bodies moved in a rhythmic dance until they both reached the peak.

He pulled her head to his and reclaimed her lips, draining her of her remaining breath. Exhausted, she slumped on top of him and for several moments only the sound of their rasped breathing invaded the silence.

Finally, Thomas rolled over, sliding her off him. She got out of bed and pulled on her robe. "What's the matter, Rory?" he asked.

Usually after they made love she felt drowsy, but tonight her nerves felt on edge. Sleep was out of the question. "I don't know. Just restless, I guess." Having no other room to go to, she tossed aside her robe and climbed back into bed. She lay stiffly on her side beside him with her hands tucked under her cheek.

"Something's bothering you."

She turned over on her back and brushed the hair away from her face. "I don't know what you mean."

"I hope to God this has nothing to do with your father."

"I still don't know what you're talking about," she snapped back angrily, recognizing that he had touched on the very truth she hadn't been willing to admit even to herself.

"I think you do. You're angry about the incident with your father, aren't you?"

"Well, as long as you've brought up the issue, I do think you could have handled it differently. Was it really necessary to pull a gun on him?"

"No, I suppose not. I could have let him hang an innocent boy."

"That's not what I mean and you know it," she said angrily.

"He would have. And you all would have stood by and let him. Well, I'm sorry, Rory. These scars on my back may be souvenirs from the Circle C, but I'm not wearing its brand."

Rory sat up, clutching the sheet to her breasts. "What are you implying? I am? I'm tired of being in the middle between you and my father, Thomas. You knew who I was when you married me."

"Sure, but when I married you, I never bargained on T.J. Callahan climbing in bed with us every night."

"And when I married you, I never bargained on sleeping alone most of my nights, either," she shouted back.

"Well, then, I'll remind you of something as well. You knew I was a doctor when you married me."

"And I don't like your patients climbing in bed with us either." Rory bolted out of bed again.

"I have a responsibility to my patients, Rory."

Her red hair flared out in a swirl as she snapped her head around and glared at him. "And I have one to my father."

Thomas Graham had always been able to address most confrontations calmly and rationally. However, he suspected that T.J. Callahan would always be a threat to his marriage. He also feared Callahan's mocking word held more than a grain of truth. Rory's attachment to her father appeared to be a grave issue that would continue to rise between them.

"That's what this is all about, isn't it? This argument has nothing to do with responsibilities. Your father was right, wasn't he? Daddy's little girl can't be loyal to any man except Daddy. Right or wrong, *Daddy* will always be right."

"That's unfair. I recognize my father's weaknesses, but I still love him. Whatever he says and does regarding our marriage, he's acting out of hurt pride because he's losing his daughter. I would think you would understand that. But you won't even try."

"I find it difficult to feel sympathy for a man who would shoot down an unarmed young boy and was prepared to hang another one."

"Daddy is used to range justice. That is what helped him to stay alive all these years. He'll change now that the territory is changing. You'll see."

"No, Rory. You're deluding yourself. Your father will never change."

"Then pity him, don't condemn him. You're tolerant of others. Or is your sympathy and understanding only reserved for your patients because there you get to play God? The omnipotent Doctor Thomas Graham. Knows all. Cures all. To hell with a wife's needs—or her father's."

Thomas rose from bed. Naked, he walked over and grasped her by the shoulders. "You don't really believe that, do you, Rory? I love you. Your interests come ahead of anyone in my life. But I've taken an oath to try to save lives."

"To play God, you mean," she lashed out.

She saw the pain in his eyes. "Think what

you want, Rory. You always have. Nobody can change your thinking. But if you believe I presume to play God by trying to save lives, what do you think your father does by destroying them?"

A loud rapping at the door interrupted them. Pulling on his trousers, Thomas opened the door to a distraught woman holding an unconscious young boy of about ten.

"I'm Mrs. O'Grady. Me husband is a gauger with the railroad, and we're livin' in Tent Town. I'm sorry to be botherin' you at such an hour, but my son Danny's real sick, sir. You've got to help me. I'm fearin' the lad is dyin'."

Thomas lifted the boy out of her arms and laid him down gently on the examination table. "What are his symptoms, Mrs. O'Grady?" After taking the youngster's pulse, he grabbed his stethoscope.

"Oh, Doctor, the lad's feverishly high and he says he has a pain in his side."

"Watch him while I finish dressing, Mrs. O'Grady. And try to keep him from moving if possible."

"I will, Doctor, and God bless you," she said, casting aside her shawl.

Thomas returned to the bedroom and began to dress. "I'm sorry, Rory. This is an emergency."

"I heard," she said.

"We can finish our talk when I'm done."

"I won't be here, Thomas. I'm going to the Circle C. I think my father needs me much more at this time than you do. Besides, it will give

313

me something to do with my time during the day . . . and night."

"When do you intend to return?"

"I don't know."

His eyes deepened with frustration. "Rory, I don't have time for this. A boy could be dying. Please wait and we'll discuss this as soon as I'm through."

Her eyes softened and she felt the swell of tenderness and love in her heart for him. "Go to the boy, Thomas. You'll save him. I know you will." For a long moment his pleading eyes remained fixed on her, then he turned and left the room.

As he performed surgery on the herniated appendix of the young boy, Thomas was unaware when Rory slipped out the door.

Chapter Eighteen

Keene's instincts had been right when he figured Rafferty would head west rather than east. He picked up the trail of two horses—one a deep impression, the other carrying a much lighter rider. He was certain they were Rafferty's and Kathleen's.

At midday, from the vantage point of a high ridge, he caught sight of the two riders in a distant clearing below, not more than a couple of hours ahead of him. He glanced up at the sky. Dark clouds were rolling in, and he knew they were in for a storm.

About a mile farther, he reined up sharply at the sight of the muddled hoofprints that crossed the trail. At least four horses from what he could observe. The tracks indicated that the riders had begun to follow the same trail.

After several more miles, he climbed down

from Duke to examine some horse spoor. The animal had been fed on wild grass, with no sign of oats in the droppings. Keene figured they must be Indian ponies.

Evidently, he wasn't the only one trailing the Raffertys.

Now, concerned for Kathleen's welfare, he climbed on Duke and goaded him to a gallop.

Kathleen reined up her horse and climbed off. "Mike, my horse is limpin'. I'm thinkin' there's somethin' wrong with it."

Disgruntled, Mike Rafferty turned, mouthing an angry snarl. "What'd you say?"

"My horse is limpin'." She stooped to examine the animal's leg.

Rafferty dismounted and walked back to her. "Get out of the way," he grumbled and shoved her aside. After a cursory examination, he stood up. "Horse has gone lame."

"What do we do now, Michael?"

"Shut up, so's I can think."

"Should I make coffee while we're waitin'?"

"Coffee? Whatta ya think I'm gonna do? Stay here 'til the damn horse gets better?" he snarled. "Give me a hand transferrin' this stuff in your saddle." He started stuffing her few pieces of clothing into his saddlebags.

"Don't know why I bothered bringin' you with me anyway. All you're doin' is slowin' me up." When he finished, Rafferty tied her blanket to his saddle.

Fatigued, Kathleen brushed aside the hair from her face. A rolling rumble caused her to

316

glance skyward. "It's blowin' up to a storm."

"We'll haveta find some cover." He climbed back on his horse. When Kathleen didn't follow, he snapped, "Whatta ya waitin' for?"

"What about the horse? It's lame and defenseless. We just can't leave it."

"I ain't got time to worry about a damn horse. And I sure as hell ain't gonna waste a bullet on it." Rafferty didn't add that if they were being followed, a gunshot would attract a posse.

"You comin' or ain't ya?" he said when she continued to hesitate. "Don't much matter to me one way or another."

With a sorrowful glance at the lame horse, Kathleen climbed up behind Rafferty.

After about a mile, large raindrops began to splatter the dust on the trail. Rafferty headed for a nearby copse of trees. "We'll take cover in here."

Dismounting, he immediately issued an order. "I'll take care of the horse. You find some wood before it all gets wet."

Wood was plentiful, but Michael insisted that she build just a small fire to avoid attracting attention. In a short time, Kathleen sat huddled before the fire, waiting for a pot of coffee to brew.

"Why did we leave Ogden in such a hurry, Michael?" Nothing about their hasty departure made sense to the confused woman.

"I had another big fight with Casement," he grumbled.

"Well, fight or not, there's no cause not to be packin' our belongings and bringin' some food."

"You tellin' me now what to do?" he snorted. "Just somethin' more to be totin'. We can get grub in the next town."

"Where are we anyway?" she asked out of curiosity. "How far *is* it to the next town?"

"How would I know?" he growled. "We're headin' west on a trail. You don't hafta know more than that. If you're so worried about eatin', try chewin' on your tongue and quit the damn yappin'," he snarled.

"Well, why would you be stealin' the horses, Michael? And what if you hurt that boy?"

He backhanded her across the face. "Stop naggin' me with questions. Go to sleep or somethin' because as soon as it stops rainin', we're leavin'." He wrapped himself up in a blanket and closed his eyes.

Kathleen tried to do the same, but sleep failed her. As she had throughout the day, she began thinking about Keene MacKenzie. Knowing she would never see him again, she shut her eyes to squeeze back her tears. Her heart ached so much, she thought it would burst. Never again to see his tall figure striding toward her, never to look again into his silvery eyes, and never again to her the sound of his husky drawl. But this was the penance she must serve for her sinful feelings about him, she told herself.

In torment, she lay listening to the distant thunder until the nearby snoring of her husband distracted her. Finally, she abandoned the attempt to sleep and decided to put on a shawl to ward off the rain when they continued the ride.

Kathleen went over to the horse. As

she rummaged through the saddlebags, she pulled out a thick pouch. Perplexed, she couldn't remember ever seeing the sack before. She lifted the pouch out of the saddlebags and sat down to examine its contents.

Her eyes rounded with astonishment when she discovered that the sack was filled with currency. "Saints alive!" she exclaimed. "There must be thousands of dollars here!"

Kathleen glanced at the sleeping figure of her husband. Michael had told her he couldn't afford to buy horses, yet he had a pouch full of money. And wherever did he ever get such an amount? she wondered.

Then, with shocking clarity, she realized the truth. He had stolen this money. That explained why they'd had to leave Ogden so hurriedly—to sneak out of town like thieves in the night.

She jerked in alarm and dropped the pouch when Rafferty coughed and rolled over. Her frightened glance swung to the figure on the ground as she held her breath, too afraid even to breathe lest he discover her.

Her fears were justified. He opened his eyes. "Whatta ya doin' back there, woman?"

"I'm just relievin' myself," she replied in a quavering voice. She nudged the pouch into the shrubbery with her knee.

As Rafferty stood up, something flew past his head that sounded like the whirring flutter of a bird's wings. He ducked instinctively and turned his head to see the quivering shaft of an arrow embedded in the tree behind him.

319

Another arrow whizzed by.

"Indians!" Michael shouted, throwing himself to the ground. Drawing his pistol, he scanned the trees around them. He fired a shot when one of the Indians dashed between trees. When another followed, Rafferty fired off several more shots.

"They're tryin' to move in closer," he said. Petrified, Kathleen hunched lower.

Rafferty pulled the trigger several more times until only a hollow click sounded. With a vile curse, he threw down the empty pistol and crawled over to the horse.

"Gotta get out of here before we're surrounded." He clambered into the saddle. In a low crouch, Kathleen ran over to climb up behind him.

"Can't take ya." He shoved her aside. "It'd be too slow carryin' two."

He goaded the horse, and Kathleen clutched at his leg in desperation. "Don't leave me behind, Mike. Please," she pleaded.

"Get away," he snarled. He kicked free, knocking her to the ground and galloped away. Whooping, two feathered riders burst from nearby trees in pursuit.

Kathleen lay sobbing. "Don't leave me, Mike. Please, don't leave me."

She sensed their presence rather than heard them. Raising her head, she stared up horrified at the two red-skinned figures standing above her.

They looked to her like specters from hell. Their faces were painted hideously with wide black circles around their eyes and red-and-white stripes streaking their foreheads and cheeks.

At her terrified scream, their mouths twisted into cruel leers and the two pounced on her, ripping at her clothing.

A rifle blast literally lifted one of the savages off her. He was dead before he hit the ground. When the other Indian reached for a knife, Keene grasped the rifle barrel and swung the stock, striking the savage across the side of the head. The blow knocked him aside. Sobbing hysterically, Kathleen crawled away.

Blood streamed from the Indian's temple as he rolled over and jumped to his feet. Brandishing a battle axe, he leaped at Keene.

The scout raised his rifle and pumped a shot that caught the attacker in mid-air. The Indian sprawled dead at Keene's feet.

Keene rushed over to where Kathleen sat huddled. He fell to his knees and pulled her into his arms. Flinging her arms around his neck, she clung to him, choking on the wrenching sobs that racked her body.

"Hush, little one," he murmured soothingly. He laid his cheek against her head and held her. "You're safe now, Kathleen. Nobody's going to hurt you."

"It's . . . it's really you?" she managed to babble between sobs. "It's really you?"

When her sobs had subsided somewhat, Keene said softly, "Kathleen, we've got to get out of here before those other Indians come back." With a shuddering sigh, she released her grasp from around his neck. "Do you think you can stand?"

She nodded, but her knees threatened to buckle as she rose to her feet. Her fingers clutched at the torn front of her gown.

Keene pulled off his buckskin tunic, and slipped it over her head. "Here, wear this. Can you walk? I've got Duke in the bushes about a quarter of a mile from here. I don't want to leave you alone."

Hearing the words leave you sent her into a panic. She grabbed frantically at his hand. "No, don't leave me, Keene," she cried out desperately. "I'm beggin' you, Keene, please don't leave me."

He faced her, clasping her shoulders in a firm grasp. "Kathleen, look at me," he said kindly. She shifted her eyes to meet his steady gaze—the calm silvery eyes she had feared she would never look into again. "I won't leave you, Kathleen. You must trust me. I won't leave you."

His glance swept the small circle. Seeing the abandoned blankets, he stooped down and picked up Rafferty's. Kathleen saw her own blanket near the bushes and went over to get it. As she bent down, she saw the pouch that she had taken out of the saddlebags.

"The money," she murmured, picking up the pouch.

"Money?" he asked warily. He didn't want to believe she had been a party to Rafferty's crime.

"I found this pouch in Michael's saddlebags. 'Tis full of money, Keene. And I'm thinkin'

Michael got it by no good means."

"Yeah, like murder," he said laconically.

"Murder!" Her blue eyes rounded with shock.

Keene took the pouch. "I'll tell you about it later. We've got to get moving. When those bucks get back, they'll probably try to pick up our trail." Taking her by the hand, he hurried through the trees.

Glancing behind, Michael Rafferty saw that the two riders were gaining on him. He tried to goad the horse to a faster gait, cursing the animal when it did not respond.

The first arrow caught him high in the back, the second one lower. He lost his grip on the reins and toppled to the ground. The riderless horse sped on.

Mike tried to run, but the next arrow slammed into his right thigh, knocking him off his feet. The big Irishman clambered to his feet and stumbled forward. His pursuers began to play with him. Riding up on each side of him, they bumped him with their horses. Laughing in enjoyment at their sport, they continued to jostle the stumbling man from one horse to another.

Too weak to go on, Mike fell to his knees. The sound of a gunshot echoed through the hills. The two riders glanced back at the trail they had just covered and ended their sport with Mike. One leaped off his horse and sunk a tomahawk into Mike's skull.

While the other Ute grabbed the reins of the horse, Mike's attacker drew a knife and ripped the scalp off the dead man.

As the Indian climbed back on his horse, a rifle blast knocked him to the ground. Before the other startled rider could even react, he met the same fate.

Two bearded mountain men, leading Mike's horse, rode up to the three bodies on the ground. After checking to make sure the Indians were dead, one of the trappers nudged Mike over with his boot.

"You ever seen him before?" His companion shook his head. "Looks like he cud be one of 'em railroaders."

"Well, he sure ain't gonna be drivin' nothin' but daisies anymore. Let's tie him to his horse and take him on in to Ogden with us. Maybe somebody there'll know who he is."

When Keene stopped to rest Duke, Kathleen bowed to exhaustion and managed a short nap before they continued on to Ogden.

Now, shortly past twilight, rain began falling steadily. Snuggled behind Keene with her arms wrapped around his waist, Kathleen was too content to pay any mind to the rain or the low rumble of thunder. She wished the two of them could go on like this forever. Lost in these dreams, she was taken by surprise when he suddenly reined up before the entrance of a cave and dismounted.

"We're in for a bad storm." He pointed toward the flash of lightning in the distant sky. "We'll take cover in there. Wait for a moment while I check it out."

His momentary absence brought a return of

her fear. As the rain poured down around her, she began to shiver. Sitting stiffly in the saddle, she waited nervously for his return.

"All clear," Keene said, reappearing.

He swung her down, then led the horse into the cave. "There's dry wood in here. Just stay near the entrance 'til I get a fire going."

"Is it safe to have a fire?"

"I've been watching the trail for the last couple of hours. I don't think we're being followed." Keene didn't tell her that before he cut off the trail, he had spotted two mountain men leading the gray that her husband had been riding.

As soon as the fire began to warm the small cave, he unsaddled the dun and tossed her a shirt and blanket from the saddlebags. "Here. Get into something dry while I take care of Duke."

While Keene rubbed down his horse, Kathleen huddled in the corner and removed the wet buckskin, hurriedly replacing it with the dry garment. The cotton shirt felt good against her body even though the tails hung below her knees. Quickly buttoning the front, she rolled up the sleeves past her wrists and sat down on a blanket to dry her wet hair.

Keene came over carrying the saddlebags and squatted down before the fire. He pulled out a coffeepot and set about making coffee.

"I can do that," she volunteered.

"I'm used to it."

"I'm thinkin' you're the kind of man who likes doin' things for himself, Keene MacKenzie," she said with a soft smile.

"Reckon so. Man living alone kinda falls into the habit."

He was still naked from the waist up, and her gaze repeatedly strayed to the puckered scar on his shoulder. "I see the wound on your shoulder has healed just fine."

He looked up and grinned. "Must have been the nursing."

Her heart seemed to leap to her throat. For the first time in eight years, she knew pure contentment. The threat of Indians, Michael Rafferty, all the demons in her life were now forgotten as she sat in the snug warmth of the cave and listened to the pleasant drone of his voice.

When he began to rummage through the saddlebags, her gaze shifted to watch the corded muscles ripple across his broad shoulders and slope down to his biceps. Everything about him fascinated her.

"You can use this if you want." He handed her a hairbrush. She had remembered seeing the tarnished, silver-handled brush on the dresser in his room.

Kathleen took it gratefully and began to brush out the long strands of her wet hair. "I'd never be thinkin' you're the kind of man to be havin' a silver-handled hairbrush," she said lightly.

"It was a gift," Keene said. For an instant, the image of Rory handing him a brightly covered package one Christmas played across his mind. Shoving aside the intruding memory, he handed Kathleen a piece of jerky. "Don't guess you've eaten today, Mrs. Rafferty."

The light remark was a teasing reminder of their shared meals while she had nursed him. Their eyes exchanged the common memory as she took the food from him—not because she was hungry, but to please him.

He pulled on a shirt, and as he repacked the saddlebags, she saw the grim reminder that returned her to reality—the money pouch. "Keene, tell me how Michael got that money."

A nerve twitched in his jaw. "He murdered the railroad's paymaster." She closed her eyes, trying to close out the information. "You've been implicated because you left with him."

Her eyes popped open, wide with shock. "I swear on the Holy Mother, I didn't know."

"Don't worry, Kathleen, once they know the whole story, you'll be cleared. The evidence speaks for itself, and Rafferty had a bad reputation."

"Maybe . . . maybe they can find Michael and he'll admit the truth," she said hopefully.

Keene cleared his throat. "Ah . . . there's something else I haven't told you."

Her worried glance swung to him. "What is it, Keene?"

"While you were napping earlier today, a couple of trappers passed us leading that big gray your husband had been riding."

Her gasp was barely audible. "Why didn't you stop and ask them about it?" she asked with shock.

"You don't mess with strangers on the trail, Kathleen. It can be dangerous." He saw no other way to say it, so he got out the words quickly. "I didn't see it 'til they passed, but there was a body tied to the horse. I think it may have been your husband."

She gasped, and made a quick sign of the cross. "May the Lord have mercy on his soul."

"I'm sorry, Kathleen," Keene said awkwardly.

She glanced up at him, tears trickling down her cheeks. "I'm not. God forgive me, but I'm not sorry he's dead." She turned away. Lying back on the blanket, she buried her face in her hands, sobbing. Her tears were not from sorrow, but from a feeling of guilt.

Keene wanted to hold her, comfort her, but he knew she must get through this moment alone.

He picked up his rifle and went to sit down by the entrance of the cave. He would keep watch through the night in case those two Utes were still trailing them.

Eventually, Kathleen cried herself to sleep. Sometime during the night, a crash of lightning and a loud boom of thunder woke her from a nightmare. She sat up, crying out Keene's name. He hurried over and gathered her into his arms.

"Sh-h-h-h," he soothed. "Everything's okay."

She huddled in his arms. "I dreamt you had left me."

"I'm right here. It was just a dream, Kathleen. I'm not leaving you. I promised. Remember?"

He lowered her back down, and tucked the blanket around her. "Now go back to sleep. I'll be right here."

Keene returned to his post at the entrance of the cave. Kathleen lay watching him. Feeling her eyes on him, he turned and their gazes locked. For a long moment, they stared in silence at each other.

Then, barely above a whisper, her voice broke the hushed stillness. "I don't know what I would ever do without the thought of you."

Keene and Kathleen were back on the trail at daylight. As soon as they rode into town, he took her to her tent. "Stay here, Kathleen, until I get back from seeing the sheriff."

He had no sooner said it than Sheriff Bellows hurried up to them.

Andy Bellows had known Keene since he was a boy. He nodded to the scout. "Howdy, Keene."

Keene dipped his head in response. "Sheriff."

Bellows turned his attention to Kathleen. "You Mrs. Rafferty?"

"Yes, sir," Kathleen replied solemnly.

"Glad to see you're safe, ma'am." Bellows half-smiled at Keene. "Heard you was trackin' them, Keene."

"Mrs. Rafferty had nothing to do with the robbery and murder," Keene said.

"I know that. Some drifter sleeping near the depot admitted to seein' Rafferty sneakin' away from the payroll car that night."

With a grim face, he turned to Kathleen. "'Fraid I've got some bad news to tell you. 'Bout your husband, Mrs. Rafferty. Couple of trappers brought in his body this morning. Seems he ran into some Ute bucks on the trail."

"I know, that's when he left me and rode

off. Mr. MacKenzie found me in time to save my life."

"Well, the trappers said they got there too late to do your husband any good. They finished off the bucks, though."

"Are you sure it's Rafferty?" Keene asked.

Bellows nodded. "That construction boss from the Union Pacific just identified his body." He looked at Keene. "'Tweren't a pretty sight."

"Jack Casement?" Keene asked.

"Yeah," Bellows said.

"Is he still in town?"

"Reckon so. Last I saw of him, he was at his office."

"I have to see him." Keene untied his saddlebags and slung them over his shoulder. "Do you want to stay here, or come with me?" he asked Kathleen.

"If nobody cares, I'd be grateful to be stayin' here in me tent," she said.

"Hey, Keene," Bellows shouted as Keene hurried away, "You get back that missin' payroll?"

"What do you think?" Keene yelled back.

Bellows grinned. "Figured you would."

Keene walked into Casement's office and threw the pouch on the table. "Here's your missing payroll."

The little construction boss looked up with a grin that appeared to be as wide as he was long. He opened the pouch and quickly thumbed through the contents.

"Looks like the sonofabitch never had a chance to spend any of it. Did you hear he's dead?"

"Yeah. I was just talking to the sheriff."

"What about Rafferty's wife?"

"She's safe. I brought her back with me. She didn't have anything to do with the robbery. The bastard forced her to go with him, that's all."

Casement got to his feet. "Good job, MacKenzie." He slapped Keene on the shoulder. "You'll pull a bonus for this."

Chapter Nineteen

That evening, Keene MacKenzie entered Jake O'Brien's, and his glance swept the interior of the smoke-filled saloon until his eyes came to rest on a solitary figure sitting alone at a table in the corner. A shot glass and an open bottle of bar whiskey sat before him. Ambling over, he pulled out a chair and sat down. "Hi, Doc."

Thomas lifted his head. Dulled by alcohol, his brown eyes lacked their usual luster. "How you doing, Keene?" He shoved the bottle of whiskey across the table.

"Have a drink of Jake O'Brien's incredibly bad whiskey."

Keene picked up the bottle and took a swig. "What are you celebratin', Doc?" He returned the bottle to the table.

"Celebrating?" Thomas asked. His mouth curled in derision as he raised the glass in a toast. "Here's to retribution, my friend."

" 'Fraid you've lost me, Doc," Keene said with his laconic drawl.

"Women, Keene. I've spent the better part of my adult life loving and leaving them. Guess you could say I deserve what I'm getting."

"Not me, Doc. Can't say if you deserve it or not, 'cause I don't know what you're talkin' about."

Thomas poured himself another drink, then shoved the bottle back to Keene. "I'm talking about Rory, my friend. Rory . . . the redheaded avenger. Rory . . . with green eyes that a man could drown in."

"Might still be better than drownin' in that whiskey, Doc," Keene advised.

Thomas rested his cheeks in his hands and fixed a steady stare on Keene. "You loved her, didn't you?"

"Reckon I still do," Keene said candidly.

"Then why'd you give her up without a fight?"

"I already told you, Doc, Rory and I ain't sweet on each other. Thought a smart guy like you would have figured it all out by now."

Thomas began to sober. "Figure out what, Keene?"

"That Rory's my sister." The shock hit Thomas like a punch to his stomach. He gaped in astonishment. "Guess I should say, she's my half-sister. I was born on the wrong side of the blanket. My ma was T.J.'s cook before he married Sarah."

"Oh, I see," Thomas said reflectively. "And why didn't he marry your mother?"

333

"Ma was part Indian," Keene replied in explanation. "She died when I was six years old. T.J. kept me around but never 'fessed up to being my pa. He married Sarah shortly after that. She took me under her wing and kind of raised me like a son. T.J. didn't like it none, but he worshipped Sarah and let her do anything she wanted. Then when Rory came along the next year, I kind of got in the habit of looking out for her. That's how we came to be close."

"What happened to cause the bad feelings between you and Callahan?" Thomas asked, the glass before him forgotten.

Keene sat silently for a long moment. When Keene picked up the bottle and took another draught of whiskey, Thomas thought he didn't intend to answer. Then Keene resumed the story in his low drawl.

"When the war broke out, I left the Circle C and went east to join the army. Didn't get back 'til sixty-six. T.J. was already mad at the railroad. They had come through and surveyed the route. Originally the plan had been to lay the track through Salt Lake City and around the south end of the lake—the way Brigham Young wanted it. That way it would have bypassed the Circle C, which was the way T.J. wanted it too," Keene explained.

"Well, the surveyors discovered the water was too deep at that end of the lake and overflowed too often, so they were forced to go around the north end of the lake over Promontory Point. Because of it, the railroad ended up runnin' through Ogden and alongside the Circle C."

"Oh, I get the picture now," Thomas said.

"Yeah, T.J. was all hot and bothered about it, and when I told him I had signed up to scout for the Union Pacific, he blew his top. Him and me had a big fight and I left."

"You mean to say he's carried this grudge just because you took a job with the railroad?" Thomas asked in disbelief.

"Well, I didn't see much of him for the next year or so. I'd come back now and again to see Sarah and Rory. Then right after the snow melted, I came back with an advance crew of graders. T.J. and me had another big fight about the railroad, and he ordered me off the Circle C. Next week, Sarah came to the camp to try to smooth over the fight. I was out huntin' so I wasn't there. While she was there, the Utes hit the camp and Sarah was killed in the attack."

"I'm sorry, Keene," Thomas said.

Absorbed in deep thought, Keene stared into space. "Yeah, Sarah was a good woman. She didn't have a mean bone in her. I loved her very much."

"And I imagine Callahan blamed the railroad for her death," Thomas commented.

"That's right, Doc. The railroad . . . and me." He shoved back his chair. "Hell, I didn't mean to run off at the mouth like this. Just wanted to set the record straight about Rory and me."

"Well, gotta tell you, my newly discovered brother-in-law, I've got just enough booze in me to be looking for a shoulder to cry on."

Keene managed to avoid grinning. "Fire away, Doc."

Thomas studied the bottom of his glass. "From the beginning?"

"Sure, why not?" Keene shoved his battered cavalry hat to the back of his head and settled down in his chair.

Cocking a brow, Thomas asked, "Have you ever stopped to wonder what attracts a man to a woman?"

"Never had to." Keene grinned. "It always kinda popped up on its own."

The bawdy innuendo went unnoticed by Thomas. "In the beginning, I guess what attracted me to Rory—besides her beauty, of course—was her courage." Thomas leaned across the table in confidence. "Want to know something, Keene? It's been my observation that a woman's courage is a solitary thing. She kind of keeps it to herself. Men get to demonstrate their bravery in massive units—like marching shoulder to shoulder into battle. But women, well—their courage is usually manifested more privately."

Keene immediately thought of Kathleen and how she'd had to face the brutality of Michael Rafferty each day. "You'll get no argument from me, Doc."

"But I'm getting off the subject, aren't I?" Thomas asked.

"Reckon so," Keene said.

Blurry-eyed, Thomas leaned over and glanced at Keene. "What was I talking about?"

"Rory." Despite an effort to avoid it, the reticent scout grinned.

"She even warned me that she was spoiled

and used to getting her own way. I'm thirty years old, Keene. I've had more than my fair share of women, so I should have had enough sense to listen to her. Right?"

"Reckon so, Doc."

Thomas shook his head. "But I didn't. Guess I'm getting what I deserve."

"Doc, Rory's got a lot of loyalty for the people she loves. She's not gonna desert T.J. when his ship is sinkin'. But she loves you too, so she's not gonna give you up. She just needs time to work this out."

"Well, Keene, it's getting to 'fish or cut bait' time because as soon as the railroad is completed, I intend to return to Virginia."

"And I'm willin' to bet my gelding that Rory'll have everything all worked out by then."

Thomas smiled at Keene's reassuring words. "You like listening to drunks, Keene?"

"Not usually, Doc. But I figure I've got a stake in this one."

Thomas's expression softened. "Tell me what she was like when she was younger, Keene. Every now and then I catch a glimpse of that little girl in her eyes. I wish I could have known her then."

"Kinda hard to remember what she looked like, Doc. All legs, I guess, like a young colt. Pesty as hell. Trailed around on my heels like a hound dog. Always gettin' herself into some kind of trouble that I had to get her out of. Sarah had been a schoolmarm before she married T.J., and she schooled the two of us together."

Keene shook his head. "I was seventeen, Rory

was ten when she heard the talk about T.J. being my father. I guess that's the gal I can remember the most. She came to me all serious-like. Her eyes were as round as saucers, and she asked me if it was true. I told her to ask her pa, but she said she wanted me to tell her. Well, I said I thought it was true, but T.J. never admitted to it."

Keene grinned, recalling that moment. "Rory started crying and she threw her arms around my waist and hugged me. I figured she was cryin' because she was upset. I felt like hell. I didn't know what I could say to ease her hurt, so I told her that maybe it was just all bunkhouse palaver and she shouldn't pay it no mind. She raised her head and looked up at me with the tears streaming down her cheeks and told me she hoped it was true, 'cause if I was her brother, she now had a better reason for loving me more than she already did."

"So you're saying she never resented your position? She accepted you as her brother."

"Position?" Keene scoffed. "Hell! I didn't have no position. I pulled my wages like the rest of the crew. I think T.J. even worked me harder. Sarah and Rory were the only two that treated me like family. Sarah even insisted I live in the big house."

"Do you believe Callahan's your father, Keene?" Thomas asked grimly.

Shrugging, Keene said, "My ma told me as much on the day she died."

"And you've never confronted Callahan with this knowledge?" Thomas asked.

"Look, Doc, if T.J. wanted to admit I'm his

son, he would have done so long before."

"But it's your birthright, Keene."

"Birthright?" Keene shook his head. "Naw. A bastard's got no birthrights."

"Well, you certainly do to the Circle C."

"I've got no claim on the Circle C. T.J. built it. It's his to do with what he wants." Having revealed more of his past to Thomas than he ever had to anyone, Keene MacKenzie shoved back his chair and stood up. "Guess I'll be catchin' some shut-eye, Doc. Need any help gettin' back to your place?"

"No, I'm fine, Keene. I'll see you in the morning."

Watching the scout walk away, Thomas thought T.J. Callahan was even a bigger bastard than he had previously considered him to be.

Returning to his room, Keene struck a match and lit the lantern. He shed his gunbelt, draped it over the headboard, then sat down on the edge of the bed to pull off his boots. Deep in reflection, he sat with a boot dangling from the ends of his fingertips. As much as he hated to get involved in other people's troubles, he figured he had better ride out to the Circle C first thing in the morning and get Rory's version of the whole mess. He sure as hell hated to see a good man like Thomas Graham hurting the way he was, and he knew damn well that Rory was probably suffering the same way.

Keene stood up and had just removed his shirt when the door creaked open. Pulling the Colt from the holster, he spun around. Kathleen stepped through the opening. Silently, the two people stared at each other for a long moment, their eyes transmitting the message their mouths failed to do. Then Keene returned the pistol to its holster and crossed the room. He closed the door and turned the key in the lock.

Grasping Kathleen by the shoulders, he drew her into his arms. She lifted her head and met his steady stare. "With me husband not even cold in his grave, 'tis a sinner I am for comin' to the arms of another man. But I've not the strength to be stayin' away from you, Keene MacKenzie."

He was tired of words of recrimination, of forbidden love. There had been too much talk between them already. Too much denial. Too much restrained desire. He needed to hold her, to kiss her, to thrust into her and feel that sublime moment of release.

Urgently, he covered her mouth with his own. The intense kiss drew the breath from her, leaving her gasping for air as he rained kisses on her face and eyes. He reclaimed her lips, and as his hands swept her slender body, he realized that she was wearing nothing beneath the cotton gown. This fueled his passion to lust. He was so aroused that he wanted to take her on the spot. Lifting her, he suspended her off the floor and his hard arousal slipped between her dangling legs. Just touching her and feeling the heat of her chamber almost caused him to ejaculate, but somehow he managed to reach the bed and lower her until her feet touched the floor.

As he started to raise the gown to pull it off her, he glanced at Kathleen and saw the fright in her eyes. She looked like a mouse staring at a snake. And he was the snake. Too late, he realized that this must have been the same animalistic treatment she had suffered at the hands of Michael Rafferty.

His ardor cooled as quickly as it had been aroused.

Remorseful, Keene's face softened with a tender smile. "Oh, God, Kathleen, I'm sorry." He gently stroked her cheek. "I just got carried away. If you're not ready for this, we can wait," he said in a husky drawl. His warm breath at her ear felt stimulating. Sighing, she relaxed in his arms.

"Have you ever been kissed, Kathleen?" he said softly.

Her blue eyes were filled with confusion when she lifted her head and glanced at him. "Of course."

"I mean, did you ever enjoy the kiss?" Keene corrected.

"No," she said simply, lowering her glance. He saw her blush, and a sadness settled in his gray eyes. Kathleen kept her eyes downcast. "I'll not be lyin' to you, Keene. I'm not a . . . warm woman. Time and again, Michael told me as much," she confessed.

Keene saw her as one of the gentlest, warmest women he had ever known. Hooking his fingers under her chin, he tilted her head to meet his probing gaze. "A warm woman? What does that mean, Kathleen?"

The blush rose again on her cheeks. "You know . . ." She tried to divert her eyes. "Michael

341

said I'm . . . I'm . . . cold. In bed."

"Did he ever attempt to make love to you?"

She turned her head aside, unable to look at him. "I'm thinkin' you're laughin' at me, Keene MacKenzie."

"I'd never laugh at you, Kathleen," he said solemnly.

Her gaze swung back to him. Tears welled in her blue eyes. "Then why would you be askin' me such a question when you know I've been with child many times?" She shook her head, hurt and confused by these cruel questions. This was a Keene MacKenzie she did not know or understand. "'Tis not your nature to be unkind."

He gathered her in his arms. "Oh Lord, Kathleen! Is that what you think? I'd never try to hurt you." His arms enfolded her, and he pressed her head to his chest, laying his cheek on her head. "I know Rafferty had his way with you, Kathleen." His mouth slid down to the slender column of her neck. "But that wasn't making love." The warm timbre of his voice was as provocative to her as his touch.

Pulling her onto his lap, he kissed her. It was a gentle kiss, yet his lips felt warm and exciting. It was a kiss far different from any she had ever known. Lying back in his arms, she felt a sense of security and contentment, yet every nerve in her body responded to him.

How she loved this man. As she looked up at him, her adoring gaze conveyed that love. He studied her face, a face that had become very dear to him.

Her blue eyes, now wide and rounded, were underlined by shadowed depressions. He hoped his love would erase those circles.

The hollows of her high, Celtic cheeks flushed when his fingers moved to the buttons of her gown. When she made no effort to prevent the slide of the gown off her shoulders, he stood up and turned around. Laying her down gently, he pulled the gown past her hips and tossed it aside. Then his gray eyes surveyed her nakedness.

She was so tiny.

He was amazed by her tininess. She had always appeared to be petite—but naked she looked elfin, childlike.

Her frail body bore the ravishment of the years of marriage to Michael Rafferty; she was thin, almost to the point of being emaciated. Her breasts were small, but they were the breasts of a woman. And the male in him responded to the sight of the dusky aureoles. He felt a tightening in his loins.

She lay silent, studying every nuance of his expression for the same signs of disappointment that had always materialized in Mike's eyes. Instead, she saw adoration gleaming in the silvery depths.

Had she not already loved him, Kathleen knew that from this day forward she would always love Keene MacKenzie, if for no other reason than this cherished moment when she looked up and saw that passion in his eyes.

She smiled with unrestrained joy. "The sight of my frailty isn't displeasin' to you?" she asked, amazed.

Keene shook his head. "Of course not." He finished shedding his clothes and joined her on the bed. Stretching out, he gathered her in his arms. "I don't think you have any idea how beautiful you are, Kathleen."

"I'm wishin' I could be beautiful for you, Keene," she said sadly with her soft Irish lilt.

Keene MacKenzie never hated any man as much as he hated Michael Rafferty at that moment.

Now that they had reached this milestone, there could only be one satisfying conclusion. Keene smiled down into her worried eyes. "Kathleen, you are beautiful to me," he said tenderly. "Believe me."

From the time she had first looked into his gray eyes, Kathleen's forbidden dreams had fantasized such a moment between them. She no longer felt ugly or ashamed; Keene made her feel desirable. She loved him and desired him with equal passion. She knew there could never be a more perfect moment between them.

And the conviction of that belief transformed her face to radiance as she smiled up at him. "I'm believin' you, Keene MacKenzie," she whispered through trembling lips.

The sight of his tender smile coaxed her to reach up and stroke his cheek, as if to capture that tenderness in her palm. He grabbed her hand and pressed his mouth to it. Her hand tingled as dozens of tantalizing shocks radiated from the spot where his lips had touched. Gasping, she clenched her fist as if to keep the sensation from escaping.

He covered her mouth and face with light kisses. She closed her eyes and lay back in his arms, feeling the flutter of her heart each time his lips found her temple, her eyes, the hollow of her throat, or took a lazy slide to her ear. Always they returned to reclaim her lips.

The flutter in her chest became a wild throbbing when his tongue began to trace the outline of her lips.

During her eight-year marriage to Michael Rafferty, Kathleen had been abused, humiliated, and brutalized by the man she had wed. She had never known a man's loving touch, the thrill of warm lips seeking and arousing; thus she had never yearned for the brutal pawing or craved the ravaging mouth of the insensitive brute she had married.

But now, for the first time in her life, Kathleen discovered the incomparable feeling of being a woman held in the arms of a man who loved and desired her.

Their kisses deepened, his tongue exploring and probing, seeking and finding hers as he drew her deeper into the fervor of her escalating passion. But he was determined not to rush her.

Gingerly, he slid his hand to her breast. He felt her tense, but she made no effort to brush aside his hand. He cupped the round firmness in the warmth of his palm and his callous thumb tantalized the nub to a hardened peak. When she shifted in a restless response, he gave the same attention to the other breast. A whimper of pleasure slipped past her lips.

Keene lowered his head and gently closed

his moist, heated mouth around one of the quivering mounds.

Kathleen trembled and arched against the pressure of his mouth in response to the arousing titillation. His tongue joined the play, lazily tracing patterns across the taut peaks. She felt a tightness low in her stomach, and her heartbeat quickened with her first taste of sexual arousal.

He shifted back to reclaim her lips, drawing her tighter in his embrace. The curled hair on his chest pressed against the sensitized peaks of her breast, creating a new and erotic sensation.

He traced a slow trail of moist kisses to her ear and began to draw circles on the tiny shell. When his tongue dipped into the chamber, a responsive shiver rippled her spine.

He raised his head and a grin softened his chiseled features. "You liked that," he said, pleased.

Her blue eyes were glazed with arousal. "I'd be lyin' if I said I didn't," she said breathlessly.

He slipped his tongue into her ear again and his hand began a leisurely exploration down the curve of her slender body. Exquisite sensation streamed from her loins.

His mouth returned to her breast, this time drawing one of the peaks between his teeth. He began a moist suckling, and a blur of indistinguishable, flashing colors began to whirl in her head. She gripped his shoulders and clung to him.

From what she had said earlier, Keene feared

she would be frigid, but her response was more than he had hoped for. He grew bolder and slid his hand into the dark curls at the junction of her legs. Cautiously, he probed until he found the sensitive nub. Her body erupted as an exquisite, unrestrained delirium enveloped her.

She writhed beneath the gentle assault—his mouth and tongue at her breasts, his fingers creating a rapture she never suspected existed.

The intensity of her response raised him to the same incredible heights in which she now swirled helplessly. He parted her legs and shifted between them, then slipped into her as he covered her mouth with a driving, intense kiss.

"Oh, Sweet Mary," she cried out as the rhythm of his thrusts increased. She soared to ecstasy, and her body erupted in a glorious burst of blinding sensation as he discharged the moist seed of his love into her body.

They remained entwined until their breathing steadied and he lifted his head. For a long moment they gazed deeply into each other's eyes.

The faint trace of a smile played across her face. "I never knew . . . I had no idea how wonderful it could be."

"You never came before," he said, suddenly grasping her meaning.

She nodded. "No. Never."

Struck by the full impact of her words, Keene felt his astonishment turn to incredulousness.

347

Naked joy split the usual enigmatic countenance of the taciturn scout. "This was your first time!"

Tears glistened in his gray eyes as he hugged her with unrestrained happiness. "Oh, Sweet Lord, this was your first time."

Chapter Twenty

Rory sat in a copse of trees and stared desolately at the majestic grandeur of the Wasatch Mountains. Every day since her return to the Circle C, she had come to this same spot—the vista she and Thomas had once shared. Almost a week had passed since she had left him in a huff of anger. The anger had cooled; and now only heartache remained. She loved him and missed him beyond reason. Separation out of necessity was hard enough to bear, but separation out of anger was intolerable. Every moment of loneliness was magnified into hours that soon seemed to swell into years.

Absorbed in her misery, she jumped in shock when hoofbeats sounded beside her, then clutched her hand to her heart in relief when she recognized the rider.

"Oh, Keene, I didn't hear you coming."

"That red hair of yours would look right pretty dangling from a Ute coup stick," he said, swinging out of the saddle. He tied Duke to a tree and hunched down beside her. "Not like you to be that careless, Rory."

Rory sighed deeply. "No Indian would ever come this close to the house. But I have to admit that lately I've made more than my share of mistakes," she said. "I suppose you know about me and Thomas."

He sat down and stretched out his legs. "Just enough to know that a damn good man's been keeping company with a whiskey bottle these nights." He glanced at her. "How are you sleeping?"

"I'm not." She glanced down at her hands in her lap. "I miss him so much, Keene."

"You got a good reason for what you're doing, Rory?"

"No. That's the worst tragedy of the whole thing. Thomas and I fought over Daddy."

Keene nodded. "Figured as much."

"Thomas stopped Daddy from hanging Stalking Moon."

"Spotted Deer's son!" Keene let out a low whistle. "T.J. must be aiming to set this territory on fire."

"Thomas drew a gun to keep Daddy from doing it. When I tried to defend some of Daddy's actions to Thomas, we ended up quarreling." She cast a fretful glance at Keene. "I never should have sided with Daddy. I knew he was wrong, Keene, but I feel so sorry for him. He's so bitter these days."

Keene sat gazing out at the mountains. "You better talk to him, Rory. His bitterness is going to get him into serious trouble with the government. I trailed some missing railroad ties to the Circle C."

Her worried glance swung to him. "What do you mean?"

"If T.J.'s interfering with the building of that railroad, he's asking for more trouble than he can handle. The government will come down his throat with a troop of cavalry."

"He's not himself. This whole situation's driven him to distraction."

"Well, the railroad's here to stay, Rory. T.J.'s gotta accept that. If he don't back off the trail he's been riding lately, he's the one who's gonna end up at the wrong end of a rope. Government ain't gonna stand for it. My God, they've fought every Indian nation between here and the Mississippi. You think they're gonna tolerate T.J.'s interference?"

He stood up and walked over to his horse. "Better try to talk to him, Rory, before the crazy fool gets himself killed."

Keene swung effortlessly into the saddle. "And get back to your husband where you belong."

With a worried frown, Rory watched him ride away, then she hurried back to the house.

T.J. Callahan was sitting behind his desk when Rory walked into the room that he called his office. When Sarah Callahan had been alive, she had used the small study as a sewing room. After his wife's death, Callahan had had his desk moved into the room and kept Sarah's keepsakes intact, as though they were sharing the space.

He looked up from the paper spread out on the desk before him. "Daddy, I want to talk to you," Rory said.

" 'Bout what?" he asked.

"Daddy, you're gettin' yourself into serious trouble by interfering with the building of the railroad."

"Don't know what you're talkin' about."

"You know damn well what I'm talking about."

"Told you before, girl, that it ain't proper for you to be usin' that kinda language. I won't let you desecrate this room with foul words."

"Oh, Daddy, stop trying to sidetrack the issue. I'm not desecrating this room any more than you are by sitting there and denying the truth."

The old man's eyes narrowed. "You been talkin' to one of the hands?"

"No. Furthermore, you have no right to jeopardize the lives of the hands with your crazed schemes."

Callahan lumbered to his feet, his eyes blazing with fury. "Don't you try to tell me what rights I have. I'm the one who says what's right or wrong on the Circle C. Every day you're soundin' more and more like that railroad trash you married."

"Thank you, Father. That's the finest compliment you've ever paid me," she declared. "And there's something else I have to say. You're wrong, Daddy. You've been wrong for a long time. You're accountable for your actions the same as anyone. Ever since Mother's death, your thinking has become twisted with bitterness. I've been at fault for ever listening to you. Everything

Thomas said was true. I intend to tell him so, and to beg him to forgive me for the way I've treated him."

"Go ahead. Go crawlin' back to him like a slitherin' snake. You deserve each other. If anyone's changed, it's you, girl. You ain't the daughter I raised. I don't need you. I don't need anybody."

Rory stared aghast at the enraged man. "Everyone needs someone, Father. I felt sorry for you, so I came back here." Her eyes misted. "I love you, Daddy, but I won't allow your bitterness to destroy my life the way I've watched it destroy yours. Just look at yourself. Can't you see what you've become?"

"Just don't try to come crawlin' back here when your husband finds out you ain't gonna own a big ranch."

"Daddy, Thomas doesn't give a damn about the Circle C. We'll be going to Virginia as soon as the railroad is completed." She walked to the door. "Good-bye, Daddy. I'll always love you."

Talking in low tones, the couple standing in the shadow of the tent drew no attention from the few people who hurried past.

Kathleen Rafferty gazed up worriedly at Keene MacKenzie. "Mr. Casement told me today that with Michael gone, I'm to be leavin' Tent Town. In the marnin' the families will be moved to Promontory, and if I'm desirin', he'll see to my free passage back East."

Keene grasped her shoulders. "I won't let you go, Kathleen. We'll get married right away."

" 'Tis too soon after me husband's death. There must be a proper time of mournin'," she protested.

"To hell with what's proper," Keene declared. "You didn't love that bastard, so why should you mourn him?"

"Oh, but 'twould only be proper, I'm thinkin'. 'Tis the way of it, Keene."

He tilted her chin to look into her wide-eyed innocence. Her blue eyes rounded with shock at the amusement flashing in his silvery gaze. "But, Mrs. Rafferty, you and I have . . . fornicated. So 'twould only be proper for us to wed, I'm thinkin'."

Suppressing a smile, she tried to ignore the mischievous gleam in his eyes. "You're not to be takin' such an important matter so lightly, Keene MacKenzie."

"Kathleen, the only important matter here is our love. We're not separating because of what's proper. We marry right away. Agreed?"

For a moment she wrestled with conscience, then her face broke into a radiant smile. "Then marry we will, Keene MacKenzie, for you're a persuasive dev'l, you are. And 'tis no denyin' that I'm crazy in love with you."

"And there's no denyin' that I'm crazy in love with you, Kathleen Rafferty," he mocked lovingly. And as he drew her into his arms, the reticent scout marveled at how easy she made it for him to say those words to her.

Rory wrestled with her feelings on the way to town, wondering what would be the best approach with Thomas. How deep would his anger be? Or his hurt? Why had she allowed the situation to get so out of hand that she now had to wrestle with the problem of how to break the ice between them?

The closer she got to town, the greater her anxiety became. What if Thomas wasn't even there? What if he was out at the end of track? Or what if he had gone back East? One ridiculous thought after another entered her head and continued to plague her.

She found most of the town in darkness when she arrived. All the businesses appeared to be closed and the streets practically deserted. She heard only the tinny, discordant sound of an off-tune piano coming from the tavern.

Rory rode up to Thomas's office and saw a light filtering through the curtains of the bedroom window. Her heartbeat quickened. Thomas was home.

Without further hesitation, she rode to the stable and turned her mount over to a sleepy Joey Ross. Her palms felt sweaty when she picked up her valise. As she hurried toward the office, she saw Kathleen and Keene talking quietly near Kathleen's tent. Rory was about to call out to them, then suddenly changed her mind and stepped quickly into the shadows to avoid being seen. In truth, she was on a mission and could not afford a distraction. Distractions could weaken her resolve.

Like a wary thief, she slinked through the shadows of the night until she reached her destination. Her hands were shaking as she fumbled with the key in the lock. What if Thomas had slipped the bolt? She would have to pound on the door or call out to him, possibly attracting attention to herself.

God, why am I acting so secretive about the whole situation? she asked herself in disgust. The issue was between her and Thomas. What did she care what anyone else thought?

She unlocked the door to the office, entered the room, and closed the door, sliding the bolt into place.

With the sound of her heartbeat drumming in her ears, she stood for a moment in the darkened room, lit only by a faint shaft of moonlight. Then, rallying her courage to face him, Rory took a deep breath and walked to the bedroom door.

She stopped upon hearing the sound of splashing water. Thomas was bathing.

Suddenly, she was struck with a daring thought. Why not avoid an unpleasant scene by simply seducing him? Wouldn't her father's conduct be a moot point if Thomas had just made love to her? The more she thought about it, the more she convinced herself.

Why not seduction? She more than any other knew full well his strong, virile drive. Seducing Thomas would be a relatively simple task to ease the awkward situation between them.

Can't say it wouldn't break the ice, she thought with a sardonic smile. And then, once they were in one another's arms, how easy it would be for apologies to follow.

But should she stoop to the actions of a

common whore just to achieve this purpose?

With a troubled sigh, Rory decided to take the surest route. She opened her valise and removed her robe, then began to undress.

Thomas had just wrapped a towel around his midsection after climbing out of the tub. He turned his head in surprise at the sound of the door opening behind him. Speechless, he stared at his wife standing there in her robe.

Rory was doing her own share of staring as well. In the short time since they had parted, she had almost forgotten what a powerful, muscular body he had.

The towel tucked at his waist concealed only his most private area. Beads of water still glimmered on his broad shoulders and dark hair.

A dark brow arched and he broke the silence. "What a pleasant surprise. A professional or pleasure call, Mrs. Graham?"

"I had hoped it would be pleasure, Thomas." But now facing him, she realized too late that she couldn't go through with her intention; their love would be defiled by bartering it.

Her voice sounded as ridiculous to her ears as the words of her confession. "I thought if I came here and seduced you, I could persuade you to forgive my father's actions."

"Seduce me?" He grinned, and his eyes gleamed with amusement. Sardonic amusement. "Why not? Any port in the storm, so to speak," he replied in a mocking taunt. "But such frankness, Rory, takes away all the mystery, not to say the romance." He walked over and stood before her. Her breath quickened at the excitement his proximity generated.

"Although I think we both know why you came here tonight."

Thomas leisurely drew her into his arms. "Don't we, Rory?" His mouth was warm and teasing at her ear as he slid the robe off her shoulders. Slowly, his hungry glance swept her nakedness and she could feel the heat of a blush flooding through her. "You came because you've missed this as much as I have."

The smug confidence in the remark made her feel like the whore she had believed she could play. She had tried to kid herself, to disguise her desire with a harebrained scheme which Thomas had seen through the moment she showed up.

Angry with herself, she brushed aside his hands. "Take your hands off me." Her emerald eyes were as icy as the frigid command. What a fool she had made of herself. Picking up the robe, she quickly slipped it back on. "I can't compromise my principles any more than you can yours," she said.

Thomas felt the reins of his control sliding through his fingertips. *Dammit, she was his wife! It was time she began acting like one, instead of like the spoiled offspring of T.J. Callahan.*

His fingers bit into the soft flesh of her shoulders. "You knew that before you stepped into this room. How much more of this childishness do you think I'll tolerate, Rory?" Unconsciously, his hands tightened, and she felt as if they would crush her bones.

"Well, I've changed my mind, so let me go,

Thomas. You're hurting me."

He loosened his grasp, but did not release her. His dark eyes glowed with anger. "Changed your mind? What game is Daddy's Little Girl playing now?" he taunted. "Have you thought of trying to play your husband's favorite game for a change? It's called Conjugal Rights. I remember a time when it used to be your favorite too."

With that, he captured her mouth with a hard kiss. Wrenching her mouth from the plundering pressure, she tried to avoid his angry gaze by focusing on his lips. When she realized the danger of that temptation, her gaze shifted higher. She saw no sign of compassion; the once handsome face had become hard with resentment.

She turned her head aside to evade his descending mouth. He knew her vulnerability, but this time she would not allow herself to give in to his persuasive kiss. Twisting her head from side to side, she avoided his marauding mouth.

"Damn it, Rory, you started this. You're not leaving without finishing it." His arm encircled her like a band of steel and he pulled her tighter against him. Grasping the nape of her neck with his other hand, he held her head to meet the descent of his mouth.

She clenched her teeth to keep his tongue from invading the chamber of her mouth. Undaunted, he traced the circle of her lips with tantalizing sweeps that inflamed her until she parted her lips and his tongue slipped past.

The kiss was hot, a branding expression of possessiveness.

Nuzzling her throat, he nibbled a path down the slender column of her neck. Each bite sent exquisite sensations surging through her, and she squirmed against him in an effort to free herself. She couldn't breathe. The powerful arms holding hers, the exciting masculine scent of him, the heat from his body pressing against her, and the demands of her own escalating passion all combined to weaken her resistance. She felt the hardness and heat of his arousal pressed between them. With a whimper of panic, she intensified her struggle.

"Let me go. Let me go," she sobbed. "Don't you think I feel enough shame for what I've done?" She attempted to shove him away.

When a gap opened between them, she thought she had succeeded, then discovered he had merely stepped back. He stared at her as if she had struck him.

She drew a shuddering breath. Her arms felt too heavy to even raise. They slid down the wall of his chest and dropped listlessly to her sides. She lifted her head to meet the naked pain and confusion in his dark eyes.

"If you really don't want me to touch you, Rory, I won't."

That was not what she wanted. She wanted to remain in his arms forever. She loved him with all her heart. And she knew he loved her. What had happened to them? How could their love have been reduced to this tragic moment?

Her lips trembled as she stared into his wounded brown eyes, and her own eyes welled with tears. "I should have told you the truth the

moment I stepped into this room. I'm so sorry
for the way I've acted. I love you, Thomas."

The confession dissolved all his anger and
resentment. These were the words he wanted
to hear—her realization that their love had
been threatened by *her* actions, not by her
father's. No more anguishing over her father's
misdeeds. Someday T.J. Callahan would have to
make an accounting to a greater authority than
his daughter.

With a husky growl, he pulled her back in
his arms. "Oh God, sweetheart, I love you,"
he whispered. "I've missed you so much." He
rained kisses on her face and eyes, then his
mouth closed over hers and his tongue speared
her parted lips, piercing the honeyed chamber
of her mouth.

With a groan of surrender, she slipped her
arms around his neck. His mouth on hers
continued to press hot kisses until she became
oblivious to everything except the throbbing
demand between her thighs, building with an
increasing intensity that threatened to explode
within her.

His hands moved to her shoulders, then hesitated. He shifted his gaze to meet hers, the air
charged with tension. "I love you, Thomas," she
whispered. "Can you ever forgive me?"

Forgiveness had come with her confession
of love.

Slowly and deliberately, he slipped the robe
off her shoulders. It fell to the floor and lay in
a crumpled heap around her ankles.

Her palms and back pressed against the wall,

she stood naked—as tall and slender as an exquisite alabaster statue carved by a master sculptor. Her eyes were slumberous, emerald slits as his brown velvet gaze caressed the firm roundness of her breasts, moved down the flat plane of her stomach, the curve of her hips, and then paused at the vee of her legs.

"Your body is perfection, Rory," he murmured in a husky whisper.

"A medical opinion, Doctor Graham?" she managed in a throaty murmur.

She reached to slip her arms around his neck, but he caught her hands and pressed her arms against the wall above her head. "No. Husband to wife. Man to woman," he whispered in a raspy growl that sent a shiver rippling down her spine.

He reclaimed her lips and slowly slid his hands down the silken length of her raised arms, his mouth and body pressing her even tighter against the unyielding wall. His hands continued the sensuous downward trail until he cupped her breasts and his thumbs toyed with the hardened nubs.

"Thomas," she pleaded when his hands left her breasts. She opened her eyes, now suffused with passion, only to close them in ecstasy when his warm mouth enveloped a breast and his tongue began to lave the peak. A feeling of exquisite rapture began driving her to the brink of mindlessness.

The near tragedy of love threatened by pride and misunderstanding made each kiss, each touch, each shared sigh much sweeter. And more intense.

Her whole body pulsated and throbbed with passion. She pleaded for him to stop—but prayed he wouldn't.

His hands spanned her waist and he sank to his knees. Her nerves jumped beneath his tongue as he traced a moist trail across her stomach.

"Oh, God, no, Thomas. Oh no," she gasped when his mouth drew ever nearer to the sensitive mound of her sex. Her fingers dug into the corded sinews of his powerful shoulders, and an instinct for fulfillment caused her to separate her thighs.

Her ragged breath became harder to draw. He closed his mouth over the throbbing source of desire, and she became inundated with divine sensation. She pressed his dark head even closer and his tongue penetrated.

"I love you, Thomas. I love you," she moaned incessantly as her body, her mind, and her consciousness floated on the edge of a spinning black abyss. She wanted to hold on, but every second brought her nearer to plummeting over the edge. She cried out as wave upon wave of tremors racked her.

She was still sobbing his name when his mouth returned to silence her moans. She clung to him, returning his kiss, ravenously devouring any taste of him in an explosive, uncontrollable response.

"Rory. My beautiful, beautiful Rory." Covering her face and neck with quick, moist kisses, he whispered his love.

Rory returned his kisses, her hands clutching at the muscular chest, her fingers digging into the corded brawn of his shoulders. She fought for the return of her sanity, but in vain. She wanted more of him—more of his hands, more of his mouth—and she wanted his hard, hot sex inside her.

But if she desired more, he was aflame with his need for her. Sweeping her off her feet, he carried her to the bed, and shoving the quilt aside, he gently laid her down.

For a long moment he allowed his urgent gaze to devour the sight of her, and she reveled in his hungry perusal. Shamelessly, she reached up and removed the towel that covered him. Her green eyes deepened to emerald, and her heart pounded wildly at the sight of his arousal.

Shifting to her side and leaning on an arm, she grinned. "You see, Thomas. I'm shameless where you're concerned." She dangled the towel over the side of the bed and dropped it to the floor.

"One of the things I love about you, sweetheart," he replied. The husky caress in his soft, Southern drawl escalated her passion.

She felt consumed by the smoldering desire in his dark eyes. She lay back and, for a long moment, each saw love's absolute surrender reflected in the eyes of the other. Unable to withstand the urgency any longer, she raised her arms to receive him.

He lowered himself to her. As he dipped his head, she rose to meet him, the long lashes of her eyelids sweeping her cheeks. Their breaths mingled. Lacing her fingers through his thick hair, she murmured his name. His mouth devoured hers, consuming the word from her mouth. Arching against him, her breasts pressed into the wall of his chest, and he drew one of the buds into his mouth.

The scent and feel of him was intoxicating, and she soon became drugged by an indescribable sensation of pure pleasure, a pleasure she abandoned herself to in an uninhibited expression of her love for him.

She stroked and explored the taut muscles of his shoulders and felt them jump beneath her fingertips. Her hands traced the powerful sloping biceps to the wall of his chest.

"Rory," he rasped when her roaming fingers sought his hot, throbbing phallus. Unable to prolong his control for another second, he levered himself above her and slipped into her tight, moist chamber.

The knot that had been stretched to tautness finally snapped with her cry. She strained against him and cried out his name at the moment of their shared rapture. Together they soared to a divine summit far beyond the earthly limitations of their bodies.

Thomas lay slumped on her until their heartbeats slowed. A fine sheen of perspiration coated their bodies, joining them together with a salty moisture.

"I just took a bath. Now I have to take another one," he moaned. He lifted his head, his eyes alight with devilishness. "Of course, we could take it together."

The mischief in her eyes matched his. "I know what that would lead to."

"Yeah," he agreed. "But then we would have to take another bath."

"And then?" she challenged.

"Then . . . we would take another bath," he grinned. Still slumped on her, he nuzzled his head in the curve between her shoulder and neck. Rory slid her arms around his waist. Even the heavy weight of him felt glorious. She never wanted to let him out of her arms. "I like bathing with you," he mumbled in a drowsy whisper.

After a few moments, she thought he had drifted off to sleep until he stirred slightly and began to idly rub his leg along hers. Its hairy roughness was tantalizing, arousing. Her nipples hardened and her body shook with a quick tremor.

Without raising his head, his breath ruffled the hair at her ear as he murmured, "And that's another thing I like about you."

His hand slid to her breast.

Chapter Twenty-one

Since it was Sunday, and Thomas's day off, he and Rory decided to take a train ride up to Promontory Point to take an early peek at the site where the Union Pacific and Central Pacific would join. Both railroads had already reached the summit with less than a hundred feet of rail separating them. The final plans had been made to have the official spike ceremony, linking the two tracks, on the following Saturday, May eighth.

Since most of the railroad crews had already gone back east, only a few hundred of the original thousands of men remained. Bright and early the following morning, the freight trains would be running again, pulling cars of supplies from Ogden to Promontory, but the Sunday train was nothing more than a passenger shuttle with only a cab, a tender, and one car.

Promontory had grown into a typical hell-on-wheels rail town; a muddy street lined with cheap saloons, a company store, and the element of people attracted to that kind of site.

"So this is the spot where history will be made in a few days," Rory moaned, looking around in dismay.

"I doubt that anyone will hang around too long after next Saturday," Thomas predicted. "Ogden will still remain the terminus for the Union Pacific."

Hand in hand, they walked around the town, peeking in the windows of shops and doors of saloons. Rory tried to appear impassive when several whores brazenly tried to entice Thomas into their sporting house.

Being Thomas, he waved good-naturedly to the women and continued on his way.

"Thomas, must you always be so friendly to *everyone* you meet?"

"Why not? That person could be a patient someday."

Rory glanced back. Two prostitutes had moved out onto the street and were standing with their heads together openly ogling Thomas's broad back.

"Well just don't go around passing out your business cards," she mumbled, with a final disgruntled look behind her. Unintentionally, she tightened her grasp on his hand.

Upon returning to the depot, much to their pleasant surprise they encountered Keene and Kathleen.

"You're looking well, Kathleen," Thomas said,

after greetings had been exchanged. "You must be feeling better."

Since the news of her husband's death, neither Thomas nor Rory had made any pretense of offering condolences to Kathleen. Rafferty's brutality toward her had been common knowledge, and both felt she was better off with the bully gone.

"Thank you, Doctor." Kathleen blushed and glanced shyly at Keene. Their open admiration for each other made their intentions apparent.

"How long are you going to continue to call me Doctor?" he asked.

"'Tis a habit that's hard to break, Doc . . . Thomas," she corrected hurriedly. "But I'll be tryin' to set my mind to the way of it," she promised with a beguiling smile.

How lovely she looks. Love has transformed her, Thomas reflected, studying her flushed face. Her eyes glowed with adoration when she glanced at Keene.

"What do the two of you think of Promontory?" Rory asked. "We're rather disappointed."

"Come Saturday, I reckon this place is gonna be the most famous town in America," Keene replied.

"Well, I've seen enough for today," Thomas said. "I'm glad it's almost time to catch the train back to Ogden, where we can have a good dinner—"

"In a *clean* diner," Rory finished for him. She hooked her arm through Kathleen's. "Let's get on that train, Kathleen. I'd hate to have it pull out of here without us."

369

After Thomas retrieved his medical bag from the cab of the train, the two couples entered the passenger car and found themselves the only passengers returning to Ogden. Once the train got underway, they shifted around. Rory and Kathleen sat together chatting, while Thomas and Keene each stretched out to snooze in the empty seats.

Their relaxing journey ended suddenly when one of the nearby windows shattered. The startled women looked out to see more than a dozen painted Indians racing on ponies along both sides of the train. Awakened by the attack, Thomas and Keene had drawn their weapons and began returning the fire from opposite sides of the aisle.

"Keep your heads down," Thomas yelled to the women, who were already crouched low between the seats.

As the train slowed to ascend a sharp incline, two of the more aggressive attackers leaped onto the observation platform to uncouple the car.

Guessing their intent, Thomas rushed to the end of the car. By the time he opened the door, the Indians had succeeded in uncoupling the car. He shot one of the attackers, and for a brief moment he stared into the equally surprised eyes of Stalking Moon. The train had almost reached the top of the incline. When the engine pulled away, for a scant second their car rattled to a stop, hesitated, then began to roll backwards, gathering momentum as it slid back down the incline.

The Indians stopped their pursuit and turned

their ponies, following the runaway car.

As Stalking Moon leaped from the platform, the sleeve of his tunic hooked on to the loose coupling, and the young Indian began to be dragged alongside the train. He tried unsuccessfully to grip the railing with his other hand and pull himself up before being dragged under the crushing wheels of the car.

Seeing his plight, Thomas instinctively went to his aid. Slipping his pistol back into its holster, he grabbed the railing and leaned out over the side of the speeding car. Stalking Moon grasped the helping hand offered him, and Thomas succeeded in pulling the boy back onto the platform.

Keene's supply of ammunition was exhausted by the time the car reached the bottom of the hill and rolled to a stop. The Indians immediately surrounded them and herded the helpless prisoners off the train.

The Indians stopped their yelping when their chief and half-a-dozen braves slowly trotted out on horseback from the cover of the trees. Spotted Deer halted before Thomas and climbed down from his horse. Stalking Moon walked over to him, and for a brief moment the two spoke in soft tones.

Spotted Deer turned to Thomas. "Medicine man of the Iron Horse, you have come to be called Hands That Heal among my people. Two times you have risked your life to save the life of Stalking Moon. Spotted Deer will spare the lives of you and your squaws."

Yelping and whooping, several of the bucks

converged on Keene and pulled off his boots and shirt. They dragged him over to a tree and tied his arms behind him, then bound his ankles.

"If you are grateful, Spotted Deer, then release my friend too," Thomas said.

"MacKenzie has killed many of my warriors," the chief declared. "He must die."

"You and your followers are not worthy to be called warriors, Spotted Deer," Keene replied contemptuously. "You crawl on your stomach like snakes. Your enemies, the brave dog soldiers of the Cheyenne, do not even count your scalps as coup. Even your Shoshoni brothers call you Bad Lodges."

The chief's eyes flared with anger. "Your death will be slow, MacKenzie. We will skin you slowly and gnaw on your flesh before you. MacKenzie will scream for death many times before he meets it."

"Oh, Dear God, no," Kathleen cried out, straining to free herself from the hold of her captors.

The chief nodded to one of the braves holding a knife. The Indian walked up and made several slashes on Keene's shoulder. Keene grunted with pain but did not cry out when the Indian peeled off a strip of the skin. A film of perspiration dotted his brow, but Keene's eyes remained impassive.

Rory and Kathleen continued to struggle unsuccessfully to free themselves from their captor. Thomas was more successful. He broke free and raced to Keene's assistance, shoving aside the brave who was about to peel away another strip of skin.

The Ute lunged at Thomas. Spotted Deer barked a sharp order, which brought the brave to a halt.

"Stay out of this, Doc, and get the women out of here," Keene yelled.

Turning to the chief, Thomas shouted, "Is this how the chief of the Ute shows his gratitude?"

"Spotted Deer has promised that Hands That Heal and his squaws can pass unharmed. But MacKenzie is the enemy of my people. He has killed many of my warriors. Hunted the game that feeds our squaws and papooses."

"And Spotted Deer is the enemy of my people. But that did not stop me from helping the son of Spotted Deer," Thomas declared. "A few years ago my people, the Confederacy, warred against the Great Father in Washington. Thousands of our young warriors died, our homes destroyed because their numbers were too great, their medicine too powerful for my people to defeat them," Thomas said earnestly.

"The Iron Horse cannot be stopped. It has come to stay. The great Sioux and Cheyenne Nations to the East failed to stop it; and their numbers are greater than the Ute. More people will come by the thousands. More numbers than all the Indian Nations combined."

Thomas walked up to Spotted Deer and stood before him. "Why destroy your young in a battle you cannot win? Did I save Stalking Moon only to see him die from starvation, or be hunted down like a jackal by the soldiers that will soon follow?

"Your cause is a lost one, Spotted Deer. The

time of the Ute has passed. Make your peace with the Great Father in Washington. Your other Shoshoni brothers have. Great chiefs such as Black Tail Deer and Lodge Pole's Son have all signed treaties with the Great White Father. These chiefs have been given beef to feed the bellies of their hungry, bulls to begin to raise their own herds, blankets to warm their people in the winter. These chiefs have given their people a chance for life—not death."

A murmur ran through the crowd as the Indians whispered this latest news among themselves.

"Spare your people further suffering. Show *your* wisdom as a chief by making peace," Thomas continued. "Begin now. Prove your good intentions with the release of MacKenzie."

"MacKenzie has killed the Ute!" Spotted Deer lashed out.

"But not until the Ute tried to kill him," Thomas pointed out. "MacKenzie and the Ute lived in peace until the arrival of the Iron Horse. MacKenzie is a son of these mountains the same as the Ute. He is not your enemy."

For a long moment, Spotted Deer stood silent. The rest of the camp waited. Finally, the chief raised his hand and spoke to his tribesmen.

Turning to Thomas, the chief declared, "Hands That Heal speaks with wisdom. Spotted Deer has watched the passing of many moons with a heavy heart as our young warriors fell under the steel hooves of the Iron Horse. Once the prints of the mighty buffalo, the swift deer, the wily fox lay heavy on the trail. Now they vanish in number with each passing moon. Even the cry of the gamecock echoes softly in the forest, for it too has been driven from these hills.

"If the Iron Horse is more massive than the mighty buffalo, more swift than the fleet deer, and more cunning than the wily fox, then the moccasin of the Ute must vanish too. For he does not have medicine more powerful.

"We will go to the West to join our Shoshoni brothers. Tell your chief of the Iron Horse that Spotted Deer will no longer wage war on him. His people can walk in peace the paths once trod by the Ute and Gosuite."

"And what of MacKenzie?" Thomas asked, daring to hope.

"An eye for an eye." When Thomas started to protest, Spotted Deer raised a hand to stop him. "An eye for an eye, Hands That Heal. Spotted Deer will return MacKenzie's life to you—as you have returned a son to Spotted Deer."

Drawing his knife, Spotted Deer cut the skin on his arm. After doing the same to Thomas, the chief rubbed the bleeding cuts together.

"Now we are blood brothers, and the wisdom of Hands That Heal has flowed into Spotted Deer."

"And Hands That Heal has become wiser and braver because he now carries the blood of Spotted Deer," Thomas replied. A glimmer of pride gleamed in the chief's eyes at this tribute from one whom he respected.

The chief climbed on his horse, and the other braves followed him into the trees.

"Well, Doc, I'm beholdin' to you," Keene said as Thomas untied him. Kathleen flung herself into his arms.

Rory cast an adoring smile at Thomas. "You're not the only one grateful, Keene."

"Let me take a look at that shoulder," Thomas announced, brushing aside the compliments. "Good Lord," he said grimly, glancing at the bloody, exposed flesh. "Man's inhumanity to man never ceases to amaze me. Let's get back to the train where I can treat that wound."

They returned to the car, and Thomas retrieved his medical bag. "Try not to move your shoulder around too much," he warned as he worked over the wound. "The sooner a scabrous membrane forms, the less chance we'll have to worry about infection."

Keene looked confused. "You saying as soon as the skin grows back?"

"Or a scab forms," Thomas grinned.

"Should have said that in the first place, Doc," Keene said.

"Oh, that would be too simple. The *doctor* must always sound wise and omnipotent," Rory teased. She leaned over and kissed the top of Thomas's head. "Right, Doctor?"

Thomas cast her a tolerant smile. "That's right, the doctor knows everything."

"He's sure convinced me. With his gift of gab, if I were you, Rory, I'd try and talk him into hanging around these parts and running for governor."

"I had the same thoughts," she said. "Might have to call on you for help, though."

Thomas winked at Keene as he finished dressing the wound. "I must be suffering sunstroke. Did I hear Rory Callahan Graham admit she might need somebody's help?"

"You notice she said, help, Doc, not advice," Keene joshed.

"Whose side are you on, Keene MacKenzie?" Rory declared with a sassy flash of her green eyes.

"Let's get out of here," Thomas advised. "Just in case Spotted Deer reconsiders."

"Is the war really over? Has peace finally come to these hills?" Rory asked.

"Well, I'm not gonna hang around here to find out," Keene replied. He squeezed Kathleen's hand.

"We've got about a twenty-mile hike back to Ogden. Let's get moving, sweetheart."

Chapter Twenty-two

Ephriam Anderson not only acted but also looked like a no-nonsense kind of individual. A smile rarely crossed his face—a laugh, never. Lacking the vibrant coloring of his Swedish ancestry, he appeared to be a vague, silvery abstraction. He had a gray beard trimmed closely to his chin, gray hair groomed neatly to his neck and round gray eyes which never seemed to blink from behind a pair of gold-framed glasses. He was never seen wearing anything other than a gray suit and vest, a white shirt with a high starched collar, a gray cravat, a gray top hat, and highly polished black shoes.

Ephriam usually wore a pained expression caused by a strong headache, the result of inhaling the potent vapor uniquely related to his chosen profession. He had neither friends nor visitors—also characteristic of his chosen profession. Ephriam Anderson was a chemist with the Union Pacific.

Each day, Ephriam combined three common and widely used chemicals—sulfuric acid, glycerine, and nitric acid—to form a compound known as glyceryl trinitrate, a light, oily, yellow liquid more commonly referred to as nitroglycerine.

With the final swing toward the summit of Promontory, the heavy blasting through mountains had been completed, and all that remained was minor leveling of a few rock outcroppings which had been encountered while laying the bed of the track. The men would drill small holes into the resistant rock, pour a few drops of nitro into the hole, plug the opening with straw, and detonate with a fuse. This procedure saved not only time, but energy. Since nitroglycerine was eight times more powerful than the black powder previously used, a smaller hole could be drilled and the force of the blast also pulverized the rock so that it could be used for ballast.

But this compound was volatile and unpredictable. Since his arrival in Ogden, Ephriam had lived and worked in an isolated hut at the far end of Tent Town. He would rarely process more than one ounce because it was so sensitive to heat and impact. For the same reason, Ephriam would never transport at one time more than one centiliter of the fluid, a quantity more understandably described as "a mite more than a third of an ounce."

On this particular morning, with daylight a

379

pink and gray promise on the horizon, Ephriam was preparing the last batch he would make before leaving Ogden—a small quantity for some minor blasting by the clean-up crew.

His spirits were high. Within hours, he would be on a train heading back to Minnesota, having saved enough money to open a small pharmacy. He had no desire to remain in Utah to witness the Golden Spike ceremony. He had endured more than enough of the Union Pacific Railroad and the people associated with it.

The temperature was unseasonably warm for the first week in May, so he propped open the door to allow some fresh air to circulate in the tiny, windowless hut.

The chemist divided the liquid equally into two vials and capped them tightly to avoid any leakage. After placing one of the vials in a square carrying case made from six-inch steel plates, he cautiously picked up the remaining vessel and put it into a grooved niche beside the other in the case.

Absorbed in the task, he was unaware of the figure that stealthily slipped through the open door. Ephriam never anticipated the blow that rendered him unconscious.

Physically, Anthony Concetti was the antithesis of Ephriam Anderson. The young Italian was short in stature and had a handsome, beardless face that usually wore a roguish grin. Outgoing by nature, he laughed easily, and women found him irresistible—possibly due to the long, black hair that hung to his shoulders, and the thick, dark lashes that tipped his deep brown eyes.

But despite these sharp contrasts, Anthony Concetti and Ephriam Anderson had one thing in common—both men indulged in a dangerous profession.

Anthony Concetti was a cardsharp. A cardsharp who entertained a weakness for a flirtatious smile or flashing eye.

When Tony wasn't cheating at cards or wooing a pretty girl, he traveled with a small medicine show, doing whatever odd job was required of him, whether masquerading as Professor Omnipotent under a long, black beard, flowing robe, and jeweled turban, or an animal tamer with a trained bear.

And while the garb worn by Ephriam Anderson was as predictable as the man himself, Tony Concetti wore many hats; no disguise was beyond the imagination of the handsome ne'er-do-well who always managed to get out of town just one step ahead of the local sheriff, an irate card player, or an indignant father with a shotgun.

While departing from a late-night tryst, Tony's attention was drawn to the hut at the far end of town. From the time Tony had heard about the nitroglycerine, he had been fascinated with the mysterious structure. Seeing the open door of the hut only piqued his curiosity more. He stepped back into the shadows to observe it. After a few minutes, he walked down to take a closer look.

*   *   *

As Rory pulled on her robe, she glanced out of the window. It was barely dawn. The urgent knocking that had awakened her became louder, and she hurried to the door. Anticipating someone from Tent Town in need of immediate medical attention, she widened her eyes with astonishment at the sight of Tony Concetti, recognizing at once her nemesis.

"It's you!" she exclaimed. "I mean, you're him! The man on the train."

Flashing his irresistible grin, Tony doffed his hat. "How do, Mrs. Graham. Pleasure to see you again." His dark eyes swept over her. "I seem to be always catching you in your robe."

Instinctively, she tightened her robe around her and eyed him with suspicion. "What do you want?"

"The doctor, ma'am. There's a man who needs some medical attention."

"Doctor Graham isn't here. He spent the night at the railroad camp. You'll have to get the town doctor."

Distrustful of the bizarre character who now appeared before her as a man, Rory quickly slammed and bolted the door. She rushed to the window and watched him race down the street toward the home of Doctor Jensen.

This time Rory was determined not to let the fellow get away without a full explanation. She dressed quickly in time to follow the two men hurrying to Anderson's hut.

The town sheriff arrived on the scene by the time the chemist regained consciousness.

Anderson related his knowledge of what had happened. When Rory looked around for Tony, she discovered that he had disappeared. Exasperated, she left the hut and began to search for the evasive scoundrel.

Her efforts proved futile. She checked out every facility she could think of, even the saloons and the hotel, but saw no sign of him. Finally, after another fruitless hour of searching, Rory realized where she would find him. She hurried to the railroad station.

The depot was deserted except for the station master, fast asleep on a cot behind the ticket window. As she turned to leave, Tony stepped out of concealment and clamped a hand over her mouth, pulling her into the shadows. "Please don't scream, Mrs. Graham. I don't intend to hurt you," he cautioned.

Ever since the incident in Omaha, when he had disguised himself as a woman in order to get out of town in one piece, Rory had held a certain fascination for the young man. The cat-and-mouse game he played with her was unintentional, but thoroughly entertaining to the young rogue. And it was out of consideration for Rory that Tony had not told the sheriff what he knew about Anderson's attacker.

"Will you promise not to scream if I release you?" he asked. "Please trust me, Mrs. Graham."

Rory nodded and Tony dropped his hand. "Just who are you?" she demanded, her eyes glaring with anger.

"Who I am is of no importance, Rory." His

dark eyes flashed roguishly. "You will forgive me for my informality, but remember we did share a bunk."

"Ha! I hope you don't think you'll buy my silence with that threat. Well, you just try, sir. My husband can swear you were masquerading as a woman."

Tony shook his head, shutting off her tirade. "This has nothing to do with what happened on the train, Rory. I planned on just getting out of town without saying anything, but I've been watching you search all over town for me, so I figure I'd better tell you the truth before I leave. Your father was the one who knocked out Anderson and stole the nitro. I saw him."

The accusation sounded ludicrous to Rory. "I don't believe you. You're making this up," she scoffed. "You probably tried to rob Mr. Anderson yourself and are attempting to shift the blame to my father."

"Rory, if I wanted to falsely implicate your father, I would have told the sheriff. I feel bad about the way I frightened you on the train. That's why you're the only one I'm telling this to."

"Why would my father steal nitroglycerine?" she argued.

"You'll have to ask your father that, not me."

Despite her protests, Rory already suffered a sense of foreboding. But she would never admit it to this stranger. "Furthermore, why should I believe anything said by a man who—who dresses up in women's clothing and terrorizes innocent girls?"

"I had no way of knowing there'd be a train accident, Rory. I dressed in women's clothes because it was the only thing I could think of at the time to get out of town."

"What'd you do? Rob the bank?" she snorted.

A wide grin sparked a mischievous gleam in his dark eyes. "It was merely a—ah, romantic indiscretion. The young woman was kind enough to offer me the use of some of her clothing as a means to elude her shotgun-toting husband."

Rory's reservations were beginning to weaken. The outrageous rogue had a devilish charm. "And what's your excuse for Laramie, *Doctor Omnipotent?* Don't think I've forgotten about that."

Shrugging, he spread his hands in a gesture of apology. "What can I say?"

Relenting, Rory turned away from the persuasive dark eyes. "Well, I'll ride out to the Circle C and talk to my father. I still don't believe you. Maybe you mistook someone else for him."

Tony knew he wasn't mistaken; having been around Ogden for the past couple of weeks, he recognized the well-known rancher. But his Latin heart swelled in sympathy for the girl's wasted loyalty. Smiling compassionately, he took her hand and raised it to his lips. "Maybe I did, Rory."

Within minutes, Rory was on a horse racing to the Circle C. When she thundered up to the ranch house, Pete Faber stepped out of the stable to greet her. "Where's my father?"

"Ain't seen him around all morning, Rory.

Charlie said he ain't in his room either."

Her eyes clouded in alarm. "I think he's stolen some nitro, Pete," she said worriedly.

Suddenly a distant reverberation that sounded like the rumble of thunder shattered the morning stillness. The glances of the two startled people swung to one another and locked. Both knew it was not thunder.

The force of the blast knocked Thomas off his cot. He grabbed his medical bag and hurried out of the tent. A cloud of dust obliterated the scene. Coughing and brushing aside the suffocating haze, Thomas finally managed to survey the damage.

Part of the face of the mountain had collapsed, blocking the entrance to a cave where several of the crew had spent the night to get out of the rain. The area was full of these large caverns, dug by French Canadian trappers decades earlier for storing their furs and supplies.

Pandemonium now reigned as rescuers shouted and scrambled over the rubble, trying to open a passage.

After much effort, they succeeded in gouging a large opening which finally enabled Thomas's voice to be heard by the men trapped inside. "This is Doctor Graham. Can anyone hear me?"

"Yeah, Doc," a voice responded, feebly.

"Any wounded in there?"

"Yeah, we need help, Doc."

"Can you move around?"

"No, we're pinned down. Half the ceiling came down on us."

Turning back to the other men, Thomas said, "I have to get in there. We'll have to widen this hole enough for me to get through."

"If more of that ceilin' collapses, you could get buried in there," Michaleen declared. "Why don't you wait 'til we can be gettin' them out, Doctor?"

"They could bleed to death by that time," Thomas said. "I'll worm my way through. Just widen that hole a little more."

The men put their picks and shovels to the task, but progress was slow. For every shovelful they removed, it seemed that a dozen more took its place.

"Oh, you're a stubborn man, Doctar," Michaleen declared a short while later after watching several of Thomas's unsuccessful attempts to squirm through the opening. "Well, step aside, lads. The situation is now needin' the services of Michaleen Timothy Dennehy." Anchoring his tam firmly on his head, the little cook started to wiggle through the hole.

"Michaleen, you don't have to do this," Thomas protested.

"That I don't, Doctar," Dennehy agreed and disappeared through the opening.

Working from the inside, Michaleen managed to dig out enough to allow Thomas to worm through. "Now my medical bag," he called out. He snatched the bag as soon as it was shoved through the opening.

T.J. Callahan had slipped into the black hole of madness. He moved around in brooding silence, snarling and cursing at anyone who approached him. Not many did; even his long-time, most trusted aides now avoided him. Charlie Toy tiptoed when serving Callahan meals, in fear that the rancher would turn his wrath upon him. Pete Faber stopped making morning visits, since he and his boss could no longer agree on what had to be done.

Each day since Rory's departure, Callahan had ridden alone to the boundary of his ranch. With malevolence gleaming in his eyes, he would watch the railroad crew laboring at the few tasks remaining to be done.

Each day he would watch them set their charges, destroying the land with their explosives and machines.

And each minute that he watched, his hatred for the railroad increased along with his madness.

The railroad had killed his wife, purloined his daughter, and continued to ravish the land. He knew it must be stopped.

And then he had gotten his inspiration on how to do it.

Unnoticed by the rescuers, Callahan watched their efforts from the ledge above. Crazed by hate and bitterness, he grinned at the sight of the frantic rescue attempt because he knew it would all be in vain. Then his eyes glowed with malice when he recognized Thomas Graham among their ranks. He still had one more vial of nitro.

Callahan's pleasure spiraled when he saw

Thomas Graham crawl through a hole in the rubble. This was more than he had hoped for. He reached for the case containing the second vial.

Below, one of the guards looked up and saw the rancher on the ledge above. "Hey, what are you doing up there?" Suspicious, he raised his rifle.

Callahan removed the vial of nitroglycerine. The second explosion would permanently seal the entrance and entomb Thomas Graham, killing two birds with one stone: he would drive the railroad away from the Circle C, and Rory would now come back home. Fortune had smiled on him again.

He stood up to toss down the vessel on the men and debris below. The guard guessed his intention. "Look out," he shouted to the rescuers. He fired, and the bullet found its mark in Callahan's chest.

The warning shout and the shot that followed sent the rescuers scrambling for cover. The impact of the bullet spun Callahan around. Stumbling, he fell backward and the vial flew forward out of his hand as he plunged over the edge of the cliff. The volatile liquid exploded on impact when it hit the ground, blasting a hole at the top of the cliff. Tons of rock and dirt tumbled down from above, further sealing the cave.

Attracted by the sound of the first explosion, Keene MacKenzie rode up to the scene in time to see Callahan fall an instant before the second explosion toppled more of the mountain down on the camp. When the dust had cleared, the camp began to stir again, and the men moved to the mound of rubble and dirt which now had become insurmountable.

Dismounting, Keene knelt over the broken figure lying on the ground. "Why'd you do it, T.J.?"

"Wanted to blow up the damn track," Callahan said, barely able to whisper.

The clatter of hooves caused Keene to look up. Rory, Pete Faber, and several of the Circle C riders came thundering into camp. Seeing Keene kneeling over a body, they rode over to him. It was then that they recognized the wounded man on the ground.

"Daddy!" Rory cried, and jumped off her horse. "Oh, God, Daddy." She knelt over him and her frantic glance swung to Keene. He shook his head in answer to her silent question. Sorrowfully, the Circle C riders removed their hats and gathered around the dying man.

Tears trickled down Rory's cheeks as she picked up her father's hand and brought it to her lips. "Don't cry, gal. Ain't got time for tears." The rancher's face grooved with pain. "Made a couple mistakes. Gotta set 'em right before . . . I go." He closed his eyes, grimacing with pain.

"Don't try to talk now, Daddy," Rory cried fearfully. She raised her head and looked around frantically. "Where's Thomas? He'll help you, Daddy."

"Love you, gal. You know that, don'tcha?"

"Yes, Daddy," Rory sobbed. "And I love you too."

"Don't think you will . . . when you learn what I did." Then a dark mist began to shroud his vision, and Callahan reached out a groping hand. "Son? Son, where are ya?"

Keene MacKenzie had waited his whole life to hear that single word pass the lips of his father. Despite the stoic shield the reticent scout had maintained throughout his life, Keene's eyes now glistened with moisture. "I'm right here, Father." He kneeled down beside the dying man.

"I've always been proud of you, son. Should have . . . should have told ya sooner. Take care of your sister and the Circle C. Don't let 'em . . . destroy it." Callahan's body contracted in a seizure, then he closed his eyes for the final time.

Sobbing, Rory buried her head against the dead man's chest. "Come on, Rory," Keene said gently. He took her by the shoulders and lifted her to her feet. For several long moments, he held her in his arms and let her spend her tears.

Finally, with a shuddering sob, Rory raised her head and looked at her brother. "He's responsible for the blasts, isn't he?"

"I think so."

No one paid any attention to Pete Faber. The grizzled foreman had ridden at Callahan's side for over twenty years. Shuffling his crushed hat from one hand to the other, he stared down at the still figure, confused and broken-hearted.

"Why'd he go do a fool thing like this? Just weren't his way. Man went plum loco these

391

last couple years. The old T.J. would of rode up bold-like, maybe even pump some lead into the air to scare 'em off, but he'd sure never blow up the place." The old-timer sniffled and brushed his sleeve across his nose. "T.J. just weren't himself no more."

Rory stood and put her arms around him. "He hasn't been himself for a long time, Pete." For a lengthy moment, the two people who had continued to love Thomas Callahan despite his misdeeds embraced, drawing comfort from each other. Then Rory stepped back and kissed the old man's weathered cheek. "He's out of his misery now."

"Reckon so, Rory."

The foreman turned to Keene. "Boys and me will take T.J. back to the ranch . . . Boss."

Keene's nod silently acknowledged acceptance of his new station.

"Rory, why don't you go with them?" Keene said.

"No," she said wearily. "I'd better go and find Thomas. He must have his hands full and probably could use some help." As one of the men hurried by, Rory called out to him. "Where's Doctor Graham?"

"Doc? Ain't you heard, ma'am?" he said. He cast a helpless glance at Keene, hoping for assistance.

Her chest constricted, and Rory felt the quick rise of panic. "Heard what?" Keene sensed what the man was about to say and instinctively reached out to her.

"The Doc's buried behind that rock," the

worker said. Unable to look her in the eye, he hurried away.

The sky began to spin around her, and Keene caught Rory just before the ground rose up to hit her in the face.

Chapter Twenty-three

Thick whorls of dust swirled through the air, filling the inside of the darkened cave with a smoky haze. Thomas had to stoop and even crawl in some sections. The moans and pleas of the wounded sounded like a dirge from hell.

Many were bleeding and unconscious. Most of the ceiling of the cave had collapsed, pining them under rock and rubble.

"Michaleen, can you give me a hand?" Thomas asked, trying to free one of the victims. "We have to move him gently."

The two men moved as swiftly as the cramped area would allow. Thomas had just wrapped a dressing around the head of an injured gauger when a second explosion shook the ground like an earthquake. With apprehension, he glanced up and then threw himself protectively across the helpless man on the ground as more of the makeshift ceiling fell down upon them.

The chamber was pitched into total blackness; the faint light that had filtered through the small opening had been instantly obliterated by the landslide.

After the ground ceased to vibrate, the silence in the cave became terrifying. Thomas raised his head and tried to adjust his vision to the darkness.

With a powerful thrust of his upper body, he raised his shoulders, casting off the heavy layer of dirt that covered him. Working hurriedly, he managed to free his legs.

He brushed the dirt off the body of the man beneath him and groped for the wrist of the wounded victim. Relieved, he felt a pulse.

"Michaleen," he called out. "Michaleen, where are you?"

There was no reply. Alarmed, Thomas crawled over a mound of dirt to where he knew another injured man lay. He scooped away the dirt with his hands, made the man as comfortable as possible, then crawled to the next one.

A flurry of activity caused him to again peer through the darkness toward the far corner. "Is that you, Michaleen?" he asked hopefully.

Sputtering and spitting, Michaleen Dennehy raised himself from under a blanket of fallen earth. "And who else would it be in this dark hole 'cept the dev'l himself," he carped. He shook the dust off his tam and plunked the hat back on his head. "Didn't I warn you, Doctar? Didn't I tell you this would happen?" he declared, with typical Irish pessimism.

395

"Save your breath, Michaleen, and stop getting yourself excited," Thomas warned. "You'll breathe less oxygen."

"What are you tryin' to say, Doctar?" Michaleen asked suspiciously.

"I'm saying that in a short while, I imagine every bit of oxygen will become very precious to us. Who knows how long it will take to dig us out of here."

The little cook was finally struck with the startling reality of their desperate straits. "Saints preserve us," he mumbled softly. "We're buried alive."

Already behind schedule, Caleb Murphy pulled "Betsy" into the depot at Ogden. Heavy rains had slowed him on the trip from Laramie. After maneuvering the train to a siding, he waited impatiently for a switchman to uncouple several cars. Chewing on a piece of straw, Murphy watched with interest as one of the Circle C ranch hands came riding up at a full gallop.

"There's been a big explosion a ways down the track. Some men are trapped, including the Doc," he shouted to Murphy. "Need all the help we can get to dig 'em out."

The tall man disembarking from the private railroad car had just assisted his wife off the train. Overhearing the urgent words of the excited cowboy, he jerked to attention. "Doctor? What's his name?" Ruark Stewart asked with apprehension.

"Doc Graham," the cowboy said.

Angeleen's hand flew to her mouth to smother

a startled gasp. "Oh, dear God!"

"What happened?" Ruark said.

"There was two blasts. From what I was told, the first blast trapped some of them railroaders in a cave or something. The Doc crawled in to treat the wounded, and the second blast trapped him along with 'em."

"So they all could still be alive," Ruark said.

"Not for long, mister. That whole damn mountain is between them and us."

Ruark Stewart bolted into action. "Young man, what's your name?"

"Curly Masters, sir," the young cowpoke replied.

"All right, Curly, you go and find the town doctor. Tell him to bring along all the medical supplies he has on hand. Mr. Murphy, start yanking on that whistle and don't stop until everybody in this town shows up here."

Something about the mien of the tall stranger automatically commanded authority. The two men complied without further comment.

Ruark turned to his stunned wife and hugged her. "Honey, we'll get him out."

Angel's chin quivered as she smiled at him through her tears. "I know you will, Ruark." Struck with a sudden thought, her sapphire eyes rounded in alarm. "Oh, Lord! Where is Rory? If she's heard about this, she must be half out of her mind by now."

"It might be better if you try to find her. You and Tommy wait here in town with her."

"I am not waiting here, Ruark Stewart," Angel declared. "I'm going with you."

"I figured as much."

He hopped up into the cab of the train. "Do you know if there are any steam shovels at the camp?" he shouted in an effort to be heard above the shrill blast of the whistle.

Murphy lifted off his cap and scratched his head. "Naw. All the heavy equipment was moved toward Promontory a couple weeks ago. There's just a clean-up crew left behind to finish whatever had to be done to the bed. Matter of fact, I was supposed to pick up the Doc and take him on up to Promontory."

"Well then, let's couple those cars of mine back onto this train."

"Good idea, Mr. Stewart." Murphy stuck his head out of the window of the cab. "Hey, O'Reilly, hitch those cars back on," he shouted. Grumbling, the switchman began to insert the pins relinking the cars that he had just disconnected.

Murphy had worked up a full head of steam by the time most of the town's citizens arrived on the scene. Ruark explained the situation and called for volunteers. Those who were able climbed on the train wherever they could find room.

Two of the women stepped forward and asked to come along. "Ladies, I don't think it will be a fitting place for a woman," Ruark said kindly.

Unblinking, one of the women shoved past him. "Mister, if my husband's hurtin', there's no more fittin' place for me to be."

Angel agreed with the sentiment. "You come with me, ladies." Linking her arms through theirs, she led them to the private car.

"Excuse me." Angel turned to the young woman who had stepped forward to address her. "Would you mind if I come along?" Kathleen Rafferty asked.

"Is your husband there too?" Angel asked kindly.

"No, but—but someone I care about," Kathleen said, visualizing Keene buried under the rubble.

Angel smiled in understanding. "Of course." As Angel followed Kathleen onto the observation platform of the car, she voiced a worried thought. "Are you acquainted with the doctor's wife?"

"Oh, yes," Kathleen nodded. "And a saint she is, too."

"Do you have any idea where I can find her?"

"She rode off like a bolt of lightnin' this morning. I'm thinkin' she went to the camp," Kathleen said.

"Are you well acquainted with Mrs. Graham?"

Kathleen noticed that the woman spoke with the same, pleasant-sounding southern drawl as Doctor Graham. "Better than most here," she acknowledged.

Angel took a longer look at the frail, but lovely young woman. "Then you must be Kathleen."

"Yes, ma'am. Kathleen Rafferty."

"I remember Rory bought you a pair of hose in St. Louis."

For a moment, a tinge of pleasure heightened

Kathleen's face. "Then I'm thinkin' you must be Angel. Rory speaks of you often." *And no wonder,* Kathleen thought with awe as she studied the beautiful and gracious lady.

The volunteers were boarded and waiting by the time Curly returned with the doctor. As soon as the medical supplies had been loaded into the private car, Ruark hopped up into the cab. "Okay, Murphy, let's roll," he ordered.

A short time later, when the train arrived at the camp, the small work force had made little progress in digging through the debris.

Ruark took command at once. Jumping down from the cab before the train had come to a full stop, he barked out a command. "All right, let's get this equipment unloaded."

The workers stared in surprise at him and then gaped in disbelief at the heavy-duty machines lashed to the flat cars. "Any of you fellows ever work one of these donkey machines before?" Ruark asked, pointing to the mammoth steam shovel he had brought west for his mining operation.

"I have," one of the men said, stepping forward.

"What's your name?" Ruark asked.

"Tommy O'Shaughnessy, sir."

Ruark reached out and shook the man's hand. "O'Shaughnessy, I'm not going to waste time on long introductions. My name's Ruark Stewart and I'm president of Stewart Enterprises. I've got a friend trapped behind that rubble, and I'm offering you a thousand dollars to get that machine powered up and start moving that rock," Ruark said.

A thousand dollars was more than O'Shaughnessy made in a year. "You can consider it done, mister, but I'll not be doin' it for the money. I've got friends under that rock, too."

He turned to the other stunned workers. "All right, you sons of—Erin—let's be gettin' this equipment movin'."

Ruark grinned and slapped the man on the back. "O'Shaughnessy, you've just earned yourself a foreman's job with Stewart Enterprises anytime you want it."

Ruark rolled up his shirt sleeves and joined the crew that began to unlash a big steam winch and several steam percussion drills.

When he heard his name called out, he spun around to see Rory running toward him. "Oh, Ruark," she cried, rushing into his arms.

Ruark hugged her for a long moment, then tipped up her chin to meet his concerned gaze. "We'll get him out, Rory," he said. He kissed her cheek and then released her to Angel's outstretched arms.

Tearfully, the two women clung together. "Oh, I'm so glad you're here," Rory sobbed. The emotional impact of seeing these cherished friends of Thomas gave her a renewed faith in the outcome.

As soon as Kathleen Rafferty stepped off the train, her worried glance swept the small compound in search of Keene. Spying the buckskin-clad figure approaching her, Kathleen made a quick sign of the cross, closed her eyes, and said a short prayer of thanks.

She opened her eyes to meet his steady, silvery gaze. "You shouldn't have come. This is no place for you, Kathleen."

"I had to know if you were safe," she said.

Keene and Kathleen had long been private and lonely individuals. Both had learned through the sadness in their lives to disguise their true feelings behind impassive facades. But at this moment, Kathleen was so relieved that she wanted to throw herself into his arms. She yearned for the warmth of his touch, the feel of his arms around her.

Although her gentle heart ached for the suffering of those who had loved ones at risk, for now she selfishly savored the joy of knowing the man she loved was safe.

The tiny woman stared into the face she so cherished. Then Kathleen smiled. And for those few, revealing seconds, unobserved by those around them, Keene MacKenzie knew the full glory of love.

In a short time, the powerful steam shovel began to scoop up the earth, but tons of rock and gravel would have to be dug away.

"Let's get a couple of those drills working and start sinking some parallel shafts," Ruark ordered. He pointed to a spot midway up the hillside. "A couple of you men get up there with a drill and start driving a shaft from above."

"You're daft, man. That's solid rock. It'll take days to drill through any of that wall," one of the men scoffed. "We're just wastin' our time.

There ain't nobody gonna come out of there alive." He threw down his shovel and started to walk away.

A strong hand clamped down on his shoulder and spun him around. Ruark Stewart clutched the shirtfront of the rebellious man and almost yanked him off his feet.

"Dammit, I've got percussion drills here. They can bore through six feet of solid rock in less than two hours. If nothing else, we can run in pipes to get air to them," Ruark shouted. "Now stop saying it can't be done, and get your ass moving." The man was too intimidated to argue. He picked up his shovel and returned to work.

Rory had stood in stunned silence listening with the rest of the men. Mesmerized, she barely felt the arm that slipped around her waist. "I believe I once hinted how much of a 'mover and shaker' he can be when provoked," Angel whispered in her ear.

Soon the steam winch couldn't haul away the dirt and gravel as fast as O'Shaughnessy scooped it up. The crews drilling the shafts were carting the debris away in wheelbarrows. Circle C cowpunchers worked side by side with the Union Pacific track layers, past rivalries forgotten in their urgency to free the trapped men.

Nightfall came, and Murphy turned on the powerful headlamp of the train to light the area as the workers continued, driven by the relentless taskmaster who swung a shovel or pick right along with them. The men paused in their labor only long enough to take a few sips of hot coffee from the women who passed among them.

And no one further challenged the demands put on them by the tall stranger from the East.

Woodenly, Rory continued the task of preparing sandwiches and pots of coffee. Her hope for an early rescue dissipated with each passing hour. But she firmly held to the conviction that Thomas would be found alive.

As the night lengthened, deepening feelings of sorrow and guilt added to her heartache. Her father's death and the knowledge that he was responsible for the tragedy filled her with despair. And with this misery came self-recrimination.

Was her father solely to blame? Had her actions led him to journey beyond the boundary of sanity into a world of madness? Had she now destroyed Thomas too?

You are not dead, my love. I would know it. I would feel it, she told herself, shaking off her gloom. Then a few minutes later she would begin the torturous mental exercise again.

The first encouraging sign came when one of the percussion drills broke through the side of the wall. "Get a pipe up here," Ruark shouted.

He and Keene MacKenzie rammed the long, narrow pipe into the opening. Ruark picked up a rock and tapped on the hollow, metal rod. The two men listened intently.

Thomas jerked awake. He sat leaning against a wall, his head slumped forward. Dust had settled on the film of perspiration that coated his body. He had long since disposed of his shirt. Part had been used as a sling for one of the men with a broken arm, the rest ripped into strips to secure gauze dressings. His medical supplies had long been exhausted.

He wiped his brow with his forearm. He figured it had to be more than one hundred degrees in the cave. Nobody spoke or stirred. Most were sleeping or in a soporific state from lack of oxygen. It was just as well, since talking or moving used up the oxygen faster than just sleeping. And the supply was almost exhausted. He could tell that by the effort it took to breathe.

Having dropped in and out of slumber, he had no idea how much time had passed since the second explosion. Was it still morning? Afternoon? Evening? Had another day come and gone? *It couldn't have; he'd be more dehydrated.*

Thomas recalled a story by Poe about a man accidentally entombed, who had imagined himself to be starving. By the time he was freed, the man had eaten the candles in the tomb. How long had he been in that tomb? It had been a ridiculously short amount of time, Thomas reflected. He searched his memory, but the answer eluded him.

Well, he wasn't hungry . . . but a cool glass of water . . . he drifted off to sleep.

A scraping sound awoke him. Or could it have been one of the men just shifting their positions? He closed his eyes, but this time he didn't sleep; he thought about Rory.

If only he could see her, just one more time. To hold her in his arms just once again. To tell her how much he loved her.

He wondered if his suspicions were true, and she now carried his child. The child he might never come to know. Would it be a girl or a boy?

I'm grateful we had at least a short time together, my beloved.

A faint scraping sound drew him out of his meditation. "You're wasting your time, Michaleen. You can't dig your way out of here."

"What did ya say, Doctar?"

"What are you doing over there?"

"I was thinkin' o' a pup I once had when I was just a lad. One day he ran off after a bitch in heat, an' I never saw the little bugger again."

Ruark half-smiled. *Funny what men think about when they are preparing to die.* "I've been thinking of my wife."

"An' a fine figure of a woman she is, Doctar."

"Yeah," Thomas said. A smile of longing softened his face. "She's very beautiful." For a long moment, he sat with the vision of Rory's smiling face before his eyes. Suddenly, he sat up. "There it is again. Don't you hear it, Michaleen?"

Both men listened to the sound of faint tapping. Thomas inched along the wall toward the source of the sound. His hand encountered the end of a metal pipe.

Buoyed with renewed hope, his heartbeat quickened to send blood surging through him. Groping, he found a rock and began tapping on the pipe. Michaleen crawled over to him, and with renewed hope surging through them, the two men listened intently.

* * *

Ruark glanced with relief at his companion when a faint tapping sounded in response. "Thank God! Someone's still alive in there." Hearing the news, a cheer went up from the workers. The knowledge that they would find someone alive revived their enthusiasm, and their efforts intensified. Minutes later, they began pumping air through the pipe.

Angel approached them holding a cup of coffee in each hand. "I think you two could use this right about now."

For a brief moment, Ruark's eyes met Angel's gaze and held it as they exchanged a silent message of love. "Thanks, honey," he said. He reached out and lightly stroked her cheek. "You aren't overdoing it, are you? Remember your condition. Why don't you climb into the car, lie down, and rest for a while."

"There will be plenty of time for resting when this is over with," she said.

"How's Tommy doing?"

"Sound asleep in the car," she said with a soft smile.

"I'd be happier if Tommy's mommy was too," Ruark said.

"Not on your life, Ruark Stewart," she said with a backward glance.

Relinquishing the pump to willing volunteers, the two tired men slumped down for a much-needed break; both of them had worked non-stop since arriving. Grinning, Ruark reached out to shake the hand of the man who had labored steadily beside him. "Ruark Stewart."

Keene accepted the handshake. "Keene MacKenzie."

"Pleasure to meet you, Mr. MacKenzie."

"We're beholdin' to you, Mr. Stewart."

"Too soon to celebrate yet. We still don't have them out, but I figure we'll break through in the next few hours. Just hope we got air to them in time."

Unaware of the pressure he had applied, Ruark clenched his tin cup until it bent. "Do you think we'll get to them in time?" For the first time since the man's arrival, Keene saw a break in Stewart's confidence.

"Reckon so," Keene said solemnly.

"I gather from your dress, you must be one of the ranchers."

"Kind of straddlin' the fence," Keene said, taking a deep draught of the coffee. "Been scouting' for the railroad, but I rode for the Circle C before the war." The fact that Callahan's dying admission had made him part owner of the ranch had already been shoved to the back of Keene's mind.

"Circle C?" The name strummed a familiar chord to Ruark. "Is that the Callahan ranch?"

"Yep," Keene replied.

"Then you're acquainted with Rory."

"Oughta be. She's my sister." Keene felt a surge of pride by saying the words that had remained unspoken for so long.

"Your sister! Then you're T.J.'s brother-in-law," Ruark said with pleasure.

Keene glanced curiously at Ruark. He admired Stewart's authority and leadership; such traits were crucial in the emergency. *But the strain must be getting to the man*, he thought.

"Brother-in-law? Rory's my sister. T.J. was my father." Keene put down his cup. "Pleasure talkin' to you, Mr. Stewart." He hurried away and returned to his job.

Perplexed, Ruark stared into space. "T.J. his father? What the hell is he talking about?"

Seeing her husband's distressed look, Angel hurried over and sat down beside him. "What's wrong, Ruark? You look confused."

Ruark slipped an arm around her shoulder and pulled her to his side. "You know, honey, I thought you Rebs were hard to figure out. But some of these Westerners are really peculiar."

Relieved to hear that there was no unexpected setback, Angeleen patted his hand consolingly. "I understand just what you're going through, sweetheart. I suffered the same misgivings about you Yankees." With a saucy flash of her eyes, she picked up Keene's abandoned cup and moved on.

Ruark shook his head as his adoring gaze following his wife. Grinning, he finished the coffee and went back to work.

Within the hour, two other shafts were feeding air to the entombed survivors.

"I reckon whoever's alive in there could probably use a drink along about now," Keene said. "Too bad we can't do something about that."

Ruark glanced at him askance, his mind already spinning. "Maybe we can do something."

"Whatta you got in mind, Mr. Stewart?"

"We'll get one of the pumps, attach it to the water barrel and feed a hose into the pipe."

"But the pump can only draw water, it can't push it," one of the men said.

"That's right," Ruark agreed. "But what happens when the pipe fills up?"

Keene grinned. "It's gonna overflow at the open end." He shouted to one of the men near the rain barrel. "Couple of you men hitch a sledge to a mule, and tote that water barrel up here."

By sunrise, the steam shovel had plowed through to within a few feet of the entrance of the cave. A crew with picks and shovels moved in to finish the job. After those men tired, others were there to take their place.

A cheer rent the air when the first hole poked through to the opening of the cave. As they were enlarging the opening, suddenly a grizzled mole wearing a red tam poked out its head.

"Saints preserve us!" Michaleen Dennehy declared. "Fresh air and sunlight."

The percussion drills made quick work of enlarging the hole, and the rescuers were soon able to begin removing the wounded. With buoyed spirits, they joked with the victims as they pulled them out and carried them to the tent where Dr. Jensen waited. Then sadly, the mood shifted to grimness as the bodies of the men who had perished were extracted. Finally, Michaleen crawled out.

Ruark Stewart peered through the opening. Grinning, he reached in and clasped the outstretched hand of the last man who emerged.

"Dammit, old friend, didn't I tell you to stay out of trouble?"

Chapter Twenty-four

A weary but saddened group converged on the Circle C in the early hours of the morning. With everyone in a state of shock, the only logical place to go was the ranch, where they all could be together and collect their thoughts. Even Ruark and Angeleen joined them.

So much had to be decided and resolved. The ownership of the Circle C was the most complex problem. Over Keene's objections, Rory signed away any legal claim to her half of the Circle C.

Thomas supported her decision and assured Keene that his sister would be comfortably provided for in Virginia. Nevertheless, Keene prevailed further upon Ruark Stewart's legal expertise to draw up a provision for Rory to be awarded an annual apportionment of the profits of the Circle C and, in the event of an unforeseen tragedy, she could always return to the ranch.

Jack Casement made a short visit to thank Ruark for his help. He informed them that because of flooding in Weber Canyon that prevented trains getting through from the east, the Golden Spike ceremony had been postponed for two days and was now scheduled for May tenth. All were relieved to discover that they would not have to miss this long-awaited occasion.

Due to the circumstances of her father's death, Rory had planned a quiet funeral, with only family and the Circle C riders in attendance. Her hopes vanished when the first carriages and riders began to arrive the next morning.

T.J. Callahan had been as much a visible presence in the community as Brigham Young. Once the word of the rancher's death had spread, the town merchants who had long done business with him, as well as the ranchers and their families from the surrounding community, descended on the Circle C. Even the Mormon leader himself had made the journey from Salt Lake City to pay his last respects. The people came with pies and cakes, breads and relishes, smoked hams and fried chickens, and casseroles wrapped in embroidered towels and tablecloths to keep them warm.

By the time of the burial, a large crowd had assembled at his gravesite, and T.J. Callahan was laid to rest in the ground he had so cherished and shielded. The solemn-faced mourners stood silent as the minister offered the eulogy.

"Finally, I direct my message today to those among you who are critics of this man," the minister said, nearing the end of his dedication.

"Thomas Callahan was a man of courage . . . a man of conviction . . . of iron strength . . . iron will. A man who might stumble but who would not fall. History has always had a season, and a need, for this breed of man, has always looked to him to write the first chapter more often than the last."

The minister's gaze solemnly swept the faces of the mourners as he continued. "And perhaps America might still stand huddled between the Appalachians and the Atlantic shores, or decades might pass before iron rails spanned our coastlines, were it not for this breed of man who paved the path for a nation to follow.

"Such a man was Thomas Callahan. He faced and fought the savagery of this land—be it God-given or man-driven—only to lose the final confrontation to the demons of his own human frailty."

Thomas heard a sob escape from Rory, and he hugged her tighter to his side.

"The great English author, William Shakespeare, eloquently reminded us that a man's evil remains behind him long after his good has been buried with him. And yes, Thomas Callahan did transgress against man. But surely not mankind.

"So as we commit this man's soul to his Maker, I pray, my friends, that we will heed the wisdom of the poet's words and not allow the memory of this man's good to be interred with his bones."

Throughout the ceremony, Thomas had stood beside Rory reflecting on the words of the clergyman. Was this message directed to him alone? Were there others present who struggled with memories so bitter that there seemed to be no room for forgiveness in the heart?

Thomas knew that for Rory's sake, he must put aside all memories of the evil that Callahan had perpetrated. That too must be buried. The specter of T.J. Callahan must never loom between them again. He tightened his grasp on Rory's shoulders.

Later, after long tables were lined with the abundance of food brought for the occasion, Rory thanked the pastor for his help. With hat in hand, Keene MacKenzie approached them. "Pastor Johnson, may I ask a favor of you?"

"Of course, Keene."

"I know this is an improper time, but I would like you to perform a wedding ceremony. I want to get married, sir."

The clergyman was flabbergasted. "Well . . . ah, it's quite unusual to conduct a marriage right after a burial, son."

"I understand that, sir. But Kathleen and I want to get married now, before Rory leaves for the East."

"And Thomas and I will be leaving tomorrow, right after the ceremony at Promontory, Reverend Johnson," Rory added.

"What of the religious complications here? Isn't your intended of a different faith?"

For a brief moment, resentment flared in

Keene's gray eyes. "No, sir. Her *faith* is the same as mine—we believe in the same God. As for her church, we'll do whatever is expected later, but for now, I want us to be wed in the eyes of the law."

The kindly pastor nodded and patted Keene on the shoulder. "It would be my pleasure to join you and your intended in holy matrimony, son."

"Married? Now?" Kathleen exclaimed, flabbergasted, as Rory and Angeleen pulled her away from where she had been slicing ham and quickly hustled her into the house. "But how can we wed now? There's been no banns read, or—"

"Forget the ritual for now," Rory said, looking more excited than the bride. "Keene has arranged for Reverend Johnson to marry you right now. You can have your priest marry you later."

Angeleen grasped the hand of the startled young woman. "You do want to marry Keene, don't you, Kathleen?" she asked in a calm voice.

"With every breath in my body," Kathleen said fervently.

Angeleen's sapphire eyes sparkled with mirth. "Well . . ."

"Then what are we waiting for?" the three women cried out in unison.

Rory brushed the bride's long black hair into a satiny sheen, and Angeleen draped a lacy black shawl on Kathleen's head and shoulders. Then, arm in arm, they left the room giggling like schoolgirls.

With widow's weeds as a wedding gown, Kathleen Rafferty took her place beside Keene MacKenzie. With love gleaming in his gray eyes, he took her trembling fingers in the warmth of his own steady and firm grasp.

Even in a black mourning gown, the bride looked ethereal as she gazed up adoringly at the tall figure at her side. For the funeral, Keene had exchanged his familiar buckskins for black trousers and coat. A white shirt now contrasted sharply against his deeply tanned face and hands.

When the ceremony began, unlike the bride, whose eyes glowed with excitement, Keene's gaze appeared serious, his usual impassive mein replaced with a frown of concentration.

As a gentle breeze ruffled his dark hair, Rory realized that she had never noticed Keene's handsomeness, had always taken her laconic, reticent half-brother for granted.

After this day, nothing will ever be the same, she thought with bittersweet emotion. *Our lives will soon follow different paths. Keene has come home to say, but this time I will be the one leaving the Circle C.*

That sad thought did not dampen the joy in her heart. Happiness for the bridal couple shone in her eyes as she turned her head to gaze at Thomas. He looked more handsome than ever, and her heart swelled with love for him. *But I will be with Thomas,* she thought with a secretive smile.

Thomas grinned and winked at her. Rory smiled back as he squeezed her hand.

Ana Leigh

If there were any skeptics among the assembly that had gathered to mourn and remained to witness the marriage of the young couple, their misgivings went unheeded in the glowing evidence of the bridal couple's love.

As the ceremony progressed, an awkward moment developed when Reverend Johnson asked Keene to place the ring on Kathleen's finger. In the hasty arrangements, that important detail had been overlooked.

Standing beside Thomas, Angeleen Stewart glanced down at a costly sapphire ring on her right hand. She looked at Ruark over the head of their son, whom he held in his arms. Always attuned to her thoughts, Ruark smiled and nodded his consent.

Angeleen slipped the ring from her finger and passed it into Thomas's hand. His dark eyes crinkled with a grin. Then, as best man, he handed the expensive band to the groom.

The slight-of-hand had gone unobserved by the assemblage. Keene slipped the ring onto the finger of his astonished bride.

A short time later, with his hands raised in benediction above the head of the couple, the Reverend Johnson proclaimed Keene and Kathleen to be husband and wife.

And what had begun as a day of mourning had been miraculously transformed into a time of rejoicing.

At sunrise the following morning, Rory and Thomas strolled to the privacy of their familiar ridge. Hand-in-hand, they gazed down into the floor of the canyon. The tree-laden mountains abounded with pine, juniper, and piñon. In the distance, the splendor of the mountain range seemed to stretch to infinity as the rising sun illuminated the rocky ridges and canyons with shifting color. In one single, awesome moment, cinnamon became red, red became orange, and orange became gold; like mighty sentinels, tall green aspen trees reached up to touch the brilliant blue of the sky.

"It's overwhelming, isn't it, Thomas?"

"And very humbling," he said. "You can't help but recognize how insignificant we all are in the scope of His magnitude."

His dark eyes deepened with affection. "I'm proud of you, sweetheart. Knowing how much you love this land, I know it took a great deal of sacrifice to surrender your rights to the Circle C."

"Keene's entitled to the ranch. He's been denied for so long. I'm just thankful Daddy finally acknowledged him." Her green-eyed gaze swept the countryside. "But now that the railroad is completed, we'll come back often, won't we, Thomas?"

He slipped his arms around her waist and drew her back against his chest. "Of course we will, honey. This track is only the beginning. Soon the rails crisscrossing this country will be as plentiful as rivers. We'll never be more than a few days away." She turned in his arms. "Do you regret leaving?" he asked.

Hugging him around his waist, she pressed her cheek against his chest. "Saddened, perhaps.

I grew up in this country. It has always been my home. But regrets, never. There's no place I want to be except with you, Thomas. I found that out those days we were apart."

"Honey, if it really matters to you, we can stay here. I can set up a practice. Once the transcontinental trains start running, people will flock West by the hundreds of thousands. There certainly will be a big demand for doctors."

Tears glistened in her eyes as she smiled up at him. "I love you for that, Thomas." Then she surprised him by shaking her head. "But I want to go to your Virginia. I want to walk those rolling green hills that you've talked about so often. I want to come to know your roots, as you have come to know mine.

"For the land will always be here, Thomas. People might pass, but the land goes on forever."

He cupped her cheeks between his hands and gazed down into her eyes. "And someday, when we bring our children to this very spot, we can show them the grandeur of this country and they'll come to understand the reason for their mother's strength of character."

His arms enfolded her, and he lowered his head and claimed her lips.

An hour later, Thomas and Rory loaded their luggage onto the train. With Keene and Kathleen accompanying them, they joined Ruark and Angeleen in the Stewarts' private car for the trip to Promontory Point.

Chapter Twenty-five

Despite a chill in the air, all the spectators had assembled by noon on the windswept summit at Promontory to witness the historic moment. Red, white, and blue bunting hung from every store, saloon, and railroad car in the gaily decorated town.

Luminaries from both railroads lined up on each side of the track—Leland Stanford, the Central Pacific's president and former governor of California, and Doctor Thomas Durant, the Union Pacific's vice-president, being the top-ranking officials. Samuel Montague, Sydney Dillion, General Grenville Dodge were but a few of the other visionaries in attendance who had helped to conceive, engineer, or survey the railroad.

But to the remnant force of railers, bolters, gaugers, and ballasters present, the most noteworthy dignitaries in attendance were the two men who had actually built the railroad—the two construction bosses, the Union Pacific's hard-driving Jack Casement and his Central Pacific counterpart, Jim Strobridge. A relentless and merciless taskmaster with an awesome proclivity for profanity, this gangling New Englander had become a railroad legend. Strobridge had gained the appellation "One-Eyed Bossy Man" from his Chinese coolies because of the black eye patch he wore due to the loss of his right eye in a powder blast.

Extending from a tall pole, a telegraph wire paralleled the route of the iron rails, stretching across the nation from the crashing surf of the Pacific to the canyons of Wall Street.

For days, Americans had waited for the news. And not only Americans. The world was waiting for this momentous event. More than a hundred foreign dignitaries were present to witness the joining of the rails.

As soon as the 21st Military Band began to play, the Central Pacific's Jupiter and the Union Pacific's No. 119 puffed forward into position. Face-to-face, the two engines were separated only by two missing rails.

The crowd surged forward, angling for a better view. Reporters and photographers shoved and jostled for positions. The workmen swarmed over the two engines, perching wherever a spot could be found.

After a clergyman led a prayer, a commemorative "last" tie of polished laurel, which had been especially made for the occasion, was laid on the bed. The tie bore several special spikes of precious metals, among which was a golden spike that weighed fourteen ounces, engraved with the inscription, "The Last Spike."

With popping cameras recording the event for posterity, Stanford and several of the other dignitaries took a silver sledge and lightly tapped these spikes, which were too malleable to pound into the tie.

Then the excitement mounted when a crew from each railroad moved in to lay the final rails. The Union Pacific's crew went to work first, lowering their thirty-foot section to the roadbed. The spectators watched as the gaugers aligned the rails, then the spikers moved in, and with the usual three steady strokes, ten spikes were driven into each rail.

Then tension mounted when the Chinese crew of the Central Pacific prepared to lower their final section of rail.

As the scene unfolded before the hundreds assembled, from the observation platform of a nearby car, a laconic Utah cowboy clasped the hand of his immigrant Irish bride; a Yankee entrepreneur from Missouri lifted his three-year-old son to his shoulders, then tucked his wife's arm through his own; and an ex-Confederate doctor slipped his arm around the woman beside him. For even though publishers would soon chronicle the events of this momentous day, the roles enacted by these players, as well as so many others, would remain unrecorded.

The much-anticipated moment neared, and

the crowd hushed and seemed to breathe as one. Only an occasional restless shuffling sounded from their ranks.

The Chinese crew lifted the last rail and, in his eagerness to capture this final moment on film, a photographer shouted, "Shoot!"

The startled Chinese, anticipating a hail of bullets, dropped the rail and fled. The tension of the crowd exploded in an outburst of laughter.

The dramatic moment was lost forever.

After much cajoling, the crew was enticed to return, and the final rail was anchored except for one remaining spike. In deference to his ranking position, Leland Stanford was handed a sledge to drive in this remaining spike. Both sledge and spike were attached to copper wires that were strung to the pole and spliced to the telegraph line. As soon as the spike was struck, the signal would trip a magnetic ball on the Capitol dome in Washington D.C. and other cities across the nation.

A few feet away, a telegraph operator sat at his key, prepared to inform America as soon as the event transpired.

Stanford swung the heavy sledge. The blow missed the spike, drawing a few titters from the crowd and loud guffaws from the spikers. Thomas and Ruark exchanged an amused glance.

Leland Stanford passed the heavy mallet to Thomas Durant. The Union Pacific vice-president took a mighty swing—and the sledge came down on the tie, missing the spike. Thomas and Ruark exchanged a disgusted glance.

"This could take longer than it took to build the whole damn railroad," Thomas mumbled aside to Rory.

With all of America waiting expectantly, the telegrapher saw the need to take matters into his own hands. His finger inched toward a key.

"Yeah, do it," Ruark Stewart said tersely, seeing the man's hesitation. "Do it, mister."

"Do it, mister," Tommy Stewart shouted, parroting Ruark's words from a perch on his father's shoulders.

As if the telegrapher heard the words of encouragement, he followed his instincts and pressed down on the key. Three dots went out across the open line—the sign that the blows had been struck.

Jim Strobridge grabbed the sledge and struck the spike. Then he handed the sledge to the Union Pacific engineer beside him to share the honor. Two more swings of the heavy mallet anchored the final spike, and the telegrapher transmitted the letters, "D-O-N-E."

And on May 10, 1869, at 12:47 P.M., America's first coast-to-coast railroad was completed.

The trains' engineers inched their locomotives forward until the two cowcatchers touched. As if they were christening a ship, each train engineer broke a bottle of champagne against the engine of the other.

As a final gesture, Leland Stanford and Thomas Durant sent a telegram to President Grant. *"We have the honor to report the last rail laid—the last spike driven. The Pacific Railway is finished."*

425

Throughout the thirty-seven states and territories, Americans proudly hailed the accomplishment in a star-spangled jubilee. Cannons boomed in San Francisco and New York, people paraded on the streets of Chicago and St. Louis, Mormons offered prayers of thanksgiving in Salt Lake City—and the spectators at Promontory went wild.

Champagne and beer flowed like water, compliments of the railroads. The saloons threw their doors open, but the crowd overflowed onto the streets, oblivious to the mud.

As soon as the two trains backed off to sidings, the commemorative laurel railroad tie was torn apart by the souvenir hunters who wanted a memento of the event. Several replacement ties met the same fate.

"I didn't see this big a celebration when the war ended," Ruark said as they joined the merrymakers.

"Could be some of us didn't have anything to celebrate," Thomas remarked.

"Well, you can't say that now," Ruark shouted to him, trying to be heard above the din. "We're all Americans today."

"I don't understand it," Rory remarked, observing one of the visiting foreign dignitaries dancing enthusiastically in the street with a local dancehall girl. "Most of these people aren't even Americans."

"Ruark's right, honey. Everyone's an American today. And that music's too inviting to ignore." Grabbing her hand, Thomas pulled her into his arms and led her into the center of the dancers.

Watching Thomas and Rory laughing and sashaying, Ruark grinned good-naturedly. "I can see that marriage hasn't changed that guy one bit."

Angeleen glanced up at Ruark, who was holding their son in one arm. "Are you sorry you're not out there indulging in those hi-jinks, too?"

Slipping his free arm around her waist, he hugged her to his side. "Angel, I wouldn't want to be doing anything other than what I am right now. I've got my whole world right here in my arms."

He dipped his head and whispered in her ear. "Besides, I can get all the hi-jinks I want later in bed."

Angeleen shook her head in loving indulgence. "I thought that speech sounded a little too straitlaced for the Ruark Stewart I know and love."

A short distance farther on Keene and Kathleen stopped to watch Murphy and Michaleen kicking up their heels with reckless abandon in an Irish jig. "They'll soon be movin' on," Kathleen said with a sad smile. "I'll be missin' them, Keene."

He tipped up her chin and smiled into her troubled eyes. "There'll be a lot of good-byes soon. But not between us. That's the important thing, Mrs. MacKenzie."

Kathleen's blue eyes glowed with adoration. "I'm thinkin' it's too good to be true. I love you, Mr. MacKenzie." She tucked her arm into his, and they rejoined Ruark and Angeleen.

By this time, Tommy Stewart had grown

tired of the festivities. The three-year-old fell asleep with his head nestled against his father's shoulder.

"We're going to get this young fellow back to the train and into his bed," Ruark told them. "You two enjoy yourselves. Tell Rory and T.J—ah, Thomas that we went back to our car."

Almost an hour passed before the other two couples returned to the train. The Stewarts had ordered a champagne buffet, and a delicious meal was now laid out awaiting the arrivals.

"Gee, it's nice to know a rich man," Thomas said, piling baked ham on a slice of bread.

Ruark approached Kathleen as she eyed the succulent spread with awe. "Mrs. MacKenzie, you ought to try one of these freshly baked croissants. They're delicious." He handed her a plate. "Did you ever hear how the croissant was invented?"

"Oh, no! Not the Marie Antoinette story." The groans came simultaneously from Angel and Thomas.

"Marie Antoinette?" Kathleen asked, confused.

Ruark continued to pile food on her plate. "Remind me to tell you, my dear, when there aren't so many unappreciative listeners around."

Carrying a plate stacked high with food, Kathleen went over and sat down in a chair next to Thomas. She began to eat ravenously.

Pleased by this unusual sight, he said with amusement, "I'm glad to see your appetite has returned, Kathleen."

"Yes, I've not the understandin' of it meself."

"Well, it must be the tonic I gave you," Thomas

said, not believing it for a moment.

"Tonic?" Kathleen looked up surprised with her mouth full of food. The bottle of tonic had been lost a long time ago. However, she did not want to embarrass Thomas by contradicting him.

"Why, that it must be, Doctor," she managed to mumble, swallowing a mouthful of lyonnaise potatoes.

"Thomas," he reminded her. Grinning, he winked at her when Keene came over carrying a plate and sat at the floor near her feet.

A short time later, not a morsel of food remained on her plate and Kathleen rose to her feet. "I'm thinkin' I'll be havin' a piece of that chocolate cake."

"Kathleen appears to have regained her appetite, Keene. She's put on some weight, too. It looks good on her," Thomas said.

Keene glanced over just as Kathleen popped a spiced crab apple into her mouth. Grinning, he said, "Yep, Doc, sure looks that way. She's really been chowin' down lately."

Thomas chuckled. "My guess would be she's most likely eating for two."

The levity left Keene's eyes, and he glanced up worriedly at Thomas. "I sure hope not."

"Wouldn't you like a child, Keene?"

" 'Course I would, Doc. But I sure don't want Kathleen riskin' her health again."

Thomas studied the Irishwoman as she talked with Rory. Kathleen's blue eyes were bright and alert; her cheeks glowed with color. "No, I don't think it would be a risk any longer, Keene. Look at her; she's the picture of health. Kathleen is a woman in love. Maybe that's the key to her successfully carrying a baby to full term. Of course, no longer being brutalized as she was in the past makes a considerable difference too. You've turned her life around, Keene."

"Well, you know I ain't one to spill my insides too easy. And I wouldn't say this to anyone but you or her, Doc. But she's turned my life around too."

Kathleen came back carrying two plates holding enormous slices of chocolate cake. She handed one to Keene, then offered the other to Thomas. Rising to his feet, he shook his head. "No, Kathleen, you eat it. I've got to go and annoy my wife." Patting Keene on the shoulder, he moved over to where Rory stood talking with Angel and Ruark.

The loud whooping and hollering of the merrymakers carried to their car. "How long do you think this celebration will continue?" Angel asked.

"Probably will still be going strong this time tomorrow," Ruark said.

"And by tonight, there won't be a sober breath on those streets," Thomas interjected.

"I bet you wish you could go back and join them," she teased.

"Listen, redhead, Thomas Graham always remains as sober as a judge." Ruark started choking on the bite he had just swallowed, and Angel began to pound him on the back.

"Are you in need of a doctor, old friend?" Thomas asked.

"It was the *doctor's* remark that almost just did me in," Ruark said. "*Always remain sober? Are we talking about the same Thomas Graham, old friend?*"

"Regardless," Rory said, "I'm just glad this train is pulling out soon and heading back to Ogden. I for one will be anxious to get to bed tonight."

Thomas grinned smugly at Ruark. "As you can see, the woman's mad about me. She just can't keep her hands to herself."

"Physician, cure thyself," Rory said, taking a bite of cake.

"Honey, you've got some crumbs in the corner of your mouth." Rory started to raise the napkin. "Here, let me." He took the napkin, then bent down and boldly licked away the cake.

"M-m-m-m, tastes good."

"Thomas!" Rory said, shocked. Blushing, she cast an embarrassed glance in the direction of the Stewarts.

Ruark feigned indignation. "See, just as I said earlier. You'll never outgrow some of your youthful habits, will you?"

Thomas nodded toward Keene and Kathleen. The young couple were now sitting on the floor with their heads together, talking quietly to one another. "See them? Newlyweds. Rory and I haven't even had our honeymoon yet." He shook his head sympathetically. "Hate to remind you, old friend, but you and Angel are the only *old* married couple in the crowd. You probably can no longer recall the sights and sounds of *young* love."

"Old married couple!" Angeleen protested.

"See, Angel, how quickly he'll turn on you," Ruark exclaimed. "I've been trying to tell you this all these years. You just can't trust the guy. Now maybe you'll believe me."

And never conceding the last word to Thomas, Ruark added, "Besides, *young lover*, experience is the best teacher."

"Still comparing quantity with quality, aren't you, old pal?"

"Before you two aged campaigners go any further in comparing your medals," Angel said, interrupting the two men, "I still have a question about today. After that commemorative laurel tie was removed, who finally replaced the missing tie and drove in the final spike?"

"Who knows?" Thomas said. "Probably one of the Chinese crew."

"Well, if I were a reporter, I certainly would have hung around to get his name," Angel said. "After all, that is the man who made history because he really drove in the last spike."

"Honey, by that time it was just academic. The railroad had been completed. He would just be doing maintenance," Ruark said.

"Completed—then vandalized by souvenir hunters," Thomas said, amused.

"Well, I don't need a souvenir to remember this day," Ruark said. "Ladies and gentlemen, I would like to make a toast." He picked up a champagne bottle and filled each of their glasses.

All heads turned toward him as the celebrants waited with expectant smiles and raised glasses.

"I apologize in advance if the toast may sound verbose—"

"And probably reflect the effects of too much champagne," his laughing wife added.

"But I'm bursting with pride this day and I have to say it," Ruark continued, sliding his free arm around Angeleen's waist.

"Then say it and get it over with," Thomas declared. "The champagne's going flat and my arm's getting tired from holding this glass in the air."

Ruark raised his glass. "To America, my friends. To this young upstart nation, not even a hundred years old, torn asunder less than a decade ago, that has risen from the ashes, hammered itself back together with each driven spike, and fulfilled the prophecy of its founding fathers. For today, we have truly become a nation indivisible. To America, ladies and gentlemen, and the visionaries it has nurtured."

"Well put, old friend," Thomas said.

And as Keene nodded in accord, as Kathleen glanced up adoringly at him, as Rory squeezed Thomas's hand, and as Angeleen smiled lovingly into the eyes of her husband, all echoed the sentiment in unison—"To America."

Suddenly the shrill of the train whistle warned the celebrants of the impending departure. Those interested in returning to Ogden that evening scrambled to the train.

"All aboard!" The conductor's shout sounded above their shouts and laughter. A few minutes later, the train pulled out of Promontory.

When they reached Ogden, the moment

arrived to say good-bye to Keene and Kathleen.

"I'm beholdin' to you and Angel," Keene said aside to the Stewarts. "I want to pay you for the ring."

Ruark shook his head. "It was our pleasure, Keene. Consider it a wedding gift."

"Mighty costly wedding gift," Keene said.

"But this way we know you'll always cherish it," Angel said, kissing his cheek.

Thomas and Rory followed Keene and Kathleen off the train after the departing couple finished their farewells to Ruark and Angel.

"I hope you're not riding back to the ranch tonight," Rory said. She was trying to sound practical in order to disguise the tears that were misting her eyes.

"No, Keene's rented us a room in the hotel," Kathleen said. The two women embraced. "I'm thinkin' I'll never have a friend like you again." She brushed aside her tears with her hand.

"We'll come back and visit you often," Rory said.

"You promise," Kathleen said.

"I promise," Rory said through her own tears. "And you insist that Keene bring you to Virginia sometime too."

Rory stepped away and faced Keene. "Funny, as often as we've said good-bye on sadder occasions, I don't understand why I should be crying now." The sister and brother hugged and kissed.

"I'm gonna hold you to the promise you made Kathleen," Keene said. "We'll be expectin' you back soon."

"Hey, not real soon," Thomas said, moving from Kathleen to shake Keene's hand. "We've got some settling down to do ourselves."

As Thomas assisted her back onto the train, Rory turned her head and glanced back at them. "Soon," she mouthed with a devilish grin and waved good-bye.

For a long moment, Rory and Thomas stood on the observation platform until the couple disappeared. Then, hand in hand, they joined Ruark and Angel.

"Saying good-bye is always hard," Angel said with a sigh. Grasping Rory's hand, she pulled her down beside her on one of the velvet sofas. "I hate to think of leaving you two when we get to St. Louis."

"Now don't start, or T.J. and I will have to suffer two crying females all the way back to Missouri," Ruark said.

"Men are so stoic, aren't they, Rory?" Angel sighed. "While you were saying good-bye, we transferred Tommy into our compartment. You and Thomas can take the other room."

"That wasn't necessary, Angel. Thomas and I could have slept out here on these couches."

"Why, we wouldn't think of it."

"They're a hundred times more comfortable than one of the berths in an ordinary sleeping car," Rory insisted. "Are you sure we aren't inconveniencing you?"

"Of course not. We're just thrilled having you. We'll have a great time on the trip back," Angel replied.

Ruark handed Thomas a drink, and they

leaned against the bar, listening.

"Will you listen to those two?" Ruark commented. "Does that conversation make any sense to you?"

"For some reason, women believe these formalities are necessary," Thomas said.

"Yeah." Ruark nodded in understanding. "What do your medical books say about it?"

Thomas took a deep swallow of his drink and put aside the glass. The two men exchanged a grin of long-time camaraderie. "Not much you can do except to thank God every day when you wake up and find them beside you."

A rap sounded on the door, and Ruark opened it to the porter. "Sorry to bother you, Mr. Stewart." The redcap turned to Thomas. "There's a sick woman in one of the berths, Doctor Graham. We're wonderin' if you'd take a look at her."

"Of course," Thomas said.

"We put your medical bag in your compartment," Angel said.

Thomas hurried to retrieve his bag. "This probably won't take long," he assured them and quickly followed the porter onto the next car.

An hour later, bowing to the exhaustion caused by her condition, Angeleen retired to her sleeping compartment. Ruark gallantly remained with Rory, waiting for Thomas's return.

Promptly at twelve, the train steamed out of the Ogden depot, first stop Laramie, Wyoming. Yawning, Rory settled back in the comfortable stuffed chair. The exhausting day had drained her energy. Within minutes, despite Ruark's presence, she fell asleep.

A short while later, Rory awoke with a start and discovered that she was alone. Assuming Ruark had abandoned his effort to wait up for Thomas, and concerned over her husband's long absence, Rory rose to her feet and set out to find him.

Bathed in black shadows, canyon walls loomed on both sides of the track as she passed from one car to another. The Pullman cars were dark except for a dim light above each door. The sounds of snores emanated from the draped berths.

There was no sign of Thomas.

Rory felt a rising sense of panic as she passed through several more cars. She finally found the conductor and porter asleep near the front of the train. Worriedly, she shook the porter's shoulder.

"I'm Mrs. Graham. Can you tell me where I can find my husband?"

"You mean the doctor?" the porter asked.

Rory nodded. "Yes. I haven't seen him since you came and got him some time ago."

Awakened by their voices, the conductor joined the conversation. "Oh, yes. We had a sick woman in one of the berths."

"Yes, that's what I understand," Rory said.

"Doctor said she was too ill to make the trip."

With her anxiety mounting with every tick of the clock, Rory wanted to scream when the conductor appeared not to have anything further to say. "Can you tell me where I can find them?"

"The doctor had her carried off the train on a stretcher."

"And what happened to Doctor Graham?"

"The last I saw of him, ma'am, he left the train with her."

"Left the train!" Her panic escalated. "Well, did he get back on?"

"Figured he did, ma'am. Said he'd be right back."

"Well, did you see him return?" Her voice had begun to rise with hysteria.

The conductor removed his hat to scratch his head. "Can't say I did." He looked sheepishly at the porter. "You see the doctor get back on, Henry?"

"No, sir. Got real busy with the passengers—making up their berths and all."

"Are you telling me my husband got off this train in Ogden, and you left without checking to see if he had reboarded?" Rory had lost all patience with them.

"Please keep your voice down, ma'am. You'll disturb the other passengers," the conductor declared. "We'll get a wire off to him. Worse that can happen is that you'll have to get off at Laramie, and he can catch up with you tomorrow."

"Well, thank you for that advice, sir," she snapped. "I'm sure I would never have thought of it myself."

Flustered, she turned in a huff to depart. Suddenly her head spun with dizziness, and she leaned against the wall to keep from falling.

The porter quickly hastened to her side. "You okay, ma'am? I'll go with you just to make sure you get back to your car safely." However, he had to quicken his step to keep up with her.

By the time she reached Ruark's private car, her anger had dissolved into disappointment. She entered the car quietly. Nothing would be gained by disturbing the Stewarts at such a late hour. Dejected, she went into the privy to change into her nightgown.

A slight feeling of nausea had combined with her dizziness. *Where is the doctor when I need him?* she reflected, disgruntled. She poured water from the ewer into a basin to wet a cloth. For several moments, she pressed the cool cloth to her brow and neck.

The illness passed, and she entered their darkened compartment. Gasping with alarm, she drew up sharply. Silhouetted in moonlight, a tall figure stood gazing out of the window.

Thomas turned and smiled at her. He had removed his suit coat, and the ends of his cravat dangled loosely from around the collar of his shirt.

"Hi, honey. I was surprised not to find you in bed. What are you doing still awake?"

"What am I doing?" she asked, aghast. "Thomas Jefferson Graham, where have you been? I've been half out of my mind worrying about you and chasing up and down the length of this train like a crazy woman."

"What were you worried about?"

"The conductor told me you got off the train

in Ogden. I thought we'd left you behind. Where have you been all this time?"

"When I came back, you were asleep in the chair, so Ruark and I stepped out on the observation platform to have a smoke. We got to talking about old times, and I guess we lost track of time."

Thomas walked over to her and, as he kissed her cheek, he began to undo the buttons of her nightgown. "I'm sorry, sweetheart. I never meant to alarm you." The boyish grin she so loved appeared on his face, melting her displeasure. "And of course, Ruark and I had to toast my future son."

Her eyes rounded with surprise. "How did you guess? I wasn't certain myself, so I haven't mentioned it to a soul. I was saving the news as a surprise to tell you tonight."

He pulled the gown over her head, then lifted her into his arms and carried her over to the bed. Laying her down gently, he sat on the edge of the bed and leaned over her. "Don't you know by now that the doctor knows everything?"

"Really? So it appears that I'm sharing a berth again with Doctor Omnipotent," she replied. Pulling on the end of his cravat, she tossed it aside. "I thought I got rid of that rogue in Ogden."

"And besides," he said, lowering his head to press a light kiss to her stomach, "I know this body of yours like the back of my hand. I can detect the slightest change in it."

She slipped the shirt off his shoulders. "Well, then you can tell me when we can anticipate our son to be born. I do assume it will be a son, since the mighty renowned and unrivaled astrological physician said so."

"Well, fortunately, due to my vast acquaintance with Egyptian and Arabian astrological science, not to mention Persian Magi and Hindu something or other, I would venture to guess we can anticipate his arrival about the middle of January." His grin flashed again. "I should also add, that as your husband, I have an added advantage of knowing when you had your last menses."

She slid her hands down his chest and stopped at the feel of the bulge in his loins. A delicate brow arched naughtily. "I'm impressed, Doctor. *Really impressed*, Doctor."

He matched her double entendre with a wicked grin. "Not as much as you soon will be."

He stood up and hastily disposed of his remaining clothing. Lowering himself on her, he claimed her lips in a passionate kiss that left her breathless.

"So have you any more predictions for our future, Doctor Omnipotent?" she asked with a breathless throatiness.

"I predicate a long"—he pressed a light kiss to her eye—" . . . slow"—he kissed her other eye—" . . . ride," he whispered, kissing the tip of her nose.

Her jade eyes deepened with desire. "I would say it's about time. The delay has been long enough." Smiling seductively, she slipped her arms around his neck.

"All aboard, Doctor."

Epilogue

Rory's hand trembled when the young delivery boy handed her the telegram. With trepidation, she opened the envelope, and her eyes rounded with surprise as she quickly scanned the wire.

SEAN THOMAS AND SHANNON RORY MAC-
KENZIE ARRIVED LAST NIGHT IN THAT
ORDER STOP MOTHER AND FATHER DO-
ING FINE STOP SON AND DAUGHTER CRY-
ING TO MEET THEIR AUNT UNCLE AND
COUSIN MATTHEW STOP HOPE YOU CAN
HOP THE NEXT TRAIN WEST CAUSE WE
NEED YOU STOP
                              KEENE

The door opened, and Thomas entered the house. With a wide smile and outstretched arms, Rory rose to greet him.

Said the Union, "Don't reflect, or
I'll run over some Director."
Said the Central, "I'm Pacific,
But, when riled, I'm quite terrific.
Yet today we shall not quarrel,
Just to show these folks this moral,
How two Engines—in their vision—
Once have met without collision."

This is what the Engines said
Unreported and unread;
Spoken slightly through the nose,
With a whistle at the close.

—Bret Harte

CREOLE NIGHTS

Deborah Martin

"A Must Read...I Loved It!"   —Rexanne Becnel

Elina Vannier's life can't get much worse. Her father is missing, her brother dead, and the most attractive man she's ever met thinks she is a lying cheat. And soon she discovers her whole past might be a lie.

Convinced that Elina wants to destroy his family's reputation, Rene Bonnange lures the young girl to his lush plantation. But as the languid days pass, Rene finds himself longing for the deceitful beauty. No matter what the cost, he vows to uncover the truth about Elina—and to share with her a tempestuous ecstasy that will forever change their lives.

_3368-2 $4.50 US/$5.50 CAN